"A nerve-wracking battle of ruse and counter-ruse and explosive ambush ... Edwards keeps the pacing brisk and the action taut ... an engrossing tale of cutting-edge naval warfare."

Kirkus Discoveries

"A timeless warrior epic. Jeff Edwards spins a stunning and irresistibly believable tale of savage modern naval combat."

Joe Buff, bestselling author of *Seas of Crisis* and *Crush Depth*

"Here is a writer at the top of his game. The result is a brilliant techno-thriller, the kind a young Clancy would be proud to call his own."

Homer Hickam, bestselling author of *October Sky*, *Torpedo Junction*, and *The Ambassador's Son*

"TORPEDO *kicks ass! Smart and involving, with an action through-line that shoots ahead like its namesake—fast and lethal. I read it in one sitting."*

Paul L. Sandberg, producer of *The Bourne Supremacy*

"Unfamiliar and exciting territory—a magnificent yarn!"

Greg Bear, bestselling author of *Darwin's Radio*, *Eon*, and *Blood Music*

"A great and enjoyable read. Edwards has been there and knows how to show it."

David E. Meadows, author of *Sixth Fleet*

"Edwards wields politics and naval combat tactics with a skill equal to the acknowledged masters of military fiction."

Military Press

"The best naval action novel I have ever read."

W. H. McDonald, President of Military Writers Society of America

"An action-packed, five-star thriller, filled with passion and intensity!"

Toronto Free Press

"The realism in Edwards' writing is phenomenal, and the word pictures he paints put you right in the middle of the action."

Armchair Interviews

"TORPEDO *pulls you along as it dives beneath the surface, powers through unexpected twists and turns, locks on, and then accelerates to attack speed! This book kept me up all night and made me late for work."*

Jak Koke, bestselling author of *Liferock*, *Dead Air*, and *The Terminus Experiment*

"One of the year's best! The action and suspense never let up."

J. T. McDaniel, naval historian and author of *Bacalao*

"As the former Commanding Officer of a U.S. Navy warship, I was awestruck by the realism and plausibility of this novel."

David Armstrong, Commander, USN (Retired)

"This is the book that Surface Warriors have been waiting for."

Vincent Fenty, Chief Petty Officer, USN (Retired)

"Jeff Edwards writes with a high-voltage pen. This right-off-the-headlines sea story crackles and pops in a continual shower of sparks! Great climax, great read!"

Don Gerrard, editor and former publisher,
Random House—Bookworks books

"TORPEDO *runs hot, straight, and normal from the first page!"*

Frank Hogan, former U.S. Navy Torpedoman

"An incredible novel! Highly accurate, tautly paced, and disturbingly prescient, TORPEDO *takes a hard look at a real naval threat that has been given too little consideration in this age of cruise missiles."*

Tom Mays, nautical engineer and author of *The Falling Sky*

"TORPEDO *is the book I've been waiting for since the sinking of my ship, USS* Truxton *(DD-229), in 1941. A must-read for everyone."*

Lanier W. Phillips, Sonar Technician, USN (Retired)

"TORPEDO *grabs you from the first page and doesn't let go. Edwards brings an experience-based edge of authenticity to his writing.*"

Elizabeth Baldwin, Mysterious Galaxy Books

"*If you liked* THE HUNT FOR RED OCTOBER, *you will love* TORPEDO."

Steve West, *Northern Islander* newspaper

"TORPEDO *will leave you breathless and unable to sleep until you've finished the very last page.*"

Kerry L. Marsala, Capitol Hill Coffee House

"*Fast-moving and technically accurate in the best Clancy tradition.*"

Terry M. Badger, Captain, USN (Retired)

TORPEDO

TORPEDO

Jeff Edwards

iUniverse Star
New York Lincoln Shanghai

TORPEDO

iUniverse Star
an iUniverse, Inc. imprint

iUniverse books may be ordered through booksellers or by contacting:

iUniverse
2021 Pine Lake Road, Suite 100
Lincoln, NE 68512
www.iuniverse.com
1-800-Authors (1-800-288-4677)

The tactics described in this book do not represent actual U.S. Navy or NATO tactics past or present. Also, many of the code words and some of the equipment have been altered to prevent unauthorized disclosure of classified material.

This novel has been reviewed by the State Department, the Department of Defense, and the Department of the Navy, and is cleared for publication in accordance with Chief of Naval Operations letter 5511.1 (Ser N09N2/32532242).

ISBN-13: 978-1-58348-465-4 (pbk)
ISBN-13: 978-0-595-67523-4 (cloth)
ISBN-13: 978-0-595-81933-1 (ebk)
ISBN-10: 1-58348-465-5 (pbk)
ISBN-10: 0-595-67523-9 (cloth)
ISBN-10: 0-595-81933-8 (ebk)

Printed in the United States of America

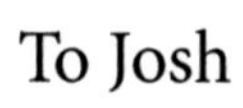

To Josh

ACKNOWLEDGMENTS

I would like to thank the following people for their assistance in bringing this book to life:

Bill Keppler of the State Department Office of Protocol; Michael A. Petrillo, Arabic linguist and Middle Eastern cultural specialist; Cathy Monaghan of the British Embassy in Washington, DC; the staff of the Los Angeles office of the British Consulate-General; the Chinese Studies Program at the University of California, San Diego; TM1(SW) Gary D. Johnson; TM1(SW) Charles Copes; Peter H. Zindler, marine engineer; and several others, some of whom asked not to be named, and others whose names have slipped my leaky brain. The information I received from these fine people was flawless. Any errors that have crept into this work are mine, not theirs.

I also owe a debt of gratitude to my lovely wife, Maria, for her excellent research and for jealously guarding my writing time so that I could stop talking about this book and actually write it.

And last, but certainly not least, I would like to thank my editor, for believing when I had forgotten to, and for making me go back and do the hard parts until they were right.

Missiles are fast. They're dangerous. They're sexy. So when we think about warfare at sea, it's natural that missiles are the first things we think about. But we can shoot down missiles. We can decoy them with chaff—jam them—hide from them with infrared suppression systems and minimized radar cross-sections.

Our Kingfisher sonars can detect mines, and we can destroy them or maneuver to avoid them.

Our ships are hardened against chemical and biological weapons.

But how do you stop a torpedo? Thirty years of R-and-D, and we still don't have a viable system for intercepting torpedoes. We can't shoot them down; we can't jam them; we can't hide from them. And, even third-world torpedoes can do upward of fifty knots, so we sure as hell can't outrun them.

We *do* have decoy systems that have shown some effectiveness, and a couple of tricky torpedo evasion maneuvers that work pretty well. But, they depend on split-second timing and perfect execution. Activate your decoys ten seconds too soon (or five seconds too late) and an enemy torpedo will eat your lunch. Hold an evasion turn a little too long, or not long enough, and it's *game over*.

We build the toughest warships on the planet, but the best engineers in the business agree that nearly every class of torpedo currently being deployed has the capacity to sink one of our ships with a single shot. To make matters worse, none of our potential adversaries believe in shooting torpedoes one-at-a-time. Typically, they shoot salvos of two or three.

It's inevitable. One day soon, maybe next year—hell, maybe next week, maybe an hour from now—one of our ships is going to end up on the wrong end of a spread of hostile torpedoes. And, when that happens, we're going to discover that *we* are the poor bastards that brought a knife to a gunfight.

—Excerpted from the Chief of Naval Operations' comments to the graduating class at Annapolis

PROLOGUE

In the language of its builders, the weapon's name was *Ozeankriegs fuhrungtechnologien Deutsches Exportmodell DMA37-R5092*—Ocean Warfare Technologies German Export Model DMA37 (Serial Number R5092). On the munitions inventory, its name was shortened to *R-92*. But the weapon did not know either of these names. It had no name for itself. It was not even aware of its own existence. It waited in its shipping canister, cradled as snugly in the cylindrical steel container as a high-powered bullet in the chamber of a rifle. Cold. Sightless. Unfeeling. Not sleeping, merely unawakened.

R-92 was a state-of-the-art acoustic homing torpedo. It was a cybernetic predator: an electro-mechanical killing machine. Fast. Smart. Unbelievably lethal. Every component, from the shark-like hydrodynamic form of its fuselage—to its multi-spectrum acoustic sensors—to the axial-flow turbine that formed its engine, was optimized for the undersea environment. Its brain was a fifth-generation digital computer, hardwired for destruction with a machine-driven relentlessness that no living predator could match. R-92 and its brethren had been honed for the chase and the kill by two and a half centuries of technological evolution.

But R-92 knew none of these things. It simply waited.

CHAPTER 1

USS *TOWERS* (DDG-103)
NORTHERN ARABIAN GULF
SATURDAY, 05 MAY
1114 hours (11:14 AM)
TIME ZONE +3 'CHARLIE'

Bowie timed it carefully, lifting each foot at just the right second as he ducked through the hatch combing of the open blast door and ran out onto the forecastle of his ship. Twenty-one laps around the deck today and his breaths were still coming evenly, but the air was hot and so humid that it felt like breathing soup. Sweat plastered his short black hair to his forehead, and his sleeveless U.S. Naval Academy T-shirt stuck to his skin, the faded goat mascot logo blending into the perspiration-darkened fabric. It wasn't even noon yet, and the sun was already fierce enough to blur the visual horizon with rapidly evaporating water. At least the seas were calm at the moment—not exactly a given in the Arabian Gulf this time of year.

His crew called him Captain Jim Bowie, which was a technical misnomer on two counts. In fact, his name was Samuel Harlan Bowie, and his actual rank was commander. The title of *Captain* was honorary; by ancient nautical tradition, the commanding officer of a naval warship is always referred to as "Captain," no matter what actual rank he carries. The *Jim* part had been following him around since childhood, a nearly inevitable consequence of having grown up in San Antonio, Texas, with the last name of Bowie. He'd long since given up the battle and accepted his nickname. It beat the hell out of what his buddies had called him at the Academy, anyway.

Bowie curved to his left, cutting between the ankle-high platform of the forward missile launcher and the low wedge of the 5-inch gun mount.

From a visual perspective, the gun was the most arresting feature on the forecastle. Its strange geometric shape and steeply angled sides gave it little resemblance to any of the generations of naval artillery that had preceded it, but the long steel barrel that protruded from the forward slope of the wedge left no doubt as to its purpose.

Situated aft of the gun, the forward missile launcher was not nearly as visually impressive. To the untrained eye, the launcher looked like a grid of square hatches set flush into an ankle-high steel platform. The innocuous-looking hatches were armored with Kevlar-reinforced steel, and every hatch concealed a vertical missile silo, known as a "cell." Loaded in those cells, and their twins in the aft launcher, were the missiles that comprised the ship's real destructive force.

When he reached the far side of the launcher, Bowie curved left again, back toward the superstructure. Another of the tricky step-duck maneuvers carried him through the port side blast doors and into the port break. This short stretch of enclosed passageway shielded him from the sun, giving him a few seconds of shade and relatively cool air. Then he dashed out into the sun again, running down the port side main deck toward the stern.

At first glance, Bowie was more likely to be taken for an accountant than a naval officer. His long face and narrow cheekbones gave him a clean and efficient look that his neatly trimmed black hair seemed to echo. His lips were thin and slightly turned down at the corners, creating a permanently thoughtful expression that reinforced the image of humorless efficiency. The laugh lines around his mouth were the only giveaways of the imaginative and playful spirit that hid behind his somber brown eyes.

A shade under six feet tall, he had a compact physique that was neither skinny nor overtly muscular. At thirty-eight, he was in the best shape of his life. He was also at the pinnacle of his career, and he knew it. No matter where he went from here, it would be downhill.

Certainly there were more promotions in his future (barring death or major screw-ups), but this was his one shot at his lifelong dream: command of a warship. He was trying very hard not to count the days, but he knew he had less than four months left to enjoy it. Then Bowie would have to turn command of the *Towers* over to someone else and move on to the next phase of his career. He didn't like to think about that, but he knew the Navy's advancement pipeline all too well. After the *Towers*, he'd be transferred to a shore duty billet, probably a career-enhancing staff position at the headquarters of one of the major commands—part of the Navy's plan to give him political seasoning that he didn't want, in preparation for selection to full-bird captain.

His next chance to command at sea would probably be as commodore of a destroyer squadron, overseeing other people's ships. Command of a squadron was an important job, but it was too much like being an astronaut's boss, instead of an astronaut. If he was very, *very* lucky, he might be able to wrangle command of one of the Aegis guided missile cruisers. But there weren't very many of the old *Ticonderoga* Class cruisers left to go around, and the Navy wouldn't be willing to waste a valuable full-bird captain on a destroyer or a frigate.

He reached the amidships break, where the forward deckhouse ended and a narrow section of open deck separated the forward superstructure from the aft superstructure. He edged closer to the lifelines as he ran, giving himself a cushion of space in case someone opened one of the watertight doors without warning. He'd made that mistake years ago, as a boot ensign on the USS *Bunker Hill*. A second class Signalman had opened a door right in front of him, and Bowie had slammed into the reinforced steel while running at full-tilt. A sprained wrist and two black eyes had given him a personal reminder of one of the most basic principles of physics: *Force = Mass × Acceleration*.

Bowie passed an exhaust vent and caught a half-second blast of what seemed to be cooler air. The temperature differential was a sensory illusion, caused by the movement of the air over his skin. In reality, the exhaust from every vent on board was precisely monitored and alternately heated or cooled to match the ambient temperature of the air surrounding the ship. The system was expensive, and a pain in the ass to maintain, but it made the ship functionally invisible to infrared sensors or heat-seeking missiles. And in this age of three-dimensional Battle Space Management, stealth was paramount.

His ship, USS *Towers*, had been built from the keel up with stealth in mind. She was 529 feet long, 66½ feet wide, and (if the media hype was to be believed) virtually invisible. The fourth (and last) ship in the heavily modified third "Flight" of *Arleigh Burke* Class destroyers, *Towers* was an example of cutting-edge military stealth technology. She was not, however, the "ghost ship" suggested by news magazines and Internet Web sites. In fact, from his vantage point running circles around her deck, it was difficult for Bowie to imagine how the destroyer even rated her official classification as a "Reduced Observability Vessel."

The low pyramid shapes of her minimized superstructure and the severely raked angle of her short mast gave her a decidedly strange profile, but she was far from invisible—up close anyway. From a distance of a few thousand yards, however, that began to change. Ninety-plus percent of her exposed surfaces were covered with polymerized carbon-fiber PCMS tiles. Although designed primarily to absorb enemy radar, this newest generation of the Passive Countermeasure System had another handy feature: the rubbery tiles were impregnated with a phototropic pigment that changed color in response to changes in lighting. In bright sunlight, the tiles were a dusty blue-gray that blended into the interface between sea and sky remarkably well. As the light dimmed, the PCMS tiles would darken accordingly, reaching a shade approaching black when the ship was in total darkness.

Although the cumulative effect was a far cry from invisibility, it camouflaged the ship's outlines enough to make her hard to see at a distance, not only reducing the range at which she could be detected visually, but also making it difficult for any optically based sensor—from the human eyeball to high-resolution video cameras—to determine her size, course, or speed.

A state-of-the-art thermal suppression system performed similar magic for the ship's infrared signature, while the radar-absorbent PCMS and the carefully calculated geometries of her hull and superstructure gave the long steel warship a radar cross section only a little larger than the average fiberglass motorboat.

Every cleat, chock, and padeye was designed to fold down and lock into its own form-fitting recess in the deck when not in use. Although intended strictly as a means of shaving another fraction off the ship's radar cross section, the hide-away fittings made for a remarkably uncluttered deck—which in turn made it a pretty good place to run.

The high-tech razzle-dazzle extended to the ship's acoustic signature as well. Seventh-generation silencing, including an acoustically isolated engineering plant, active noise-control modules, and the venerable (but still effective) Prairie and Masker systems, made *Towers* a difficult target for passive sonar sensors. Popular rumor held that she, and her sister ships in the Flight Three *Arleigh Burke* Class, were quieter cruising through the water at twenty knots than most warships were tied to the pier. That was an exaggeration, but not by much.

When he came to the aft end of the superstructure, Bowie curved to his left, dodging a pair of Gunner's Mates engaged in lubricating Mount 503, the aft-starboard .50-caliber machine gun. The arc of his improvised running track took Bowie around the aft missile launcher and back to the starboard side of the ship. The aft missile launcher marked the halfway point for each lap.

Only four more laps to go. Bowie's daily routine called for twenty-five and a half laps, which he had worked out to be about three miles. Once upon a time he'd done five miles a day, but then he'd discovered that while on board ship he didn't eat the right kinds of foods to fuel that sort of regimen. The extra mileage had pushed his metabolism into the catabolic zone, burning up muscle tissue as well as fat.

Maybe when he returned to shore duty he'd need to crank back up to five miles a day to keep away the nearly inevitable swivel-chair spread. But that was in the future, a future that he wasn't quite ready to think about. A future in which he would no longer command what he considered to be the finest warship in the Pacific Fleet.

Bowie increased his stride a little as he turned up the starboard side. The ship's motion through the water generated relative wind, and running toward the bow, he was headed back into it.

Off to his right, an oil tanker was passing down the starboard side. It was an enormous thing—a supertanker—nearly twice as long as *Towers*, with an unloaded displacement of about three hundred thousand tons, rising maybe fifty feet above the water and obscuring his vision to starboard. The paint on its orange hull and white superstructure was bright and well maintained. It rode low in the water now, a sure indication that its tanks were full. Based on its size, Bowie estimated that it was carrying somewhere around two million barrels of oil.

The supertanker was about fifteen hundred yards out and nearing its closest point of approach. Bowie already knew that the big ship would pass *Towers* with a comfortable safety margin, but he couldn't stop himself from rechecking its position and heading every time he came around the deck for another lap. He knew that the Officer of the Deck had the situation well in hand, but—when it came to collision avoidance—it never hurt to have another pair of eyes open.

In the distance astern of and beyond the tanker, a pair of oil platforms squatted on the horizon, their images wavering like mirages in the desert-heated air. The larger of the platforms belched enormous plumes of fire into the sky as its flare tower burned off the natural gas that accumulated as a natural consequence of the oil-pumping process. It was a routine procedure that the local oil rig crews referred to as "off-gassing." The Middle Eastern oil fields were so productive that it was marginally cheaper to incinerate natural gas than to containerize and ship it.

The wind was hot in Bowie's face, and he was beginning to look forward to the brief stretch of cool air he would find in the starboard break. He checked an urge to put on a burst of speed. Running in the heat was all about pacing yourself. *Patience,* he thought. *Patience.*

He glanced at the supertanker again. Oil. In the end, *everything* came down to oil. The light-sweet crude that these fields held in such abundance was easily fractionalized into kerosene, diesel fuel, and gasoline—the very lifeblood of the industrialized world.

Bowie had done an experiment with a globe once. He had discovered that he could cover all of the Arabian Gulf and most of the OPEC nations under the tips of two fingers. The idea that such a disproportionately small area had the power to influence events all over the planet was frightening. When you factored in the region's political instability, the whole situation got scary as hell.

Bowie reached the boat deck and ran past the RHIBs, the ship's two Rigid-Hulled Inflatable Boats.

Suddenly, an alarm sounded: a jarring electronic klaxon that pounded its discordant rhythm out of every topside speaker. Bowie's easy jog turned instantly to a sprint. He was already into the starboard break and opening the outer door to the airlock when the alarm was replaced by the amplified voice of the Officer of the Deck.

"General Quarters, General Quarters. All hands man your battle stations. Set Material Condition Zebra throughout the ship. Commanding officer, your presence is requested on the bridge."

Five seconds later, Bowie was climbing the first of the four steeply inclined ladders that would take him to the bridge. He passed a dozen Sailors, all headed in different directions, toward their battle stations. Those who got caught in his path were quick to leap out of the way. One did not delay the captain under the best of circumstances, and certainly not when he was headed toward the bridge for General Quarters.

Bowie's running shoes pounded up the aluminum steps two at a time. He hadn't approved any training drills for this morning, so the emergency (whatever it was) had to be real.

He nearly ducked into his at-sea cabin to grab a set of coveralls and a pair of boots, but the OOD's amplified voice came over the 1-MC speakers again. "Away the Small Craft Action Team. Now set Tac-Sit One. This is not a drill."

Bowie put on a burst of speed as he hit the last ladder. *Screw the coveralls. If the OOD was declaring Tactical Situation One, he was expecting immediate combat. Something was getting ugly fast, but what in the hell could it be?*

* * *

The bridge on board *Towers* was a break with a centuries-old tradition in shipbuilding. In place of a customary "walk-around" style pilothouse that ran from one side of the ship to the other, the *Towers*' design offered a small angular module that protruded from the leading edge of the superstructure like a faceted bump.

Seen from the inside, it resembled the cockpit of a jumbo jet. Two contoured chairs, each surrounded by instrument-packed control consoles, dominated the small amount of floor space. The forward-most of these chairs belonged to the Helmsman, a junior petty officer whose primary duty was to steer the ship and issue speed commands to its engines. Behind the Helmsman sat the Officer of the Deck; his chair was mounted on a platform to give him an unrestricted view through the angled bridge windows. In another break with nautical tradition, there were no chairs for the commanding officer, or his second in command, the executive officer.

Bowie stepped through the last watertight door and edged into the cramped control room. The Helmsman's voice announced his presence before he had closed and dogged the door. "The captain's on the bridge!"

Bowie squeezed in next to the OOD's chair and grabbed the overhead handrail that was the only real provision for visitors. He began to shiver almost instantly as cool air from the circulation vents hit his sweat-drenched skin. "What have you got, Brett?"

Lieutenant Brett Parker looked up from his console. His boyishly good-looking features were taut, his normally mischievous green eyes dark and intense. He pointed out the window toward a pair of dark shapes skimming rapidly across the water: small boats, moving fast. The Bridge Heads-Up Display projected targeting symbols on the inside of the windows, superimposing red diamond-shaped brackets around each of the rapidly moving boats. "Sledgehammers, sir. Two of them, off the starboard bow—about a thousand yards out. Looks like they came in on the far side of that tanker and pretty much used it for cover until they got in close."

Sledgehammer was the current Navy code word for a motorboat armed with an over-the-shoulder missile launcher.

Bowie felt his stomach tighten a fraction. "Damn." He stared at the target symbols, and then at the small boats behind them. "Are you sure they're Sledgehammers?"

"Pretty much, sir. They've made two high-speed runs on us already, sheering off suddenly both times. It looked like they were practicing missile approaches. And my Helmsman thought he saw a laser flash on the last pass."

"I did, sir," the Helmsman said. "A red dot, dancing on the side of the gun mount. I think it was a targeting laser, sir."

Bowie nodded and looked around. "Did anybody else see it?"

The OOD shook his head. "I don't think so, sir."

"I saw the tanker when I was out there," Bowie said. "But I didn't see anything else."

The Helmsman piped up immediately. "With all due respect, Captain, I *know* what I saw."

The corners of Bowie's mouth curled up in the faintest hint of a smile. "Relax, son, I believe you. I was just wondering if anyone saw a laser from the second boat."

A speaker crackled in the overhead. "Captain? This is the TAO. Are you watching these guys on MMS?"

The voice belonged to the ship's Combat Systems Officer, Lieutenant Terri Sikes, currently standing duty as the Tactical Action Officer.

Bowie pressed the *talk* button on the comm box. "Not yet, Terri. Give us half a sec to get it punched up." He nodded toward his OOD.

Lt. Parker tapped out a rapid-fire sequence of keys on his wraparound control console. A burst of video static blossomed on one of the three display screens and then instantly resolved itself into a coherent image: a direct video feed from the mast-mounted sight, a high-definition video camera mounted near the top of the mast.

The video was black-and-white, but the picture was exceptionally crisp. The camera was locked on the nearer of the two speedboats. It was a cigarette boat: long and dagger-shaped, very fast and very low to the water. A continuous rooster tail of spray shot out from under the stern of the narrow fiberglass hull. The image jerked occasionally as the boat took a dip or a roll that the *Towers*' optical tracking computer hadn't anticipated.

Suddenly, the image froze and the Tactical Action Officer's voice came over the speaker. "There!" she said. "Right there, sir. Do you see *that*?"

Bowie pressed the *talk* button on the comm box. "What am I looking for?"

A pixelized oval appeared on the screen, drawn in by the TAO using a light pen. The area inside the oval magnified itself to show a grainy image of the interior of the cigarette boat. Two men were visible, or people, anyway—it was impossible to tell more from the frozen image. One of the figures was hunched over a console, obviously driving. The second figure was half-crouched, hanging on to the windscreen with one hand. His other hand was wrapped around a rectangular object draped over his right shoulder.

Bowie's stomach tightened another notch. "Got it."

The oval disappeared, and the image leapt back to life. "Sir," the TAO's voice said, "that's got to be a missile launcher. I think those bastards are going to light us up. Request permission to engage."

Bowie watched the screen. "Not yet," he said.

The boats were circling back around for another pass at the ship.

"Two boats," Bowie said to himself. "No markings. They're not terrorists, or they would have shot at us on the first pass. There's no way to tell if they're Siraji or Iranian, but it's a decent bet that it's one of the two. I don't think anybody else around here is mad enough to shoot at us."

Lt. Parker cleared his throat. "Uh, Captain … I have to agree with the TAO. Those boats are showing classic Sledgehammer attack profiles. We need to take them out before they get off a shot at us."

An enunciator on the Helmsman's console beeped once, lighting a green tattletale on his display panel. A second later, it beeped again, lighting another tattletale. "Material Condition Zebra is set throughout the ship," the Helmsman announced. "All gunnery stations are reporting manned and ready for Tac-Sit One."

Bowie kept his eyes on the black-and-white video. Something was funny here. If the cigarette boats really were Sledgehammers, why hadn't they attacked yet? "I'm not sure that's a missile launcher."

"What else could it be, sir?"

Bowie glanced up for a half-second into the eyes of his Officer of the Deck. "It could be a video camera, Brett."

The OOD's voice nearly squeaked. "But they trained a laser on us. They're targeting us, sir. It's obvious."

Bowie shook his head. "What's obvious is that they're trying to provoke us."

The TAO's voice came over the speaker. "Sledgehammers are inbound. I say again, Sledgehammers are *inbound*. Request permission to engage, sir!"

Bowie watched the video screen as the cigarette boats raced through the water toward his ship. The conditioned air of the bridge was turning his sweat-dampened skin to ice.

Sledgehammers were every skipper's nightmare. They were the poor man's navy: a boat, a shoulder-launched weapon, one idiot to drive, and another to shoot. Presto: instant navy. Not enough firepower to take out a warship, but more than enough to damage it. And even modest damage to a U.S. warship would be an incalculable propaganda coup for a third-rate nation.

Of course, if he blew the boats away and it turned out that they were not armed, then *that* would be a propaganda coup against the United States as well. The local nutcases weren't above sending out boats armed only with bulky old-fashioned video cameras and harmless laser pointers, hoping to spook a warship into attacking them.

Bowie's mouth felt suddenly dry. His intuition told him that the boats would have attacked by now if they were going to. He hoped like hell that his intuition wasn't about to get somebody killed. "Negative. Do not engage." Bowie could feel the crew on the bridge stiffen.

A flicker of red light shot through a side window and played around the interior of the bridge for a split-second before vanishing.

The Helmsman shouted, "Targeting laser!"

"Do *not* engage!" Bowie repeated. He waited about two heartbeats and then added, "I have the Conn. All engines ahead flank! Right full rudder!"

The ship heeled over instantly as the Helmsman executed his orders. "Sir, my rudder is right thirty degrees! No new course given. All engines ahead flank!"

The big destroyer surged forward as all four of her gas turbine engines wound up to top speed, pouring 105,000 horsepower into each of her twin propeller shafts. The acoustic suppression systems muted the rising scream of the turbines to a barely audible wail, like the sound of a jet taking off in the distance.

"Captain," the OOD said, "that's going to take us right into them!"

"You're damned right it is!" Bowie snapped. "If they want to play chicken, then we'll show them how we do it back home!"

The course change spun the bow of the ship around toward the charging cigarette boats. When they were centered in the front bridge window, Bowie said, "Steady as she goes."

"Helmsman aye! She goes two-seven-three, sir!"

Bowie nodded. "Very well. Brett, stand by to launch chaff."

"Sir, we're too close for chaff. It'll be on the other side of the boats before it blooms."

"I know that," Bowie said. "It's not worth a damn against laser-guided weapons anyway. I just want to scare the shit out of them." He pressed the *talk* button on the comm box. "Terri, I want every gun on this ship pointed at those boats! Now!"

"Yes, sir!"

Bowie watched the boats through the front bridge window. They were getting larger fast, the range closing rapidly as they barreled toward a head-on collision with his ship. There would be no collision; Bowie was sure of that. The boats would sheer off, or the reinforced steel bow of the destroyer would crush their fragile fiberglass hulls like eggshells. They would turn, all right. But would they launch missiles first? And if they did, what would they target? The bridge windows? That's what he would do in their position.

The TAO's voice came over the speaker. "All guns are trained on the Sledgehammers, sir."

Bowie glared at the onrushing boats. "All right, you bastards," he said quietly. "Let's see what you've got …"

He waited another five seconds while the boats grew ever larger in the window. Then he said, "Launch chaff, port and starboard!"

Lt. Parker's response was nearly instantaneous; he slammed a button on his console. "Chaff away, sir!"

Blunt projectiles rocketed out of the forward RBOC launchers. Super Rapid-Blooming Overboard Chaff rounds hurtled through the air, passing over the charging cigarette boats and exploding on the far side of them, littering the sky with aluminum dust and metallic confetti.

Designed to fool enemy radar with false targets, the chaff had no electronic effect on the small boats, since they had no radar. But the effect Bowie wanted was psychological, not electronic.

He tried to imagine what his ship looked like to the men aboard the cigarette boats: 9,794 tons of steel rushing down on them like a freight train; chaff exploding overhead; and every gun on board pointed down their throats.

His grip tightened on the handrail above his head. "Come on, you bastards, *turn* ..."

There wasn't a sound on the ship except the muted wail of the turbine engines. Everyone on the bridge seemed to be holding their breath.

The boats grew larger in the window. They couldn't be more than fifty yards away now. This was not going to work. The boats weren't going to sheer away. They were waiting to get close enough to make their missiles count.

Bowie glanced up at his Officer of the Deck. The young lieutenant's eyes were locked on him.

Bowie pressed the *talk* button on the comm box. "Stand by your guns."

The boats weren't going to turn. The bastards were calling his bluff.

A chill washed down his spine that had nothing to do with the air conditioning or his damp running clothes. It had come on him suddenly, the moment that every military commander secretly dreads. The crux of a decision in which there was no good choice, where both action and inaction were equally likely to lead to disaster.

If he sank the boats and they turned out to be unarmed, the United States would find itself neck-deep in an international incident, and Bowie's career would be over. A lifetime of hard work and sacrifice, gone in a matter of seconds. It would play out in the U.S. media as monumental incompetence at best, and criminal disregard for human life at worst. In the current political climate, the Arab press wouldn't bother with half-measures; they'd cut straight to the chase and call it murder. And, under all the flack and the political posturing, four men would be dead. Four men who might not be guilty of any crime more serious than harassing an American warship.

On the other hand, if he *didn't* shoot the boats and they *did* turn out to be armed, the safety of his ship and crew were at risk. This could end with some of *his* men going home in body bags. And, of considerably lesser importance, his career would *still* be at an end.

How ironic was that? Ten minutes earlier, he'd been feeling sorry for himself, decrying the lack of excitement in his future career prospects. Now, he was about to watch his career self-destruct, and it was the very least of his worries.

He watched the boats continue to close. His first duty was to protect his crew. He couldn't wait for the Sledgehammers to take the first shot. It wasn't really a very hard decision to make, but it hurt like hell to have to throw away everything he had ever worked for.

He opened his mouth to give the order to fire, but he was interrupted by a shout from the Helmsman. "They're turning, sir! They're running away!"

Bowie looked at the boats. Sure enough, they had peeled off and appeared to be running. He let out a breath that he didn't even realize he'd been holding.

The TAO keyed her mike for a few seconds to let him hear the cheers coming from the crew in Combat Information Center. In the background, a male voice cut loose with a rebel yell.

The boats grew smaller in the window. Bowie watched them until he was certain that they weren't coming back. Then he turned to his Officer of the Deck. "Stand us down from General Quarters."

The young lieutenant was still a little pale. "Yes, sir!"

Bowie looked down at the cold, sweat-drenched T-shirt sticking to his skin. "Take the Conn, Brett. I need a shower."

CHAPTER 2

WASHINGTON, DC
SUNDAY; 06 MAY
8:27 PM EDT

The Americans had an idiom: "*It's not so much what you say, it's how you say it.*" Although the phrase had no direct corollary in Mandarin, Ambassador Shaozu Tian of the People's Republic of China had long since puzzled out the meaning behind the words. There was a certain sort of wisdom in them. Not exactly Lao Tzu, or even Confucius, but an identifiable kernel of truth nonetheless.

His hand slid across the seat to touch the folded black-leather shape of his diplomatic pouch. In the darkness he could feel the reassuring creases and nicks left by years of faithful service. His hand trembled slightly, and he stilled it with an act of will. *It was unfortunate,* he thought wryly, *that one could not become a wise old master of statecraft without first becoming old.*

The lights of the American capital city slid by the rain-streaked windows of his embassy limousine. Discrete shapes smeared into prismatic blurs of light and color as rivulets of water snaked down the glass beside him. Beautiful images, but confusing. An apt metaphor for his years in America.

The car was one of the new Zhonghua M-1s that the Party was so proud of. Five and a half meters of sleek, lacquered black steel, which they were heralding as the first truly all-Chinese limousine. When he'd first seen it, Tian had found himself smiling at the irony posed by the car's very existence. China's leading auto manufacturer, the state-owned Brilliance China Automotive, had been forced to partner with BMW (German capitalists) and Italdesign (Italian capitalists) to produce their all-Chinese masterpiece of communist automotive engineering.

The Politburo had chosen to carefully ignore strategic parts of that partnership, the same way that they had chosen to ignore a hundred other changes brought on by globalization and the Information Age. They were so confident in the inherent superiority of the communist social and economic model that they continued to operate as if their actions took place in a vacuum. If Tianamen Square had taught them nothing else, they should have learned that the world was watching China. To act in ignorance of this fact was to court trouble. Which was, ultimately, why Tian found himself being called across town in the rain and the dark to answer for the actions of his government. He sighed. His country still had much to learn.

Tian fidgeted with his coat buttons and drew the collar more tightly around his neck. He did not yet know why the American president had summoned him at this hour, and that lack of knowledge left him with a cold spot in the pit of his stomach. He did not know what the Americans were going to say, but he knew from the way they had chosen to say it, that it was not going to be good.

At the beginning of his diplomatic career, Tian had viewed the intricacies of state protocol with a critical eye. In the vanity of his youth, he had dismissed the diplomatic ceremonies and rules of political etiquette as nothing more than useless rituals. But thirty years in his country's diplomatic service had opened his eyes to many things, not the least of which was the foolishness of his own youth. Protocol (and the Americans thought of it that way in their own language—with a capital "P") went far beyond ritual. As the Americans practiced it, Protocol was more than a system of rules for diplomatic communication; it was a language in and of itself. It was a rich and subtle language, in which every detail had meaning.

Tian checked his watch. Tonight's meeting was an excellent example. To begin with, the president wanted to meet directly with Tian. That was a most disturbing development. Other than the little ceremony that took place when he accepted the diplomatic credentials of a new ambassador, the president rarely met with ambassadors at all. Meetings with foreign ambassadors were usually entrusted to the secretary of state or an appointed underling. For the president to call for a personal meeting with an ambassador was nearly always a signal of extremely unusual circumstances. The very thought made Tian nervous, and he checked his watch again. No, traffic was light, and he would be on time. He took a breath.

The Americans had given Tian another hint of possible problems when they'd asked him to come alone. Under normal circumstances, he would have been accompanied by his deputy chief of mission. By excluding Tian's deputy from the invitation, the Americans were forcing the ambassador to face them alone. This was, of course, their prerogative, but it was one that the Americans rarely exercised. It was another bad sign, and Tian was not at all pleased with the prospect of walking alone into a room full of angry Americans.

The designated location for the meeting was yet another clue. There were three traditional choices for diplomatic meetings in the White House. The Roosevelt Room had a neutral connotation, and the majority of diplomatic meetings were conducted there. The West Wing Lobby was *Dao shan huo hai—a mountain of swords and sea of flames.* The Americans had an equivalent expression. What was it? The doghouse? Yes … the West Wing Lobby was the *doghouse.* An ambassador called to a meeting there could be certain that he had angered the American government.

But no, tonight's meeting was scheduled for the Oval Office, the third and by far the least common site for diplomatic conferences. The selection of the Oval Office meant one of two things, each of which were—oddly enough—at opposite ends of the spectrum. If the president wanted to ask a favor of China, or of Shaozu Tian himself, he *might* call for an Oval Office meeting. The favor would have to be *enormous* for the Americans to invoke such a rare privilege. And, though Tian had racked his brain to the point of a headache, he could not think of a single favor China could bestow that might warrant such treatment. Which meant that, in all probability, the Oval Office had been selected for the second reason: the president was angry at China. Not just angry either, spectacularly angry. Too angry for the doghouse—a thought that made Tian squirm uncomfortably in the limousine's leather seat. Maybe even *dangerously* angry. And he was calling in the ambassador of the People's Republic so that he could vent his wrath in person, in the Oval Office—the very seat of his country's power.

Such a meeting could conceivably lead to the disruption of diplomatic ties, or even trade embargoes and the loss of Most Favored Nation status. It was even conceivable that a meeting of that sort might serve as a precursor to war. Tian realized that his armpits were damp. The more he thought about it, the more this promised to be an ugly night.

* * *

As the limousine slid to a stop before the black steel bars of the diplomatic security gate that led to the White House grounds, Tian peered out the windshield through the rhythmic sweep of the wipers. The limousine had diplomatic license plates, which made the interior spaces sovereign Chinese territory, and therefore, immune to inspection. But the exterior of the car was—through the vagaries of diplomatic custom—classified as U.S. territory and was subject to inspection.

The steel gate slid open, and Tian's driver eased the big car forward into a three-sided enclosure built from the same black steel bars that supported the rest of the White House fence. As soon as the limousine braked to a stop, the gate slid shut behind it, leaving the car boxed and helpless in a steel cage. *My predicament exactly,* Tian thought. *Boxed in and helpless.*

An expressionless armed Marine guard stepped out of the concrete guardhouse and walked over to stand in the rain near the driver's window—hands tucked behind his back and feet spread shoulder-width apart in the formal posture known as parade rest. A pair of dark-uniformed Secret Service agents with powerful flashlights and inspection mirrors conducted a thorough search of the car's wheel wells and the underside of the chassis, working smoothly from the front of the car toward the rear. The men moved with determination and precision, not letting the pouring rain deter them, or hurry their procedures in the slightest.

When their visual inspection was finally complete, the Secret Service personnel backed away from the limousine and took up positions near the inner gate. One of them raised his right wrist to his mouth and spoke quietly into a microphone concealed in his sleeve.

A few seconds later, another pair of Secret Service agents stepped out of the guardhouse. Each of these men carried a device that looked like a cross between a lunch box and a vacuum cleaner. They were smaller than the models in use at the Chinese Embassy, but Tian had no trouble recognizing them through the rain-blurred window. They were ion-spectrometers: machines that sucked in air and sniffed it for the specific trace molecules given off by explosive chemicals. It was the electronic equivalent of a dog's nose.

Tian hoped that the smaller American spectrometers were smarter than the Chinese models. The ones at the embassy had a tendency to sound their alarms upon detecting the nitroglycerin in Tian's heart medication.

Despite the downpour, the Secret Service agents went to work at once, letting their machines sniff the exterior of the car, in a pattern that closely duplicated the visual inspection that their fellow agents had just completed. And, like their fellow agents, they gave no hint of even noticing the rain that pounded down on them from the dark Washington sky. Tian could not help but admire their patience and determination.

Satisfied at last, the Secret Service agents retreated into the guardhouse. The Marine guard took a step backward, came to attention, and saluted. As if in response, the inner gate slid open, allowing Tian's limousine access to the White House grounds. With barely a nod of acknowledgment, Tian's silent driver steered the car into the White House driveway and turned toward the famed West Wing.

Tian reached across the seat for his diplomatic pouch, pulled it to him, and held it in his lap. The esteemed members of the Politburo could not seem to grasp the fact that the Americans were different now. The terrorist attacks on New York and Washington had changed them, *hardened* them—as fire hardens steel. They were less trusting now and a good deal less naive about world affairs. And—after decades spent trying to broker peace at nearly any price—they had become awfully eager to reach for their guns. Surely the American invasions of Afghanistan and Iraq were ample evidence of that.

Tian tightened his grip on the diplomatic pouch, rubbing the largest, most familiar nick in the old leather with the ball of his thumb. He had not been told why he was being called to task, so he was reduced to guessing—a thoroughly uncomfortable situation for an international diplomat to find himself in. If the Americans were truly angry, it might well be over his country's most recent ballistic missile test. Based on that as yet untested assumption, his staff had drafted extensive notes on potential arguments that he might employ. His diplomatic pouch contained twenty-two pages of Chinese pictographs in the neat calligraphy of his deputy chief of mission. Tian did not anticipate having to refer to those notes. He had read and re-read them until he could nearly recite them from memory. Still, there was a vague comfort in the knowledge that they were available to him if needed—the same sense of sufficiency that came from knowing that your vehicle carried a spare tire, even if you did not expect to need it, or know how to change it.

His staff had done their work well, and Tian intended to score some points—provided that the missile test did, in fact, prove to be the subject of this meeting. Despite his preparations, he had no desire to argue this point. Unfortunately, he had no choice—his orders from the Politburo were unmistakable. If the Americans raised the issue of the missile test, he was to give no ground. The words of Premier Xiao had been quite clear on this: *Bu huan er san—to part on hard terms*—was acceptable. He was not to bend, or even *appear* to bend on this matter.

Tian shifted in his seat and hoped fervently that he had guessed wrong. This was an issue on which it was not even remotely wise to anger the Americans. They had become quick to react to anything they perceived as a threat, and these days it was difficult to predict what would fall into that category.

Despite his hopes to the contrary, he had little doubt that the missile test would be the topic of this meeting. He would know in a few seconds. The Laws of Protocol were about to give him a final clue. He would be able to take a reading on the disposition of the Americans according to who was waiting to meet him at the entrance to the West Wing. If tempers were reasonable, he would be greeted by David Spiros, the National Security Council country officer assigned to China. If the Americans were pleased with China, or if they wanted to ask a favor, they would send Gregory Brenthoven, the national security advisor himself. If they were truly angry, they would send a minor functionary from the NSC, probably someone whom Tian would not recognize.

The limousine pulled out of the rain under the curved overhang of the West Wing portico and stopped opposite the marble steps that led into the White House. The rhythmic whunk-whunk of the wipers swept the windshield uselessly a few times before the driver shut them off. Heart in his mouth and lips pressed tightly together, Tian peered through the steamy window toward the door at the top of the steps. It was guarded by a pair of United States Marines in full dress uniforms. As was the custom, one of the Marines came to attention and honored the Chinese Embassy's vehicle with a crisp salute. Then the guard dropped his salute and marched down the steps to open the rear door of the limousine.

Able to learn nothing further from his vantage point in the back seat, Tian uttered a sigh and, clutching his leather diplomatic pouch, pulled himself from the automobile. Then, as Tian stood and straightened his suit, the Marine came to attention again, and rendered a second salute.

Tian acknowledged the salute with a nod and started walking up the steps. The damp night air enveloped him like an evil spell; he felt flares of arthritic pain in his knees and hips, echoed dully by an ache of anxiety in his chest. He concentrated on keeping his steps even and his face implacable. One did not show weakness in the face of a potential adversary.

The Marine remaining at the top of the steps opened the door, and Tian caught sight of the person assigned to greet him. It was a youngish woman, and Tian did not recognize her at all.

"Bao tian tian wu," he said under his breath. Literally *a reckless waste of grain*, but in this context it meant *an ill omen*. This was not going to go well. He smiled and extended his hand for the woman to shake.

This was not going to go well at all.

CHAPTER 3

DEUTSCHE MARINE NAVAL ARSENAL
KIEL, GERMANY
MONDAY; 07 MAY
0951 hours (9:51 AM)
TIME ZONE +1 'ALPHA'

Dirty-looking clouds scudded across an iron-colored sky. In a few hours, the spring sun would burn away the overcast, but for now, the damp remnants of winter hung over the harbor. The water that lapped up against the rusting steel pilings seemed oily and dark, its froth the color of a dead fish's belly.

Kapitan Stefan Gröeler leaned against the dock railing and watched the huge yellow ammunition crane lift the last of the torpedoes off the ordnance barge. Suspended from the crane's heavy cable by a four-way sling, the weapon swung slowly out to hover above the aft deck of Gröeler's submarine, the *U-307.* Crewmen in gray coveralls grabbed the dangling weapon's tag-lines and began to guide it into the proper attitude for lowering through the main hatch. The men worked in near silence, as they should have, with the Team Leader watching closely and issuing brief commands. "Hold fast on the forward line," or "Bring the nose down farther," or "Check the crane," or "Watch your deck clearance!"

Gröeler nodded almost imperceptibly. They were good men—a good crew.

His eyes lingered on the weapon suspended above the deck. It hung nose down and tail high, close to the thirty-seven–degree angle needed to lower it through the weapons hatch.

The Team Leader issued another command, and the nose dropped a few more degrees. Satisfied, he turned, made eye contact with the crane operator, and opened and closed the fingers of his right hand several times like the quacking of a duck: the hand signal for *lower slowly*.

The polymerized coating of the *Ozeankriegsführungtechnologien* DMA37 torpedo gave the weapon a shiny green look, as though it were a child's toy made of plastic. In comparison, the rounded profile of the Type 212B submarine seemed especially menacing: a sleek, dark-skinned predator floating low in the water. It was a false impression; *both* machines were dangerous. The quietest, most capable diesel submarine ever built, paired with one of the most sophisticated and lethal undersea weapons that modern military science could devise.

The morning sun found its way through a hole in the clouds, and Gröeler squinted slightly. The skin around his eyes was crosshatched with heavy crow's feet. Not laugh lines, but rather a cumulative network of wrinkles caused by thousands of hours spent peering through periscopes and attack-scopes.

He was a short, solidly built man, with ice-blue eyes that moved quickly and missed very little. Behind his back, the men called him *das Armkreuz*—the spider. Under another circumstance, the nickname might have been disparaging. But Gröeler knew that his crew considered it a compliment. It signified their respect for his skill as a hunter. He moved quietly, worked meticulously, and killed quickly.

He rummaged in the pocket of his gray Deutsche Marine coveralls for a cigarette. Smoking was forbidden at the ammunition piers, but he was in command here. It was *his* submarine, they were *his* torpedoes, and the gray-coveralled crewmen working down on the deck were *his* to command. He lit the cigarette with a slender butane lighter made of good German steel. He drew a lung full of smoke. It was a stupid rule anyway. The plasticized-hexite explosive used in the torpedoes was incredibly stable. Without a precisely measured electrical charge from an arming mechanism, it was just so much harmless chemical modeling clay. *With* the proper initiating charge ... well, *that* was a different matter. But ten cartons of smoldering cigarettes and a hundred butane lighters couldn't hope to set one of those weapons off.

He took another hit off the cigarette, exhaling fiercely through his nostrils. Still, it was good to have such rules. They gave the men direction: road signs for separating acceptable behavior from unacceptable behavior. And it was good for the men to see their kapitan breaking such rules. They needed to be reminded that his was the final word on all subjects. As commanding officer of the wolfpack, his orders were not subject to question. He, and he alone, would decide when to follow regulations and when to break them.

He looked at his watch. They would finish with the torpedoes shortly, and then they could begin loading the missiles. It was obvious that his crew would finish ahead of schedule. He stepped away from the railing, executed a precise turn to the right, and began walking with a crisp, deliberate stride.

It was time to inspect the other three submarines under his command and check the status of their weapons onloads. No doubt they would also be ahead of schedule, but probably not so far as his own crew. He had, after all, personally selected every one of his men. They were, quite literally, the best that the German Navy had to offer. And after six months of intensive pre-mission training, they meshed like the proverbial well-oiled machine.

As he walked, Gröeler pulled off his officer's cap and rubbed his fingers briskly through his blond crew cut. There was more than a little gray in his hair now. That too was a good thing. The other wolves in the pack should be reminded that the *lead* wolf was the oldest and wisest, as well as the strongest.

He pulled his cap back on and straightened it with a practiced gesture: no wasted motion. Let his men see the outward evidence of his self-assurance. Let them note the steadiness of his hands and the easy grace of his movements. They would take confidence from these things, and they were going to need that confidence, along with every scrap of advantage they could get.

The mission was achievable; he was certain of that. It would require exceptional skill and more luck than he cared to think about, but it *could* be done. He knew the tactics of the American Navy and the capabilities of their hardware. He could bluff the Americans. Avoid them. And if he couldn't ...

It wasn't failure that worried him. He had made every possible preparation. His men were handpicked and expertly trained. His boats were in superb condition. All of the necessary support mechanisms were in place. The plan could work. He would *make* it work.

But what about afterward? Would the Americans really react as the Bundeswehr's military Security Council predicted? Did his superiors really understand the Americans at all? Gröeler certainly didn't, and he'd been studying them and their military tactics for his entire adult life.

The Japanese had critically misjudged the Americans in 1941, hadn't they? Their attack on Pearl Harbor had devastated the U.S. Pacific Fleet. The mission had succeeded. But the Americans had not sued for peace, as the expert strategists and tacticians had assured the Japanese High Command. The carnage inflicted at Pearl Harbor had enraged the normally placid Americans in ways the Japanese psyche could not even comprehend. The Americans had risen from the wreckage of the attack and crushed Japan like an insect. Finally, it had taken the nuclear extermination of over a quarter of a million Japanese citizens and the utter destruction of Hiroshima and Nagasaki to slake the American thirst for revenge.

Japan had nearly been destroyed as a result of wishful thinking on the part of its leaders. And now, the chancellor and his cronies in the Bundeswehr seemed to be poised to make the same mistake. They were gambling the fate of Germany on their projections of how the Americans would react. What if their guesses were wrong? What if the American response was military instead of political?

Gröeler shook his head. He had spent his entire life in submarines. He didn't know much about international politics, but this whole thing struck him as the worst sort of wishful thinking. The kind by which nations were destroyed.

He had nearly turned the mission down. For the first time in his life, he had come within a centimeter of refusing to obey his orders. Only one thing had stopped him—the knowledge that the Bundeswehr would find someone else to carry out the plan. Someone less capable. Success might bring consequences that the Bundeswehr and the chancellor had not foreseen. But, if the mission was botched, the consequences would be ungodly.

Gröeler shook his head again. Either his superiors had forgotten their history, or they hadn't noticed the date. The seventh of May. The anniversary of the Nazi High Command's unconditional surrender to the Allies at the end of the Second World War. Germany had lain in ruins then, Berlin still burning from the American fire bombs, the countryside torn by the boots of soldiers and the treads of tanks. And the Bundeswehr had selected *this* date to launch their operation. Had they done so out of blind ignorance? Or was their choice of dates intentional? Some delusion that Germany was destined to recapture its former glory? Gröeler couldn't decide which idea was more frightening.

He sucked a last lung full of smoke from the cigarette and thumped it over the rail into the water. In the split-second before the butt left his fingers, he caught a glimpse of the brand name: *Ernte 23.*

The name brought a bitter smile to Kapitan Gröeler's mouth. *Ernte* meant *harvest.* And, if the mission didn't go as planned, there would be a harvest all right. A harvest of blood and fire. He looked down at the piers where the young Sailors were rushing to carry out his orders and wondered if any of them would survive it.

CHAPTER 4

WASHINGTON, DC
SUNDAY; 06 MAY
8:45 PM EDT

President Francis "Frank" Chandler swiveled his chair a few degrees to the left and stared out the window across the White House grounds. It was really coming down out there tonight, the rain driving across the manicured lawn in torrents. Occasionally the wind would manage to whip a burst of raindrops far enough under the edge of the colonnade to splatter on the marble flagstones of the covered walkway. But even those violent bursts fell well short of the windows.

Some small part of him wished that the wind would pick up enough to drive the rain against his windows. He loved the sound of rain on glass; it conjured up memories of boyhood summers in Iowa cornfields and of the clatter of a good spring rain on a corrugated tin roof. Of course, he probably wouldn't have been able to hear it anyway; the windows were triple-paned bulletproof glass.

He watched for a few seconds in silent fascination. There was something strange about seeing the rain without hearing it; something vaguely disconnected: a little like the feeling that came from watching television with the sound turned down.

He leaned a little farther back, rested his elbows on the padded leather arms of the chair, and wondered for the thousandth time at the strange chain of events that had led him to the Oval Office. The thought, as always, brought an odd half-smile to his lips. There were men—powerful and influential men—who spent their entire lives fighting for a chance to sit in this office. Struggling one rung at a time up the twin ladders of politics and public opinion—waiting for a chance to sit in *this* chair, behind *this* desk. But the job had very nearly fallen into Frank's lap. He sure as hell hadn't planned his life around it, anyway.

He was a latecomer to politics, and he had entered the political arena by the back door. (Some of his more vocal critics preferred to say he had tunneled under the back fence.)

The son of an Iowa corn farmer, he had inherited three major things from his father: a passion for the land, an iron-hard work ethic, and the shambling big-boned frame of a farmhand. Six foot four and broad shouldered, he had a roughness about him that spoke more of flannel shirts and work-scuffed blue jeans than of suits and neckties.

His love of the land had not led him to the farm, as it had his father and grandfather before him, but to the laboratories of the University of Iowa. Armed with a master's degree in organic chemistry, he had climbed through the ranks of the Iowa Department of Agriculture and Land Stewardship, where his fierce determination to improve the lot of the American farmer had eventually earned him an appointment as the state secretary of agriculture.

With the appointment had come the realization that the future of the farmer was being decided not in the fields or in the laboratory, but in the boardrooms and on the floors of the legislature. Frank had decided to throw his hat into the political ring. After an extremely successful term as the state secretary of agriculture, he had made a dark-horse bid for governor of Iowa. He'd never really expected to win. At best, he had hoped to drag the plight of the farmer into the forefront of Iowa's political system. To raise important issues in the hopes that more viable gubernatorial candidates would have to deal with them.

But his plain-talking grassroots campaign had resonated with the voters of Iowa, and they had surprised him (and everyone else in the state political machine) by electing him governor.

Four years later, he had entered the race for the presidency, running a distant second to Martin Bridgewater: an archly conservative senator and the fair-haired boy of the Republican Party. Bridgewater was a charismatic speaker and a political heavyweight. The cameras loved him, and so did the crowds. He had started with a thirty-point lead over Frank in the CNN, *USA Today,* and Gallup polls, and had widened it quickly.

Frank had been poised to lose the election by the widest margin in history, when fate dropped another surprise in his lap. Martin Bridgewater's pregnant nineteen-year-old mistress had decided to take her story to the media. Bridgewater had lost twenty polling points in the first forty-eight hours. Even so, he might well have weathered the storm. After the predictable outcry, his supporters had settled down pretty quickly. They seemed prepared to forgive him for his transgressions. Other powerful men had succumbed to the temptations of the flesh, after all. Some of them had even been presidents.

But Bridgewater's girlfriend had sold six cassette tapes to one of the more sensational cable news programs. The young woman had recorded many of her private phone conversations with Bridgewater. The news anchors had apparently delighted in playing sound bytes of the more lurid parts, bleeping out questionable choices of language in a manner that made the tapes seem even more sordid than they actually were. At the climax of the exposé had come the most damning revelation of all: Senator Bridgewater—a rabid pro-lifer—had tried to convince his mistress to have an abortion. He had offered the girl a quiet cash settlement to get rid of the baby and disappear into the woodwork.

Bridgewater's campaign had disintegrated in a matter of days. The resulting backlash of public opinion had hurled Frank Chandler, the hayseed candidate, into the highest office in the land.

* * *

President Chandler's eyes were still locked on the rain falling soundlessly outside the bulletproof windows. His odd little smile faded slowly. He'd been sitting in the big chair for thirty-nine months and sixteen days, and he still couldn't believe he was here. In the few quiet moments that the job afforded him, the surreal quality of the entire situation filtered back to the surface of his mind, leaving him with a disjointed feeling. Disconnected. Like the strangely silent rain.

He sighed and, for a brief second, entertained the notion of opening one of the French doors that led to the columned walkway. That way, at least he'd be able to *hear* the occasional spatters of rain on the flagstones.

"Mr. President?" The voice belonged to the White House chief of staff, Veronica Doyle.

The president snapped his mind back to attention and swung his chair around. "Yes?"

"They're ready for you, sir."

"Good," the president said. He rubbed his eyes and blinked several times. "Where is the ambassador?"

"In a holding pattern in the West Wing lobby."

The president nodded. "Show our people in. We'll give them a minute to get settled before we call for the ambassador."

Doyle nodded to the Secret Service agent standing by the door to the office of the president's secretary. The agent opened the door, and the team for the China meeting began to filter into the Oval Office.

The president beckoned them into the room and waved them toward the rectangle of couches and chairs at the end of the room opposite his desk. "Have a seat in the bullpen. Make yourselves comfortable, I'll be with you in a couple of seconds."

He turned back to his chief of staff. "What else have we got tonight?"

The chief of staff flipped open the lid of her palm-top computer and scanned the small LCD screen. "At nine-thirty, you've got a phone conference with the assistant secretary of state for Eastern European affairs. The Russians are asking for increased wheat subsidies. Assistant Secretary Chernja thinks it's a bad idea, but she wants your permission before she shuts the door on this one. You also promised the vice president you would sit down with him and look at his numbers on the handgun bill."

The president nodded. "Move the vice president up to nine-thirty and bump Assistant Secretary Chernja to tomorrow morning. The Russian thing isn't going to self-destruct any time soon, and I'd much rather hit it when my brain is fresh."

Doyle nodded and made rapid notes on the input screen of her palm-top. "Good idea, Mr. President. I'm starting to fade myself, sir."

Her appearance belied her words. Her short black hair was flawlessly styled, her turquoise silk business suit was immaculate, and if there was any fatigue behind her flint-gray eyes, it certainly wasn't visible to mere mortals.

The president stood up. "All right. Send for the ambassador. Let's get this over with."

* * *

The bullpen consisted of two couches and four chairs, laid out in a rough rectangle around a low-topped French Empire bureau that served as a coffee table. The table was an authentic piece from the President Monroe collection, burnished ebony with curving saber-style legs that were chased with gold leaf. The source of a minor point of contention, the date of the table's manufacture could be set at either 1827 or 1830, and a fairly good case could be made for either date. The chairs and couches—which appeared to be matching French Empire pieces—were actually excellent reproductions, crafted by the famed Kittinger Furniture, suppliers of White House furnishings for nearly a hundred and fifty years.

The president had given the bullpen its name during his first week in office. In baseball, the bullpen was a designated area of the ballpark where the pitchers warmed up before they trudged out to the pitcher's mound, where the real work began. The nickname had not proven to be very accurate, because he generally accomplished more serious work in the bullpen than he did at his desk—which (according to the metaphor) should have been the pitcher's mound. But, apropos or not, the nickname had stuck.

The president walked over to the bullpen and spent a few minutes greeting the members of his meeting team and shaking hands. Not counting himself and his chief of staff, Veronica Doyle, the team consisted of Secretary of State Elizabeth Whelkin; National Security Advisor Gregory Brenthoven; Assistant Secretary of State for Southeast Asian Affairs William Collins; and a designated note taker, Marine Corps Lieutenant Michael Summers, on loan from the National Security Council. There would be no need for an interpreter, as the Chinese ambassador spoke excellent English.

*　　*　　*

The hallway door opened and the ambassador was ushered in by a deputy assistant to somebody-or-other in the National Security Council. The young woman, who probably didn't know that she had been selected on the basis of her obscurity, was visibly nervous over what was obviously her first visit to the Oval Office. Despite her nervousness, she made her announcement flawlessly. "Mr. President, may I present Ambassador Shaozu Tian, minister plenipotentiary of the People's Republic of China."

The president smiled and stepped forward to shake the ambassador's hand. "Good evening, Ambassador Shaozu. Thank you for coming on such short notice."

The ambassador returned his smile. "I am honored to be of service, Mr. President. And I bring you greetings on behalf of the citizens and government of the People's Republic of China."

The next few moments were dedicated to handshakes and pleasantries as the ambassador was introduced to the rest of the team.

When the members of the team took their seats, they fell silent. In accordance with the dictates of protocol, the president would speak as the sole representative of the United States—just as the ambassador would speak as the sole representative of his own government. The other members of the team were there to watch, gather information, and formulate ideas for the discussion that would immediately follow the meeting. During the meeting itself, they might pass the president notes or documents, but they would not contribute directly to the conversation.

There was an additional point to having so many non-speaking members in the room. Few people are comfortable under close scrutiny. Having a room full of people watch your every gesture and listen to your every word—all without speaking themselves—can be highly unsettling. It is difficult for even the most accomplished of diplomats to concentrate properly under such circumstances. In Washington circles, the technique has often been likened to a low-intensity version of Psychological Warfare.

* * *

When everyone was finally seated, the president said, "I hope you will forgive me if I come directly to matters of business."

The ambassador smiled slightly. "An excellent idea, Mr. President. I am an old man, and I must confess that the passage of years has somewhat blunted my taste for polite small talk."

"Good," the president said. "I would like to discuss the matter of your country's most recent ballistic missile launch."

The ambassador's eyebrows went up slightly. "I see. Is there a problem?"

"Yes," the president said. "There is a problem, or rather—there are *two* problems. The first is with the trajectory of the missile, and the second is with the timing of the launch."

"Oh? And why should either of those pose difficulties? To my understanding, the launch was conducted safely, without incident or threat to life."

"Without incident—yes," the president said. "It's the 'threat to life' part that we are not so certain about."

"How so?"

"The missile in question was a DF-21C, designed to carry the NV-6 nuclear warhead; is that correct?"

"I believe that is so."

"Does the DF-21C have the capability to carry any non-nuclear payloads?"

The ambassador's hand stole down to the black leather diplomatic pouch in his lap. He made no move to open it. His fingers began to play over the creased leather, almost as though the pouch were some sort of worry stone, or talisman. "I … cannot speak on this issue," he said. "That is, I am not an expert on the subject of ballistic missile systems."

The national security advisor scribbled something on a slip of paper, folded it, and passed it to the president. The president read it and then paused for a second before continuing. "I'm sure that it will come as no surprise to you that I have numerous ballistic missile experts at my disposal, some of whom are quite knowledgeable on the subject of the weapons systems of your People's Liberation Army. My experts assure me that the DF-21C has no conventional warhead capability."

The ambassador tilted his head slightly to the side. "If your experts are—as you say, *expert*—then I am sure that their assessments are correct. May I now ask the point of this question?"

"The point is this," the president said. "Your military fired a ballistic missile directly over Taiwan, less than a week before the Taiwanese national election—an election in which the front-running candidate just happens to be a strong proponent of Taiwanese independence. The missile in question is designed solely for offensive nuclear strikes. You have to admit, that sounds an awful lot like deliberate intimidation. What my grandfather used to call strong-arm politics."

The Chinese ambassador shot to his feet, his black leather pouch falling to the carpet. "You accuse my country of playing politics with nuclear weapons?" His voice was a near shout. Then he seemed to realize where he was and sank slowly to his seat, groping around the floor for a few seconds before he recovered his diplomatic pouch and set it in his lap again.

President Chandler raised his eyebrows a fraction. "What would *you* call it?"

The ambassador paused for a few seconds before speaking. His tone was much calmer now. "I would call it ... I believe ... a routine test-launch of an unarmed missile. A launch, I might add, that traveled entirely through Chinese airspace, passed over only Chinese territory, and landed safely in Chinese national waters. As for the timing? I would call *that* a coincidence."

The secretary of state passed a folded slip of paper to the president. He scanned it before continuing. "A coincidence," he said slowly. "Would that be the same sort of coincidence that led your government to launch three missiles into Taiwanese territorial waters on the eve of their first national election in 1996? Was it *also* coincidence that your country moved several hundred CSS-6 and CSS-7 missile systems into Fujian province—directly across the straits from Taiwan—in the weeks just prior to their election in 2000?"

Ambassador Shaozu stiffened. "Mr. President, are you now suggesting that the defensive deployment of the People's Liberation Army within our *own* borders is somehow the business of the United States?"

"Perhaps not," the president said. "But firing a ballistic missile directly over Taiwan is an overtly hostile act."

"Hostile to whom, Mr. President?"

"To Taiwan, the Democratic People's Republic of China."

The ambassador smiled. "Mr. President, there is no Democratic People's Republic of China. It does not exist. It never *has* existed."

"I understand that your government holds such an opinion," the president said. "But you must realize that the United States does not share your view."

"There is only one China, Mr. President—a simple truth that even the United Nations acknowledges. There are two chairs for Korea in the General

Assembly, one for South Korea and another for North Korea. That is because there are two Koreas.

"You will note that there is only one chair in the United Nations General Assembly for China. That is because there is only one China. If there were two Chinas, there would be two chairs, would there not? The citizens of our troublesome island province may style themselves as renegades, but they are Chinese citizens nonetheless."

"The citizens of Taiwan have a democratically elected government," the president said. "They have their own laws, their own currency, their own national identity. They do not wish to be part of your country."

The ambassador sighed. "We cannot let the wishes of a few million miscreants threaten the integrity of our sovereign nation. Their desires are irrelevant."

"How can the wishes of millions of people be irrelevant?"

"Perhaps my memory for American history is a little fuzzy," the ambassador said, "but I seem to recall that your country was faced with a similar situation in the latter half of the nineteenth century. A number of your Southern provinces … excuse me … you call them *states*, do you not? A number of your Southern *states* decided to secede from your Union. If I am not mistaken, your government used military force to repatriate the renegade states. I believe the casualties from that war totaled something just short of seven hundred thousand people. Yet, your citizens seem to regard the loss of nearly three-quarters of a million lives as a reasonable price to pay for reacquiring the lost territories and reabsorbing the inhabitants."

"A fair point," the president said. "But we are in the twenty-first century, not the nineteenth. The world is a different place. The tools and attitudes that served us well a hundred and fifty years ago have no place in the modern age."

"Perhaps things have not changed as much as you would like to believe," Ambassador Shaozu said. "What if the situation arose again tomorrow? Suppose that the citizens of your island state of Hawaii decide next week that they are disillusioned with the direction that your government is taking. Suppose they elect their own president, draft their own constitution, and print their own money. Will your country let them peacefully secede, merely because they wish it?"

The president didn't say anything.

"It's not such an easy question when the problem is in your backyard, is it, Mr. President?"

The president leaned back and made a steeple of his fingers. "An interesting argument, Ambassador, but it fails to take into account the two enormously powerful effects in the evolution of nations. Time … and acceptance."

The ambassador's eyes narrowed. "I do not understand."

"Consider your hypothetical example," the president said. "Suppose the people of Hawaii *did* declare their independence and form their own government. Then suppose that the United States chose to wait a while before acting to repatriate Hawaii. If Hawaii were self-governing and self-sufficient, at what point would they cease to be a renegade state and actually *become* an independent country?"

The ambassador frowned. "I am not following your argument."

"Your People's Republic of China and our own United States have much in common," the president said. "Both of our nations were given birth by revolution. Each of our countries managed to fight its way out from under the yoke of a repressive government. Both of our countries began as renegade states. And yet, today, China and America exist as two of the most powerful nations on Earth, due—in large part—to the passage of time and the acceptance of other nations. I'm sure you will agree that far too much time has passed for Great Britain to recoup the United States as lost territory. Similarly, far too many nations have acknowledged the existence of your own People's Republic of China for the Kuomintang or the descendants of the Empress Dowager to attempt to regain your citizens as outlaw rebels."

The ambassador did not speak.

"Time has passed for Taiwan, Mr. Ambassador," the president said. "You haven't made a serious move to repatriate them in over sixty years. In that time, they have become self-governing, and they have gained the acceptance of many nations. Taiwan now enjoys formal diplomatic ties with over thirty countries and maintains trading partnerships with over a hundred and fifty countries. At last count, they were the fourteenth largest trading nation in the world. It is true that they do not hold a seat in the United Nations General Assembly, but we both know that your country has blocked every attempt to formally admit them to the UN." He smiled gently. "Rebel republics are transformed into nations by time and acceptance. And the Democratic People's Republic of China on Taiwan has had both."

The ambassador did not speak for several seconds. When he did, his voice was tight and low. "You are welcome to accept the make-believe sovereignty of our renegade province, if you so choose. The People's Republic of China is under no obligation to do so."

The president nodded. "I understand your position. And I acknowledge that it's likely that our countries will continue to agree to *dis*agree on matters concerning Taiwan—at least for the foreseeable future. In the meantime, the United States is willing to support whatever diplomatic overtures your government wishes to make toward peaceful reunification with Taiwan. I must caution you though, the U.S. cannot and *will* not sit back and allow military threats to Taiwan to go unchallenged. Our policy on this matter dates back to 1950, when President Truman deployed the entire U.S. Seventh Fleet in defense of Taiwan. Please convey this message directly to your premier: we are willing to give you the benefit of the doubt on this recent missile launch. You say that it was a routine test, and we will accept your word for that, despite the evidence to the contrary."

He leaned over the coffee table and flipped open a heavy leather-bound book to a pre-marked page. A glossy color image of mainland China covered two pages. "My world atlas tells me that your country has about eighty-seven hundred miles of coastline." He flipped to another marked page. The map of Taiwan took up a half-page. "It also tells me that Taiwan is about two hundred and thirty-seven miles in its longest axis." He closed the book with a thump. "If we add a twelve-mile buffer to the north and south of the island, to account for Taiwanese territorial waters, we discover that your country has over eight thousand four hundred miles of coastline to fire missile tests from—without impinging on the airspace, territory, or seas of Taiwan." His voice hardened. "I suggest you consider using another piece of ocean for your next missile test."

"I object to your tone," the ambassador said. "I have given you my assurances that the launch was a routine test, yet you insinuate that it was a deliberate act of … what did you call it? Strong-arm politics?"

The president beckoned to his secretary of state, Elizabeth Whelkin, who leaned over far enough to hand him a folded newspaper. It was an English-language edition of the *Tokyo Times*.

"The Japanese press has picked up on a rumor that your missile launch was code-named *Tongyi De Zhongguo*," the president said. He unfolded the paper and laid it on the coffee table with slow, deliberate motions. "My Mandarin is a little rusty, Ambassador Shaozu. Could you refresh my memory? How does *Tongyi De Zhongguo* translate into English?"

The ambassador's cheeks reddened. His fingers seemed to spasm as they roamed the surface of his old diplomatic pouch. "I give you my assurance, Mr. President; I have no knowledge of any such code name."

The president nodded. "I'm relieved to hear that. Perhaps you'd be kind enough to translate the phrase anyway, for the benefit of those of us who do not speak the language of the Middle Kingdom."

"Of course," the ambassador said in a quiet voice. "It means … *United China*."

The words hung in the air for several seconds before the president spoke again. "United China," he said. "Used in the context of a nuclear missile launch, might that phrase be interpreted to mean that your country is prepared to use any sort of force necessary to achieve a United China? That is to say, the return of Taiwan to Chinese control?"

"That might be one interpretation," the ambassador said slowly.

"If you have a different interpretation to offer, I would be interested in hearing it," the president said.

Ambassador Shaozu said nothing.

The president allowed the silence to drag on for nearly a minute. He was tempted to rake the ambassador over the coals again, but there wasn't anything to be gained by it. He had gotten his message across, and the rules of protocol required diplomatic meetings to end with pleasantries and handshakes.

"Thank you for coming," he said finally. He climbed to his feet and extended his hand. "Please convey my greetings to Premier Xiao and the esteemed members of the Politburo."

The ambassador got to his feet and shook the president's outstretched hand. "I will, Mr. President."

The ambassador shook hands with the other members of the meeting team before taking his leave. The note taker, Lt. Summers, escorted him from the room.

* * *

The president waited nearly a minute after the door had closed behind the ambassador before he clapped his hands together. "Talk to me, people."

The secretary of state spoke first. "Did you notice his eyes, sir? He was blowing smoke the entire time, and I don't think he was at all happy about it."

The president waved a hand in a circle. "Continue."

"The diplomacy game is sticky," she said. "An ambassador is sometimes forced to present his government's position, even when he thinks his government is screwing up. This is especially true of diplomats who represent communist governments; they have little or no latitude to deviate from the official party line."

The president leaned back in his chair. "You think Shaozu disagrees with the Politburo's position on this missile launch?"

"Maybe, sir," the secretary of state said.

"Something is definitely bothering him," added William Collins, the assistant secretary of state for Southeast Asian affairs. "I've worked with Tian for years, and I have to agree. Tian put on a good show tonight; he's too good a diplomat not to put his best into every session, but his heart wasn't in it tonight."

"All right," the president said. "He was distracted, and that threw his game off a little. The next obvious question is: what's got him rattled? Is it just frustration over having to spout Party rhetoric? Or is he worried about something?"

"If I had to guess," Assistant Secretary Collins said, "I'd say Tian is worried."

"About what?" the chief of staff asked.

Gregory Brenthoven, the national security advisor, loosened his tie. "We've got two good possibilities. On the one hand, he may be worried about our response to the missile launch—possible military reprisals, diplomatic or economic sanctions—hell, he may even be worried that this will goad us into extending formal diplomatic recognition to Taiwan. On the other hand, it may be his own government he's worried about. Either something they've done, or something they're about to do."

"That doesn't exactly narrow the field," the president said. "Do you have any sense for what it might be? At the moment, I'll settle for a hunch."

"I have no idea, sir," Brenthoven said. "But it's liable to be something we're really not going to like."

Veronica Doyle looked around at the members of the team. "Anybody got any idea how far the Chinese might go?"

"They just launched a ballistic missile over Taiwan," said Secretary Whelkin. "I'd say they're feeling pretty bold."

"And in this case," the president said, "bold might equate to stupid." He nodded slowly and then turned to his national security advisor. "Greg, round up the Joint Chiefs; I want an aircraft carrier off the coast of Taiwan by the time the sun comes up tomorrow, and a second carrier on scene as soon as we can manage it."

The national security advisor frowned. "Two carriers, Mr. President? We've only got four deployed. That's going to spread us pretty thin. If we're trying to show the Chinese that we're not happy with them, I should think one carrier will more than do the job."

The president shook his head. "I don't want China to think we're unhappy. I want them to know that we're mad as hell and not interested in playing games where Taiwan is concerned. Besides, the people of Taiwan have an election coming up in a few days. If we let the Politburo have their way, that election will take place in the shadow of a Chinese sword. Let's show the Taiwanese people a little of the American shield instead."

He looked up. "Okay guys, all we've got are guesses. If the Chinese are planning some kind of move, we're going to need a lot more than that. Get out there and beat the bushes. We need numbers on the Chinese economy, readiness assessments on their military, and trend analyses on their logistics. If they're stockpiling anything—I don't care if it's rice, bullets, or canned peaches—I want to know about it." He stood up. "That's all."

The members of the team began filing out the door. In a few seconds, only the president, his chief of staff, and the national security advisor remained.

"Something I can do for you, Greg?"

"Yes, sir. I do have one more item I'd like to run by you, if you have a couple of minutes."

The president nodded.

Brenthoven reached into the inside breast pocket of his jacket and retrieved a small leather-bound notebook. He opened it and read for a couple of seconds before looking up at his boss. "February of last year, Niedersachsen Six, the nuclear reactor outside Hanover, Germany, had to be shut down because of a primary coolant leak. There wasn't a great deal of contamination, but the European media had a field day with it anyway."

"I remember," the president said. "They trotted out every China Syndrome reference they could lay their hands on, from Three Mile Island to Chernobyl."

"Taken by itself, I wouldn't assign it much importance," Brenthoven said. "But Niedersachsen Six was the third significant incident in the German nuclear power program in less than two years."

"I read a white paper on Niedersachsen," Doyle said. "They shut down the reactor for inspection and repair. They're going to restart it at the end of this month."

Brenthoven shook his head. "No, they're not. The Green Party has cobbled together a sort of ecologist's coalition to block the restarting of the reactor. In fact, they managed to whip up enough public backlash to push their case all the way up to the Bundestag for a formal vote. It's official: they're shutting them all down. Every reactor on German soil."

Doyle pursed her lips for a half-second. "Germany was moving in that direction anyway. Now they'll have to do it a little faster."

"Not a *little* faster," Brenthoven said. "A *lot* faster. In less than a year, the Germans are going to have one hell of an energy crunch. Nearly thirty-five percent of their electricity comes from nuclear power, and their per capita usage is through the roof. Over six thousand kilowatt-hours per person, per year."

"How bad is it going to get, Greg?" the president asked.

Brenthoven checked his notebook again. "Bad, sir. Catastrophic. We could conceivably be looking at the collapse of the entire German economy."

Doyle curled a finger under her chin. "That doesn't make any sense. Why would the German people vote for a plan that could bankrupt their economy?"

"It's a classic argument," the president said. "The pro-Earth lobbies push for environmental safety at any and all cost; they try to frighten people with dire predictions of impending ecological disasters. The pro-industrial lobbies counter with their own brand of scare tactics. Factory shutdowns, loss of jobs, and the crippling economic impact of tighter environmental restrictions. Both sides run around screaming that the sky is falling, and the only way to stop it is to vote the way they tell you to." He smiled. "And the irony of it is, both sides are probably right. We *are* poisoning our planet at an alarming rate. And the cost of stopping this catastrophe-in-progress may well be higher than we can afford to pay."

He sighed. "It comes down to a tug-of-war between the tree huggers and the polluters. Most of the time, industry wins out. People have a hard time picturing ecological catastrophe; but they *can* picture themselves unemployed. It's hard to get the man on the street to see past his job. Usually, the only way to do it at all is to scare the hell out of him. I would guess that the Green Party has been capitalizing on the recent spate of accidents in the German nuclear power industry."

"I would call that an understatement, Mr. President," Brenthoven said. "A group called *Leben Zuerst*, Life First, has blitzed the German media with grisly commercials. One of them, the so-called *Dance of the Condemned*, uses movie-quality special effects to morph a playground full of laughing children into a pile of smoldering corpses, with a voice-over of German children reading the names of people killed in and around Chernobyl." He shuddered. "Nasty stuff, sir. The more so because there's a grain of truth in it."

"I get the picture," the president said. "But I have to admit that I'm a little puzzled by your sudden interest in German politics." He stared at his national security advisor. "There's more to this, isn't there?"

Brenthoven nodded. "Yesterday morning, British military intelligence intercepted what they believe to be an internal memorandum from German Chancellor Shoernberg to his chief attaché officer. The memo alludes to a letter-of-intent from the German government to Abdul al-Rahiim, the president of Siraj. The CIA and British MI-5 are trying to get their hands on a copy of the letter itself. If the Brits are right, the letter formalizes a secret deal between Germany and Siraj."

The president leaned forward slowly. "What kind of deal?"

"British intelligence thinks it's an exchange: military hardware for oil. The boys at Langley think the Brits could be right."

"Shoernberg will never be able to get the UN Security Council to lift the standing embargo against Siraj," Doyle said. "Abdul al-Rahiim may call himself president of Siraj, but everyone knows he's a dictator and a thug. His regime can be linked to half the terrorist organizations in the Middle East. The last thing anybody wants to do is *arm* the bastard. If Germany brings this up before the UN, there's going to be a very loud splat when it hits the floor."

"I agree," Brenthoven said. "The Office of Naval Intelligence thinks the Germans might just sidestep the embargo."

"You mean ignore it?" the president asked.

Brenthoven nodded. "Yes, sir. They may just try to deliver the goods in broad daylight and dare anyone to do anything about it."

"I don't see that happening," the president said. "But we'll worry about that part later. Do you have any details on this supposed deal?"

The national security advisor shook his head. "Not anything concrete, Mr. President. But ONI has thrown together a rough projection, mostly based on production figures from the German military-industrial complex. Recently, quite a bit of hardware has been earmarked for sale to the German military. I asked State to have a look at the German federal budget and any recent appropriations bills. They couldn't find any sign at all that the German government has plans to allocate money for upcoming major military purchases."

The president's eyebrows furrowed. "So the German military never intended to buy all this new hardware they're building?"

"Not as far as we can tell, Mr. President."

"What's ONI's best guess on this?" the president asked. "How much hardware, and when does it get delivered?"

The national security advisor tugged at his collar. "Uh … again, I remind you that these are rough figures, sir. But right now, we're looking at something like four Type 212B diesel submarines, to be followed by at least three Type 214s when those start rolling off the block."

The president frowned. "Obviously we don't want any new military hardware going into Siraj at all, but why are we getting so bent out of shape over diesel submarines? Nuclear subs I could understand …"

"With all due respect, Mr. President," Brenthoven said, "your information is about a half a century out of date."

The president whistled through his teeth. "I've been accused of being behind the times before, but never a half century."

Brenthoven smiled. "Sir, when I say *diesel sub*, you're picturing something out of an old black-and-white war movie—back when diesel subs had no real speed or endurance, and they were easy prey for surface ships. But those days are ancient history.

"Over the past three decades, there have been about a hundred quantum leaps in diesel submarine design and engineering. The new boats are equipped with air-independent propulsion systems and hydrogen fuel-cell technology straight out of the aerospace industry. They can run submerged for weeks without having to snorkel or come up for air. Their hull metallurgy is incredibly advanced, giving them operating depths comparable to our nuclear subs.

And the new Austenitic steels are non-magnetic, making the most advanced diesel subs difficult or impossible to detect with magnetic sensors. To top it all off, nearly all of the new diesel subs are capable of firing Exocet anti-ship cruise missiles, as well as highly advanced acoustic homing torpedoes."

The national security advisor looked at the president. "Sir, I could go on for an hour."

"You make them sound better than our nuclear attack subs," the president said.

Brenthoven shook his head. "Not better, sir. Nuclear subs can still stay down longer. But when you're chasing a diesel boat that can stay submerged for a month at a time, the difference starts to seem academic. And in a reasonably confined body of water, like the Persian Gulf, an advanced diesel submarine is every bit as deadly as one of our nuclear fast-attack subs."

"Jesus," Doyle said softly. "The Germans are actually thinking about selling these things to Siraj? Abdul al-Rahiim has stirred up enough trouble with obsolete Soviet hardware. I don't even want to think about what a madman like that can do with cutting-edge submarines. What little stability there is in the Middle East will go right down the toilet."

"I'm afraid that subs aren't all of it." The national security advisor swallowed before continuing. "It looks like the deal may include somewhere between thirty and fifty of the new Joint European Strike Fighters."

The president took a breath and let it out slowly. "Are we certain about this weapons deal?"

"Not yet, Mr. President. The CIA and ONI are both out shaking the trees for independent corroboration."

"So this whole thing could turn out to be a pig in a poke?"

Brenthoven nodded. "It's possible, sir. But the intelligence boys don't think so, and neither do I. Do you want me to bring the Joint Chiefs in on this?"

"Not yet," the president said. "Let's push this one onto the back burner until we get some sort of corroboration. Right now, Germany rates about a zero-point-nothing on my threat scale. I'm worried about China. Those boys have stuck their dick out, and I've got a bad feeling that they're not going to be really happy until they've stepped on it."

CHAPTER 5

BRITISH EMBASSY
WASHINGTON, DC
MONDAY; 07 MAY
2:14 PM EDT

Sarah Bexley leaned on the sink basin and rested her eyes for a moment. Here, in the quiet coolness of the ladies' toilet, her throbbing headache seemed to recede to something approaching a bearable level. It had to be the flu—some nasty little American variety of the virus with a particular taste for fair English flesh. At least it seemed that way, since everyone in the office appeared to be catching it. A third of the staff had already gone home ill.

Sarah felt for the handle of the cold-water tap and turned it on, cringing instantly at the sound of the water cascading into the marble basin. Her head was killing her. The two Motrin she had taken had done a bit to ease the body aches, but they weren't doing much for the pounding symphony of pain behind her temples. Why couldn't the Yank pharmacies stock a decent painkiller, like Nurosen? Oh they said it was all ibuprofen, didn't they? But it wasn't really the same, now was it? A couple of Nurosen would have had this headache on the run by now, whereas the bloody Motrin wasn't doing a thing.

She opened her eyes and looked at her reflection in the mirror. It took a few seconds to force her eyes to focus. She barely recognized the face staring back out of the glass; it was flushed, puffy looking, and inhumanly tired. Her eyes were the worst: red-rimmed and bloodshot. There were dark circles under them that her makeup couldn't disguise.

Sarah was twenty-eight, and she prided herself on having inherited something of her mother's Anglican beauty. Not that you could see it at the moment. The face in the mirror might have belonged to a forty-year-old barfly after a month or two of pub crawling.

She pulled a hand towel from the neat stack next to the wash basin, moistened a corner of it under the running water, and then folded it and dabbed it against the back of her neck. The cool wetness felt good against her overheated skin.

She swallowed with a painful effort. Her throat felt raw and swollen. This was ridiculous. She couldn't work like this. She needed to go home and curl up on the couch with a blanket and a cup of tea. Maybe she *would* go home. She sighed, and something rattled deep in her chest, a burbling, phlegmy sort of sound. She really couldn't go home, could she? Sir Anthony had the economic conference on Wednesday, and his presentation materials weren't ready yet. Or rather, they *were* ready, but Mr. Nitpicky-Hammersmith wasn't through fussing over them yet. She could already hear his voice … "Nothing reaches the ambassador's desk until it is letter perfect. Let-*ter per*-fect. England's hopes ride on Sir Anthony's shoulders, and *his* hopes ride on *our* shoulders."

Hammersmith was a grumpy old bastard. If she tried to leave before he was happy with her presentation materials, she might as well pack up her desk and move back down to the second floor.

She sighed again. *Back to the desk, old girl. Don't give Hammersmith an excuse to shuttle you back to the administrative pool.*

Her bleary eyes came to rest on the delicate curves of the marble sink basin with its sculpted supporting column and the elegant fluting of the water spout and tap handles. It had taken her five years to make it to the fourth floor—up here, where the desks were polished mahogany, the floors were tiled with exquisite mosaics, and the fluffy hand towels were emblazoned with the Royal Crest. Up here, where Sarah's opinion mattered, where influential people depended upon her work and listened to her words with interest. Up here, where men found her ideas more compelling than her breasts.

She laid the towel on the countertop and turned off the water tap. She stood up straight, doing her best to ignore the surge of pain her movements sent coursing through her aching muscles. She nearly had to lean on the sink again as her knees trembled and threatened to give way. But the weakness passed after a few seconds—most of it anyway. She could tough it out. Another hour or two, at least. Perhaps long enough for Mr. Hammersmith to admit that her economic presentation was ready for the ambassador's desk. Or at least long enough for Hammersmith to throw in the towel himself and go home sick. He looked even worse than Sarah did. She suspected that he was running more on his stiff upper lip than he was off of any internal reserves of strength.

Well, if he could do it, Sarah could do it. She squared her shoulders and turned away from the sink.

She pulled the door open, stepped into the corridor, and immediately tripped over a heavy bundle of rags lying on the floor. She lost her footing and pitched forward, just managing to turn her face to the side as she half-stumbled, half-fell into the far corridor wall. Her shoulder banged painfully into sculpted plaster and she nearly fell down entirely. Still swaying and half-dazed, she looked over her shoulder at the bundle of rags.

But it wasn't a bundle at all. It was a person ... A young woman, lying on her side with her arms and legs sprawled limply in impossible directions, like a rag doll dropped on the floor and forgotten. She wasn't moving. Was she breathing?

Sarah tried to bend over the woman, but the pain in her head ramped up so violently that she thought she was going to lose consciousness. Her blood roared in her ears, and her vision seemed to shift and waver. A hot flash swept over her like a gust of air from a blast furnace.

She slumped against the wall, panting and praying for the pain in her head to subside just a little. Through the nauseous fog of her pain, she could see the young woman's face. The woman's eyes were open, staring vacantly into the distance. Her lips were parted, and a trickle of blood-tinged saliva dropped from the corner of her slack mouth to a spreading pool on the floor. Another trickle ran from her right nostril and down her cheek.

Oh god! What was wrong with this woman? Was she ... dead? Sarah opened her mouth to scream, but all that came out was a hoarse croak. She looked around for help. Someone. *Anyone.* She was alone in the corridor with the dying woman.

Sarah began staggering toward the door of the closest office. She couldn't remember whose office it was, but it didn't really matter. She needed to call someone. Call for help.

The door couldn't have been more than seven or eight meters away, but the distance appeared to stretch and then contract in a dizzying manner that seemed to be keeping rhythm with the pounding in Sarah's head. Leaning against the wall, Sarah made for the door, step after trembling step, her knees becoming weaker with every movement. The door ... the ... door ... She stumbled and nearly went down. It was becoming difficult to breathe.

There was something in her throat. Some sort of hard knot. She tried to swallow and tasted something strange but distantly familiar. Her nose was running. She swiped at it blindly with one hand. Her fingers came away red. She was bleeding ... Oh God ... What was happening to her? What was happening to *all* of them?

She reached the door, fought with the knob for a desperate second, and then stumbled through. "Help me ..." Her voice sounded feeble in her ears, guttural and strangely distant. "Help ... me ..."

It took a few seconds for her eyes to focus on the contents of the room. It was a charnel house. Bodies lay scattered about like so much wastepaper. Men. Women. In chairs; collapsed on the floor; slumped over desks. Sightless eyes staring into infinity, blood streaming from noses, ears, and mouths.

Sarah stood in the doorway, her lungs laboring for air, her mind refusing to take in the reality of what she was seeing. They couldn't all be dead. They couldn't …

Her legs gave way, and she collapsed to her knees. "Somebody … help …"

A man was lying face up on the carpet, his head a few centimeters from her left knee. An older man, his lower face a mask of blood and sputum. In some dark recess of Sarah's brain, the man's face connected with a name. Hammer … smith.

And then Sarah did scream, the sound wrenching itself free from somewhere deep in her chest, clawing its way up her tortured and swollen throat like a wild beast rending flesh. She screamed until the last of the air was gone from her lungs.

CHAPTER 6

Los Angeles Chronicle C-3

Pentagon Denies Siraji Destruction of U.S. Jet

By Laura Sherman
Chronicle Staff Writer

BARAKAT, SIRAJ — General Abdul Khaaliq, a senior officer in the Siraji Ministry of Defense, announced this morning that Siraji surface-to-air missiles brought down a U.S. Air Force fighter jet operating over the Eastern No-Fly Zone late Monday night.

"We have the sovereign right to protect our airspace," Khaaliq said. "This so-called no-fly-zone is a fiction created by the United States. It is not recognized by the United Nations, the Arab League, or the Gulf Cooperation Council. It was illegal when the United States imposed no-fly-zones on Iraq, and it is no less illegal now.

"It is a reprehensible attempt by the American Government to meddle in the internal affairs of my country. Let the destruction of this aircraft serve as a reminder that the United States does not and cannot control the skies over Siraj."

In a statement to the press, Pentagon spokesman Col. William Harris confirmed that U.S. war planes were fired upon in the no-fly-zone, but denied any damage.

A photograph provided by the Siraji Ministry of Defense shows wreckage.

"All our aircraft are accounted for," Harris said. "A pair of Air Force F-16s did exchange fire with a Siraji missile battery last night, but neither plane was damaged, and the pilots were not injured."

When questioned about the photographs of aircraft wreckage being circulated by the Siraji government, Harris said, "They're recycling old photos. Our analysts haven't made a formal determination yet, but we believe these are pictures of a plane that went down in Saudi Arabia nearly eight years ago."

See **CRASH,** C-6

WASHINGTON, DC
MONDAY; 07 MAY
2:46 PM EDT

The president finished the article and dropped the newspaper on his desk with a sigh. What did the Sirajis think they stood to gain by making up stories like this? Did they think there was some political edge to be had? Was it just the need to see their names in the paper? Or were they just full of shit?

The door opened and Agent Allain LaBauve walked in. "Excuse me, Mr. President, we have a Condition Firestorm." LaBauve's voice was cool and professional. The two agents who had followed him into the room stood behind him without speaking.

President Chandler glanced up at LaBauve. The Secret Service agent's poker face was firmly in place. His neutral expression gave no clue that he had just barged into the Oval Office without knocking, dragging a pair of agents in his wake. "Say again, Alan?"

LaBauve was the head of the President's Personal Security Detail, his so-called body man, because he was never more than an arm's length away when the president was in a non-secure location. The president called the big Cajun man Alan, LaBauve's preferred version of his first name.

LaBauve had a talent for languages; he spoke French, German, and Russian—all with near-perfect accents. He had a master's degree in criminal justice from the University of Virginia, and double bachelors in systems theory and political science. His speech was clipped, precise, and bore no trace of his dirt-poor southern Louisiana upbringing. And still he couldn't escape nicknames like Swamp Thing and Gator. The last came from a persistent rumor that LaBauve—in his young and wild days—had once beaten an alligator to death with a half-empty jug of moonshine.

"Mr. President, we have a confirmed Condition Firestorm," LaBauve said again. "We need to evacuate you immediately, sir."

The president pushed back his chair and stood up. "Evacuate? What's going on?"

LaBauve shook his head. "The British Embassy has been attacked, sir."

A surge of ice water rushed through the president's veins. His mind immediately started dreaming up worst-case scenarios. His brain was suddenly flooded with images of burned and mutilated bodies. He shook his head and blinked rapidly. "What? A bomb?"

"I don't know, sir," LaBauve said. "I don't have any details."

The president hesitated for a few seconds and then nodded. "All right. Where are we going? Down to the bunker?"

"Negative, Mr. President. We don't yet know how the attack was carried out, or whether or not more attacks are imminent. Command Post's assessment says you'll be safer outside of the White House until we can be certain that the residence is not a target." He walked toward the French doors to the West Wing colonnade and opened the nearest one.

The president followed him, with the two other Secret Service agents a half-step behind. His legs seemed heavy, his steps stiff, as if the news had somehow weighed him down. He forced himself to think. "If the White House was a target," he said, "we would have been hit first."

"CP concurs with your reasoning, Mr. President," LaBauve said. "But we can't rule out the possibility that somebody jumped the gun and attacked the embassy ahead of schedule. It's still possible that the embassy is just one of a series of coordinated attacks."

The president walked out onto the colonnade. LaBauve slid smoothly past him into the point position, and the other agents took up positions behind the president's left and right shoulders, putting the president in the center of a tight triangular formation. LaBauve's position in front of the president was a clear sign of how seriously the Secret Service was taking the threat. As a rule, the president walked in front, and the agents assigned to his protection walked to the side and slightly behind.

LaBauve raised his right wrist to his mouth and spoke quietly into the microphone concealed in the cuff of his black suit jacket. "Eagle is moving."

A rhythmic thumping in the sky announced the approach of Marine One, the presidential helicopter. The president stared up into the clouds, trying to spot it. He could hear sirens in the distance now. But that must have been his imagination. Massachusetts Avenue was too far away.

"Where's my family?" he asked.

"Susan and Nicole are still in school, sir. Their agents have been alerted, and CP is preparing to evacuate them by motorcade. The first lady is at Bradford Hall, speaking to the Daughters of the American Revolution. Her agents have also been alerted, and CP has a scramble squad and evacuation team in route to her position. They'll meet us at the Marine Barracks at Eighth and I."

The president nodded. "Good." Marine One appeared as a dark speck against the blue sky and grew rapidly as it dropped toward the White House lawn. He couldn't help wondering how many people were dead. How many might be dying right now? "What about the vice president?"

"His security detail is evacuating him from OEOB now, sir."

The vice president's regular office was in the Old Executive Office Building.

"They're moving him to the emergency response bunker?"

"Yes, sir."

The president nodded. "Good. Any word on casualties at the British Embassy?"

"CP didn't brief me on the details of the attack, sir," LaBauve said.

"Of course," the president said. His words were lost in the thundering winds churned up by the helicopter's rotors as the big machine settled gently on the lawn.

LaBauve began shepherding the president toward Marine One the second the helicopter's wheels touched the grass. A door swung down from the side of the helicopter and then unfolded itself into a set of stairs. A young Marine lieutenant trotted down the stairs, stopped to ensure that they were properly extended and locked, and then snapped to attention and saluted.

As the president and his security detail walked into the downwash of the helicopter's rotors, LaBauve sidestepped to the left and slowed his own pace for a second or so, putting the president in the lead position for the last few steps to the stairs.

The president returned the Marine's salute and climbed the short metal stairs into the interior of the helicopter.

He was belting himself into his seat when LaBauve climbed into the cabin, followed by his two flanking agents and then the Marine lieutenant. Thirty seconds later, the pitch of the rotors climbed an octave, and they lifted off the ground.

LaBauve spoke into his sleeve again. "Eagle is airborne."

* * *

The Marine lieutenant's chair was mounted backward from all the other chairs in the cabin, which left him facing the president. His eyes traveled quickly around the interior of the cabin, making sure that everyone was properly seated and belted in. He turned his eyes to the president. "Sir, Lieutenant Charles Donahue, Marine One in-flight Tactical Officer standing by to report."

The president stared out the window as the ground dropped away. "Make your report."

"Sir, the disposition of the Joint Chiefs of Staff is as follows: The chairman of the Joint Chiefs, J1, J4, and J6 are at the Pentagon. J2 is at Langley. J3 is in the White House Situation Room. J5 is on an inspection tour in San Diego. J7 is aboard USS *Mobile Bay* in the Sea of Japan, and J8 is currently unlocated. The national security advisor is at Fort Meade."

"Got it," the president said, without looking at him. "What else have you got for me?"

Lt. Donahue held out a red satellite phone. "I have the secretary of homeland security patched in on this line, sir. He's in his car. He has a secure-capable phone, but he can't get his crypto to sync up, so this call is not secure.

The president accepted the phone and held it up to his ear. "Where are you, Clark?"

"On the beltway, Mr. President," said Secretary of Homeland Security Clark Chapman. "In route to the Pentagon. ETA about fifteen minutes. Maybe ten if this traffic lets up."

"All right," the president said. "How much can you tell me over a non-secure line?"

"I can sketch in the basics, sir, and then fill you in on the details when I get to a secure phone that actually works."

"Fair enough," the president said. "Give me what you've got."

"Sir, the British Embassy has been hit with some kind of biological warfare agent."

The ice water was back with a vengeance. "Oh God. Is it anthrax?"

"We don't know yet, sir. But whatever it is, it's nasty as hell. We'll have to get a team in there to look around. But the initial report seemed to indicate that nearly everyone in the embassy is either dead or dying."

"Jesus Christ."

"Excuse me, sir?"

The president sighed. "Nothing, Clark. Please, continue with your report."

"Well, sir, the initial stages of this thing are all pretty much standard operating procedure."

The president interrupted him. "We have an SOP for this?"

"Yes, sir," Chapman said. "At least we have one for a biological or chemical attack on a U.S. government building. We're following that plan until the British are ready to take over. The British deputy chief of mission has assumed temporary duties as ambassador. He's given us the green light to drive the containment and response until they can fly their own people in."

"I take it the British deputy chief of mission wasn't at the embassy during the attack."

"No, sir. He's in Seattle for the latest round of World Trade Organization negotiations. At least, he *was* in Seattle. He's probably in the air by now, on his way back here."

"I'm sure he is," the president said. "Okay, we're following our SOP, for the moment at least. Is it any good?"

Chapman sighed. "We don't really know, sir. It looks great on paper, and it's played pretty well in training exercises. I guess we're about to find out how well it works in real life."

"Looks like it," the president said. "What have we done so far?"

"Sir, step one is to notify the U.S. Army Medical Research Institute of Infectious Diseases and the Centers for Disease Control and Prevention. That's already been done. USAMRIID is working on airlifting in a biohazard response team from Fort Detrick, and CDC is sending us a couple of advisors. No ETA on either team yet, but they're shaking a leg."

"Okay," the president said. "What's step two?"

"Emergency Services evacuates a three-block radius around the attack site. That's already in progress. As soon as the initial evacuation is complete, they will extend the evacuation zone to five blocks in the area downwind from the attack site, to create a buffer zone for wind-borne contamination.

"Step three is to get a medical team into the embassy—in biohazard suits, of course—to rescue and treat survivors. The British deputy chief of mission has already given us permission to enter the building."

"We have a medical facility standing by to receive the victims?"

"Yes, sir. The infectious disease isolation units at Walter Reed are equipped and trained for this sort of scenario. They'll have to ramp up their staff, but they're already recalling off-duty personnel. I've authorized them to draw from other military medical facilities in the area to augment as needed."

The president looked out the window. The flight to the Marine barracks at Eighth and I was little more than a hop. They were already descending toward the helicopter pad. "I'll be on the ground in a couple of minutes," he said. "I'm going to have to call the prime minister before too much longer to extend my condolences and to make a formal offer of support. I don't envy whoever did this."

"I don't either, Mr. President," Chapman said. "Prime Minster Irons isn't going to rest until she tracks down every last one of them and nails them to a tree."

The president nodded. That wasn't much of an exaggeration. Emily Irons, better known to political satirists as "Iron-Balls Emily," was widely regarded as the least tolerant and most volatile prime minister Britain had seen since Margaret Thatcher. Very quick to anger, she was utterly unforgiving of anyone she considered to be an enemy of her country.

Someone had just poked a stick into a hornet's nest. And if Frank knew anything at all about Emily Irons, there would be hell to pay.

CHAPTER 7

TORPEDO: THE HISTORY AND EVOLUTION OF A KILLING MACHINE

(Excerpted from an unpublished manuscript [pages 84–87] and reprinted by permission of the author, Retired Master Chief Sonar Technician David M. Hardy, USN)

It is an axiom in both philosophy and politics that a single determined person can change the world. Anyone who dares to argue the point is likely to face an exhaustive litany of famous names—Louis Pasteur, Robert Goddard, Sir Isaac Newton, Thomas Edison, Ferdinand Magellan, Albert Einstein, Marie Curie, Alexander the Great, Henry Ford, Grace Hopper, Adolf Hitler, Alan Turing—some of whom have changed the world for the better, and some of whom have changed it for the worse, but all of whom have inarguably left an imprint on the pages of history.

As citizens of the human race, we are well prepared to accept the idea that human beings can alter the fate of mankind. But we are far less likely to consider the effect of non-human influences on the course of world events. Perhaps it is a sort of species-centric conceit that blinds us to the effect of the inanimate object—the thing—on history.

And yet, through the sharply focused lens of hindsight, we can see that objects—tools, devices, or weapons—have often become the axis on which history itself has turned. Some of these incidences are easy to spot. On a cold December morning in 1903, a crude biplane clawed its way into the air over Kill Devil Hill at Kitty Hawk, North Carolina. The homemade aircraft's maiden flight lasted only three and a half seconds, but it carried the future of aviation on its spruce and cotton muslin wings. And after that nothing would ever be the same.

Forty-two years later, a single bomb (with the innocuous nickname of Little Boy) devastated the Japanese city of Hiroshima. In a single instant of fire and destruction, the world was catapulted into the nuclear age.

At just before 1:00 PM on November 22, 1963, a rifle bullet killed John F. Kennedy. The president was struck by at least one other bullet (conspiracy buffs count a third), but medical opinions are virtually unanimous in saying that Kennedy would have survived his other injuries if not for the head shot. Popular theories argue for a second, or even a third gunman in the shooting, but no one seriously disputes the fact that a single 6.5mm bullet ended John F. Kennedy's life. It's impossible to know if the world was changed for the better or the worse in the wake of JFK's assassination. But there's no doubt that Lyndon Johnson's vision for America was different from Kennedy's. LBJ had different views on Vietnam, human rights, and the future of the space program. And he led the most powerful nation on Earth down different paths than Kennedy might have taken.

Are these examples proof of the concept that inanimate objects can drive the forces of history? To verify the validity of the assertion, we must work the problem in reverse, in the same manner that we can check our answer to a mathematical equation by working backward from the answer. To determine if the bullet that killed Kennedy was truly responsible for altering human events, we can ask two simple questions: If that particular bullet had misfired, or gone astray, would the world be a demonstrably different place than it is today? And, in natural corollary to the first question, would JFK have made different decisions as president than did his successor, Lyndon Johnson? If the answer to either question is *yes*, we must conclude that a single 6.5mm rifle bullet seized control of the destiny of the most powerful nation on Earth, and therefore the destiny of mankind.

The same sort of reverse check can be run on the atomic bomb question. If the bomb at Hiroshima had failed to detonate (for whatever reason), would the world be a different place? Would the nuclear arms race have ever come to pass? Would mankind have ever been forced to live under the threat of nuclear annihilation?

These examples are relatively easy to recognize: the airplane, the A-bomb, the bullet that killed a president. But there are other instances, other objects or machines that have shaped the fate of our planet.

One particular device has been the engine of history on numerous occasions, and yet its impact is almost entirely overlooked. The torpedo. On at least five verifiable instances in recorded history, the torpedo has become the lever of Archimedes: the machine that moved the world.

To examine the influence of the torpedo, we must examine the history of the torpedo itself. When was the torpedo invented? How did this influential and deadly device come into being?

Some military historians trace the origins of the torpedo back to the Roman Empire, and the fire ships that the ancient Romans would send drifting amongst the fleets of their enemies. Others prefer to attribute the invention of the torpedo to a sixteenth-century Italian inventor named Zambelli, who used a drifting boatload of explosives with a delayed fuse to destroy a bridge in 1585.

But the actual word *torpedo* was first applied to naval warfare in the late eighteenth century by a young colonial American named David Bushnell. Graduating from Yale University at the dawn of the American Revolution, Bushnell was inspired to use his engineering expertise to support the fight for American Independence. With the help of fellow Yale graduate Phineas Pratt, Bushnell designed an underwater bomb with a clockwork-delayed flintlock detonator. By modern standards, the device would be more properly classified as a limpet mine, but Bushnell chose the name *torpedo*—in reference to the harmless-looking (but dangerous) torpedo ray. A member of the electric ray family (Torpedinidae), the torpedo ray can deliver a crippling electrical shock to its prey and its enemies alike. Bushnell hoped to emulate the torpedo ray's nasty underwater surprise by attaching his clockwork bomb to the bottom of one of the British warships that were currently blockading New York harbor.

The blockade gave the British control of the Hudson River Valley, allowing them to effectively split the colonial forces in two. The situation was becoming increasingly desperate for the Americans. If the blockade remained unbroken, the revolution would likely fail.

Without a navy of their own, the colonials could not challenge the blockade. Although generally unrecognized by scholars and students of history, Bushnell's torpedo—as crazy and as unproven as it must have seemed—held the only real hope for American independence.

Shortly after midnight on September 7, 1776, a young Army sergeant named Ezra Lee climbed into a tiny one-man submarine, pulled the hatch shut over his head, and submerged beneath the waters of New York harbor. His target was HMS *Eagle*, a sixty-four–gun man-of-war that served as the flagship of the British fleet. (In a tiny stroke of irony, the British Admiral Lord Howe had anchored *Eagle* within a few hundred yards of Bedloe's Island, which would one day be renamed Liberty Island—the site for the Statue of Liberty.)

The submarine used in the attack was another of David Bushnell's inventions. Constructed from curved oaken planks and strengthened with iron bands, the little one-passenger craft was shaped very much like a peach. Bushnell called his submarine the *Turtle*, and he equipped it with hand-operated propellers, ballast tanks, and a pair of hand-pumps that enabled the vessel to submerge or surface.

The torpedo was carried near the top of the little submarine, just above the rudder. Built into the top of the submarine was a vertically mounted auger, which the operator could use to screw the torpedo to the bottom planking of the target ship.

Without electricity, the only illumination inside the *Turtle* came from the glowing foxfire moss that surrounded the compass and depth gauge. Battling unfamiliar tides and physical fatigue from manually powering the submarine through the water, Ezra Lee had only about thirty minutes of air with which to conduct his attack and make his escape. Laboring, sweating, and—perhaps—grunting and swearing in the darkened confines of the tiny vessel, Lee managed to maneuver the *Turtle* under the hull of HMS *Eagle.* He set to work with the auger, but several minutes of unproductive drilling convinced him that he could not penetrate the hull planking of the British ship. He rested for a few minutes and then tried again, still without success. With his air supply running low, Lee was forced to abandon the attack.

Nearly exhausted and starving for breathable air, Lee pumped out his ballast tanks shortly after he was clear of *Eagle*'s hull. He was probably hoping that the darkness would hide the top of his strange little craft as it protruded from the water.

Luck was not with him. The British spotted his craft almost immediately and sent out a boat to capture it.

Lee jettisoned the torpedo in the hopes of lightening his vessel enough to escape the pursuing boat. His tactic worked. Gaining speed, he managed to out-distance the British long enough for them to lose his tiny craft in the darkness. Lee escaped, with the *Turtle* intact.

To all appearances, the first torpedo attack was a failure. But the night was not yet over. Lying forgotten on the bottom of the river, the torpedo's clockwork detonator continued its countdown. One hour after Lee jettisoned it, David Bushnell's weapon went off. The resulting explosion was huge, throwing an enormous plume of spray into the air and illuminating the darkened harbor like a flash of underwater lightning.

Not one British ship was damaged, but Adm. Howe was shaken by it. Strange machines were prowling about beneath the waters of New York harbor—and the next underwater attack might well succeed where this one had failed. Adm. Howe moved his ships. The blockade was broken.

Thanks (in part) to a crude weapon, with an even cruder delivery system, America became a nation. And, from the very moment of its infancy, the torpedo began to shape world events.

CHAPTER 8

MARINE BARRACKS AT EIGHTH AND I
WASHINGTON, DC
MONDAY; 07 MAY
7:03 PM EDT

"First off, Mr. President, it looks like the British Embassy was the only target." The secretary of homeland security's voice warbled slightly over the secure phone. "The Pentagon, the Capitol Building, and the White House are still under security lockdown, but there don't seem to be any follow-on attacks. We've issued warnings to all of the other embassies, and they're taking whatever precautions they deem appropriate. We'll be releasing the lockdowns shortly, but I've directed all federal and military facilities to remain at an increased threat condition for the next seventy-two hours, just to be safe."

"Good call," the president said. "Continue."

"Sir, we've got four biohazard teams working the embassy: one forensic survey team and three rescue teams. We're concentrating on survivors first. We can start thinking about moving bodies after we're sure nobody else is left alive in there. We don't have a formal casualty report yet, but we've got a head count from the initial rapid sweep. Forty-two dead, so far, and about sixty survivors, nearly all unconscious or comatose."

"I see," the president said.

The secretary's voice changed. "I'm afraid that Sir Anthony is among the dead, sir."

"I see," the president said again. He stared across the conference room that had become his temporary Situation Room. The wall on the far side of the long oak table was dominated by a floor-to-ceiling bas relief of the Marine Corps emblem—the globe, eagle, and anchor, topped by a banner proclaiming *Semper Fidelis* (Always Faithful)—the words by which the U.S. Marines lived and died. Proud words, symbolizing the honor, courage, and sacrifice of men and women who were both warriors and keepers of the peace.

But where was the honor in killing an embassy full of civilians? He had no doubt that the attackers considered themselves warriors. Whoever they were, whatever their agenda was, they were probably congratulating themselves on their bravery and declaring their attack a victory for their cause. But it wasn't a victory, and it wasn't the act of warriors. It was murder.

"Sir?"

The president flinched. It took a second to remember that Chapman was still on the phone. "Huh? What?" The president tightened his grip on the receiver and jerked his mind back to the phone conversation. "I'm sorry, Clark. What were you saying?"

"Sir, we can go over this later."

"No," the president said. "Now. Go ahead."

"We still don't know very much about the bio-warfare agent, except that it's a powerful hemorrhagic—the victims all show signs of bleeding from the nose, ears, and mouth. We also know that it works quickly, in hours rather than days. And that eliminates a lot of agents, including Ebola, plague, Q-fever, botulism, hantavirus, anthrax, smallpox, and most of the other commonly weaponized bugs."

"Do we know how the attack was carried out?"

"Yes, sir. The attack vector appears to have been the carpet."

The president's eyebrows arched. "Say that again?"

"Sir, I know how crazy that sounds," Secretary Chapman said. "The bio-survey team can't identify the agent—that's going to take some lab work—but they *can* detect it. There are traces of the agent all throughout the building, but the highest concentrations by far are in the carpeting. Apparently, the carpet was pretty much saturated by the agent."

"How in the hell did that happen?"

"We don't know, sir. Not yet."

"All right," the president said. "What's our next move?"

"Well, sir, there are going to be victims outside the embassy. Personnel who went home sick at the first sign of symptoms. Visitors, couriers, reporters, people who passed through the embassy but don't work there. We'll find some of them in clinics and emergency rooms. Some will be at home in bed. Some of them are probably dead by now."

The president sucked air through his teeth. "How contagious is this thing?"

"We don't know, sir," Chapman said. "We won't know that until we've identified the agent that was used."

"Or when the hospitals start filling up with sick people," the president said.

"CDC and USAMRIID don't think that's going to happen, sir"

"How can they possibly know that?"

"It's an educated guess, sir," Secretary Chapman said. "The agent concentration levels are massive. If this bug was really toxic in low concentrations, the attackers wouldn't have had to use nearly as much to achieve the desired effect. They could have dropped an aerosol spray can in a bathroom trashcan, instead of saturating the carpets."

"Sounds like a reasonable assumption," the president said. "But bear in mind that the people who did this are not reasonable. We don't know what motivates them, or even what their goal is, short of murdering British diplomats." He sighed. "Anything else?"

"Not at the moment, Mr. President."

"Okay," the president said. "When can I go home?"

"The Secret Service should be giving the all-clear on the White House any time now. If you go ahead and whistle for your helicopter, the residence should be clear by the time you get there."

"Good," the president said. "I've got work to do."

CHAPTER 9

USS *TOWERS* (DDG-103)
NORTHERN ARABIAN GULF
WEDNESDAY; 09 MAY
1826 hours (6:26 PM)
TIME ZONE +3 'CHARLIE'

Standing on the port side main deck of USS *Towers*, Capt. Bowie was just about as hot as he could ever remember being—and for a man born and raised in San Antonio, Texas, that was no small feat. He was facing west, into the setting sun, but the sky was still painfully bright. Behind him, the coast of Iran was only a few miles over the horizon, and the winds blowing in from the Iranian desert showed no signs of cooling down. The back and armpits of his blue coveralls were dark with sweat. The bill of his USS *Towers* ball cap drooped across his forehead like some dead—but still soggy—sea creature.

He propped a steel-toed boot on a Kevlar life rail and looked out across the five hundred or so yards of water that separated his own ship from the merchant ship that was causing all the trouble.

The motor vessel *Lotus Blossom* wallowed uneasily on the water, bulling her way through the waves rather than cleaving them cleanly. She was an ancient rust-bucket of a freighter, probably built in the postwar shipbuilding boom of the mid-1950s, and she had not aged gracefully.

Bowie watched the old cargo ship bob and roll. The seas were calm, the waves low and almost lazy under the fierce Arabian sun, but the MV *Lotus Blossom* heeled alarmingly with each swell that passed under her keel. To Bowie's trained eye, it was obvious that the old ship's weight was not properly trimmed; in all probability, her cargo was not distributed evenly. Such an obvious oversight spoke of sloppiness and neglect. Not that Bowie needed any clues to tell him that the aging vessel was poorly maintained (and probably poorly manned). The ship's appearance told that story all by itself.

The *Lotus Blossom* was a Type-3 freighter, with her superstructure situated well aft. The forward three-quarters of her deck were dominated by two large cargo hatches and the V-shaped booms of a cargo crane that had once lowered crates and pallets into the twin cargo holds. The crane was gone now, or mostly gone. At some time in the past—possibly in the 1970s, when containerized shipping had become the cargo industry standard—the old ship had been converted from a bulk cargo carrier to a container ship. The conversion had been none too neat. The crane, which had obviously been too light to handle the standard twenty-foot–long steel shipping containers, had been hacked off with welding torches, leaving two truncated stubs sticking out of the winch housing like the stumps of poorly amputated arms.

The ship's superstructure had been white once, and the hull had been green, but the colors were nearly masked by the scabrous orange and brown of new rust over old. The ship's name, painted across the stern in two-foot–high capital letters, had faded into near invisibility.

Bowie looked at the ship and exhaled slowly through his teeth. *Lotus Blossom*. What an utterly inappropriate name. He had trouble associating the battered old tub with any sort of flower. To his mind, it required a liberal stretch of imagination to call the damned thing a ship—never mind a flower.

The *Lotus Blossom* looked harmless enough, though. Even from five hundred yards away, the old girl looked tired to the bone, as though she might decide to give up the ghost in a minute or two, and slip beneath the waves for some long overdue rest. And, for all Bowie knew, the old freighter might do just that, which certainly didn't make the ship any less dangerous to his crew. The *Lotus Blossom* was a suspected smuggler, and Bowie's Visit, Board, Search, and Seizure teams were preparing to board the ship to search for contraband cargo. His teams would have their hands full confronting and controlling a potentially hostile crew, and trying to worm their way through every nook and cranny of an unfamiliar vessel while covering each other's backs. They didn't need the added angst of worrying about whether or not the ship was going to sink beneath their feet.

From a tactical standpoint, Bowie wasn't crazy about being this far away from the ship that his crew would be searching. His teams would be armed, but that didn't make them invulnerable if things turned ugly over there. His gun crews were standing ready to rake the freighter with machine gun fire, or even the 5-inch deck gun, but Bowie couldn't very well order them to shoot at the ship if his own crew members were aboard.

If he could bring the *Towers* in closer, his gun crews would be able to see the tactical situation clearly and pick their own targets. For years, that had been the standard operating procedure for Visit, Board, Search, and Seizure teams. But the terrorist attack on USS *Cole* had demonstrated the folly of allowing any unknown vessel to get too close to a warship. The Navy had learned the hard way that the most powerful warship afloat is vulnerable to a close-in suicide attack.

Capt. Bowie gave the MV *Lotus Blossom* another careful once-over with his eyes. The crew of the old freighter probably had some small arms aboard, possibly quite a few—if they really *were* smugglers. But he was ninety-eight percent certain that the old tub was not crammed to the gunwales with explosives and rigged for a suicide attack on a U.S. warship.

Odds were he could order his ship in nice and close to the old girl so that his gun crews could give good cover to his VBSS teams as they boarded. Unfortunately, he was not *one hundred* percent certain. And, like it or not, it was tactically smarter to risk *some* of his crew by maintaining a stand-off distance, than to risk *all* of his crew (and the ship) by getting in closer.

* * *

A watertight door opened behind Bowie, and he looked over his shoulder in time to see a small group of junior ensigns file out onto the deck. There were five of them: three men and two women. They stood for a moment, blinking and shielding their eyes against the unexpected brilliance of the setting sun.

Bowie looked them over. They were a good crop of kids. Young, physically fit, and so desperately eager that their enthusiasm nearly shone out of their eyes like the beams of searchlights.

Bowie had been a junior ensign himself once, and he had a pretty fair idea of what was racing around in their minds. Each of them had spent the last four years having his or her head crammed full of information on a dizzying array of subjects: naval history, tactical doctrine, theory of leadership, uniform regulations, military custom and law, formal dining etiquette, shipboard firefighting, and damage control. And now, they were itching to put all that knowledge to good use.

In their own eyes, they were educated and dedicated professionals, ready to seize the reigns of authority and prove themselves as warriors and leaders of men. To the men and women who served under them, they were *sea puppies*—no experience, no common sense, and prone to sticking their little puppy dog noses where they didn't belong.

It was Bowie's job, with the assistance of his officers and chief petty officers, to turn these sea puppies into by-God naval officers. Hands-on training would do some of the work. So would practical experience and the time-honored school of hard knocks. The majority would be well on the way to becoming useful officers by the end of this deployment. The real trick would be making sure they didn't get anybody killed along the way.

The hardest part for most of them would be the eventual realization that they would never master the technologies under their command. It would be a difficult and painful lesson for them to learn. They were intelligent, educated, highly motivated, and hungry for the respect of their peers and subordinates. It was natural and predictable that they would want to become experts on the equipment and procedures under their control. And many of them would spend their first sea tours trying to do just that. But Bowie knew from experience that it was an impossible task. The equipment and tactics involved were so complex that a person could spend half a career mastering *one* warfare area, and the other half of that career studying and working to stay on top of the rapid changes brought on by evolving technologies.

An effective naval officer had to be the proverbial jack-of-all-trades and master of none. He or she needed a strong working knowledge of radar systems, sonar systems, cruise missiles, anti-aircraft missiles, communications systems, combat support logistics, torpedoes, turbine engines, firefighting systems, chemical warfare defense systems, navigation technologies, ship-handling techniques, weather patterns, electrical power generation, naval gun systems, infrared sensors, and about a hundred other disciplines, *each* of which required years to master. It simply wasn't possible to become an expert in all of them, so a good officer had to be satisfied with becoming a capable leader for his subordinates: the enlisted men and women who were the Navy's *real* experts.

Successful officers learned to accept the limitations of the human brain and concentrated on knowing enough about each discipline to command effectively. Naval aviators tended to learn that lesson quickly. You didn't need to know how to field-strip an F-18 engine in order to fly the aircraft.

But some junior officers never quite got the message. They drove themselves unmercifully, trying to learn *everything* about *everything*, piling more and more pressure on themselves to achieve the impossible, until they either burned out or snapped.

Bowie scanned the faces of his latest crop of junior officers. How many of them would not make it over the hump? How many of these bright young men and women would resign their commissions and limp home with their spirits in tatters, never really understanding where they had failed? One of them, probably. Perhaps even two. But wouldn't it he great if, just once, *all* of them could make the cut?

"If wishes were fishes," Bowie said under his breath. He turned his attention back to the motor vessel *Lotus Blossom*. He would do everything in his power to help these puppies along, but only time would tell.

"Gather round, ladies and gentlemen," he said over his shoulder. "School is now in session."

Still blinking as their eyes adjusted to the sunlight, the young officers collected around him in a loose semicircle.

"Let's start with your assessment of the tactical situation," he said. "And then we'll go from there." He looked at Ensign Patrick Cooper, the ship's Undersea Warfare Officer. "Why don't you kick us off, Pat? Take a look at our problem child out there and tell us what you see. Throw in anything you think might be tactically useful."

Cooper nearly flinched at the sound of his name, and then stood up straighter and squared his shoulders. "Yes, sir." He looked out at the *Lotus Blossom* for several seconds. "Aft superstructure," he said slowly. "So she's a Type-3 freighter. It looks like she's a converted bulk carrier. From here it doesn't look like the shipfitters did a very clean job."

Capt. Bowie smiled. "Is that a tactical observation, or are you just offended by sloppy work?"

Ensign Carol Harvey snickered until Bowie caught her eye, then she chopped it off instantly.

Ens. Cooper reddened. "It's … uh … a tactical observation, sir."

Bowie's eyebrows went up. "Explain your thinking."

"Well, sir," Cooper began, "it seems to me that those old cranes make for a lot of deck clutter. They'll provide good concealment for anyone who wants to hide from our search teams. It probably wouldn't take much for someone to stage an ambush from one of those old cable housings. On another note, I wouldn't be surprised if our guys run into that same sort of crappy workmanship in other parts of the ship. Bare electrical wires, rusted ladder rungs, leaky steam pipes, missing deck plates—that sort of thing. A lot of opportunities for our people to get hurt over there, especially with the sun going down."

The captain nodded again. "All good points, Pat. These are the kinds of things you have to think about *before* you send your people into a tight spot." He shifted his eyes to Ens. Harvey. "Let's talk about the *sunset* issue for a moment. Carol, why *are* we sending our teams out to board a potentially hostile vessel while the sun is going down? More specifically, why don't we order the *Lotus Blossom* to heave-to and drop anchor? Then we could sit here and keep an eye on her until the sun comes up and send our boarding teams over in daylight."

Ens. Harvey cleared her throat. "I can see two reasons for boarding tonight, sir. First, if the *Lotus Blossom* really is a smuggler, any contraband cargo she's carrying is going to get tossed over the side as soon as the sun goes down. The only way to prevent that is to seize the ship now and post a guard on the crew while we search the cargo."

"Good," the captain said. "What's your second reason?"

Ens. Harvey grinned. "I just came from Combat Information Center, sir. The *Lotus Blossom* is still ignoring all attempts to establish contact. They won't respond to our signal flags or our flashing light, and they refuse to answer on bridge-to-bridge radio channel 16, which international law requires *all* major vessels to monitor at *all* times. In other words, Captain, they're ducking our calls. And we can't very well order them to heave-to and drop anchor if we can't even establish communication with them."

"True," Capt. Bowie said. "I'll bet ten dollars against a month's pay that—when we *do* finally establish contact—we'll discover that their bridge-to-bridge radio is broken, and somehow they just didn't see our signal flags or our flashing light."

"By the looks of things," Ensign Elliot La'Roche said, "they haven't noticed us at all. Personally, I think if I had a ninety-seven hundred–ton destroyer cruising a few hundred yards off my starboard beam, I'd probably notice."

"I agree," the captain said. "And that brings up another point of discussion. Why did we position ourselves on her starboard beam? This puts us close to Iranian territorial waters, and the Iranians do *not* like foreign warships in their water. If we crowd the line too closely, they'll send a couple of missile boats out to keep us company. Wouldn't it have been smarter for us to come in on *Lotus Blossom's* port side? That would have kept us farther away from Iranian waters and less likely to provoke a nasty international incident, or—worse—a missile attack."

Ens. La'Roche rubbed his chin. "It might have been a little *safer* to do it that way, sir, but it definitely wouldn't have been *smarter*."

The captain nodded once. "Go on."

"When we first picked the *Lotus Blossom* up on radar," La'Roche said, "she was well east of the established shipping lanes and hugging the territorial waters of Iran. According to our TACMEMOs, that's a tactic favored by smugglers who are trying to penetrate the naval blockade against Siraj. It gives the smugglers a chance to dart into Iranian waters if they think they're about to be intercepted. As I understand it, Iran has no particular interest in harboring smugglers, especially ones who are bringing aid to Siraj, but the Iranians are fiercely protective of their national waters. If we go in there, even in pursuit of a known smuggler, we're going to get shot at. By coming in on *Lotus Blossom's* starboard side, we cut off her escape route into Iranian waters."

"Excellent," the captain said. "You kids have done your homework. One final question before recess ..." Something caught his attention: the sound of approaching footsteps. He held up a hand. "Just a second."

Lieutenant (junior grade) Mitchell Hayes walked up to the little group. He came to an abrupt stop about two paces away from Bowie, drew himself up to attention, and snapped out a salute. "Sir! All equipment checks and communications checks are complete. The boats are ready and at the rail. VBSS teams Blue and Gold are manned and ready to deploy."

Capt. Bowie returned the salute. "At ease, Mitch."

Lt.(jg) Hayes relaxed his posture a notch and held a radio headset out to Bowie. "Your crypto is loaded and keyed, sir."

The captain nodded and took the headset. "Thanks. Your teams can stand easy for a few minutes. We have to establish comms with our suspect vessel."

"How are we going to do that, sir?" Ens. Harvey asked.

"We're going to give them a little technical assistance in repairing their radio," the captain said. He pulled the radio headset over his ears and positioned the throat mike in front of his mouth. When he was satisfied with the setup, he keyed the mike. "TAO, this is the Captain, over."

The Tactical Action Officer's voice came back in his ear a second later. "Captain, this is the TAO. Read you Lima Charlie. Standing by for orders, over."

Bowie keyed the mike again. "TAO, this is the Captain. Lay a 5-inch round across the bow of motor vessel *Lotus Blossom*. You have batteries released, over."

"Captain, this is the TAO. I copy—lay a 5-inch round across the bow of suspect vessel. I understand I have batteries released, over."

The captain reached into the pocket of his coveralls and pulled out a pair of flanged rubber earplugs: a standard part of the at-sea uniform. "Well, kids ... I suggest you put your hearing protection in."

* * *

A few seconds later, the 5-inch gun mount spun ninety degrees to the left with a speed that seemed impossible for so large a machine. The rifled barrel of the large-bore cannon locked instantly on the bridge of the *Lotus Blossom* and tracked it with an eerie electro-mechanical precision, continuously making minute adjustments to compensate for the pitch and roll of the *Towers* and of her target. It hung there for a few seconds, and then suddenly it swung forty degrees to the right and fired. The ninety-six–pound steel projectile rocketed out of the barrel with a flash and a thunder that would have shamed a Norse god. Bowie knew that it had broken the sound barrier before it was even clear of the gun.

The shell impacted the water less than fifty yards off the *Lotus Blossom's* bow, throwing up a surge of spray that looked like a golden fountain in the failing sunlight.

The spray had barely settled back to the wave tops when a voice came over Bowie's headset radio. "Captain, this is the TAO. Apparently the motor vessel *Lotus Blossom* has repaired her bridge-to-bridge radio. Her captain is on Channel 16 screaming his head off in Arabic, over."

Bowie smiled and keyed his mike. "TAO, this is the Captain. Put our interpreter on bridge-to-bridge Channel 16 and ask the motor vessel *Lotus Blossom* to kindly heave-to and drop anchor, over."

"TAO, aye."

Bowie looked at his small group of junior officers. Every one of them was grinning from ear to ear. "I do believe," he said, "that those boys have managed to repair their radio."

* * *

Forty minutes later, Lt.(jg) Hayes stood on the starboard bridge wing of MV *Lotus Blossom* and looked out across the five hundred yards of water that separated the old freighter from his own ship. The destroyer's phototropic PCMS tiles were darkening steadily in response to the failing sunlight, making the warship's squat angular profile increasingly more difficult to see as the sun went down. On the one hand, it was impressive to witness the technology at work. On the other hand, this mission was making Hayes nervous enough, without having to watch the vessel that represented home and safety pull a slow-motion disappearing act. Although the logical side of his mind was well familiar with the limitations of phototropic camouflage, his imagination harbored a tiny (and admittedly irrational) image of the ship continuing to fade until it vanished completely, perhaps with a tiny plop, like a soap bubble bursting.

Hayes turned his eyes back to the ship he was standing on and keyed the mike built into his headset, "*Towers*, this is VBSS Team Leader, over."

Capt. Bowie's voice came back in his left earphone. "VBSS Team Leader, this is *Towers*. Standing by for your report, over."

Hayes keyed the mike again. "*Towers*, this is VBSS Team Leader. VBSS Gold Team has secured the bridge and engineering spaces. The vessel's crew is assembled on the fantail, under guard. The head-count is fourteen, that is one-four. VBSS Blue has completed an initial sweep of all spaces with the exception of the cargo holds, over."

The captain's voice came back. "*Towers*, aye. Say again your head-count for the crew, over."

"*Towers*, this is VBSS Team Leader. Head-count is fourteen, that is one-four personnel, over."

There was a brief pause before the reply came. "VBSS Team Leader, this is *Towers*. Be advised, the vessel's paperwork indicates a crew of seventeen, that is one-seven personnel, over."

"VBSS Team Leader, aye. My interpreter has been questioning Captain Isam on the matter. Supposedly, two of the crew jumped ship in Jakarta, and the third was medically evacuated at sea due to an apparent heart attack. We've asked for documentation on the changes to the crew manifest, but Captain Isam is putting a lot of effort into carefully misunderstanding our questions, over."

"*Towers*, aye," Capt. Bowie's voice said in his ear. "I'd say the good captain is giving you the runaround. His vessel is based out of Singapore. Unless he's fluent in Cantonese, it's a pretty safe bet that he speaks English, over."

Hayes wiped sweat from his forehead with the back of a sleeve and grimaced when some of the stinging liquid found its way into his left eye. He squinted and rubbed at the eye. "*Towers*, this is VBSS Team Leader, copy that and concur. GSM3 Rashid tells me that Captain Isam switches back and forth between Farsi and an Egyptian dialect of Arabic, depending on whichever gives him the best opportunity to be obscure and difficult. The man is definitely taking us for a ride, over."

"*Towers*, aye," the captain said. "That's why we're boarding his vessel in the middle of the night, over."

Lt.(jg) Hayes nodded to himself. "Roger that."

Yusuf Isam, the captain of the *Lotus Blossom*, had been acting suspiciously almost from the second his ship had appeared on the *Towers*' radar scopes. The issue of the three missing crew members was just the latest in a whole string of evasions, accidents, and deliberate misunderstandings on the part of the Arab captain and his crew.

In view of Isam's evasive behavior, Hayes was in total agreement with Capt. Bowie's decision not to wait until morning to board the *Lotus Blossom*, despite the fact that he didn't care for nighttime boardings. He glanced over his shoulder in time to see the last sliver of the sun sink behind the horizon. He did not like this at all. The fact that he agreed with the necessity did not make him any more comfortable about being on an unfamiliar ship in the dark. Factor in the thinly veiled hostility of the crew, three of whom were missing, and the situation became even sketchier.

He keyed his mike again. "*Towers*, this is VBSS Team Leader. Request permission to set Modified Security Condition Two, over."

Capt. Bowie's voice came over the headset almost immediately. "VBSS Team Leader, this is *Towers*. Do you have an emergency or an escalating situation? Over."

"This is VBSS Team Leader. That's a negative, sir. But I'm not crazy about the vibes we're getting from Isam and his crew. Nobody's done anything snaky yet, but I get the feeling they've been waiting for the sun to go down. Don't ask me what they're expecting to happen, but they do outnumber my teams by two men, even if we don't count the three who may or may not be missing. If those guys are hiding on board, we're outnumbered by *five*. They might be armed, and they *definitely* have the home-field advantage, over."

He didn't voice the other half of his thought; any or all of the crew under guard could be armed as well. The United Nations guidelines did not permit VBSS teams to conduct body searches of suspect crew members unless they committed acts of physical hostility. Hostile attitudes and general lack of compliance were not considered sufficient grounds for a personal search. VBSS teams were permitted to *ask* the crew members if they were carrying weapons, which worked about as well as asking politicians if they were crooked.

"VBSS Team Leader, this is *Towers*. Understood. Stand by on your request, over."

Hayes suppressed the urge to lay a hand on the butt of the Navy-issue 9mm Barretta automatic riding in the speed holster on his web belt. The sky was full dark now, and though a few operational deck lights had come on, they didn't seem to be making much difference. He keyed his mike. "VBSS Team Leader, aye."

Hayes had expected a delay. VBSS teams normally operated in Security Condition One, with their Barretta 9mms loaded but holstered. Condition One would cost the team a few seconds if they encountered a threat, but the risk caused by the delay was balanced by the fact that holstered weapons were less threatening and (theoretically) less likely to provoke a hostile response from the crew of the seized ship.

It made sense that the captain would want to think for a few minutes and maybe call in a couple of senior officers for a quick powwow before deciding whether to authorize the change to a more aggressive posture.

Security Condition Two, which called for the teams to operate with their weapons drawn, was inherently more threatening. It also slowed the search process, as it required his team members to work one-handed, the other hand being constantly occupied by a weapon.

Hayes had requested *Modified* Security Condition Two instead, which would require only the odd-numbered members of his teams to operate with weapons drawn, allowing them to protect their even-numbered buddies. To Hayes' mind, it was a decent compromise; half of his team would have two hands to work with, and all of them would have some protection.

Isam was a snake. The VBSS teams hadn't found any contraband yet, but Hayes was certain the man was a smuggler. Everything about the cagey old bastard and his crew pointed in that direction.

Hayes leaned on the railing of the bridge wing and looked down toward the darkened forecastle. The fore deck was cluttered with equipment and deck fittings, visible now only as dark shapes. There were a hundred places to hide down there. A hundred good places for somebody to ambush his teams. "Shit," he said softly.

* * *

Three decks below, Operations Specialist Chief Harry Deacon stood at the entrance to the forward cargo hold. He scanned the darkened compartment and felt his jaws begin to tighten. "This looks like a real good place to get somebody killed," he said softly.

The cavernous space was crammed with Conex boxes. The huge shipping containers were stacked far closer together than international shipping laws allowed, forming a maze of narrow passageways with walls of corrugated steel.

The lighting system, inadequate when the ship had been designed, had seen fifty-odd years of hard use. Less than half of the fixtures worked, and those had been fitted with energy-saving sodium-vapor lamps. What little light they produced was largely eclipsed by the towering rows of shipping containers.

Deacon counted thirty Conex boxes in this hold. With the twenty-two they had found in the aft cargo hold, his team had fifty-two shipping containers to search. Deacon had six men, including himself, to do the job. There were no ladders or catwalks to the containers on the upper level, so his team would have to haul themselves up with climbing harnesses.

He shook his head in disgust. The United Nations bureaucrats who had drafted the Security Council resolution that mandated these searches had not had a clue of what they were really asking; that much was patently clear. He shook his head again. This was going to take all goddamned night.

"Come on," he said. "Get that first box open. And don't forget to write down the number off the box car seal *before* you cut it off."

* * *

Electronics Warfare Technician Second Class Paul Allen stepped up to the doors of the first Conex box with a pocket-sized notebook and a pair of orange-handled wire cutters. The EW2 was Chief Deacon's second in command on the Blue Team. "We've got it, Chief."

The chief nodded. "I'm going to head aft and check on Carlin and Finch." He turned and disappeared into the darkness.

Allen nudged his partner, an eighteen-year-old seaman named Steve Blandy. "Get your flashlight on this box car seal so I can get the number off of it."

Blandy pointed his flashlight as ordered. "God damn! It smells like a stable in here. What the hell are they shipping? Yaks?"

Allen ignored him. It *did* stink down here, but that wasn't exactly a surprise. A lot of these old freighters smelled like shit.

Blandy looked down and prodded the deck with the toe of his left boot. "One of these days, one of these rusty old bitches is going to fucking sink on us."

"Pay attention to what you're doing," Allen said. "Hold the light steady."

Blandy switched his attention to the flashlight. "Sorry about that," he said. "I'm not kidding, though. Last week, when we were searching that Omani freighter, Jenkins put his foot right through a deck plate. It was rusted as thin as paper."

Allen scribbled the last few digits of the serial number from the boxcar seal and slid his pen and notebook into his hip pocket. "Jenkins is always saying crap like that. He's so full of shit his eyes are brown."

"Not this time," Blandy said. "I was there. I saw it happen."

Allen latched the jaws of the wire cutters onto the thin metal of the seal. "Eye hazard—look away."

Both men turned their faces away from the door of the shipping container, and Allen squeezed the handles of the wire cutters. The seal parted with a metallic twang and fell to the deck.

Allen turned back toward the container. "Clear." He retrieved the errant seal and shoved it into a canvas pouch attached to his belt. He grabbed the latching handle of the Conex box and lifted. The handle moved slowly, with a groan of protest. "Give me a hand with this," he said.

Blandy went rigid. "Shhhh …" He swung the beam of his flashlight around to cover a narrow corridor between two rows of stacked shipping containers. "You hear that?"

Allen gave him a sour look. "Knock it off, goofball."

Blandy's hand went to his holster. He unsnapped the strap and wrapped his hand around the butt of his 9mm. "I'm serious," he said, playing the beam of the flashlight around in the labyrinth of shadows. "Somebody's down here."

"We're still in Security Condition One," Allen said. "That weapon stays in its holster."

"Do you see me drawing the damned thing?" Blandy whispered. "Anyway, we can cock and lock if we're threatened, even in Security Condition One."

"I don't see any threat," Allen said. "And I don't hear anything."

"Shut up and listen!" Blandy hissed. "There it is again!"

Something thumped in the darkness, followed by a scraping sound. Then there was silence.

Allen put his hand on the butt of his own 9mm. "I heard it that time." He keyed his headset mike and spoke in a low voice, "Blue One, this is Blue Two, over."

Chief Deacon responded immediately. "This is Blue One, go ahead, over."

"Blue One, this is Blue Two. We have somebody moving around down here, approximately ten yards forward of my position. Do you have any teams working in this part of the hold besides us? Over."

"Negative, Blue Two. Our personnel are all accounted for. I am in route your position. Take cover and don't do anything until I get there, over."

"Blue Two, aye."

Allen touched Blandy's shoulder. "Shut off your flashlight and get down."

The beam of Blandy's flashlight vanished, plunging them into the yellow-tinged gloom of aging sodium-vapor lamps. The cargo hold was not completely dark, but the shadows were numerous and thick, and the feeble glow of the overhead lamps did little to penetrate them.

Both men crouched against the doors of the steel shipping container. They were still exposed to the sides and the rear, but at least they had cover against attack from the forward end of the compartment—the direction from which the sounds had come.

They heard the noises again. They seemed to be closer this time.

"That's it," Blandy said. "I'm drawing down."

"No you're not!" Allen whispered fiercely. "Keep your weapon holstered. That's an order."

"This is bullshit!" Blandy hissed. "At least three of these fuckers are unaccounted for, and there could be a half dozen more who aren't even listed on the crew manifest. You can bet your ass *they* don't have to get a note from mommy to draw *their* fucking weapons."

Allen held up a hand. "Shhhh …"

Something else was moving—something behind them. Allen looked over his shoulder. Damn. They had no cover in that direction. Hopefully it was the chief. But what if it wasn't?

Allen bit his lower lip. Maybe Blandy was right. Maybe it was time to stop thinking about the rules and start thinking about self-preservation.

In the pre-mission briefings, the Combat Systems Officer was always saying, "*No matter how spooked you are, it's nearly impossible to accidentally shoot a man if your weapon is holstered.*" When you were suiting up on the boat deck, that sounded like good common sense. At the moment—crouched in near darkness in this foul-smelling cargo hold with possible hostiles coming from two directions—Allen thought it sounded a little thin.

He took a deep breath and let it out slowly. "Calm down," he said. "And keep your weapon holstered." He realized that he was talking to himself, more than to Blandy.

The sounds from behind them grew nearer. Someone was moving toward them rapidly. Allen was about a second and a half from throwing his safety training and Security Condition One out the window, when OSC Deacon's voice crackled in his earphone.

"Blue Two, this is Blue One. I'm coming up behind you, over."

"Copy, Blue One." Allen relaxed a fraction. At least *one* thing moving around out there was friendly.

A shape appeared, moving toward them in the gloom. After a few seconds, it resolved itself into OSC Deacon. He stopped at close whispering distance and crouched down. "Have you seen anything yet?"

"Negative, Chief," Allen said softly. "But we definitely heard something."

Chief Deacon nodded. "I've notified the lieutenant. He was already in the process of getting clearance to upgrade to Modified Security Condition Two. In the meantime, he's authorized me to use my judgment in accordance with the tactical situation." The chief paused for a second and then drew his own 9mm Barretta. "We're going to go cocked and locked. But, I swear to God, if either one of you shoots at anything, it had better be armed and in the process of cutting your fucking throat. Are we clear on this?"

Allen and Blandy both nodded and drew their weapons.

"All right," the chief said. "These corridors aren't wide enough to do right-left properly, so we're going to have to do high-low. Blandy, you're the shortest, so you're low. I'll take the high position. Make sure you keep your head down after we turn a corner so you don't foul my field of fire. Allen, you're jackrabbit."

Allen frowned. In the jackrabbit position, his job would be to lag behind whenever the others turned a corner and opened themselves up to attack. Allen would only follow when the new stretch of corridor was proven to be empty of attackers, or if Blandy or the chief went down, in which case he would jackrabbit around the corner with his 9mm blazing—providing rapid and (hopefully) unexpected backup. "Chief, I'm taller than you are," he said. "*I* should be high and *you* should be jackrabbit."

Chief Deacon shook his head. "Negative. You're the best shooter on the ship. I don't want you hit by the first bullet that flies. If one of us goes down, you're our best chance of getting out alive."

"But ..."

The chief grabbed Allen's shoulder and squeezed it. "You've got your orders, Sailor."

His words were gentle, but Allen knew him well enough to know that they were utterly nonnegotiable.

Allen nodded. "Aye-aye, Chief."

The chief stood up and shifted his 9mm to a two-handed combat grip. Allen and Blandy did likewise. The chief nodded. "Let's go."

Blandy went around the starboard corner of the Conex box, low and moving fast, his weapon swinging from side to side in short, precise arcs as he covered the shadowed corridor ahead. The chief swung around the corner a half-second behind him, his own Barretta carving a similar back-and-forth arc above Blandy's head. They moved forward at a fast walk, their eyes and weapons ceaselessly scanning the gloom ahead of them.

In accordance with jackrabbit doctrine, Allen counted to three before swinging around the corner and following at the same brisk pace, his own weapon tilted up at a forty-five–degree angle so that an accidental discharge wouldn't hit one of his teammates.

They covered the distance up the length of the first row of Conex boxes without incident. There was a five- or six-foot gap between the end of the first row of containers and the start of the second row. This space formed another makeshift corridor that intersected their corridor at a right angle, leaving short left- and right-hand passageways to investigate. They halted just short of the intersection.

OSC Deacon tapped Blandy on the shoulder and pointed to the left passageway, then he touched his own chest and pointed to the right passageway. "*You check left, I'll check right.*"

Blandy nodded. Still in his low-man crouch, he swung around the corner to the left and screamed.

Allen jumped so hard that he nearly squeezed off a round before he caught himself. He flattened himself against the steel wall of the shipping container to his left, trying to see what was going on.

Blandy threw himself backward, his arms and legs flailing as he struggled to get away. Still scrambling in a sort of crazy crab-walk, he crashed into the back of OSC Deacon's legs, bringing the chief down on top of him. Blandy screamed again.

What the hell was it? Allen lowered his 9mm to a shooting angle and rushed forward to cover the threat. He had covered about half the distance to the intersection when something rounded the corner in front of him and charged up the corridor in his direction. It was low and moving fast through the darkness, its rapid steps drumming on the deck plates. It was some kind of animal, shaggy and four-legged. A dog? Allen's 9mm jerked downward to cover the animal as it ran toward him. He sighted in on it, ready to shoot it before it could attack him the way it had attacked Blandy. Would it go for his throat or his groin? His finger began to squeeze the trigger, and then he got a good look at the animal. He broke into laughter.

It wasn't a dog. It was a goat. Blandy's terrifying attacker was a *goat*.

Still laughing, Allen stepped aside and let the frightened animal run past him.

OSC Deacon crawled to his feet and began dusting himself off. "Was that what I think it was?"

"That," Allen said with a grin that threatened to split his head in half, "was a highly trained attack goat. It's a miracle Blandy wasn't killed."

Blandy got to his feet. "That's not funny. That's not funny at all."

Chief Deacon holstered his 9mm and bent down to retrieve his boonie hat from the deck. "That is where you're wrong, kid. I can tell you already that this is one of those stories that's going to get funnier every time I tell it."

Allen holstered his own 9mm and turned on his flashlight. "You can count on that, Goat Boy."

Allen turned and walked back down the corridor to the doors of the container they had been set to inspect. Blandy and the chief followed him a few seconds later.

Allen grasped the latching handle of the Conex box and pulled. It wouldn't budge. He clipped his flashlight to his belt, freeing up his left hand. "Hey, Blandy, come help me with this."

The chief stepped forward. "I'll help. Blandy, you keep an eye out for goats, sheep, and other farm animals with terrorist leanings."

"Cute, Chief," Blandy said. "Real cute."

Between them, Allen and the chief were able to wrestle the reluctant latching handle up into the released position.

Allen swung the door open and shone his flashlight inside. He whistled through his teeth. "Uh … Chief? I think you need to take a look at this."

OSC Deacon looked over his shoulder. "What have you got?"

The beam of Allen's flashlight revealed stacks of gray crates with stenciled lettering in yellow spray paint: FALKE ANTI-AIRCRAFT RAKETENWERFER.

"Holy shit," Chief Deacon said. "I don't know what Ratken-worker means, or whatever the hell that is, but the *anti-aircraft* part I can figure out."

Allen sounded the syllables out slowly, "Rak-eten-werf-er … I think that's Arabic for '*somebody's in a shitload of trouble.*'"

CHAPTER 10

WASHINGTON, DC
THURSDAY; 10 MAY
7:22 PM EDT

On the state floor of the White House, sandwiched between the enormous East Room and the sumptuously appointed oval Blue Room, was the Green Room. Once the dining room of Thomas Jefferson, the Green Room was now a parlor, usually devoted to small receptions. It was a soothing place; the green watered-silk wall coverings and striped silk damask draperies seemed to invite introspection. President Chandler liked the Green Room a lot. He often went there to relax, and he nearly always left the little parlor with a smile on his face.

He was not smiling this evening, as his chief of staff opened the door for him and stepped back to let him in. Through the open doorway came the background murmur from the East Room: numerous voices mingled with the muted tones of light orchestral music.

Perched delicately on a nineteenth-century Duncan Phyfe settee, Gregory Brenthoven rose quickly to his feet.

The president waved him back. "Sit," he said. He nodded over his left shoulder toward the East Room. "I've got fourteen South American diplomats out there, and at least half of them are trying to pinch Jenny's bottom. So let's try to make this quick, before my lovely wife dislocates someone's jaw and causes an international incident."

Veronica Doyle followed her boss into the room and closed the door behind her. "The first lady *is* looking especially attractive tonight."

The president tugged at his bow tie, loosening it a fraction. "She is, indeed. But I still think it's rude of our esteemed guests to leave their fingerprints on her anatomy." He sighed and looked at Gregory Brenthoven. "What have you got, Greg?"

"Germany," the national security advisor said.

"All right," the president said. "We'll get to that in a minute. First, what's going on with the British Embassy?"

"Sir, you're scheduled for back-to-back Situation Room briefings at nine thirty and nine forty-five," the chief of staff said. "The topics of interest are developing events in China and the status of the British Embassy investigation."

"That's fine," the president said. "But the embassy attack is on my front burner; Greg can give me the ten-cent version now."

Brenthoven paused for a second as though mentally shifting gears. "The casualty count has stabilized. Sixty-eight people dead and forty-nine still in treatment. With the possible exception of two who are still on the critical list and could go either way, the doctors are expecting all of the remaining victims to recover."

"Both of those numbers are higher than the ones I got from homeland security," the president said.

The national security advisor nodded. "Yes, sir. The FBI has been tracking down people who came in contact with the agent at the embassy, but were somewhere else when they developed symptoms. They're using the embassy visitors' logs as a checklist, and they think they've found them all now."

"That's one piece of good news," the president said.

"Here's another one, sir," Brenthoven said. "So far, everyone who's come down with symptoms has actually been to the embassy. CDC was right. The bio-warfare agent used isn't robust enough to spread by human contact. The concentration level has to be pretty high to ensure infection."

"Have we identified the agent yet?"

Brenthoven nodded. "Yes, sir. CDC ran the micrographs, and USAMRIID cross-checked them. It's a strain of T2, a trichothecene mycotoxin that comes from corn or wheat mold."

The president frowned. "Mold? Clark told me that the highest agent concentrations were in the carpet. If we're talking about mold, that seems like something that could occur naturally. Can we be certain this isn't some kind of rare natural phenomenon? I remember reading an article on Sick Building Syndrome where the ventilation ducts become infected with mold or a virus and then spread it through the building."

Brenthoven shook his head. "No, sir. There is no room for doubt. Natural forms of this mold grow on corn or wheat, not carpets. Besides, the agent used was not actually a mold at all; it was a chemically engineered mycotoxin that is *manufactured* from mold. The T2 mycotoxin doesn't exist anywhere in a natural form. It's strictly a man-made agent."

"So we are one hundred percent certain that this was a biological warfare attack?"

"Yes, Mr. President. We also know how the agent was introduced into the building—in carpet cleaning machines. It went right past the security dogs, because they're trained to smell explosives, not biological agents. The shampooing process saturates the carpets with liquid soap, but—in this case—the liquid in the machines was about 5 percent soap and about 95 percent mycotoxin. Every carpet in the building received a massive concentration of the T2 mycotoxin."

The president tugged at his necktie. "How much do we know about the attackers?" he asked.

"There were two men, both American citizens of Middle Eastern descent—Michael Umar and Raphael Ghazi."

"Deep-cover operatives?" the president asked.

"Possibly, sir," the national security advisor said. "So far, three terrorist groups have claimed credit for the attack: Assi'rat, the Islamic Revolutionary Congress, and the Hand of Allah. Langley is pretty sure that none of those groups were actually involved in the planning or the attack itself. Most of the major terrorist groups are denying involvement. We haven't yet turned up any links between the attackers and any known organizations. There was a third man assigned to the carpet cleaning crew as well, a nineteen-year-old American Sailor named Jerome Gilbert. He was dispatched to the embassy with the other two men, but according to the logbook, he never showed up. We're looking for all three men, but no luck so far."

The president rubbed his eyes. "One of our Sailors was involved in a biological warfare attack on the British Embassy?"

"We don't know that, sir," Brenthoven said. "Seaman Gilbert was moonlighting, and he was brand new to the job. There's a good chance that he was just in the wrong place at the wrong time. My guess is he showed up for work and got assigned to a crew with a hidden agenda. It's even odds that Umar and Ghazi, the other two men on his work crew, murdered him before the attack took place—to keep him from interfering. I wouldn't be surprised if his body turns up in a ditch somewhere."

"If that's true," the president said, "then the attackers have *another* murder to answer for."

"Yes, sir," Brenthoven said. "It's a pity we'll never get a chance to bring them to justice."

The president's eyebrows went up. "Why is that?"

"They're almost certainly dead, Mr. President," Brenthoven said. "They couldn't very well arouse suspicion at the embassy by wearing gas masks or biohazard suits. They would have had to do the job in their regular work uniforms.

No masks, no respirators, no special protective equipment. I don't see any way they could have avoided absorbing lethal concentrations of the mycotoxin."

"A suicide mission," the president said.

"I think so, sir," Brenthoven said. "Standing right next to the carpet shampooing machines as they were pouring out the mycotoxin, Umar and Ghazi were probably the first people in the embassy to receive a lethal dose. It's also likely that they were exposed to higher concentrations than everyone else—again because they were right next to the machines. So they got it *first* and they got it *worst*. According to CDC, victims of T2 exposure generally begin to show symptoms about five or six hours after contact with the mycotoxin. Death usually follows an hour or two after that. So the attackers were almost certainly dead before any of the embassy staff began to show symptoms."

"So much for catching the attackers," the president said.

"I'm afraid so, sir," Brenthoven said. "We'll probably find their bodies in a day or two."

"Do we have any other leads?" Doyle asked. "Can we trace the source of the biological warfare agent?"

"We're working on that," Brenthoven said. "USAMRIID thinks the mycotoxin may have been genetically modified for increased lethality and a higher rate of contagion. That should narrow the field for us a bit. Despite the UN's efforts to stamp them out, there are a number of biological warfare laboratories in the Persian Gulf region. But most of them lack the sophistication for tinkering at the genetic level. The list of countries that could pull it off is relatively short."

"Don't tell me," the president said, "Siraj is at the top of that list."

"Pretty *near* the top, sir," Brenthoven said.

The president held up a hand. "I'll get the rest of the details at the briefing. Talk to me about Germany."

Brenthoven fished out his little leather notebook and flipped it open. "CIA has authenticated the memo."

"The one from Chancellor Shoernberg to his attaché officer?"

"Yes, sir. It looks like Germany is going ahead with the arms-for-oil deal."

The president's eyebrows went up a millimeter. "You're certain about this?"

Brenthoven nodded. "I'm afraid so, sir. Three days ago, one of the Air Force's Oracle spy satellites imaged four submarines at the naval arsenal in Kiel, Germany. A significant portion of the satellite's imaging footprint was blocked by cloud cover, but it's pretty clear that the subs were onloading missiles and torpedoes."

Doyle glanced at her watch. "Three days ago? Why are we just finding out about this now?"

Gregory Brenthoven pursed his lips and paused for a second before answering. "Three days ago, our German allies were not considered to be even a remote threat. Air Force intelligence analysts didn't regard a routine weapons onload by an allied navy as very noteworthy. It was a reasonable decision, based on the situation as they understood it. It hardly seems fair to second-guess their judgment after the fact."

"I agree," the president said. "Is there more?"

Brenthoven looked back at his notes. "Yes, sir. Langley has been chasing down a few leads. It turns out that a lot of the Indian pilots that Germany has been training over the last several months might not actually *be* Indian."

"Meaning they're Siraji?"

"That's what we're thinking, sir. We're running it down, but—at this stage—all we can say for certain is that a number of their immigration papers have strange inconsistencies."

"It's starting to sound like this deal has been cooking for a while," the president said. "So the Germans might be ready to deliver some of the hardware right now?"

"They may have already started, sir," Brenthoven said. "Yesterday evening, one of our destroyers in the Persian Gulf intercepted and boarded a cargo ship that was attempting to run the blockade of Siraj. The Visit, Board, Search, and Seizure teams discovered approximately three hundred German-built, over-the-shoulder missile launchers."

Doyle shook her head. "Greg, how in the hell did we miss something this big?"

Brenthoven closed his notebook. "A lot of our intelligence assets—too many—are electronic. We're still feeling the bite from the Clinton years; he cut our network of field operatives to ribbons. And the best electronics in the world are no substitute for good agents working on the scene. Our European network is especially thin; we've been concentrating most of our efforts on the Middle Eastern countries."

The president closed his eyes and took a deep breath. He released it slowly and opened his eyes. "Where are the subs now?"

Brenthoven blinked twice and looked at the president. "Ah … we don't know, sir. Our last satellite imagery of them is three days old. They could be through the English Channel by now."

"They'll have to transit the Strait of Gibraltar to get to the Mediterranean," the president said. "What if we blockade the strait?"

Brenthoven said, "Our nearest significant asset is the *Abraham Lincoln* carrier strike group. They're way down at the east end of the Med. Even at top speed, they'd never make it in time."

"If we can't get ships over there," the president said, "we'll have to find someone who *can*. Who are our allies in this?"

Brenthoven said, "The United Kingdom for certain, sir. Greece. Italy, maybe."

Doyle shook her head. "Not Italy. They're tied up too closely to France and Germany both. They've all got that Joint Theater Defense Missile thing going. Greece is a little shaky too."

The president ran his right index finger up and down along the bridge of his nose. "We'll get State to drum us up a list of possibles. In the meantime, we'll start with the UK." He glanced at his watch and nodded toward the door to the East Room. "I'd better get back out there before Jenny gets spoiled by so much attention." He turned his eyes to his chief of staff. "Get me Prime Minister Irons on the phone in an hour. Britain has at least as big a stake in this as we have." His eyes shifted to his national security advisor. "Wake some people up at Langley. You'd better call ONI as well. If I'm going to yell for help, I want some idea of what we're up against." He looked at his watch again. "You've got about fifty-seven minutes."

CHAPTER 11

R-92:

The signal rocketed through the fiber-optic core of the gray Kevlar cable and into the torpedo's dorsal interface module. A portion of R-92's digital brain powered itself up and awaited further instructions.

The cable, known as an umbilical in the parlance of technicians and torpedomen, served as a digital communications conduit between the weapon and the submarine's digital fire control computers.

In the seconds preceding a launch, the umbilical would upload programming commands and updated target information into the weapon's on-board computer. When the launch order came, the umbilical would relay that command to the torpedo and then automatically detach itself from the weapon at the instant of firing.

But the burst of digital codes coming through the umbilical now was not a launch order or targeting data. It was a routine maintenance signal.

R-92's on-board computer responded as ordered—transmitting power to each of its major systems in turn, running diagnostic routines to test for faults or errors—and then removing power and letting each subsystem revert to its normal at-rest condition.

The entire sequence of electronic tests took just under three seconds. All subsystems reported themselves as fully operational. R-92's digital computer relayed the reports back to the fire control computers via the umbilical.

This done, the torpedo waited another three hundred seconds for follow-on orders. When none were detected, R-92's digital brain powered itself down. Secure in its firing tube, deep in the belly of Gröeler's *U-307,* the predator was dormant.

CHAPTER 12

STRAIT OF GIBRALTAR
SUNDAY; 13 MAY
0132 hours (1:32 AM)
TIME ZONE 0 'ZULU'

The bridge of HMS *York* was rigged for darken-ship: all unnecessary lights turned off to preserve the night vision of the watchstanders. What little illumination there was came from the soft red glow of instrument lamps, and even those feeble lights were turned down to minimal intensity to preserve the night vision of the bridge crew. As was often the case on evenings when the moon was out, it was actually darker on the bridge of the old British destroyer than it was outside under the night sky.

Second Officer of the Watch, Sub Lieutenant Michael Kensington, felt the front panel of the radar repeater until his fingers located the dimmer knob. He turned the brightness up for a few seconds, just enough to get a good look at the sweep. Still just the one contact, aft and off to port. He turned the dimmer back down. That would be HMS *Chatham*, the Royal Navy frigate that formed the other half of their little task force.

The young officer raised his binoculars and peered out the window into the night. The seas were calm, and the moonlight coated the gently rolling wave tops with liquid silver. "Good moon tonight," he said, in what he hoped was an authoritative voice. "Shouldn't be very hard to spot a periscope."

Somewhere behind him, Ian Bryce, a seasoned lieutenant and First Officer of the Watch, exhaled sharply through his nose. "I keep telling you, there aren't going to *be* any periscopes. Fact of the matter is there aren't going to be any submarines. No submarines—no periscopes. Can't very well have one without the other, now, can we?"

Sub Lt. Kensington continued his binocular sweep of the waves. "I'd say Her Majesty's Navy thinks otherwise, or else we wouldn't be here."

The other two crew members on the darkened bridge, the Helmsman and the Bo'sun of the Watch, performed their respective jobs in near silence. They were both enlisted men, and—in much the same fashion that butlers and chauffeurs are paid to ignore the dealings of their employers—enlisted men were trained to stay out of the private conversations of commissioned officers.

Lt. Bryce sighed, his breath a disembodied sound on the darkened bridge. "The Germans are many things, but they are not stupid. They may posture and rattle their sabers, but when it comes down to it, they aren't going to challenge the combined might of NATO. They'd have to be pretty well deranged to pull a fool stunt like that, now wouldn't they? Use your head. If the Admiralty really intended for us to blockade the strait against those German subs, they'd have sent more than two ships." His words were punctuated by the sound of him patting something in the darkness. "This old girl has got more than twenty-five years on her, and the *Chatham*'s getting a bit long in the tooth as well. One old destroyer and one old frigate do *not* a blockade make."

Sub Lt. Kensington lowered his binoculars. "Then why send us out here at all?"

"We … are a symbol," said his unseen superior. "We are a visual reminder to the Germans, *and* to the world, that Her Majesty's government and her NATO allies are firmly opposed to the illegal sale of arms to Siraj. The Germans have rattled *their* sabers, and now it's time to rattle ours. Trust me on this, lad; it's all posturing."

Kensington shook his head, a pointless gesture in the darkness. "The captain doesn't seem to think so. You were at the briefing; he made it sound as if we're going to see some action."

Lt. Bryce laughed softly, that condescending chuckle that adults use when trying to explain difficult concepts to children. "Our fair captain is a wise man. Far too wise to cast doubt, however slight, upon the stated policies of his superiors. If you watch closely, you'll notice that his orders and opinions are *always* a close reflection of the current official rhetoric. He'd have to be a fool to do otherwise, and that man is no fool."

Kensington said, "You make him sound like a mindless puppet."

"Not at all. He's a smart naval officer who knows that his career floats as much on politics as it does on the ocean."

"Ah," Kensington said. "So a smart naval officer keeps his mouth shut and does his job. How is it, then, that you are able to speak your mind so freely?"

Lt. Bryce laughed. "*Someone* has got to teach the junior officers how the world really works." He laughed again. "We haven't fired a shot at one of Jerry's ships since Churchill was PM. Do you really think we're going to start another war over a handful of submarines? This is the voice of experience talking; if there's any fighting to be done, it will all be political."

"That's very well," Kensington said, "but if it's all the same to you, I'll be keeping an eye out for German periscopes."

"And so you should be," said Bryce. "The Royal Navy needs earnest young men like you, if only to offset the cynicism of broken-down old wretches like me."

Sub Lt. Kensington snorted. "Listen to you, playing the Ancient Mariner. You may be more experienced than I am, but you're not more than five or six years older."

"Too true," said Bryce. "But they've been *hard* years, Young Kensington. *Very* hard years. You should have a go at my life—never knowing when the Exocet is going to drop in. She did it again last month, the old bitch. Showed up for tea unannounced and didn't leave for a week."

Kensington laughed. "Why do you call your mum-in-law the Exocet?"

"That woman is not my mum-in-law," Bryce said. "She's my wife's mum. She's not *anything* to me. Not as far as I'm concerned."

"But the *Exocet*?"

"Because," said Bryce with a theatrical sigh, "she's like a ruddy cruise missile: you can see her coming, but there's not really much you can do about it."

Sub Lt. Kensington laughed again. "Right." He raised the binoculars and resumed his search of the waves.

* * *

For all his enthusiasm, two hours later, Kensington was beginning to admit to himself that the First Watch Officer might be right. German submarines weren't exactly leaping out of the water like trained dolphins. And Bryce's words, as cocky as they'd seemed at the time, *did* have a certain logic to them. Surely the Germans wouldn't let things escalate to the point of military conflict. He yawned and raised the binoculars for what seemed like the hundredth time.

He was still searching for periscopes, diligently (if tiredly) when he felt a tap on his shoulder. A voice said softly, "Second Officer of the Watch, I stand ready to relieve you, sir."

Kensington smiled in the darkness; the arrival of one's watch relief was always an agreeable thing, but especially so after a long mid-watch. He lowered his binoculars and turned toward the sound of the voice. In the gloom, he could just make out the shape of the man waiting to assume his watch responsibilities. "Sub Lieutenant Lavelle, punctual as always. I am ready to be relieved, sir."

Kensington turned up the brightness on the radar repeater to show Lavelle that the surface picture was empty of contacts with the exception of their escorting frigate, the HMS *Chatham*. He was about to crank the knob back down when he caught a tiny flash on the yellow phosphorous screen. "Hello," he said. "What have we here?"

He spent a few seconds adjusting the controls on the faceplate of the repeater, trying to refine the tiny radar contact.

Sub Lt. Lavelle yawned loudly. "Probably a bit of sea return. Just finish your turnover. I'll have a look at it later."

"It's not sea return," Kensington said softly. "It's small but consistent, and it's tracking west-to-east. Right toward us." He cleared his throat and spoke louder. "Lieutenant Bryce, could you come look at this? I think I'm getting a radar return from a periscope."

"Get on with your periscopes," Bryce said. "Turn over the watch and go to bed. Then you can dream of Jerry subs all you want."

Kensington stared at the radar screen. He made his voice as serious as possible. "First Officer of the Watch, I am *officially* requesting that you evaluate this radar contact."

"Listen to you," said Bryce with a laugh. "Go to bed, you silly bastard! There are no submarines out there. I give you my word as a British officer."

In a fluke of timing more suited to a situation comedy than to the bridge of a warship at sea, a short burst of static punctuated his last sentence. It was followed immediately by the voice of the ship's Operations Room Officer, coming from an overhead speaker. "Bridge—Operations Room. The sonar boys are tracking an active contact at bearing two-nine-zero, range of about six thousand meters. They're requesting a bearing check. My radar shows a flicker of something at that bearing and range. Request you do a visual sweep for surface contacts at that position."

Kensington swung his binoculars to the appropriate area. "I've got nothing," he said.

Sub Lt. Lavelle keyed a comm box near the radar repeater. "Operations Room—Bridge. We have negative surface contacts. Bearing and range are clear." He released the button. "Think it's a submarine?" he asked softly.

"Probably a fishing boat," Lt. Bryce said immediately. "Wooden hulls don't give much of a radar return, especially if they're small."

"We should wake up the captain on this," Kensington said.

"Nobody's waking the captain over a fishing boat," Bryce said.

The Operations Room Officer's voice rumbled the speaker again. "Bridge—Operations Room. We have six inbound Bogies. I repeat, we have six unidentified aircraft inbound! We are initiating Level One challenges at this time. Recommend we take the ship to Action Stations."

Before his First Watch Officer could object, Kensington shouted, "Bo'sun of the Watch! Sound the general alarm! Take the ship to Action Stations."

The raucous alarm whooped instantly in response, blaring out of speakers all over the ship, rousting sleeping Sailors from their bunks—as it was designed to do. Then the alarm was replaced by the bo'sun's voice. "All hands to Action Stations! All hands to Action Stations!"

"Damn it, Kensington," Lt. Bryce half shouted. "That was not your order to give!"

"Sorry, sir," said Kensington, who was not even a little bit sorry. "I was trying to anticipate your next command. Quick reaction, and all that!"

"Nothing to be done for it now, sir," Sub Lt. Lavelle added helpfully.

"I suppose not," said Bryce. "Kensington, call down to Main Engineering and tell them we'll be needing all engines on line. Lavelle, you call up the *Chatham*. Tell them we're going to Action Stations and advise them to do the same." He snapped his fingers three times. "Step lively. The captain is going to be up here in about two shakes, and I want him to see us doing it right."

"Bridge—Operations Room," the overhead speaker said. "Sonar is reporting three more active contacts!"

"That would be the rest of those submarines that aren't going to show up," Kensington said.

"Shut your mouth," Bryce hissed.

Kensington started to say something, but the overhead speaker interrupted him. "Bridge—Operations Room," the Operations Room Officer's voice said. "Bogies have ignored our Level One challenges. Issuing Level Two challenges now. Gun and missile stations reporting ready for combat."

"Very well," Lt. Bryce said. "Stand by for orders."

A watertight door banged open at the back of the bridge, and the bo'sun called out, "Captain is on the bridge!"

The captain crossed the bridge with a few long strides, his movements in the darkness carrying a confidence that only years of familiarity can bring. He climbed into his raised chair at the starboard end of the bridge and said loudly, "First Officer of the Watch, what is the situation?"

"We have six inbound aircraft, sir, as well as three active sonar contacts."

"Four," said Sub Lt. Kensington.

"Correction, sir," Lt. Bryce said. "We have *four* sonar contacts. The aircraft have disregarded our Level One challenges. Level Two challenges are in progress. Gun and missile stations are reporting ready for combat."

Over the speaker, the Operations Room Officer's voice said, "Bridge—Operations Room. Bogies have gone radar-active. I and J band pulse-Doppler emitters with a cascading pulse repetition rate. Looks like the German Air Force variant of the ECR-90C radar."

The captain exhaled audibly. "Luftwaffe. *That* narrows the field a trifle. We're either dealing with back-fitted Toranados or those damned Eurofighter 2000s."

"Bridge—Operations Room. Bogies are not responding to Level Two challenges."

"Is *that* right?" the captain asked quietly. "Second Officer of the Watch, take missiles to the rails. Shift the gun to anti-air automatic."

Sub Lt. Kensington stood for a few seconds without speaking. He'd done this a thousand times under simulated conditions, but this was no simulation. There were real planes out there, and real submarines.

"Second Officer of the Watch!" the captain said loudly.

Kensington started. "Yes, sir!"

"*Take* missiles to the rails, and *shift* the gun to anti-air automatic."

Kensington managed to catch himself before he saluted out of reflex. "Aye-aye, sir!" He keyed a comm box and repeated the captain's orders to the Operations Room Officer. Were they actually going to shoot? Surely it wouldn't go that far … or would it? The captain seemed to think so …

* * *

Out on the darkened forecastle, the twin arms of the British Aerospace missile launcher rotated up to the *zero* position. Two small hatches powered smoothly aside, and slender rails extended through the openings to mate with the arms of the launcher. A fraction of a second later, a pair of Sea Dart missiles rode up the vertically aligned rails to lock into place on the arms of the launcher. The rails retracted themselves, and the small hatches closed as soon as they were clear. The entire operation took less than three seconds.

The 114mm Vickers gun was loaded and ready a split-second later. Its barrel instantly slewed to a new position as it locked on the inbound aircraft and tracked their radar returns through the night sky.

* * *

"Missiles at the rail, sir," the Operations Room Officer reported. "The gun is in anti-air automatic."

"Good," the captain said. "Ready all torpedo tubes for firing."

"Aye-aye, sir," Kensington said. He keyed his comm box and repeated the order to the Operations Room Officer.

"Bring us around to two-six-zero," the captain said. "Don't let those subs get past us."

Lt. Bryce's voice was loud, "Helmsman, right standard rudder. Steady on course two-six-zero."

"Helm aye! Sir, my rudder is right fifteen degrees, coming to new course two-six-zero!"

The Operations Room Officer's voice came over the speaker. "Bridge—Operations Room. Bogies will penetrate our inner defense perimeter in five seconds! Request guns and missiles free!"

"Negative!" the captain said. "They're just trying to scare us into breaking formation so those submarines can get past us. We are not at war, gentlemen. We'll not fire the first shot!" His next words were drowned out by an earsplitting roar that vibrated the thick bridge windows like tuning forks.

The jets rocketed overhead, not more than ten meters above the foremast. The shriek of their engines was deafening, literally rattling Kensington's teeth. The glass faceplate of a gyrocompass repeater exploded into fragments under the sudden pressure.

A sliver of flying glass stung Kensington high on the right cheek, burying itself deep under the skin. His involuntary yelp was lost in the cacophonous scream of six pairs of jet engines running at open throttle.

And then the jets were gone, climbing away into the darkness, their afterburners carving blue arcs of flame into the night sky.

Kensington touched his cheek and felt the moistness of his own blood. His ears were still ringing from the fly-by.

"Steady, lads," the captain shouted, obviously nearly deafened himself. "We'll not fire the first shot," he repeated. "But if *they* do, I give you my word that we will fire the last one!"

The Operations Room Officer's voice came over the speaker again. It was difficult to hear him because he wasn't yelling like everyone else. Working farther down in the superstructure, he hadn't been half-deafened by the jets. "Bridge—Operations Room. Bogies are coming back around for another pass."

"Keep on those subs!" the captain yelled.

"Bridge—Operations Room. Bogies have locked on us with fire control radar!"

"Damn it!" the captain shouted. "Lock on the lead aircraft!"

Staring out the window, Sub Lt. Kensington spotted it first: an orange-white flare in the darkness, followed instantly by five more. Just as his brain was coming to grips with what he was seeing, he heard the Operations Room Officer's voice.

"Inbound! We have six inbound missiles!"

"Flank speed!" the captain shouted. "Hard left rudder! Guns and missiles free! Engage all targets!"

The deck pitched sharply to the right. Kensington grabbed the crossbar mount of the radar repeater to keep his footing as the ship heeled over into the turn.

Two brilliant flashes of light from the forecastle and twin rumbles, like freight trains passing a half-meter away, announced the launch of HMS *York*'s first pair of missiles. The British Aerospace Sea Darts hurtled into the sky on fiery white columns of smoke. Perhaps three-quarters of a second later, two Sea Wolf missiles leapt off the deck of HMS *Chatham*.

The forward chaff launchers fired six times in rapid succession. Six egg-shaped chaff projectiles arced away from the ship, four of them exploding at predetermined distances, spewing clouds of aluminum dust and metallic confetti into the sky to confuse the enemy missiles with false radar targets. The remaining two chaff rounds ignited like roman candles. They were torch rounds: magnesium flares designed to seduce heat-seeking infrared guided missiles.

The *York's* 114mm Vickers deck gun opened fire, and suddenly the night sky seemed to be filled with man-made lightning and thunder.

The starboard Phalanx fired a short burst of 20mm rounds, and was rewarded a second later by a distant explosion as the hardened tungsten bullets shredded an incoming missile. The high-tech Gatling gun swung around toward another incoming missile and fired again.

The port Phalanx mount remained silent, waiting for suitable targets to enter its arc of fire.

Out on the forecastle, a second pair of Sea Dart missiles slid up the loading rails to the launcher.

"Bogies are firing again!" the Operations Room Officer shouted over the speaker. And another half-dozen missiles leapt into the fray.

The Sea Darts blasted the forecastle with fiery exhaust as they shot away into the night.

* * *

Kormoran 2 (mid-flight):

The German missiles were AS-34B Kormoran 2s. Sea-skimmers that dropped like stones, not leveling out until they were less than two meters above the wave tops.

Following its mid-course inertial guidance program, the first missile waited twelve seconds before activating its nose-mounted targeting radar. When it did, it immediately located two radar contacts: one large and close, and a second, smaller contact fifty meters beyond. The target selection algorithm running through the missile's Thompson-CSF digital seeker instantly rejected the nearer/larger target. Large/near targets tended to be chaff decoys. The missile locked on the smaller target, and executed a short S-turn to the left to avoid the chaff cloud.

Locked firmly on the second contact, it closed in for the kill. At an optimum range of one-point-three meters from its target, the missile detonated its warhead. Fifty-five kilograms of plasticized-hexite erupted into a mushrooming shock wave of fire and shrapnel.

* * *

HMS *York*:

The concussion shook the bridge, throwing Sub Lt. Kensington up against the radar repeater hard enough to knock the wind out of him. "Holy Mother of God!" he gasped. "That was close!" His ears were still ringing, and the brilliant after-image of the close-aboard explosion still danced in front of his night-accustomed retinas. He pulled himself back to his feet. "Why are we seeding chaff so close to the ship?"

No one bothered to answer, but a second after he asked the question, he dredged up the answer from some half-forgotten training lecture. Missile manufacturers knew about chaff, and they were programming their weapons with little tricks to avoid it. Many missiles were now smart enough not to turn on their radar seekers immediately. If a chaff cloud was far enough away from the real target, a missile with an inactive seeker could fly through it without being distracted. The closer the chaff was to the ship, the better the odds that a missile's radar would be active and subject to seduction. By seeding an inner pattern of small chaff clouds and an outer pattern of larger chaff clouds, the ship could even sucker missiles that were programmed to ignore the first targets they spotted.

A fireball blossomed in the distance, as one of the Sea Darts intercepted and destroyed a German sea-skimmer. A few seconds later, a Sea Wolf from the *Chatham* vaporized another of the German missiles.

The Phalanx Gatling guns continued to spray short bursts of 20mm bullets into the night.

* * *

Flight Lead:

Two hundred meters above the water, Fliegen Oberleutnant Pieter Hulbert torqued his pistol-grip control stick to the left and nudged the rudder pedal, twisting his EF-2000S EuroStrike-Fighter into a tight turn. Mounting G-forces mashed him back into his seat as the agile jet fighter practically stood on its port wing. Stubby canard-style foreplanes gave the delta-winged aircraft a vicious midair turning radius. Hulbert grunted several times as his plane ripped through the turn, an old fighter pilot's trick for keeping blood pressure in the upper body when the Gs were stacking up.

He bumped the dorsal airbrake, and a streamlined section of the fuselage just aft of the cockpit folded open, creating a drag-stream that caused his plane to shed speed and altitude rapidly. The maneuver saved his life, as a Sea Wolf missile punched through the section of sky that his aircraft had occupied a millisecond earlier. The G-forces eased off as he rolled out of the turn into level flight less than a hundred meters above the water.

Hulbert scanned his Head Up Display for the targeting reticule. There! A wire-frame rectangle popped into existence on the HUD, outlining a fat radar blip. With the touch of a button, Hulbert called up an infrared display, superimposing the target's IR signature over its radar image. The IR signature was black: no significant heat sources. Not enough for a warship, anyway. It was a false target, a chaff cloud.

He sequenced to the next radar target and immediately called up its IR signature. An irregular oblong appeared on the HUD—gray, shot with dapplings of white. Heat sources. Heat from engine exhaust. Heat from ventilation systems. It was a warship. A target.

Hulbert shifted his right thumb up to the top of the control stick and flipped up the hinged plastic cover that protected the arming selector and fire button. He held down the arming selector, giving the missile under his starboard wing its first look at the target. A bright circle appeared on the HUD, signaling the missile's acknowledgment. He released the arming selector and gave the control stick a tiny jog to the right, improving his alignment on the target, to give the missile the best possible odds of success. His thumb shifted to the fire button.

The Kormoran missile dropped away from the wing, falling for nearly a second before its engine fired in midair. Then it dropped even closer to the water to begin the inertial-guidance portion of its attack on HMS *York*.

Oberleutnant Hulbert twisted his pistol-grip control stick to the right, peeling his aircraft away from the firing bearing as quickly as possible. It was a good tactic: what any smart fighter pilot would have done in the same situation. But in this case, it was fatal.

The 114mm cannon shell that tore through his port wing wasn't even aimed at him; he just happened to fly between it and its intended target.

Red tattletales began flashing all over his instrument panel, accompanied by a small choir of alarm bells and warning buzzers. Fly-by-wire was out and shifting to backup. Fuel pressure was dropping rapidly. The HUD lost power and went dark, and half of his instruments started fluctuating wildly.

The plane began to vibrate, and the control stick bucked crazily in his hand. A quick glance over his left shoulder told him that the carbon-fiber wing was starting to delaminate. He had perhaps ten seconds before the entire aircraft came apart on him.

He reached behind his head and groped for the looped shape of the eject handle. His fingers locked on it.

The second 114mm shell wasn't aimed at his aircraft either. It punched through the thin skin of the EF-2000S's fuselage just aft of his seat, about sixteen centimeters left of centerline. The explosion rolled through the tight little cockpit, simultaneously shredding Hulbert's body and flash-cooking it to cinders. Unable to contain the expanding pressure wave, the aircraft ruptured like an overripe fruit, spilling fire and twisted metal into the night sky.

* * *

Kormoran 2 (mid-flight):

Oberleutnant Hulbert's AS-34B flew two meters above the wave tops. In route to its target, it encountered two fat radar contacts, both of which it discarded as too large. The missile's target selection algorithm evaluated the third radar contact it detected and decided that the new candidate was of a size and shape appropriate for a valid target. Twice, the missile made mid-course corrections to improve its angle of attack, unaware that the second of these course changes snatched it out of the way of a burst of 20mm rounds from the destroyer's Phalanx Close-In Weapon System. The missile kicked into terminal homing mode and accelerated to mach 0.9 for the attack.

* * *

HMS *York*:

The starboard Phalanx mount had expended the last of its ammunition. It continued to track the incoming missile with unerring accuracy, its six Gatling gun–style barrels spinning impotently.

The missile struck the destroyer starboard side midships, just above the waterline, blowing a huge hole through the old ship's steel hull. The fireball and shock wave ripped through Engine Room Number One, buckling decks, collapsing bulkheads, shattering pipes, and severing electrical cables. Anything that was even remotely flammable was instantly incinerated—from the insulated lagging that lined the bulkheads, to the six crew members closest to the blast.

The sound wave that accompanied the explosion ruptured the eardrums of the three engineering personnel who survived the initial detonation.

Though the point of impact had been a half-meter or so above the waterline, the hole created by the explosion extended well below the waterline. The sea poured through the ragged hole in a sledgehammer torrent that drove an apprentice engineer to the deck.

Unable to fight the relentless deluge, the young man was swept across the space by the wave front. Deafened by the explosion and half-blinded by the seawater, he flailed about helplessly under the driving cascade as water forced its way up his nose and past his shattered eardrums. He opened his mouth to scream, but the water forced itself down his throat, pumping his lungs full of liquid fire. Still tumbling, his head slammed into a pump housing hard enough to crack his skull. The in-rushing sea tossed him about like a rag doll until it had driven the final spark of life from his limp body.

Electrical power to the compartment failed immediately, plunging the huge space into darkness. Battery-powered emergency lanterns kicked on, casting spheres of light into the roiling black floodwaters. Scalding tendrils of steam drifted through the semidarkness, the inevitable result of contact between cold seawater and super-heated metal.

A ruptured pipe spewed fuel onto the rising water. The volatile liquid floated on the surface, forming a slick that widened steadily.

Bleeding from their shattered ears and dazed by the concussive force of the explosion, the two remaining engineers managed to scramble up the steep ladder to the engine room's upper level. By the time they were through the watertight door at the top of the ladder and had dogged it behind themselves, the water level was halfway up the sides of the acoustic isolation modules for the gas turbine engines.

The larger of the turbines, a 50,000 horsepower Olympus TM3B, ran on—oblivious to the water swirling around its airtight isolation module. Its air supply and exhaust were routed through ventilation ducts that were still well above the water level. Closer to the blast, the isolation module for the smaller boost-turbine had been penetrated by shrapnel. Seawater poured in through several holes, quickly drowning the engine.

The ship began to slow.

Rising water reached an electrical junction box and shorted it out in a shower of sparks, igniting the fuel slick, and instantly converting the huge compartment into an inferno.

The ship's firefighting systems were more than adequate to handle the blaze. Fifteen cylinders of compressed halon gas stood ready to suppress the flames with a combustion-inhibiting chemical reaction. An extensive network of piping and sprinkler nozzles stood ready to spray hundreds of liters of firefighting foam throughout the massive engineering compartment, blanketing the fuel slick with a layer of chemical bubbles that would smother the flames and form a vapor barrier against reflash.

Neither system was activated, because neither system was automatic. Both systems required manual activation, either from control panels located inside the engine room or from duplicate control panels in the passageway outside the main entrance. Bloodied and dazed by the explosion, neither of the escaping engineers had thought to activate the fire suppression systems.

Fed by the still-gushing fuel pipe, the fire grew larger, stronger, and hotter.

* * *

On the bridge, the captain shouted, "Hard right rudder! Get us around so the port Phalanx can cover us!"

"Helm aye! Sir, my rudder is right thirty degrees, no new course given!"

A dazzling ball of flame lit up the sky as a Sea Dart missile swatted a German fighter jet out of the air. Kensington's heart jumped in his chest. His pulse was racing, and every explosion brought another involuntary flinch. Some primal part of his brain was screaming at him to run, to get away from this place. To escape this worthless stretch of water that the God of death had staked out as a playground. But there wasn't anywhere to run to …

"Kensington!" the captain said. "Find out where we were hit!"

The young sub lieutenant stared out the window. In the distance, he could see that the aft superstructure of their escort, HMS *Chatham,* was burning. They'd been hit too, then. Maybe they were *all* going to die.

"Goddamn it, Kensington!" the captain yelled. "Don't make me repeat every order!"

Kensington flinched again. "Yes, sir!" He leaned over the comm box and punched up the damage control circuit. "Damage Control—Bridge. I need a damage report."

There was no answer. Kensington tried again. He paused to wait for a reply, and that's when he saw them: two streaks of fire boring through the night. Coming right toward him. He had just enough time to scream before the first one slammed into the ship one level below the bridge. A millisecond later, the deck under his feet erupted into a volcano of fire and molten steel.

* * *

***U-307*:**

Through the lens of the Zeiss-Eltro Optronic 19 attack scope, Kapitan Gröeler watched the British destroyer surrender to the sea. Clouds of steam rolled skyward as fire and melted steel drowned themselves in the dark waves. Oily smoke mingled with the steam, creating billowing black columns against the white vapor. After a few moments, the waves closed over the old ship, leaving only a burning oil slick and a handful of floating debris to mark the destroyer's grave.

Gröeler's hands tightened on the grips of the attack scope. What were the fools doing? The fighters were supposed to keep the British ships occupied, not attack them! Some *idiot* of a pilot had pissed his pants and squeezed off a missile. And now look at this ...

The plan called for keeping the British out of the conflict. Gröeler felt his jaw tighten. *That* wasn't going to happen now, was it?

He swung the scope ten degrees to the right and centered the other ship in his crosshairs. The frigate had a heavy list to starboard, and her guns and missile launchers were motionless. Her active sonar had fallen silent as well. Probably she was without power.

For the briefest of seconds, he considered throwing the mission out the window and ordering his boats to the surface to mount a rescue operation. His country would try him for treason, of course, but that wasn't such a high price to pay for averting a war.

But his men would pay the price with him, wouldn't they? The economy of his country would still collapse into ruins. And, even then, it might not be possible to prevent war.

Gröeler flipped up the handles of the attack scope and stood back as the burnished metal cylinder lowered itself into its recess beneath the deck. He kept his face carefully neutral. It would not pay to allow his crew to see the doubt that he was feeling.

He turned to his Officer of the Deck. "Make your depth one hundred meters."

"Sir, make my depth one hundred meters, aye!" the Officer of the Deck said. He pivoted on his heal. "Diving Officer, make your depth one hundred meters."

The Diving Officer acknowledged the order and repeated it back. Almost without pause, he issued his own order to the Planesman. "Ten degree down bubble. Make your new depth one hundred meters."

Gröeler watched his men only long enough to verify that they were carrying out his order with their usual efficiency, then he turned his mind back to the

British ships. He almost couldn't believe it. With the flick of a switch, some fool had dragged the British into this—a development Gröeler was certain the all-seeing strategists of the Bundeswehr had not foreseen. One stupid, reflexive squeeze of a trigger and the plan had gone to hell. And, who knew? Maybe the world would go to hell with it …

Like nearly all senior naval officers, Gröeler was a student of history. Twice in the last century, his country had traded fire with the British. And both times, the entire world had stumbled blindly after them into war. He suppressed a shudder. *Please, God, do not let history repeat itself.*

CHAPTER 13

USS *TOWERS* (DDG-103)
NORTHERN ARABIAN GULF
SUNDAY; 13 MAY
1601 hours (4:01 PM)
TIME ZONE +3 'CHARLIE'

It appeared on the video screen without warning: a brilliant wedge of jittering green static that dominated the lower left quadrant of the SPY radar display. Operations Specialist Third Class Angela Hartford stared at the flickering green triangle with disbelief. She had been tracking three air contacts in that sector, and now she couldn't see any of them. They were totally eclipsed by the pulsing wedge of static. It was an equipment malfunction or maybe a software error. It *had* to be. Because the only other possible explanation was impossible. At least it was *supposed* to be impossible.

Hartford glanced across Combat Information Center to the Radar Control Officer's console, to the left of the Tactical Action Officer's station. She punched the channel selector on her communications panel, patching her headset into the Radar Control Officer's circuit. "RCO—Air. I'm getting some kind of weird system artifact on my air tracking display. It's gobbling up about a sixty-degree sector of my radar coverage. Can you run a quick diagnostic on SPY and check it out?"

The AN/SPY-1D(V)2 phased-array radar formed the heart of the ship's Aegis integrated sensor and weapons suite. With a power output of over four million watts and a high–data-rate multi-function computer control system, the most recent generation of SPY radar was capable of detecting and tracking nearly two hundred simultaneous air and surface contacts. In Aegis ready-auto mode, SPY could detect a contact, classify it as friendly or hostile (based on its radar signature, movement characteristics, and approach profile), prioritize it in relation to other threat ships or aircraft, and—if necessary—assign and launch missiles to attack it. Following a missile launch, SPY could even assess the target for damage and decide whether to launch additional missiles to finish it off.

But with such technological power came complexity, and the need for continuous human attention and frequent adjustment. That was the job of the Radar Control Officer: monitoring the condition of the SPY radar and keeping it tuned for optimum performance based upon atmospheric conditions and the types of ships and aircraft operating in and around its detection envelope.

The Radar Control Officer answered Hartford's call almost immediately. "Air—RCO. Copy your suspected system artifact. Running SPY diagnostics now. Stand by for updated system status."

Hartford was about to key her mike to acknowledge when another voice broke in on the circuit. "RCO—Surface. I'm getting it too. A big section of my scope is getting creamed. I can't see squat off the port side of the stern. Somebody's jamming us."

The RCO's reply was sharp. "Surface—RCO. Watch your professionalism on the comm net! Didn't they teach you anything in school? SPY frequency-hops about a hundred times a second. You *can't* jam SPY without jamming the entire electromagnetic spectrum. Now stand by while I run SPY diagnostics."

Hartford nodded. The RCO was right. Everybody knew it was impossible to jam SPY, and not just because of the frequency-hopping. At four megawatts, SPY was powerful enough to burn through any jamming signal known to man.

Hartford watched the brilliant triangle of static on her screen. It couldn't be a jammer, but it sure *looked* like one.

She punched her channel selector, patching her headset into the Electronics Warfare circuit. "EW—Air. Are you showing any sort of electromagnetic interference off the port quarter?" She shied away from the word *jammer.* Better not to get people spun up over nothing.

The Electronics Warfare Technician was obviously trying to stifle a yawn as his voice came over the comm circuit. "Air—EW. That's a negative. I'm tracking a couple of APG-79s and a WXR-2100 down in that sector. Slick-32 shows no interference in any sector. The EM spectrum looks nice and clean."

"EW—Air. I copy no interference and a clean electromagnetic spectrum. Thanks." Hartford released her mike button. The APG-79s would belong to the two F-18s she'd been tracking prior to the appearance of the artifact, and the WXR-2100 must be weather radar for the Saudi airliner she'd been tracking. Whatever the strange interference *was*, it was *not* a jammer. If it had been, the Electronics Warfare Technicians would have picked it up on their SLQ-32, or as they called it, the *Slick-32.*

Hartford frowned. If it wasn't a jammer, then it *had* to be a SPY malfunction. Either hardware or software. Hartford shrugged and turned her attention to the three hundred degrees of her scope that were *not* being blown away by the video artifact. Whatever it was, the RCO would find it.

CHAPTER 14

WHITE HOUSE SITUATION ROOM
WASHINGTON, DC
SUNDAY; 13 MAY
9:16 PM EDT

President Chandler laid both palms flat on the polished mahogany tabletop and let his eyes travel down one side of the long conference table and back up the other. The seven men and five women gathered around the table ranged in age from thirty-four to sixty-eight. Some were in military uniform, and some were not. A few wore suits, but most were dressed casually, in whatever they'd been wearing when the call had gone out for an emergency meeting. The single visible characteristic common to all of them was the grim expression they shared.

Seated directly across the table, Vice President Dalton Wainright nodded once when the president's eye caught his.

Veronica Doyle sat to the president's immediate left, in the spot traditionally reserved for the White House chief of staff. She leaned over next to him and whispered. "SecState is still shuttling back and forth between Beijing and Taipei, trying to nip the China situation in the bud. She's got Undersecretary Mitchell covering for her."

The president nodded and said quietly, "I don't see SecNav either."

"Secretary Larribee called from his car," Doyle said. "He's stuck in traffic on the beltway. I've got police escorts in route, trying to make a big enough hole to get him out of there, but it'll probably be at least an hour." She nodded toward the Chief of Naval Operations. "In the meantime, the CNO is ready to cover the Navy angle."

"Good enough," the president said. He looked at the CNO and said in a louder voice, "Bob, I understand that your boss probably isn't going to make it. Are you ready to proceed?"

Admiral Robert Casey stood up and nodded toward his commander in chief. "Yes, Mr. President." He picked up a small remote control and ran his thumb across a dial. The room lights dimmed and, at the far end of the conference table, a large projection screen scrolled down from a recess in the ceiling.

The admiral's summer-white uniform fairly glowed in the semi-darkened room. The contrast between the immaculate twill fabric and his tanned, weather-beaten face made his skin seem the color of old leather.

He pressed another button and an image filled the screen. It appeared to be an aerial view of a large industrial seaport. A good deal of the picture was obscured by cloud cover, but—judging from the clarity of the image—the shot appeared to have been taken from low altitude with a very good camera.

"This photograph was taken on the seventh of this month by a U.S. Air Force Oracle III series surveillance satellite, during a covert medium-altitude orbital pass over Western Europe. The area under surveillance, in this case, was the Deutsche Marine Naval Arsenal in Kiel, Germany."

The admiral pressed a button on the remote, and the image was replaced by an enlargement of a section of the photo. The picture was somewhat grainier than the first image had been, but the clarity was still very good. Several dark cylindrical shapes could be seen in the waters adjacent to a series of parallel docks, each attended by a large yellow crane. Workmen were clearly visible on the docks and on and around the dark cylinders.

"These are satellite photos?" asked Undersecretary of State Mitchell. "From the quality, I would've thought they were shot from an airplane."

Adm. Casey smiled briefly. "Yes, sir, they're satellite shots. I have to give those Zoomies credit; their equipment is top-notch."

"It certainly *is*," Mitchell said in a nearly reverent tone.

The admiral pressed a button. Four bright red ovals appeared on the screen, each of them enclosing one of the dark cylindrical shapes. "These are German Type 212B diesel submarines. The Office of Naval Intelligence believes that they are hull numbers *U-304* through *U-307.* Barring the new German Type 214s, which are not operational yet, these are the most sophisticated and deadly diesel submarines on planet Earth. Intelligence analysts at ONI and the Central Intelligence Agency have examined these photographs in detail and are confident that we are witnessing a complete missile and torpedo load-out for all four submarines."

The admiral looked around the room. "Under ordinary circumstances, we wouldn't be even slightly concerned by this. Our allied nations are entitled to arm their submarines, and we wouldn't expect them to do otherwise. But we believe that these *particular* submarines have been earmarked for delivery to the government of Siraj."

Eyebrows went up around the table, and a few people sat up straighter in their seats.

Undersecretary of State Mitchell said, "*Obviously*, any such delivery is in clear violation of standing United Nations resolutions."

"Obviously," Adm. Casey said.

"The repercussions would be staggering," the vice president said. "The government of Germany wouldn't dare ..."

The admiral keyed the remote. "I'm afraid they already *have* dared, sir." The image changed to a split-screen picture of two warships. "The ship on the left is—or rather *was*—HMS *York*, a destroyer belonging to the British Royal Navy. The ship on the right is her escort, HMS *Chatham*, a Royal Navy frigate. Approximately twenty-two hours ago, while attempting to blockade the Strait of Gibraltar, these ships gained sonar contact on what they believed to be the four German submarines. While HMS *York* and HMS *Chatham* were attempting to divert the submarines, a flight of approximately six German warplanes appeared. Based upon their performance characteristics, we believe they were the German Air Force variant of the EF-2000S EuroStrike-Fighter. We don't know who pulled the trigger first, but the encounter escalated into into a missile shoot. HMS *York* went down with a loss of nearly all hands. HMS *Chatham* was severely damaged and is currently being rigged for tow back into port. According to their reports, the British shot down four of the jets and may have damaged a fifth."

The admiral looked directly at Vice President Wainright. "The Royal Navy has search and rescue helicopters out combing the water for survivors, but as of their last situation report, two hundred ninety-four British Sailors are either dead or missing." He paused for a second. "Sir, I humbly submit that our German allies have already *dared* one hell of a lot."

"Where does that put us now, Bob?" the president asked.

The admiral looked at the screen and pressed the button again. The ships were replaced by a color map of the Mediterranean Sea. "The German subs are somewhere in the Med by now. Assuming that they are moving at their maximum possible speed, they should still be west of this line." He pressed another button, and a curved red line appeared on the map. "In all probability, they are somewhere between the Spanish island of Balearic and Sardinia—off the Italian coast." He turned to look at the president. "It's a big stretch of water, Mr. President. But not so big as to be unmanageable. I've got the Abraham Lincoln strike group steaming west at top speed, and a half-dozen P-3s in the air as we speak." He keyed the remote again, and a series of small black silhouettes appeared on the map: six ships at the eastern end of the Mediterranean Sea and six airplanes at the western end.

"Excuse me," Undersecretary Mitchell said. "P-3s? Those would be some sort of aircraft?"

"Yes, sir," the admiral said. "Lockheed Martin P-3 Orions. Long-range, prop-driven planes. Specially designed for Undersea Warfare, or what we call USW."

Mitchell nodded.

The admiral continued. "The plan is to blanket the western end of the Med with sonobuoys. By the time the P-3s have the subs localized, the carrier and her escorts should be on station."

Army General Horace Gilmore, the chairman of the Joint Chiefs of Staff, cleared his throat. He was a mild-looking man, with a rounded face and black-rimmed glasses that would have been at home on the nose of a librarian. The rack of ribbons on the left breast of his uniform jacket hadn't come from shelving books, though. He leaned his head forward and stared over the tops of his glasses with eyes that were nearly predatory in their intensity. "And then what, Admiral Casey?"

The admiral sat down and pulled his seat up next to the table. "I believe that's what we're here to discuss, General."

Secretary of Defense Rebecca Kilpatrick leaned back in her chair. "I get the feeling that you already have a plan of action."

"I do, Madam Secretary. I think we should hunt those bastards down and sink every one of them."

Secretary Kilpatrick smiled. "It has the virtue of being simple. And a simple plan is often the *best* plan." She looked around the table. "But I think we need to consider this situation carefully before we start shooting at people. Things may not be as cut-and-dried as we think."

"With all due respect, Madam Secretary," the admiral said, "it looks pretty simple from my side of the table. One of our allies has been attacked. If we don't cover their backs, how can we expect them to cover ours?"

"I don't dispute the fact that one of our allies has been attacked," Secretary Kilpatrick said. "The question is *which* of our allies?"

"That's pretty obvious," the admiral said.

SecDef's eyebrows went up. "Are you certain? Right now, we can't even be sure who fired the first shot. What if we investigate and discover that one of the British ships launched first, and the Germans only returned fire in self-defense?"

"I suppose it's possible," Adm. Casey said. "But I don't think it's very likely."

"You've been in combat before," the secretary of defense said. "And so have I." As a retired Army colonel, she was one of only three people in the room who had earned the right to wear the coveted Combat Infantry Badge.

"We both know how the game is played," she said. "Some yahoo crowds your airspace, so you lock on them with fire control radar. They return the favor and paint you with *their* fire control radar. Before you know it, you're both pumping enough electromagnetic energy into the air to microwave a hot-dog. Alarms are going off; adrenaline levels are sky high; people are shouting. Ninety-nine times out of a hundred, somebody eventually gets tired of the game and backs down. Everybody gets to go home claiming victory. But about one percent of the time, somebody gets spooked and does something stupid. Sometimes it's one of our guys, and sometimes it's one of their guys."

"The Brits are claiming that the Germans shot first."

"Of course they are," the secretary of defense said. "In their shoes, I'd probably say the same thing, whether I'd shot first or not."

Gen. Gilmore nodded. "I agree. We have to table the matter of the shooting, at least until we know who initiated the attack. That still leaves us with four German submarines hauling ass through the Med. What do we do about them?"

"We can't afford to attack them out of hand," Undersecretary of State Mitchell said.

"We're not going to," the president said. "I want the Abraham Lincoln strike group to intercept them and turn them around."

Adm. Casey tilted his head to the side. "That tactic didn't seem to work too well for the British, sir."

The president brought his palms together and interlaced his fingers. "A fully escorted aircraft carrier should fare slightly better than two aging British warships. I would hope so, anyway."

Gen. Gilmore nodded. "No doubt you are right, Mr. President. But Admiral Casey does have a point. While there's no conclusive evidence yet, my instincts tell me that the Germans probably pulled the trigger first. What if they start shooting at us?"

"They won't," the president said. "Somebody just got an itchy finger. It's not going to happen again." He looked at the Chief of Naval Operations. "Bob, it's your job to make *sure* that it doesn't happen again. We don't want to provoke the Germans; we just want to turn them around."

"Understood, sir," the CNO said. "We'll play it low-key. But what happens if the Germans open up on us anyway?"

"Jesus Christ, Bob!" the president snapped. "Get over it, and get over it *now*. You've got your orders. We're not going to get in a shooting war with the god-damned Republic of Germany. That is simply not an option. It's … it's unthinkable."

CHAPTER 15

TORPEDO: THE HISTORY AND EVOLUTION OF A KILLING MACHINE

(Excerpted from an unpublished manuscript [pages 91–95] and reprinted by permission of the author, Retired Master Chief Sonar Technician David M. Hardy, USN)

Following the American Revolution, naval tacticians in many countries began to see the torpedo's promise as a weapon. The torpedo still lacked a viable delivery system, but its destructive potential was nothing short of astounding.

Over the course of the next several decades, two basic design philosophies emerged. Floating torpedoes (by far the most common) were designed to drift on, or slightly below, the surface of the water until they came into contact with the hull of an enemy ship. Today, these so-called floating torpedoes would be classified as *mines*, but in the eighteenth and nineteenth centuries, the word *torpedo* was understood to include nearly any form of waterborne explosive device. During the American Civil War, when Union Admiral David Farragut shouted his famous line, "*Damn the torpedoes! Full speed ahead*!" he was referring to mines.

Spar torpedoes were second in popularity and effectiveness to floating torpedoes. A spar torpedo consisted of an explosive charge mounted on a wooden pole (or spar) and lashed to the bow of a small boat. Rigged to project several yards out in front of the bow, the spar torpedo was designed to be rammed directly against the hull of the target vessel. The resulting explosion, only a few yards from the attacking boat, would almost certainly result in damage to the torpedo boat or its crew. Understandably, spar torpedoes were unpopular weapons, and they saw very little application in combat before they fell out of use altogether.

Destructive capacity notwithstanding, the lack of a reliable delivery system severely limited the effectiveness of both spar and floating torpedo designs. It would take a major technological breakthrough to change that.

The breakthrough finally came in 1866, when a British-born naval engineer named Robert Whitehead built the first self-propelled torpedo. Whitehead called his invention the *automotive* torpedo (or sometimes, the *locomotive* torpedo), but critics and supporters alike insisted on calling it the *Whitehead* torpedo. By any title, the self-propelled torpedo represented more than a technological breakthrough; it was a quantum leap in naval weaponry.

In appearance, Whitehead's torpedo was a cigar-shaped steel cylinder with severely tapered ends. Mounted at the rear (or *afterbody*) of the weapon was a propeller, which was coupled by a drive shaft to a pneumatic motor inside the cylinder. Also mounted on the afterbody were a pair of horizontal fins and a pair of vertical fins, to guide the torpedo through the water in a straight line. The pneumatic motor was powered by compressed air from a tank built into the middle section of the weapon. The nose of the weapon was dedicated to an explosive charge, the *warhead*. Whitehead used explosive gun cotton in most of his early warhead designs, but eventually he switched to dynamite, which was more stable and packed significantly more destructive power.

The ironclad warships of Whitehead's day were defenseless against torpedo attacks. Designed to repel explosive shells from naval cannons, ironclads were heavily armored all the way down to the waterline. Since cannon shells could not effectively penetrate below the water, naval architects the world over agreed that it was not necessary to armor the underwater portion of a warship's hull. (In fact, an armored hull was considered undesirable; the increased weight would make a ship ride lower in the water, reducing its speed and its fuel efficiency.) As a consequence, in the closing decades of the nineteenth century, every warship in the world was vulnerable to torpedo attack.

Nineteenth-century Sailors found the very idea of the torpedo both insulting and terrifying. They began to refer to Whitehead's invention as the *Devil's Device*. Many prominent naval officers condemned the machine as a *barbarous method of warfare*. After all, war at sea was a gentleman's game, and a device that slipped in under a ship's armor wasn't a very far cry from a punch below the belt. It could hardly be considered the weapon of an honorable man.

Luckily (for its detractors), Whitehead's torpedo had a lot of problems. Early models had difficulty maintaining their depth in the water. A torpedo that rose too high in the water would impact on a ship's armor, which might well absorb the explosion without serious damage. A torpedo that ran too deep would pass under the target ship's hull and miss it completely. To make matters worse, since Whitehead's first models did not have steering mechanisms, they were easily pushed off course by tides or ocean currents, frequently causing them to miss their targets.

Whitehead applied his engineering skills to the first problem: depth control. It took him two years to solve it, but by 1868, he had the solution: a device that he referred to as the *secret*. Many European countries were becoming interested in the automotive torpedo, and Whitehead was intensely aware that he had a growing list of competitors. To throw them off the scent, Whitehead hinted strongly that his secret depth control device was highly complex and would be difficult or impossible to duplicate. In fact—despite its dramatic title—the *secret* was little more than a piston, a cylinder, and a spring attached to the horizontal fins by a mechanical linkage. Seawater flowed into the cylinder by means of a small vent just behind the warhead. As the water pressure increased with depth, the seawater in the chamber would exert force on the piston, compressing it against the spring. The motion of the piston would in turn move the mechanical linkage, which would change the angle of the horizontal fins, making the torpedo climb or dive. When the force exerted on the piston by the seawater became equal to the opposing force of the spring, the fins would return to a level position, causing the torpedo to level off. By adjusting the tension on the spring, Whitehead was able to pre-select the depth to which a torpedo would dive. To make depth changes even smoother, Whitehead attached a pendulum to the linkage to dampen minor oscillations as the piston shifted positions.

The basic design of Whitehead's *secret* depth control device was so successful that it remained in use—with very few changes—for nearly a hundred years.

With the depth control issue finally solved, Whitehead turned his attention to the problem of steering. Unlike the depth control issue, which had yielded to Whitehead's engineering expertise in only two years, the steering problem seemed to defy solution. Whitehead (and his competitors) spent the next several decades trying to solve it.

In the meantime, the unsolved steering problem did not prevent the torpedo from gaining popularity. Over the social and moral objections of many naval officers, nearly every navy in Europe began buying or building automotive torpedoes. Small, steam-powered *torpedo boats* began appearing in increasing numbers, and many larger warships were back-fitted to carry torpedoes. The situation escalated into an arms race, and conventional wisdom held that any navy that did not arm itself with torpedoes was likely to fall prey to one that had embraced torpedo warfare.

On January 25, 1878, the automotive torpedo found its first real use in combat. Russia, under the rule of Tsar Alexander II, had been at war with Turkey since April of the previous year. On the night of January twenty-fifth, two Russian torpedo boats, *Tchesma* and *Sinope*, conducted attacks on the armed Turkish steamer *Intibah*. Both shots were direct hits, and the resulting explosions devastated the Turkish ship. The wreckage of the *Intibah* slipped beneath the waves in less than two minutes.

In many ways, the attack was less impressive than Whitehead might have hoped for. The *Intibah*—although armed—was not an ironclad, so the torpedo's effectiveness still had not been demonstrated against a fully armored warship. (In fact, the *Tchesma* and *Sinope* had conducted earlier attacks on the Turkish ironclad *Mahmoudieh*, but both of their torpedoes had missed the target.) Still, details notwithstanding, history had been made: automotive torpedoes had struck and destroyed an armed vessel under conditions of actual combat. The torpedo was no longer a curiosity, or even a theoretical weapon. It was an engine of war. The race to acquire and perfect torpedo technology rose to a level approaching frenzy.

The torpedo, in various designs, saw use in several sea battles over the next few decades, with wildly varying degrees of success. The mixed results were the product of two factors: one positive and one negative. On the positive side, the destructive energy that a torpedo could deliver was astounding; it was not at all unusual for a single torpedo hit to cripple or sink a fully armored warship. On the negative side, the lack of a self-correcting steering mechanism made it difficult to actually *hit* a target with any real degree of reliability.

In the early 1890s, Whitehead became convinced that the torpedo steering problem could be solved by installing a gyroscope. (Invented in 1852 by French physicist Jean Bernard Leon Foucault, the gyroscope was known to have interesting properties but was generally thought to have no practical application.) Whitehead embarked on a series of experiments using a Russian-made gyro called a Petrovich. Despite its promise, the Russian gyro was too crudely made to suit Whitehead's purpose. In 1895, Whitehead turned his attention to a precision-built gyroscope designed by an Austrian naval engineer named Ludwig Obry. Unlike the Russian model, Obry's gyroscope could achieve and maintain a high enough rotation speed (about 2,400 rpm) to give a torpedo both duration and accuracy.

Whitehead attached the gyro to a two-way air valve, which directed measured quantities of compressed air to a steering engine whenever a torpedo began to deviate from its directed path through the water. The steering engine was connected in turn to the torpedo's vertical fins, which Whitehead re-engineered into turnable rudders. It was an ingenious solution to a problem that had plagued the automotive torpedo ever since its birth in 1866. Gyroscopic steering increased the accuracy of the torpedo's course to a mere half degree over a distance of seven thousand yards, or three and a half nautical miles.

Suddenly, the torpedo had striking range, accuracy, *and* the incredible destructive potential for which it had become famous. With the major engineering problems finally solved, it was nearly inevitable that the torpedo would begin to exert a significant influence on world events.

CHAPTER 16

SOUTHERN MEDITERRANEAN SEA
MONDAY; 14 MAY
1609 hours (4:09 PM)
TIME ZONE +2 'BRAVO'

Lieutenant Shari Scarlotti leaned her head against the side window and felt the bass drone of her plane's engines resonate through her skull. Dark-haired and small-boned, her slight frame looked out of scale in the pilot's seat, like a child swallowed up in her father's easy chair. The relentless sound of the turbines never ceased and rarely wavered while the big four-engined aircraft was airborne.

Her air crew had nicknamed it the *hypno-tone*, and they frequently joked that it lulled them into a post-hypnotic state and then forced them to perform acts that they would never have even considered without its mesmeric (and undoubtedly evil) influence. Any trouble they got into when they were off-duty was invariably blamed on fourteen-hour missions spent listening to the hypno-tone.

Her Flight Engineer, Chief Benjamin Lanier, took the opposite side of the argument, asserting that the steady thrum of the huge Allison turboprops was the most beautiful music audible to the human ear. With a couple of beers in him, he'd even been known to claim that he couldn't make love to his wife without a recording of turboprops droning in the background.

Shari wouldn't go quite that far, but she liked the sound; she liked it a lot. The Lockheed Martin P-3C Orion was a big plane and over thirty years old. But as long as the 4,600 horsepower engines kept pumping out that deep monotonous tone, she knew that her aircraft had a guaranteed place in the sky.

Shari's copilot, Lieutenant (junior grade) Andy Cole, squeezed past her right shoulder and slid into the right-hand seat. He held out a tall, spill-proof plastic cup. "Coffee, boss? Just the way you like it: fourteen sugars, nine creams, and then I waved the cup over the pot to give it that good coffee flavor."

Shari reached for the cup and took a sip. It *was* just the way she liked it, hot and black. She swallowed. "Thanks, wise-ass." She took another sip and swallowed again. "What's the word from Nav?"

Andy set his own coffee cup in a car-type cup holder that he had Velcroed to his side of the cockpit and went about the business of belting himself into the copilot's chair. "Our fearless Navigator assures me that we are right on track, and nine minutes ahead of profile. We should be on station in about fifteen minutes." He lifted his coffee cup out of the holder.

Shari nodded. "Good. It's just about time to start this party."

Andy furrowed his eyebrows in mock concentration. "I think Nav had his fingers crossed," he said. "So he could have been blowing smoke up my butt."

Shari looked out her side window at the brilliant blue waters of the southern Med scrolling by fifteen thousand feet below. "If I've told you once, I've told you a hundred times," she said. "If you don't put your butt where Nav can get to it, he can't blow smoke where you don't want it."

Andy grinned. "Roger that, boss."

Shari rotated her neck to relieve a crick. "How are we looking for Electronic Support?"

"The ALR-66 is still out of commission," Andy said. "Chief Lanier is back there breathing down the tech's neck, trying to get it fixed. Apparently, we need a break-while-stepping relay, whatever the hell *that* is. It's probably going to stay broke till we get back to the barn."

Shari sighed. "Have we ever flown a mission where everything on board actually worked for the entire flight?"

"Not that I know of, boss. In fact, I don't think I've ever even heard of such a thing."

"So we're hitting the Op-Area blind?"

"Not exactly. We just got an ES cross-fix from *Abraham Lincoln's* Airborne Early Warning plane."

"Better than nothing," Shari said. "Is it good news or bad?"

"Good news. There are at least two Kelvin Hughes Type 1007 I-band radars transmitting right-smack-dab in the middle of our Op-Area. Definitely consistent with German Type 212 subs."

Shari's eyebrows went up. "Two? What about the other two? Did they split off from the rest of the pack?"

Andy shook his head. "George doesn't think so."

George was Ensign George Freely, the plane's Tactical Coordinator, or TACO (pronounced to rhyme with "whacko").

"He says it's not unusual for subs in a rotating diesel barrier to alternate their depths according to a predetermined schedule. That way, not all the subs are at periscope depth at the same time."

"This isn't exactly a rotating diesel barrier," Shari said.

"True," said Andy. "But that's the closest tactical example that anyone can think of. Nobody's had to deal with a roving diesel wolfpack since the Second World War."

"I understand that," Shari said. "But we still don't know for a fact that the subs are sticking together. What if we get all our eggs in one basket, and some of those subs slip by us to the north?"

"They're going to have to refuel somewhere," Andy said. "The intel weenies think they'll head for Tobruk, Libya. That's the nearest port that's seriously hostile to the good old U.S. of A."

Shari glanced at her own fuel gauges. "Sounds like a pretty big gamble to me," she said. "How much time will we have on station before the carrier gets there and steals our thunder?"

Andy took a swallow of coffee. "Those guys are making tracks. We'll probably have the Op-Area to ourselves for an hour before AEW gets there." He shrugged. "The carrier will be, what? An hour behind that? An hour and a half, maybe?"

Shari pursed her lips and nodded once. "Let's make the most of it. I want to have those subs filleted and on a plate before the big boys even stick their toes in our Op-Area." She pulled her headphones from around her neck and positioned the left earpiece over her ear. The other earpiece she put over her right temple, leaving her ear uncovered so that she could hear her copilot. She keyed her mike. "George, let's get FLIR warmed up and ready to play."

The TACO's voice cracked in her left ear. "You got it, Lieutenant."

Down in the belly of the plane, the Forward-Looking Infrared cameras came to life and began scanning the water below and in front of the aircraft for thermal signatures. The temperature contrast between a periscope and the surrounding water was sometimes drastic enough to make it detectable to IR. But FLIR really worked best against snorkeling submarines. A snorkel was a specially designed ventilation pipe that a submerged submarine could extend above the surface of the water to allow its diesel engines to suck in fresh air and expel exhaust gasses. In the infrared spectrum, the heat plume from a snorkeling engine was like a giant arrow pointing directly back to the submarine.

* * *

A few minutes out from the Op-Area, Shari began a slow descent that would take them down to their patrol altitude of 1,500 feet. Based on the recommendations of the TACO, they didn't drop any sonobuoys on the first pass, giving the FLIR cameras and the APS-137 radar a chance to sweep the area for periscopes or snorkels.

When she reached the far edge of the search grid, Shari eased the yoke over into a slow turn that would bring them back around for another pass. She keyed her mike. "Did we get anything, George?"

"No joy. Just a merchant ship and a couple of yachts."

"So much for beginner's luck," Shari said. "Let's start planting the *Briar Patch* on this next pass."

"Roger that," her TACO said. "Stand by for waypoints."

A series of coordinates popped up on Shari's Tactical Data Display. She punched the *acknowledge* key on the TDD. "Got 'em." She brought the nose around two degrees to starboard to line up on the first waypoint. The TDD beeped to tell her that her approach vector was within acceptable limits. She keyed her mike. "I'll do the flying, Andy. You cover the numbers."

Andy said, "Roger that, boss." He paused, watching the numbers on the TDD for a moment, and then he keyed his mike. "All stations—waypoint Alpha coming up in *five* seconds … four … three … two … *mark*!"

On cue, one of the two Acoustic Sensor Operators sitting at display consoles near the center of the plane pushed a button.

An electrical signal triggered a small explosive charge, not much more powerful than a shotgun shell, propelling the first sonobuoy out of its launch tube. As soon as the metal and plastic cylinder was clear of the aircraft, a propeller-like set of spring-loaded fins popped open on the rear end of the buoy. Known in Undersea Warfare circles as a roto-chute, the fins caused the sonobuoy to spin like a helicopter, slowing the buoy's rate of fall and keeping its nose pointed down toward the water.

On splashdown, the sonobuoy performed a series of automatic operations in rapid sequence. First a flotation collar inflated, keeping the buoy floating upright with four-fifths of its length extending down into the water. Next a latch snapped open in the lower end of the device, releasing a small array of sensitive underwater microphones to dangle at the end of a cable beneath the buoy. Relays clicked; a lithium battery powered up an acoustic processor and a radio transmitter, transforming the buoy into a small disposable sonar system. Almost simultaneously, an antenna popped out of the top of the buoy and began transmitting coded signals back to the aircraft.

The P-3 continued launching sonobuoys at precisely measured intervals, turning occasionally to begin another row. Buoy after buoy shot from the launch tubes, each spinning down toward a pre-selected spot in the ocean, until they formed an integrated field of sonar sensors: a Briar Patch.

In Shari's left ear, the TACO's voice said. "Buoy 12 won't tune up. All other buoys are up and operational."

"Copy," said Shari. "How big a hole does that make in our coverage?"

"Negligible," George said in her ear.

Andy keyed his mike. "Do you want to swing back around and re-seed buoy 12?"

"It's a tight pattern with a lot of coverage overlap," George said. "We can re-seed, if it'll give you a warm-fuzzy, but it's not really necessary."

"You're the USW guru," Shari said. "I'm just the bus driver."

"Copilot concurs," Andy said. "If you're happy, we're happy."

"Roger," said George. "Looks like we're getting some LOFAR data now."

LOFAR is an acronym for Low Frequency Analysis and Recording. It's a method of acoustic processing that takes the noise detected by a sonar sensor and strips it apart into individual component frequencies. By comparing those frequencies against a catalogue of known acoustic sources, it is often possible to classify the source of a particular noise.

A skilled Acoustic Analyst can read a LOFAR gram the way an average person reads a newspaper. The process is largely one of elimination. Three-bladed propellers have different characteristics than four-bladed propellers. Engines with in-line cylinders generate different frequencies than V-configured engines. Four-pole electric motors make different tonals than two-pole motors. Chinese-built ventilation fans are different from French-built fans, which are different from Russian-built fans. Different hull designs have different hydrodynamic characteristics, which create identifiable sounds.

Sometimes, the majority of the contact's frequencies are common to several possible sources and the resulting classification may be ambiguous: *This is a non–Russian-built Type I diesel submarine—probably Chinese but possibly Korean.* Other times, the classification can be startlingly exact: *This is a Russian-built Akula submarine hull Number 8.*

From their display consoles, the two Acoustic Sensor Operators began the process of classifying the frequencies coming in from the sonobuoys.

After several minutes, George's voice came over Shari's headset. "All buoys are *cold*."

Shari and Andy stared at each other in disbelief. "Say again," Shari said.

"I repeat," the TACO said, "all buoys are cold."

"All of them?" Andy asked softly.

"Every one of them," George said. "The only tonals we've got are coming from those two yachts, and that merchant ship. We have zero possible submarine contacts."

"Have your guys go over the grams again," Shari said. "Maybe they're missing something."

"They've been over them twice," George said. "Then I went over them myself. Those grams are ice cold."

Shari's eyes went to the Tactical Data Display. "Check the numbers, Andy. First you do them, and then give them back to Nav for a cross-check. While you're at it, get Nav to run a diagnostic on GPS. Maybe we planted the Briar Patch in the wrong spot."

"I'll check, boss," Andy said. "But I've never seen a GPS plot that was off by more than a few inches." He flipped a selector switch and began talking to the Navigator on another circuit.

Shari keyed her mike. "George, have your ASOs run diagnostics on their gear."

"Already in progress," the TACO said, "but I can tell you up front that the equipment is running sweet. Whatever's wrong ain't in the ARR-78s."

"Let's swing back and re-seed that bad buoy," Shari said.

"That's not it," George said. "There isn't enough room in the blind zone for one sub to hide, much less *four*."

"Maybe all four of them aren't down here," Shari said.

Andy kept his eyes on the TDD and punched buttons, watching the changing numbers like a hawk. He keyed back into Shari's intercom circuit. "That's certainly a possibility. But AEW got solid ES cuts on at least two of their radars. Even if there *are* only two of them down here, there's no way they both just *happened* to be sitting under the only bad buoy in this whole piece of water."

"If anyone's got a better explanation," Shari said, "I'd love to hear it right now."

"These new 212Bs are supposed to be bad-ass," Andy said. "Maybe they're just so quiet that we can't detect them."

"I can't rule that out," George said. "But I'll believe it when I've seen the proof."

"Could be we're seeing it now," Shari said. "Or not seeing it, as the case may be."

"The Brits detected them by going active," Andy said. "Maybe we need to drop some active buoys."

"Not my first choice," George said. "As soon as we start pinging, those subs are going to run like scalded dogs. If they split up, we'll never catch them all."

Shari stared out the window at the Mediterranean. The water was still just as blue as it had been before, but now her eyes accused the waves of concealing the location of her enemies. "It's not like we're having a hell of a lot of luck catching them now," she said.

Andy looked up from the TDD. "The numbers are clean. We dropped those buoys right on top of the ES cross-fix."

George said, "Maybe the cross-fix was wrong. Who says the AEW guys can't screw the pooch once in a while?"

"Maybe," Shari said, "but they're never going to admit it. Let's set up a rack of active buoys and try this again."

"Yes ma'am," George said, but his voice didn't sound very confident.

Shari pretended not to notice. "Shoot me some waypoints."

*　　　*　　　*

Active buoy number 9 was going into the water when George said, "*Abraham Lincoln's* AEW is about thirty miles out. They're still picking up Kelvin Hughes I-band radars in our Op-Area."

"Where the hell are they?" Shari asked.

"Just a second," George said. "I'm getting the cross-fix now."

Shari waited without speaking; the only sound in the cockpit was the drone of the engines.

After what seemed like an hour, but was—in reality—probably more like five minutes, the accordion door at the rear of the cockpit slid open. George stepped into the cockpit and stood in the narrow strip of floor space between the pilot and copilot chairs. His disconnected comm-set was down around his neck, the cord draped around his shoulders. "Ah, boss?"

Shari looked up. George never came up to the flight deck to deliver good news. "I'm not going to like this, am I?" she asked.

"Afraid not, boss. We plotted the cross-fixes on those I-band radars we've been chasing. They fall right on top of those two yachts in the middle of our Briar Patch."

"That's nuts," Shari said. "Go out to AEW and get them to check their ES gear."

"I've already done that," George said. "Their gear is clean. Those boats are emitting I-band radar signatures consistent with German Type 212B diesel submarines."

"Leave it to the AEW weenies to screw up something simple like an ES cut."

The idea dawned on Shari slowly, like some sort of vile egg hatching deep in her intestines. "AEW didn't screw up," she said. "They got suckered. We *all* got suckered."

"Those boats are carrying decoy radar emitters," George said softly.

Shari's eyes shot over to Andy. "Get on the horn to the *Abraham Lincoln*! Tell them the subs are not in this Op-Area, and they never have been. We've got to get that carrier turned around and headed back toward the eastern end of the Med."

Andy picked up the radio microphone, his face gone suddenly the color of ash. "It's already too late, isn't it? The subs have already gotten past us."

"Forget about us," Shari said. "The carrier is out of position, *way* out of position. Those subs have a straight shot into the Suez now." She whistled softly through her teeth. "I doubt anybody can stop them."

CHAPTER 17

USS *TOWERS* (DDG-103)
NORTHERN ARABIAN GULF
MONDAY; 14 MAY
1840 hours (6:40 PM)
TIME ZONE +3 'CHARLIE'

Fire Controlman Chief Robert Lowery tapped the video screen with the tip of his index finger. A bright green wedge of static interference eclipsed an arc of the SPY radar display. "This is a playback of recorded video from the Aegis display system," he said. He looked up at the faces of the three technicians gathered on the far side of the console. "The interference lasted about two and a half minutes, which is pretty consistent with the other two times this malfunction has shown its ugly head." He tapped the screen again. That's pretty much all we know, except that it always appears in the same sector of the aft port-side SPY array, and that it tends to show up in the early to mid-afternoon."

Fire Controlman Second Class Todd Burgess rubbed the back of his neck. "That's array number four, Chief. Fish and I have run every test in the book on that damned thing. Every single module in the array is operating within design tolerances. Now we're thinking about a couple of tricks that aren't in the book."

Chief Lowery glanced back down at the partially garbled radar screen. "Like what?"

Burgess nodded toward Fire Controlman Third Class Daryl Fisher. "The problem always seems to show up during the hottest part of the day. Fish thought that some of the emitter-receiver modules might be breaking down under the heat. If he's right, we should be able to duplicate the problem by heating up the array a little bit. We have some ideas on how to do that."

FCC Lowery cocked his head and narrowed his eyes. "Why am I suddenly certain that I don't want to hear the rest of your idea?"

Fisher grinned. "Relax, Chief. We're not going to burn it up. We're just looking to crank the heat up a notch."

"It's not as bad as it sounds," Burgess said. "We just want to half close a couple of valves in the cooling loop that feeds the array. That will slow down the movement of chilled water through the modules and reduce the effectiveness of the cooling loop. Then, when the array starts to warm up a bit, we run over-voltage tests on the emitter-receivers and heat things up a little more. If this malfunction is being triggered by some sort of thermal component failure, we should be able to force the array to reproduce the interference pattern."

The chief nodded. "I see … If you *can* make the problem appear by turning up the heat, then it just becomes a matter of finding out which components are breaking down under high temperature."

"Right," Fisher said. "We'll have the problem localized to the array, and we can chase it down a module at a time. Plus, we can get the engineers to rig us a couple of fan units inside the array housing to blow extra air across the back sides of the modules. That might help us hold the heat down enough to keep the array from shitting all over itself while we look for the bad modules."

"Sounds good," FCC Lowery said. He looked at the third technician, who hadn't said a word yet. "Gordo, these clowns may be onto something, but we can't afford to get tunnel vision here. This could still be a processor error, or a software glitch, or God knows what. I want you to reload the entire Aegis software package from your archive disk packs."

Fire Controlman Second Class Bruce Gordon nodded. "Will do, Chief. And the next time we get a satellite window for Internet access, I'll log onto Navy Knowledge Online and post a note on the troubleshooting forum for SPY. It's possible that somebody has seen this particular casualty before, and there might already be a fix for it."

"Good idea," the chief said. "All right guys, you've got your marching orders. I don't need to tell you how serious this is. If we were joyriding off the coast of Southern California, this kind of casualty wouldn't be much more than an inconvenience. Unfortunately, this is the Arabian Gulf, and the natives out here don't run around in roller blades and thong bikinis. There are an awful lot of people out here who would love to stick a cruise missile up our ass while we're not looking. We can't afford to have our primary sensor go blind at a critical moment."

The three technicians all nodded.

"Right," the chief said. "Now, let's go find this bug and kill it, before it kills *us*."

CHAPTER 18

ALASKAN AIR CORRIDOR
MONDAY; 14 MAY
2319 hours (11:19 PM)
TIME ZONE-9 'VICTOR'

The flight from Narita, Japan, to Alaska was nearly sixteen hours long, and there was still an hour of it left to endure. Then, after a quick refueling, it would be back into the air for another six hours on the final leg to DC. The very thought of it made Secretary of State Elizabeth Whelkin want to bang her head against the window.

The Air Force 747 was a nice enough plane, and she and her staff had the VIP section all to themselves, but she was tired. She was sick of flying, and she was feeling cranky as hell—far too cranky to handle the kind of delicate phone call that she was about to make.

Roger Couric, her chief aide, was on the phone now, wading through the intricate barrier of political flunkies that shielded the president of Egypt from the outside world. Elizabeth had been watching Roger work the phone for nearly forty minutes. He was good at it, shifting smoothly from English to Arabic, and back again as he climbed steadily up the chain of command of the Egyptian government. Even so, from the look on his face, things were not going well.

After a while, Roger appeared to hit an impasse. Chances were, President Bin-Saud' knew why Elizabeth was calling and had instructed his staff to deflect the call.

Elizabeth yawned and stretched, the seat belt pulling tight across her well-padded stomach. Plump rather than fat, she looked like Hollywood's idea of the perfect maiden auntie. Her tightly curled hair was an aggregation of silver gray and Clairol's Born Blonde, but her bright blue eyes were pure steel.

Eventually, Roger covered the mouthpiece of the satellite phone and whispered, "Prime Minister. That's the best I can do. The big man is absolutely not talking today."

Elizabeth sighed and held her hand out for the phone. She had to endure two minutes of hold-music before it was picked up again on the other end.

"Prime Minister Amman."

"Good evening, Prime Minister," she said. "This is Elizabeth Whelkin."

"Ah, Madam Secretary," the Egyptian prime minister replied. "It is an honor to hear your voice again. Peace be unto you." His voice carried a note of well-disguised condescension.

Egyptian men were inimical toward women on the best of days, and—polite conversation aside—their distaste for having to treat female political leaders as equals was never very far beneath the surface.

"And unto you," Elizabeth said, trying very hard to keep the weariness out of her own voice. Exhaustion was a form of weakness, and weakness could be exploited.

"May the blessings of the one true God be upon your home, and upon your children, and upon your children's children," the prime minister said.

"And unto you and your family, blessings," said Elizabeth Whelkin. "May the Lord God protect you and keep you safe from harm."

"Are you enjoying your stay in Beijing?" the prime minister asked.

"So kind of you to ask," Elizabeth said. "I didn't get a chance to spend much time in Beijing. But I did enjoy what little I saw of it. I have concluded my visit, and now I'm flying back to Washington."

"I trust that your business in China was brought to a satisfactory conclusion?"

"I believe that we made some progress. It is, of course, a bit too early to tell how much."

"A pity that you could not have stayed a few extra days to enjoy the local culture. I'm told that the water-silks produced in the Xi'an province are particularly fine this year."

Elizabeth closed her eyes and massaged her right temple. The Arabic system of conversation was built around elaborate layers of small talk. Face-to-face meetings were practically rituals, nurtured carefully—never rushed—and fueled by a seemingly endless stream of thimble-sized cups of hot Arabic coffee. Luckily, the telephone version was much abbreviated. Even so, it was considered rude to attempt to arrive at the point of the conversation without first exchanging an extensive series of irrelevant pleasantries.

"I hadn't heard," she said. "But now that I know, I will certainly look for silk the next time I'm in China. Xi'an province, did you say? Please excuse me for a second, while I write that down." She closed her eyes for a moment and made no move to write anything at all. "There," she said after a short pause. "Now I'll be certain to remember. Thank you for the suggestion, Prime Minister."

"Think nothing of it," he said. "It is always my pleasure to be of assistance to a lady."

Thank God, an opening at last …

"So kind of you," she said. "In fact, that's the very reason I called: to ask for your assistance."

"Ah," said the prime minister. "And how may I help you?"

Elizabeth paused for a second. *How should she phrase it?* "We have reason to believe that four German submarines will attempt to transit the Suez Canal within the next day or so."

"How unusual," the prime minister said. "Ships of that country frequently travel our canal, but I cannot recall the last time that we were visited by German submarines. And now, four at once you say?"

Elizabeth massaged her temple again. "We believe so, yes."

"Am I to assume that your reason for calling has to do with these four submarines? Or, more specifically, with their transit through our national waterway?"

"Yes, Prime Minister, it does. My government has reason to believe that the submarines are in route to the Arabian Gulf for delivery to the Siraji Navy."

There was silence on the other end of the line. When Amman finally spoke, he did so slowly, as though choosing his words carefully. "You are prepared to accuse the Federal Republic of Germany of violating international law?"

"I understand that this is a serious allegation," Elizabeth said. "But our intelligence sources are virtually certain that Germany intends to sell military hardware to Siraj."

"I see," Amman said. "You are asking me to close the canal to these submarines, are you not?"

"Yes, Prime Minister, that is exactly what I'm asking. My president requests formal assurances from your government that the submarines will not be allowed to travel through the Suez Canal."

Amman paused for an even longer time before speaking again. "Madam Secretary, perhaps you are aware of my country's previous attempts to close the canal? On several occasions in the last century, we undertook to deny use of the canal to ships of Israel, who was—at that time—considered an enemy of Egypt. If I recall correctly, the United States government led an international movement to force us to open the canal, even to nations that had proven hostile to our country."

"Yes, Prime Minister. I am quite familiar with my country's dealings in your region during the latter half of the twentieth century. But these are extraordinary circumstances; we believe they justify an exception to ordinary policy."

"I do not believe that I can agree," Amman said. "Not unless you can provide me with some compelling evidence of hostility on the part of the Federal Republic of Germany."

Elizabeth grimaced; she had hoped to avoid the path this conversation was taking. "There have been hostilities," she said. "The day before yesterday, two British warships were attacked by a squadron of German fighter jets in the Strait of Gibraltar. One of the ships, HMS *York,* went down with a loss of nearly all hands. The other ship, HMS *Chatham,* was severely damaged. At least four of the fighters were shot down."

"Why would the Germans do such a thing?" Amman asked. "Are they not allied with the United Kingdom? Or, at the very least, peaceful neighbors?"

"The British ships were attempting to blockade the strait, to prevent the submarines from entering the Mediterranean Sea."

"Ah," said the prime minister. "Then it would be safe to assume that the German government did not consider the blockade a friendly act."

"Apparently not."

Amman said, "I am not certain that I can blame them. I would not take well to having the Strait of Gibraltar blocked to the military vessels of Egypt's navy either. I do not believe that it would be proper for my government to impose restrictions on other nations that we would not like to have imposed upon ourselves."

"I understand your reasoning," Elizabeth said. "But, if those submarines do reach Siraj, the repercussions could destabilize the Gulf region for years to come."

"If that is so," Amman said, "then this matter would best be decided by the United Nations. If there is an international ruling on the matter, my country will certainly abide by it."

Elizabeth fought to keep the frustration out of her voice. "Those submarines are moving *now*. By the time we petition the UN for a ruling, the subs will be through the canal and gone."

"*Inshallah,* Madam Secretary," said the prime minister, and he hung up the phone.

Elizabeth hung up the phone and looked at Roger. *Inshallah* ... Roughly translated, it meant: *If such is the will of Allah.*

CHAPTER 19

//SSSSSSSSSS//
//SECRET//
//FLASH//FLASH//FLASH//
//161228Z MAY//

FM CHIEF OF NAVAL OPERATIONS//

TO CINCPACFLEET//
COMFIFTHFLEET//
USS KITTY HAWK//
USS CHANCELORSVILLE//
USS FORT PULASKI//
USS BOLLINGER//
USS TRIPPLER//
USS WALLINGFORD//

INFO CTF FIVE ZERO//

SUBJ/USW TASKING/IMMEDIATE EXECUTE//

REF/A/RMG/CNO/150744Z MAY//

NARR/REF A IS MY TACTICAL SUMMARY OF LIVE-FIRE HOSTILITIES BETWEEN UNITED KINGDOM ROYAL NAVY WARSHIPS AND FEDERAL REPUBLIC OF GERMANY (LUFTWAFFE) AIRCRAFT APPROX 13MAY//

1. (UNCL) AS OUTLINED IN REF A, TWO RN WARSHIPS, HMS YORK AND HMS CHATHAM, ENGAGED IN AN EXTENDED MISSILE/GUN BATTLE WITH APPROX SIX LUFTWAFFE AIRCRAFT. HMS YORK WAS SUNK WITH A LOSS OF NEARLY ALL HANDS. HMS CHATHAM WAS HEAVILY DAMAGED AND SUFFERED HIGH PERSONNEL CASUALTIES. AT LEAST FOUR (4) LUFTWAFFE AIRCRAFT KNOWN DESTROYED WITH PROBABLE DAMAGE TO A FIFTH. REF A REFERS.

2. (CONF) EARLY REVIEW OF LUFTWAFFE AIRCRAFT PERFORMANCE CHARACTERISTICS INDICATE THEY WERE PROBABLY EF-2000S EUROSTRIKE-FIGHTERS. REF A REFERS.

3. (CONF) AT U.S. REQUEST, RN SHIPS WERE ATTEMPTING TO BLOCKADE PASSAGE OF FOUR (4) DEUTSCHE MARINE TYPE 212B DIESEL SUBMARINES THROUGH GIBRALTAR STRAIT. INTELLIGENCE SOURCES BELIEVE DM IS ATTEMPTING TO DELIVER SUBS TO SIRAJ IN VIOLATION OF STANDING UN RESOLUTIONS.

4. (CONF) INITIAL REPORTS INDICATE THAT AIRCRAFT INITIATED HOSTILITIES, POSSIBLY TO FORCE AN OPENING THROUGH BLOCKADE FOR DM SUBMARINES.

5. (CONF) DIPLOMATIC ATTEMPTS TO CLOSE SUEZ CANAL TO SUBMARINES UNSUCCESSFUL. BELIEVE SUBS STILL IN ROUTE ARABIAN GULF FOR DELIVERY TO SIRAJ.

6. (SECR) USS KITTY HAWK AND ESCORTS DIRECTED TO DEPART SOUTHERN ARABIAN GULF IMMEDIATELY UPON RECEIPT OF THIS MESSAGE. PROCEED AT MAXIMUM AVAILABLE SPEED TO ENTRANCE TO RED SEA (LATITUDE 1322N LONGITUDE 04406E) TO INTERCEPT DEUTSCHE MARINE SUBMARINES.

7. (SECR) U.S. IS NOT, REPEAT NOT IN A STATE OF WAR WITH FEDERAL REPUBLIC OF GERMANY. WEAPONS CONDITION FREEZE IS IN EFFECT. NO U.S. SHIP OR AIRCRAFT IS TO FIRE ON ANY VESSEL OR AIRCRAFT OF THE REPUBLIC OF GERMANY WITHOUT SPECIFIC ORDERS, OR EXCEPT IN THE LAST POSSIBLE EXTREMIS OF SELF-DEFENSE.

8. (SECR) KITTY HAWK CARRIER STRIKE GROUP IS TO BLOCKADE RED SEA AGAINST PASSAGE OF SUBMARINES WITHOUT INITIATING HOSTILITIES. RECOMMEND YOU UTILIZE ACTIVE SURFACE SHIP SONAR, ACTIVE SONOBUOYS, RADAR FLOODING, AND HELO HOLD-DOWN TACTICS TO HERD SUBS AWAY FROM CHOKE POINT.

9. (UNCL) I KNOW THIS IS A DIFFICULT ASSIGNMENT, AND THAT IT REQUIRES SUBTLETY AND RESTRAINT ON THE PART OF THE MEN AND WOMEN UNDER YOUR COMMAND. I M CONFIDENT THAT YOU CAN HANDLE IT; THAT S WHY

I CALLED IN THE BEST. GOOD LUCK. ADMIRAL CASEY SENDS.

//161228Z MAY//

//FLASH//FLASH//FLASH//
//SECRET//
//SSSSSSSSSS//

ARABIAN SEA (SOUTH OF OMAN)
WEDNESDAY; 16 MAY
1604 hours (4:04 PM)
TIME ZONE +4 'DELTA'

Had it been a little larger, Flag Plot aboard USS *Kitty Hawk* could have easily doubled as a movie set for the infamous *War Room*. The dimly lit compartment was crammed floor to ceiling with electronic equipment. Four large-screen tactical displays dominated the forward and starboard bulkheads. Each of the six-foot–square screens was speckled with cryptic-looking tactical symbols representing ships, submarines, aircraft, and shore installations within the carrier's area of responsibility. The symbols were color-coded: blue for friendly, red for hostile, and white for neutral.

The remaining two bulkheads were lined with computer terminals, automated status boards, radio comm panels, and radar repeaters, all designed to provide the admiral and his staff with the information required to effectively manage the aircraft carrier and her attendant strike group.

Despite the nearly continuous flurry of activity, the room was quiet. The equipment operators spoke to each other in low tones, using hands-free communications headsets very much like those used by astronauts.

Slouched in his raised chair at the center of the room, Admiral Curtiss Joiner read the closing lines of the CNO's message for about the seventh time. "What a crock of shit," he said under his breath.

The admiral's chief of staff, Commander Ernesto Ortiz, was standing next to his chair. "Pardon me, sir?"

Adm. Joiner looked up. "What? Oh, sorry, Ernie. It's just this message. It doesn't make sense. We've been asked … no—we've been *ordered* … to haul ass to the Gulf of Aden and bottle up a pack of German subs before they can sneak out of the Red Sea."

Ortiz nodded slowly. "Is this the same four diesel boats that gave *Abraham Lincoln* the slip over in the Med, sir?"

"It's the same guys all right," the admiral said.

"They made LANTFLEET look like idiots," Cmdr. Ortiz said. "Now I guess it's PACFLEET's turn in the barrel."

The admiral shook his head. "I'm an old man, Ernie, too old to worry about looking like a fool. But if I'm going to pull my pants down in public, I'd like to have some degree of confidence that nobody's going to shoot me in the ass."

Ortiz frowned. "You think that's a real danger here, sir?"

"They sure as hell didn't have any compunctions about shooting the Brits," Adm. Joiner said. He waved the message printout like a fan. "It says right here that the Germans are almost certainly trying to sell those subs to Siraj. As far as I'm concerned, that makes them proven hostiles. But we're being ordered to turn their submarines around with a kind word and a smile."

"They wouldn't be stupid enough to take on a carrier strike group, would they, sir?"

"Probably not," the admiral said, looking up at the tactical display screens again. "But I'd sure hate to guess wrong." He stopped himself before he spoke the next words on his mind: *History was written in the blood of thousands of poor bastards who had underestimated their opponents.* Instead, he said, "Turn the formation around, Ernie, and crank it up to flank speed. We've got a date with some submarines."

* * *

The carrier strike group tore across the water, heedless of the noise it was making. Six ships, all racing through the morning sun at thirty knots, their propellers churning up frothy wakes that stood out against the dark blue waves like vibrant stripes.

Stealth would come later, when they arrived on station. Until then, speed was more vital than silence. If the submarines made it through the choke point and out of the Red Sea before the admiral's blockading force arrived, the mission would be a failure before it had even begun.

At the center of the formation was the aircraft carrier USS *Kitty Hawk.* Stationed around her in a protective screen were two frigates, two destroyers, and a cruiser. The positioning of each ship was carefully calculated to provide the maximum possible amount of sensor and weapons coverage overlap.

Even the order of the ships was important. For the moment, submarines were rated as the highest potential threat, so the frigates, USS *Wallingford* and USS *Trippler,* which had been built primarily for Undersea Warfare, composed the leading edge of the formation. On the carrier's flanks ran the destroyers, USS *Fort Pulaski* and USS *Bollinger*, multi-mission ships that were also highly effective USW platforms. The cruiser USS *Chancellorsville* comprised the trailing edge of the formation, protecting the carrier from air attack along the axis that led back toward the Arabian Gulf—where the majority of potentially hostile aircraft in the region were based.

The layered screen defense concept had been around since the Cold War. Its longevity could be attributed to two simple words: it worked. Or at least it had worked against every naval threat encountered in nearly fifty years. But, despite its impressive track record, the screen concept was not flawless. To provide effective protection, a screen formation required seven or eight escort ships per carrier. Anything less left gaps in the screen, exposing the carrier to attack. But the U.S. Navy no longer had enough ships to provide that kind of coverage.

Kitty Hawk was making do with five escorts, and at that was better off than half the carriers in the Navy. Adm. Joiner's tactical staff used aircraft to plug the holes in the screen, a common tactic in an era of few ships and numerous taskings.

MH-60R Seahawk helicopters played leapfrog with the screening ships, hovering low over the wave tops at strategic moments to lower sonar transducers into the water and ping for enemy submarines. For now, the dipping sonars were especially important because the ships' sonars were virtually deaf when they were moving at high speed.

Thousands of feet above, maintaining careful vertical separation from the helos, the carrier's F/A-18E Super Hornet fighter/attack jets patrolled the sky. The twin-tailed Super Hornets were multi-role aircraft, and their flexibility saddled them with two missions: CAP (Combat Air Patrol) and SUCAP (Surface Combat Air Patrol). Any ship or aircraft close enough to threaten the carrier strike group had to get past the missiles and guns of the Hornets first.

Flying well in front of the formation, E-2C Hawkeyes scanned the sea and sky for potentially hostile radar contacts. The disk-shaped radome mounted on the back of each Hawkeye was so hugely out of proportion to the rest of the aircraft that a running Navy joke accused its designers of trying to mate a twin-engined commuter plane with a flying saucer. The sensitivity and power of the strange-looking radar dish were no joke, though. The Hawkeyes really were the eyes of the fleet.

* * *

In Flag Plot, aboard the carrier, Adm. Joiner stared up at the large-screen tactical displays, evaluating the positioning of the colored symbols that marked the ships and aircraft under his command. Between them, the aircraft he had deployed extended the carrier strike group's sensor and weapons ranges well beyond the coverage envelopes of the ships. But he would have gladly traded one of the stars on his collar for another pair of frigates or destroyers.

CHAPTER 20

USS *TOWERS* (DDG-103)
NORTHERN ARABIAN GULF
THURSDAY; 17 MAY
2239 hours (10:39 PM)
TIME ZONE +3 'CHARLIE'

Chief Lowery pushed a technical manual to the side, sat on the workbench, and waited for the rest of his technicians to straggle into Combat Systems Equipment Room #2. The three men came in slowly, one at a time, exhaustion weighing them down like lead.

The chief yawned. The compartment was nearly the temperature of a meat locker; it *had* to be to keep the rows of electronic equipment cool. Like all high-powered radars, SPY generated a tremendous amount of heat. It took the majority of the output of an industrial air conditioning skid to cool it off.

The shelves above the workbench were lined with technical manuals, and the stretch of bulkhead immediately adjacent was given over to large-scale color schematics of the air, water, and power systems that fed the radar. They had been through every one of the manuals at least once, and some of them two or three times. So far, to no avail.

His techs were wiped out. One glance at their faces was enough to tell Chief Lowery that Fisher was the worst, or at least he looked it. Fish, whose clean-cut Boy Scout handsomeness could have ordinarily been used to sell Mother's Farm Fresh Bread, looked like a crack addict on a three-day comedown. His eyes were nearly slits, half-closed with fatigue, bloodshot and underscored with dark circles. Burgess and Gordon weren't going to win any beauty contests either. The chief yawned so hard that his ears rang. How long had they been going now? Four days?

Fish flipped absently through one of the tech manuals without bothering to look at the pages. "We need some fucking chicken bones, Chief. We need to go down to Supply Berthing, wake up one of the cooks, and make them get us some chicken bones from the galley."

The chief yawned again. "Chicken bones?"

Fisher nodded. "Chicken bones. We need to do the secret voodoo ritual."

"I see," the chief said. "And what, pray tell, is the secret voodoo ritual?"

"We had some on the Paul Foster," Fish said. "Dried up chicken bones. We kept them in one of those purple velvet bags like Crown Royal bottles come in. Whenever we came across a radar problem that was kicking our asses, we'd get out the chicken bones. We'd turn on one battle lantern and shut off all the lights, so things would get real dark and spooky looking. Then, we'd shake up the bag really good and dump the chicken bones on the deck."

Chief Lowery grinned. "This helped somehow?"

"Hell yeah," Fish said. "One of the bones was bigger than all of the others, and one end of *that* bone was bigger than the other end. See?"

"Like a leg bone?" Gordon asked.

"Yeah," Fish said. "Like a drumstick. Anyway, whichever way the big end of the big bone was pointing, that's where the problem was. We would go to the nearest piece of equipment to where it was pointing and start troubleshooting."

"Bullshit," Gordon said.

Burgess grabbed the crotch of his own coveralls and squeezed theatrically. "Yeah, Fish. I've got your big bone right here!"

Fish grinned and gave Burgess a wink. "No thanks, Cowboy. I've seen your bone, and it didn't look very big to *me*."

Chief Lowery tried not to grin. "Knock it off, you knuckleheads. We've still got a radar to troubleshoot."

Fish held his hands palm up and let them drop. "That's what I'm trying to tell you, Chief. There's nothing left to troubleshoot. There is nothing wrong with this fucking radar. We've run every on-line test, every off-line test, and every dynamic and static load test ever invented. We've swapped every circuit card in Array #4 with every circuit card in Array #3. If the problem was in one of those cards, or even several cards, the interference should have moved to Array #3 with the cards."

Burgess nodded. "We've checked video processing, wave guides, primary and alternate power, and all of the digital multiplexers. We've checked for thermal problems, phase angle calibration errors, electromagnetic cross-talk between cable runs, signal shedding, and digital sync pulse errors. We've also tested the sweep raster initiators, and every clock pulse and digital incrementer that's even remotely related to SPY."

"Fish and Shit-for-Brains are right," Gordon said. "We've swapped every disk pack, and reloaded the software from scratch three times. I've used the secure sat-phones to make four tech-assist calls to the engineers at Lockheed Martin who built the system, and the software bubbas who wrote the program code. None of them have ever *heard* of anything like this problem. They're going to fly a tech rep out to help us troubleshoot it, but they've already pretty much said they don't have a clue of how to tackle this. In fact, one of the engineers as much as told me that we're full of shit. He said we *can't* have this problem, because the system isn't capable of generating this type of sector-specific interference."

The chief snorted. "What? Does he think we're making this shit up?"

"I don't know what he thinks," Gordon said. "But I'll tell you what *I* think. There is nothing wrong with this radar, Chief. Not a fucking thing. It's clean as a whistle."

"So where is the interference coming from?" It was the captain's voice.

Chief Lowery leapt off the workbench. "Attention on deck!"

They all scrambled to attention.

"Sorry, Sir," Chief Lowery said. "We didn't see you come in."

Capt. Bowie motioned for them to relax. "Don't worry about it, Chief. Carry on. Please."

All four men relaxed their postures, but no one made any move to sit down.

"Let's get back to my question," the captain said. "If there's nothing wrong with the radar equipment and nothing wrong with the software, where is this interference coming from?"

"We don't know, sir," Chief Lowery said.

"But you agree with your techs that there's nothing wrong with SPY?" the captain asked.

Chief Lowery shook his head. "No, sir, I don't. SPY is *not* designed to lose sixty degrees of coverage every day or two. And, if SPY is operating outside of its design parameters, by definition something is wrong. I don't know if it's hardware or software, sir. But something is sure as hell wrong somewhere."

The captain nodded. "Well said, Chief." He reached out and patted the side of one of the gray radar equipment cabinets. "Our primary anti-air and anti-surface sensor seems to be in the habit of losing its mind every day or two. There are no two ways about it, gentlemen. That's unsatisfactory."

Fisher squinted his eyes and opened his mouth. Then he appeared to think better of it, and he closed his mouth.

"Go ahead, son," the captain said. "Whatever it is, you can say it."

Fisher looked at his chief and then back to the captain. "Sir, it's only for a couple of minutes …" He waited, and when it became apparent that no one was going to say anything, he cleared his throat and continued. "The … um … the interference only appears for two or three minutes every other day or so. And it's only a sixty-degree arc. It's not like we lose the entire quadrant. Just sixty degrees or so, for a couple of minutes." He cleared his throat again. "I mean, I understand that there's something wrong with SPY, even if we don't have any idea what it is. But we've been killing ourselves for four days now, over a two-minute glitch that only eats up sixty degrees of our coverage."

The captain nodded. "I know you've been knocking yourselves out, son. I've talked to a couple of the engineers at Lockheed Martin, and they say your troubleshooting efforts so far have been excellent. First rate. But we can't afford to minimize the impact of this casualty. We're in some of the most hotly contested waters in the world, and every day or two, a significant sector of our radar loses its ability to scan for ships, aircraft, and missiles."

No one said anything.

"Suppose it happened to you while you were on the freeway," the captain said. "You're driving along, doing seventy-five or eighty, and a slice of your vision goes pitch black. Not all of it. Say it's just twenty degrees. The rest of your field of vision is fine, but your eyes are totally blind within that twenty-degree arc." He looked around. "Are you with me?"

Everyone nodded.

"Good," the captain said. "So, every couple of days—while you're cruising down the freeway—a twenty-degree sector of your vision goes on the fritz. It's just twenty degrees. And it's just a couple of minutes." His eyebrows went up. "How safe are you?"

"Not very, sir," Fisher said. "Point taken."

"Good," Capt. Bowie said. He looked at Lowery. "Chief, you guys have been at this long enough." He looked at his watch. "I want you and your men to hit your racks for at least the next three hours."

The chief looked surprised. "But sir ..."

"No buts, Chief. That's an order. Come to think of it, make it four hours. I don't want anybody getting electrocuted because his brain is too tired to think properly. And, I want you to set up a sleep rotation. One man in his rack at all times, and you can swap out every couple of hours. That way no one has to work for more than a few hours before he gets a chance to recharge his batteries."

The chief nodded. "Aye-aye, sir."

The captain looked at each of the men in turn. "You're all doing excellent work," he said. "Keep looking. You'll find it." He cocked one eyebrow. "And, if you don't, there's always the chicken bones."

CHAPTER 21

GULF OF ADEN (SOUTH OF YEMEN)
FRIDAY; 18 MAY
0647 hours (06:47 AM)
TIME ZONE +3 'CHARLIE'

Wolfhound Eight-Seven was the call sign for an MH-60R helicopter working the outer edge of USS *Kitty Hawk*'s formation. The gull-gray helo hovered fifty feet above the water, close enough for the edge vortexes down-drafting from its rotors to whip a swirling mist of salt spray off the wave tops.

The pilot, Lieutenant Ray Forester, checked his instruments and, when he was satisfied with the positioning of his aircraft, he turned to his copilot. "Your show, Ted."

Ensign Theodore Dillon nodded. Out of habit he scanned the instrument panel himself, and then said, "Down dome."

From his console at the rear of the cabin, the Sensor Operator responded, "Down dome, aye." He pressed a fingertip to a highlighted rectangle on the touch-sensitive control screen. The floor of the cabin vibrated slightly as the high-speed winch built into the underside of the fuselage began reeling out cable at a rate of sixteen feet per second.

At the end of the cable, the cylindrical sonar transducer slid out of a form-fitting cavity in the bottom of the aircraft and began its rapid descent toward the ocean. A little over three seconds later, the rubber-coated sensor plunged into the water, disappearing quickly beneath the waves.

"The dome is wet," the Sensor Operator said. "How deep do you want it?"

The copilot looked over his shoulder. "How deep is the sonic layer?"

The Sensor Operator studied his screen. "Just a second, sir. We haven't hit it yet."

His eyes stayed locked on the digital temperature readout relayed back from the descending sonar transducer. For several seconds, the numbers on the green phosphorous screen showed only tiny fluctuations, never varying by more than a tenth of a degree. When the depth readout passed 130 feet, the temperature began dropping rapidly. The transducer had passed from the *surface duct*, a zone of nearly constant water temperature near the surface of the ocean, into the *thermocline*, a zone of rapidly decreasing water temperature that extended down to about two thousand feet. Below that, the temperature would become nearly constant again at just above the freezing temperature of water.

The drastic temperature differential between the surface duct and the thermocline formed a barrier to sound energy. Submarine hunters called it the *sonic layer*, or sometimes just the *layer*. A well-trained submarine captain would know the depth of the layer at any given time—as well as his boat's position in relation to it. Properly exploited, the layer could make submarines—which were difficult to detect under the best of circumstances—even harder to locate.

The Sensor Operator looked at the readout. "Layer depth looks like about a hundred and thirty feet, sir."

"Let's start below the layer this time," the copilot said. "Take her down to about four hundred."

"Four hundred aye, sir." The Sensor Operator watched the descent of the transducer on his screen for another minute and then pressed a highlighted soft-key. The depth readout froze at four hundred. "Dome is at four hundred feet. Request permission to go active."

The copilot nodded. "Go active."

The Sensor Operator pressed a soft-key on his screen and was rewarded with a high-pitched *ping* in his headphones as the sonar transducer fired a pulse of sound energy into the water four hundred feet below the surface. He began scanning his screen for the telltale echo that a submarine would produce. "We are active, sir."

The copilot keyed his radio circuit and waited a half-second for the *cryptoburst*, a short string of garbled tones that the UHF transmitter used to synchronize its encrypted signal with the secure communications satellite. "Strike Group Command, this is Wolfhound Eight-Seven. My dome is wet. I am active at this time, over."

The voice that answered a few seconds later had a strange warble to it. "Wolfhound Eight-Seven, this is Strike Group Command. Roger. Good hunting, out."

The cartoonish voice modulation and the short delay caused by the cryptoburst were unavoidable by-products of the encryption-decryption algorithm that scrambled the signal at the transmitting end and decoded it on the receiving end. Ens. Dillon liked to pretend that his voice came out of the speakers on the other end as a masculine baritone, but deep down he knew that he probably sounded just as silly over the secure satellite circuits as everyone else did. It was a small price to pay for secure voice communication.

At the rear of the aircraft, the Sensor Operator watched his screen carefully. Every time the sonar transmitted, a bright green line appeared at the bottom of the search display and began tracking upward. In its wake, the search raster left random scatterings of green dots in varying shades and intensities: ambient noise in the ocean caused by everything from fish, to wave action, to distant shipping. A contact would appear as a bright cluster of dots, generally accompanied by an audible echo in the operator's headphones.

After about fifteen sweeps, the Sensor Operator said, "No joy, sir. Want to pull her up some and see what's above the layer?"

The copilot paused for a second. As a general rule, submarines liked to approach surface ships from below the layer, where they would be shielded from the powerful hull-mounted sonars carried by most warships. Still, it didn't hurt to check both sides of the fence. He shrugged. "It's worth a shot," he said. "Bring her up to about a hundred feet."

The Sensor Operator pressed a soft-key and the floor rumbled again as the winch began retrieving cable. "One hundred feet, coming up, sir."

Less than two minutes later, the Sensor Operator sang out, "Active sonar contact! Bearing zero-five-five, range three thousand eight hundred yards." He watched the screen for another sweep. "No supporting data yet, but it's a clear bearing. Could be a sub, sir!"

The copilot grinned. "Good job! Now stay on it!"

He keyed his radio circuit and waited for the crypto-burst. "Strike Group Command, this is Wolfhound Eight-Seven. I have active sonar contact, bearing zero-five-five, range three thousand eight hundred yards. Initial classification—POSS-SUB low, over."

The reply came a few seconds later. "Wolfhound Eight-Seven, this is Strike Group Command. Copy your active contact. We are vectoring Wolfhound Nine-Three in to assist. Get ready to play leapfrog, out!"

The pilot and copilot both grinned. Helicopters were a lot faster than submarines. With two dipping sonars working together, a submarine's chance of escape was virtually zero. One of the dippers could maintain the track, while the other one repositioned closer to the submarine. By alternating their dip cycles, they could maintain contact indefinitely. Dipping helicopters were every submariner's worst nightmare, because—apart from their speed and tracking abilities—they could carry torpedoes. A skillful air crew could put a torpedo within yards of a submarine's bow—much too close to evade.

Suddenly, the Sensor Operator shouted. "Launch transient! I'm getting some kind of launch transient! Same bearing as the POSS-SUB!"

"It's probably a hydraulic transient," the pilot said. "Our active pinging scared them, and they're diving for the layer."

"No, sir," the Sensor Operator said. "This is definitely not hydraulic. This is … oh shit!" He began pointing emphatically toward the window. "It's coming out of the water! We have missile emergence, bearing zero-five-five!"

All three men watched in disbelief as the missile erupted from the ocean in a fountain of salt water and fire.

"Cruise missile!" the copilot shouted. "It's gotta be aimed for the carrier!"

The pilot shook his head. "That's a SAM, and it's coming after us!" He pulled back on the control stick, breaking the helo out of its hover. The helicopter climbed steeply, snatching the sonar transducer out of the water where it swung crazily at the end of its cable.

Lt. Forester threw his aircraft into a violent series of banks and turns that were the closest thing to evasive maneuvering that a 22,000-pound helicopter could manage. "Launch chaff!"

Ens. Dillon flipped up a row of red protective covers and stabbed at two of the buttons underneath. The helo shuddered slightly as two chaff projectiles blasted clear of the airframe.

Before the chaff pods had even blossomed, Dillon was on the radio. "Sub-SAM! We've got a sub-SAM! This is Wolfhound Eight-Seven. I say again: we have a submarine-launched surface-to-air missile inbound, over!"

The Sensor Operator watched the missile blow through the expanding cloud of aluminum dust without slowing. "It's not going for the chaff, sir!" he yelled.

"Heat-seeker!" the pilot said. "Launch a flare!"

The radio warbled with the crypto burst of an incoming message; no one had time to pay attention to it.

Ens. Dillon reached above his head and flipped up the covers for another row of protected switches. His finger jabbed toward a button, but he never made it.

The missile's infrared seeker rode the heat plumes off the helicopter's engines like a railroad track. A fraction of a second before Dillon's finger touched the button, the sub-SAM slipped into the exhaust chamber for the starboard engine as neatly as a key sliding into a lock.

The warhead detonated, blowing the General Electric T700 turbine into a thousand fragments, each one blasting through the helicopter like a machine gun bullet. The flight crew was cut to shreds even before the secondary explosion hit the fuel tanks.

Bits of flaming wreckage fell out of the sky like meteors, and Wolfhound Eight-Seven ceased to exist.

* * *

<u>USS *Kitty Hawk*:</u>

Cmdr. Ortiz stared at the tactical display. Wolfhound Eight-Seven's tracking symbol flashed several times and then converted itself to a last-known-position symbol. *They were gone. They were really gone. How in the hell could this happen?*

He shook his head once and then blinked several times. "Get the admiral up here! And get on the radio to Wolfhound Nine-Three. Tell them to get a torpedo in the water *now*! I don't give a damn if it hits anything. We've got to put that sub on the defensive before it gets a bead on them."

Even as he spoke, he saw that his order had come too late. A hostile-missile symbol popped up on the tactical display and began homing in on Wolfhound Nine-Three's position.

"Goddamn it!" Ortiz shouted. He grabbed a red radio-telephone handset. "USS *Wallingford,* this is Strike Group Command. Lock on to hostile missile track zero-zero-two and kill that son of a bitch!" Without waiting for a reply, he said, "Break—Wolfhound Nine-Three, this is Strike Group Command. Forget the torpedo! Get the hell out of there, over!"

A friendly-missile symbol appeared on the tactical display next to USS *Wallingford.* It began to close rapidly on the hostile-missile symbol. The hostile-missile symbol continued to race toward the helicopter.

"It's too far away," somebody behind Cmdr. Ortiz said. "*Wallingford*'s missile is never going to get there in time."

Ortiz knew instantly that the speaker, whoever he was, was right.

Ten seconds later, the hostile-missile symbol merged with the helicopter symbol, and Wolfhound Nine-Three was gone.

Ortiz was amazed at how clean it looked from the tactical display. No blood. No fire. No screams of terror as burnt bodies fell from the sky. Not even the imaginary canned violence of a video-game explosion. Just two cryptic symbols touching on a video display, joining to create a new symbol: a last-known-position marker for Wolfhound Nine-Three. An electronic headstone to mark the death place of three men.

It took a second to hit him—the tactical display had more to show him than the last positions of two downed helicopters. Something else was staring him in the face. With the two helos gone, there was a hole in the formation. A big one. A gap in the protective screen surrounding the carrier. There was another pair of helicopters at Ready-Five on *Kitty Hawk*'s flight deck, but it would take five minutes to get them airborne and another few minutes to position them to plug the hole. And they didn't have five minutes. *Kitty Hawk* was wide open to attack.

*　　*　　*

U-307:

Leaning over the shoulder of the Sonar Operator, Kapitan Gröeler watched the acoustic display. The sounds kept playing themselves back in his mind. The distant rumbles of the exploding helicopters. The serpentine hiss of burned metal quenching itself in the ocean.

They were well and truly committed now. After this, there could be no turning back.

He almost wished that he could have fired the missiles himself, pushed the buttons with his own hands. He had no desire to kill those men. But the act of killing them was far too much like murder, and ordering someone else to do it *for* him felt like the worst sort of cowardice.

Gröeler's jaws tightened. This *was* murder. The men whose deaths he had ordered were allies of his country, both by law and by intent. Moreover, their attempt to halt the passage of Gröeler's wolfpack was in the spirit of international law and consistent with the stated intentions of the United Nations.

These killings could not even be justified under the auspices of war. The fact that they were a necessary step toward the success of the mission did not make them seem any less repugnant.

At least if he had fired the missiles himself, he could have carried the physical responsibility for the act. The moral responsibility was already his. The orders to carry out this mission had come from the Bundeswehr, far above Gröeler's rank. But *he* had made the decision to carry out those orders. And the fact that he had only done so to prevent someone less capable from carrying them out in his place was little or no comfort.

But the missiles had to come from north of the American carrier formation, and Gröeler's own battle plan demanded that he position his submarine to the south—in preparation for the next phase of the operation. So the onus of murdering the helicopter crews had fallen on Jurgen Hostettler, the young *fraggetenkapitan* in command of the *U-304*.

The Americans placed far too much faith in the invulnerability of their aircraft. It was an easy logical trap to fall into: no submarine ever *had* shot down an aircraft—therefore no submarine ever *would* shoot down an aircraft. Everyone knew that sub-SAMs were only a rumor: a spook story with which to tease helicopter pilots. No one had ever seen one—therefore they must not exist.

But the Americans had just learned the hard way that sub-SAMs were not the stuff of rumor. Like the dagger they were named for, the *Dolch* missiles had cut the American defenses to the bone.

With two quick squeezes of his thumb on the firing button, young Hostettler had changed the face of naval warfare. He had also, perhaps, branded himself a war criminal. Only time and the judgment of history could tell.

Gröeler forced his attention back to the sonar display. The hole in the American's defense perimeter was massive, a veritable *autobahn* into the heart of their carrier strike group.

He stepped through the door of the Sonar Room into the submarine's Control Room. "Take us below the sonic layer and then increase speed to all-ahead full. If we are to penetrate the formation, we must be in exactly the right position when their defenses begin to come apart."

* * *

USS *Kitty Hawk*:

The deck tilted to the left as the huge ship heeled into a tight starboard turn. To an untrained observer, it might have seemed incredible that 82,000 tons of steel could move so quickly. In fact, the carrier was by far the fastest ship in the strike group, with a top speed of over forty knots. *Kitty Hawk* was making use of that speed now, building momentum rapidly as she turned to leave her slower escorts behind. That too might have surprised an observer, but strategically the carrier was far more valuable than all of her escort ships combined. And right now, *Kitty Hawk* was running for her life.

The watertight door at the rear of Flag Plot slammed open, and Adm. Joiner made his way across the slanting deck to his chair. "Ernie, what the hell is going on? Why are we turning?"

Cmdr. Ortiz looked up from the tactical display. "The formation has been penetrated, Admiral. We've got two helos down and a hole in our defensive screen the size of Texas."

The admiral scowled. "How did we lose two helos?"

"Looks like sub-launched surface-to-air missiles, sir."

"Sub-SAMs? Jesus Christ, I thought those rumors were bullshit."

Cmdr. Ortiz nodded. "Frankly, sir, so did I. But the Germans have apparently taken the technology past the rumor stage."

Adm. Joiner looked up at the tactical display. "You did good, Ernie. *Priority One* is to protect the carrier *first*. That buys us time to think about *Priority Two*: how to turn this situation around and kick some ass!" He rubbed his chin. "Let's establish datum halfway between the last-known positions for the helos. Designate the frigates as a Search Attack Unit and get them down there to run an active sonar search. Then I want you to issue full weapons release authority to all ships for torpedoes and ASROC. There aren't any friendly subs in the area, so the order is shoot first."

Cmdr. Ortiz reached for a radio handset. "Aye-aye, sir."

The admiral's eyes were still locked on the tactical display. "How much longer before our Ready-Five helos are ready to launch?"

"About three minutes, sir."

"Get on the horn and tell the flight deck to shake a leg," the admiral said. "And tell the frigates to keep their eyes peeled for dye markers and flares. Maybe somebody made it out of one of those helicopters."

* * *

U-307:

The voice of the Sonar Operator came over the Control Room speaker. "Active sonar transmissions, bearing three-zero-five and two-eight-zero. Frequencies consistent with SQS-56 surface sonars."

"That will be the frigates, searching for *U-304,*" Kapitan Gröeler said. He nodded. The Americans were performing just as he'd expected. Their tactics were rapid, efficient, and (no doubt) lethal—at least against an adversary who was unfamiliar with them. Gröeler knew their tactics well though, and that made them predictable. And in combat, *predictable* was synonymous with *dead.*

He leaned over the plotting table and reviewed the tactical situation. The plot showed his submarine, *U-307,* at the southern edge of the strike group's defense perimeter. *U-305* would be in position to the west of the carrier formation, and *U-306* would be to the east.

He checked his watch. In exactly fifteen seconds, *U-305* and *U-306* would each fire a spread of torpedoes toward the heart of the formation. Perhaps one of them would get lucky and nail an escort ship, but it didn't matter if every torpedo missed its mark. They would almost certainly miss the aircraft carrier, but that didn't matter either.

The carrier couldn't possibly know how close the torpedoes were, so it would have to turn to evade them. It couldn't turn west, toward the torpedoes of *U-305,* and it couldn't continue east, toward the torpedoes of *U-306.* It certainly wouldn't turn north, back toward datum—the last known position of the submarine threat. The carrier would turn south, toward the only safe sector that it could identify. And that would be the aircraft carrier's final mistake.

* * *

USS *Kitty Hawk*:

"Holy mother of God," said Cmdr. Ortiz in a quiet voice. Flashing red hostile-torpedo symbols were popping up all over the tactical display—five of them so far. While he watched, a sixth enemy torpedo appeared.

Blue friendly-torpedo symbols began springing up as the ships conducted counterattacks against the submarines. At the moment, no one held sonar contact on any of the subs, so the ships were reduced to firing down the bearings of the incoming torpedoes.

The sub-surface part of the tactical plot was a few seconds behind real time. The carrier was too noisy to carry its own sonar, so it had to rely on the sonar systems of its escorts. It took a few seconds for symbols and updates to percolate through the Tactical Data Link, which meant that every torpedo that appeared on the screen had been in the water for at least two or three seconds by the time the computer assigned it a symbol.

"This is going to hell in a hand basket," Adm. Joiner said. "Tell the bridge to take us up to flank speed and get us the hell out of here."

Cmdr. Ortiz looked up at the tactical display. "We're at flank speed now, sir. Which way do we run?"

"South!" the admiral said. "It's the only clear vector. Turn us south, now!"

Ortiz relayed the admiral's orders to the bridge and then returned his eyes to the tactical display as the big ship began to come about. "We're being herded," he said. "We're being systematically isolated from our screening units."

The admiral nodded. "Just what I was thinking," he said. "But I don't see where we have a lot of options at the moment. We sure as hell can't turn back toward those torpedoes!"

* * *

U-307:

Gröeler watched the situation unfold on his tactical plot. The Americans were reacting as he had expected, which was to say in accordance with their tactical doctrine. It was good doctrine, as far as it went, but it did have a few weaknesses. He was about to show the Americans what those weaknesses were.

The carrier was running toward him now. It was close; too close to dodge his torpedoes.

According to standing tactical doctrine, it was time to come to periscope depth and take a final peek at his target through the attack scope before shooting. It wasn't just doctrine, either. The idea was so deeply ingrained into the minds of the submarine force that it had taken on nearly religious significance; you *never* launch torpedoes without making a last-second visual confirmation. Not *ever*.

Gröeler knew without looking that his Control Room crew were watching him out of the corners of their eyes. They had practiced this shot in the simulators a hundred times, but it was such a fundamental violation of basic tactical principles that none of them could really believe that he would actually try it under combat conditions. Behind his back, they called it *Schießen in dem dunklen*: shooting in the dark. The bolder of them compared their kapitan to the knife thrower in a circus—letting fly with deadly blades while a blindfold covered his eyes. They assumed he didn't know about their little jests, but they were wrong. Where his boat and crew were concerned, very little escaped his attention.

"Stand by to fire salvo one," he snapped. "Three torpedoes, shallow run, fifteen degree spread." He checked the current sonar bearing to his target. "Centered on zero-two-zero."

He took a breath and held it for several seconds. "Fire!"

Three quick tremors ran through the deck as a trio of Ozeankriegsführungtechnologien DMA37 torpedoes were rammed out of their launch tubes by columns of high-pressure water.

An instant later, the Sonar Operator called out, "I have start-up on all three weapons."

"Estimate fourteen seconds to impact," the Fire Control Officer said.

"Right full rudder," Gröeler said. "Ten degrees down-angle on the forward planes." This was one part of the tactical doctrine that he could not ignore. He had to separate himself from his firing bearing and depth as quickly as possible; without an actual contact to shoot at, the Americans would fire their own torpedoes down the bearing from which his torpedoes had come. Doctrine again.

"Sir, my rudder is right full," the helmsman said. "My dive bubble is down ten degrees."

"Torpedoes two and three have acquired," the Sonar Operator said.

Gröeler frowned. "What about torpedo one?"

"It's gone astray, Kapitan. Sounds like it's a bad fish."

"Ten seconds to impact," the Fire Control Officer said.

The Sonar Operator's voice came over the speaker again. "They've detected our weapons, sir. Target is altering course to starboard."

"Too late," Gröeler said. "Much too late."

"Target is launching acoustic decoys," the Sonar Operator said.

"Too late," Gröeler said again—a whisper this time.

"Impact in five seconds," the Fire Control Officer said. "Four … three … two … one … Weapons on top!"

* * *

USS *Kitty Hawk*:

Ortiz grabbed the edge of a radar console with both hands. "Brace for shock!"

His words were drowned out by the first explosion. The deck of the huge ship lurched violently as the shock wave surged down the length of the keel. The point of impact was on the starboard side, several hundred feet forward of Flag Plot, and at least nine decks down, but the intensity of the concussion was still unbelievably fierce.

A pipe ruptured in the overhead, spewing water in every direction. A third class Operations Specialist screamed as the shower of water shorted out the electronics in his console, making his body the path of lowest electrical resistance. For an instant, his muscles went rigid as four hundred forty volts of alternating current surged through his flesh and internal organs, finding its path to ground through the soles of his feet. Then, a circuit breaker tripped, cutting the power to the console, and he sank lifelessly back into his chair, the air around him permeated with the smells of ozone and singed meat.

The ship rolled heavily to port. Something hit Cmdr. Ortiz from behind, throwing him against his console and then knocking him to the deck. The lights flickered, and it took him a second to realize that the hurtling object that had laid him out was another person—someone who hadn't been properly braced for the explosion. The lights flickered again and then came back on. The ship had begun settling back toward starboard when the second torpedo found its mark and exploded.

* * *

The Ozeankriegsführungtechnologien DMA37 torpedo had been designed as a ship killer. Programmed to dive under the target's hull before detonating, it carried a 250-kilogram high-explosive warhead powerful enough to shatter the keel of any ship the size of a cruiser or smaller. To make matters worse, as the explosion ripped through the steel hull plates, a white-hot bubble of expanding gases would flash-vaporize the water directly below the ship's keel. Combined with the devastating effects of the explosion, the nearly incalculable stress created by the sudden loss of all support beneath the hull was frequently enough to break a ship in half.

But at 82,000 tons, *Kitty Hawk* was nearly ten times as large as any cruiser or destroyer on the planet. She could be damaged by torpedoes, but it would take more than one or two to sink her.

The wounded aircraft carrier slowed a few knots and began to list to starboard as water poured in through the two enormous holes in her hull.

CHAPTER 22

TORPEDO: THE HISTORY AND EVOLUTION OF A KILLING MACHINE

(Excerpted from an unpublished manuscript [pages 102–104] and reprinted by permission of the author, Retired Master Chief Sonar Technician David M. Hardy, USN)

On June 28, 1914, Archduke Francis Ferdinand and his wife were assassinated in the Bosnian capital of Sarajevo. The gunman was a young Serbian nationalist and a member of the Black Hand terrorist organization. Archduke Ferdinand had been heir to the throne of Austria. A month after his murder, Austria declared war on Serbia and, over the next several months, the conflict spread to every major country in Europe. World War I had begun.

Germany, a relative latecomer to submarine technology, put its *unterseeboots* (undersea boats) to excellent use. In short order, German U-boats dominated the seas surrounding Europe, stalking Allied supply ships and sinking them at will. The torpedo, which had been a relatively obscure weapon at the outset of the war, became an object of terror. The German U-boat captains wielded their torpedoes with skill and cruelty—painting the seas with fire and blood, and littering the bottom of the ocean with the broken ships of their enemies.

Situated safely on the far side of the Atlantic Ocean, the United States adopted a policy of strict isolationism. America turned a blind eye as the death toll in Europe skyrocketed. It was a European war, after all, and Americans were overwhelmingly in favor of letting the Europeans handle it themselves.

On May 7, 1915, a single event shifted public opinion in America: a German submarine, *U-20,* torpedoed the British passenger ship *Lusitania.* Two perfectly aimed torpedoes blasted through the hull of the ocean liner, sending the ship to the bottom of the ocean, along with 1,195 civilian passengers. Unfortunately for the Germans, 123 of those passengers were American citizens.

Horrified by what they saw as a barbaric attack on an unarmed ship, the American people began to scream for revenge. The United States was drawn into the war that it had struggled to avoid, shifting the balance of power to the Allies.

It is, perhaps, a supreme stroke of irony that the torpedo—the very weapon that had almost brought victory—would sow the seeds of Germany's defeat.

CHAPTER 23

USS *TOWERS* (DDG-103)
NORTHERN ARABIAN GULF
FRIDAY; 18 MAY
0732 hours (7:32 AM)
TIME ZONE +3 'CHARLIE'

Someone was shaking him …

Some distantly conscious fragment of Chief Lowery's brain detected the pressure of someone's hand on his shoulder. A million miles away, someone with a tin bucket over his head was speaking gibberish in slow motion. The voice was tinny, echoey, and totally incomprehensible. The lump of unconscious meat that sometimes called itself Chief Lowery grunted and rolled over, burrowing farther under the blankets, away from the intruder, whoever—or whatever—it was.

The hand grabbed his shoulder again, tighter this time, and shook harder. "Heep! May-buff!"

Chief Lowery flailed one arm in a half-hearted attempt to drive the intruder away. The sudden motion ratcheted his brain a couple of notches closer to consciousness. "Keef! Hay-gupp!" It was the voice again. Closer this time, and more word-like. The shaking continued.

A switch in the deep recesses of his brain clicked reluctantly to the "*on*" position. Lowery felt the rumble of his own groan as it escaped his throat. He clenched his eyes shut even tighter, preparing the muscles for the unthinkable task of opening his eyelids.

The hand on his shoulder continued to shake him toward awareness. "Chief! Way-gupp!" The voice was an urgent whisper, close to his ear.

A whiff of his dream still floated at the edge of his memory, an indistinct sweetness, like the subtlest perfume smelled at a distance. It was a wonderful dream, part of him knew. A glorious re-imagining of life, in which Charlotte was still in love with him, and he could somehow dance and sing like Fred Astaire.

He groaned again and felt his hand come up of its own accord to scratch an itch near his right ear. The movement drove the last of the dream from his mind. "What?"

The hand stopped shaking his shoulder. "Chief, wake up!"

Chief Lowery grunted and opened one eye. He didn't bother to point it toward his tormenter. "What time is it?"

"What?" The voice sounded confused. "It's, um … just a second … it's, uh … oh-seven-thirty-three, Chief."

Lowery opened the other eye and began blinking heavily to get things moving. "It's seven thirty in the morning?"

"Uh … yes, Chief. Seven thirty-three."

"Oh God …" Chief Lowery said. "Forty minutes … I got a whole forty minutes of sleep this time." He yawned. "Go away right now, and I *may* let you live."

"I need to talk to you about the radar, Chief. SPY radar."

The words brought Lowery to full consciousness. No, not the words. The voice. His uninvited guest was not one of his techs. It sounded like … Lowery grabbed his privacy curtains and slid them back, opening his coffin-sized bunk area up to the rest of the berthing compartment. He recognized his mistake immediately. It was after reveille, so the lights in Aft Chief Petty Officer's Berthing were on. He flinched away from the unexpected brightness and tried to squint out of the corners of his eyes.

Into the bleary circle of his vision swam the face of CS3 Charles Zeigler, better known to the enlisted crew as *Z-Man*, or *Zebra*. Zeigler was a Culinary Specialist—a cook.

Chief Lowery blinked. "Zeigler? Do you have any idea how much sleep I've had? Or, I should say, how *little* sleep I've had?"

Zeigler shook his head. "No, Chief, I don't. But this is real important. I know who's been … I mean I know what's wrong with your SPY radar."

Chief Lowery sighed. "Petty Officer Zeigler, you are a CS. A *cook*."

"Yeah, Chief. I'm the night baker this month. I've got sweet rolls in the oven right now. As soon as they're done, I'm going off shift."

"Sweet rolls in the oven," Chief Lowery said. "That makes you an expert on the most sophisticated combat radar system in the world?"

Zeigler grinned. "I'm not an expert on radar. I'm a cook. Which means I'm an expert on potatoes. That's what's wrong with your radar, Chief. It's the potatoes."

Chief Lowery grimaced. The potatoes? The *potatoes*? He slid one leg out of his bunk and dangled it toward the floor. "Excuse me, Zeigler. Could you back up a little? I'm getting up. This is either going to be the coolest story I've ever heard, or I'm going to strangle you right where you fucking stand." He reached for his pants. "Chicken bones … potatoes … Thank God there's not a problem with the *linguini*. That would probably sink the whole goddamned ship."

* * *

Forty minutes later, Lowery and his three technicians stood gathered around a SPY console in Combat Information Center.

Gordon yawned. "What are we looking for, Chief? I'm setting up to do some signal injection tests on Array #4. I'd like to get back to it."

"Hold your horses," the chief said. "Just watch the screen. If this works, you can forget about troubleshooting the array."

"If *what* works?" Burgess asked. "What are we waiting for?"

Chief Lowery held up his hand. "Just give it a minute. We should start seeing … There!" He pointed to the screen. "Read 'em and weep, boys!"

A jittering wedge of video static glowed bright green on the radar screen. The interference was back.

FC2 Burgess stared at it. "There it is! But it's only eight in the morning! We've never seen it before mid-afternoon …"

The interference vanished after less than a minute.

"Hey! It's gone!" Fisher said. "That was fast."

Chief Lowery grinned. "Keep watching, Fish. In about two minutes, you're going to see something you've never seen before."

They stared at the screen together. Considerably less than two minutes later, the interference appeared again, in a different part of the screen.

Fish nearly jumped. "Holy shit! It's on the *starboard* side now! That's Array #3. We've *never* seen it in Array #3!"

The chief crossed his arms and looked smug. "It all depends on where you put the potato."

All three technicians glared at him. Gordon spoke first. "What the hell are you talking about, Chief?"

The chief grinned again. "Fish had it right all along. If you can't fix your radar, go see the cooks." He uncrossed his arms and patted Burgess on the shoulder. "Come on, boys. Let's go track down the Division Officer. He's gonna *love* this!"

* * *

An hour later, they were all gathered around the SPY console for another demonstration. This time, the onlookers included Ensign Christopher Lance (CF Division Officer), Lieutenant Terri Sikes (the ship's Combat Systems Officer), Lieutenant Commander Peter Tyler (the executive officer), and Captain Bowie.

On cue, the sizzling wedge of static interference appeared on the lower left side of the screen. Like the last time, it disappeared after a minute or so, only to reappear a short time later on the starboard side of the scope.

The XO cocked his head to the side and looked at Chief Lowery. "It's not a SPY casualty, is it?"

Chief Lowery shook his head. "No, sir. It's not a hardware problem or a software problem. It's a potato."

"A potato?"

"Yes, sir. That's why we couldn't find the source of the interference. It wasn't in the radar at all. It was completely external."

"A potato," the captain said.

Chief Lowery grinned. "I didn't believe it myself, sir. But it's true."

The Combat Systems Officer gave the chief a hard look. "Would you mind telling us how a potato made its way into our SPY radar system?"

"It didn't, ma'am," the chief said. "The potato is entirely external. Or I should say *potatoes*, because there have been several of them. We've just been seeing them one at a time."

"You've dragged this out long enough, Chief," Ens. Lance said. "You'd better tell them the rest of it before they beat you to death."

"Yes, sir!" Chief Lowery tried to bring his grin under control. "The potato business has been going on for a long time. It's sort of a secret thing that the mess attendants keep to themselves. They've got these two long bamboo poles. I don't know where they got them from, but they keep them stashed in one of the dry provision storerooms. Anyway, when one of the mess attendants wants a snack, he drags out these two bamboo poles. They can plug the narrow end of one pole into the wide end of the other pole and make a single pole that's even longer."

"Where does the potato come in?" the CSO asked.

"They jam the potato onto the top of the bamboo pole, and then use the pole to hold it up a few inches from the front of the SPY radar array. SPY is pumping out more than four million watts of microwave energy. The intensity that close to the array face is really high. It's like the giant microwave oven from hell. It'll cook a potato in about a minute. If the mess attendant brings along a pat of butter and a little salt, presto! Instant snack."

Capt. Bowie half-smiled and shook his head. "I don't know whether to laugh or hang somebody from the yardarm."

"Wait a second," the XO said. "If this potato thing has been going on for so long, why haven't we seen this interference problem before this past week?"

"Well, sir, the bamboo stick and the potato are *transparent* to radar. The microwaves go right through them, so they don't show up on the screen. That's how the mess attendants have been able to do this for so long without getting caught. Then, last week, Seaman Apprentice Murphy was assigned to mess attendant duties. One of the other mess attendants shared the secret potato trick with Murphy, and *that* was when the problem started."

The captain's eyebrows went up. "Seaman Apprentice Murphy brought some new twist to the potato-and-stick routine?"

"Yes, sir," Chief Lowery said. "I guess Murphy's mother taught him to wrap his potatoes in aluminum foil before he cooked them. And aluminum is *not* radar transparent. A potato-sized piece of foil hanging three or four inches in front of the array face throws a whole lot of electromagnetic backscatter. Enough to jam the hell out of a big sector of SPY's coverage."

Lt. Sikes looked at the deck and shook her head. "Two hundred million dollars worth of state-of-the-art electronics, and we were being jammed by a potato?"

"I'm afraid so, ma'am," Chief Lowery said. "We only saw the interference on the port side, because there's a small landing at the top of the 01 level ladder, just below the Super-RBOC launchers. It makes a great place to stand when you're holding the bamboo pole up in front of the array. It can be done from the starboard side too, but there's nowhere to stand. You have to hang off the side of a vertical ladder and hold the bamboo pole with one hand. The port side is much easier."

The XO said, "Don't tell me. I'll bet I know why the jamming only happened in the mid-afternoon. That's when Seaman Apprentice Murphy gets his break, isn't it?"

"You hit the nail on the head, sir. But Murphy got rotated to the night shift. That's the only reason we found out about it at all. Murphy told the night baker about his *improved* method of cooking potatoes, and the night baker was smart enough to put two and two together. He came and woke me up." Chief Lowery looked at the captain. "If you ask me, sir, I think CS3 Zeigler deserves a Letter of Appreciation for this. He single-handedly solved the mystery of the ghost potato."

The captain snorted, tried to hold it in, and then began to laugh quietly. The Combat Systems Officer burst out with a laugh of her own, more like the bray of a donkey than anything human. The entire group dissolved into hysterics. It was one of those wild group laugh sessions, where every time it starts to die down, somebody snorts again, and it cranks up for another go-around.

It took five minutes to die down to chuckles. The XO stood, half hunched over, wiping tears from his eyes. "You want to know what's really funny?" He gasped a few times before gathering enough wind to continue. "Murphy's potatoes probably took three times as long to cook as everyone else's because he wrapped them in foil. If SPY wasn't so damned powerful, they probably wouldn't have cooked at all."

The captain shook his head. "No, Pete. I'll tell you what's *really* funny. *You* get to write the message explaining how the most advanced warship in the world got jammed by a vegetable." He snorted again. "Because I wouldn't touch that report with a ten-foot bamboo pole!"

CHAPTER 24

WHITE HOUSE SITUATION ROOM
WASHINGTON, DC
FRIDAY; 18 MAY
12:13 AM EDT

The double doors swung open, and two Secret Service agents entered the room and took up positions at either side of the doorway. The president strode into the room a few seconds later, holding up his hand as he walked. "Please, don't get up."

He slid into his chair at the head of the table and looked at each of his three advisors in turn. "We all know why we're here," he said. "Fifteen U.S. Sailors dead, nearly thirty more wounded, two helicopters destroyed, and a half-billion dollars worth of damage to an aircraft carrier." He pinched the bridge of his nose between his thumb and index finger. "The question is, what do we do now?"

Adm. Casey, the Chief of Naval Operations, cleared his throat. "My position remains unchanged, Mr. President. Our best recourse is to sink those submarines and do it now."

The president forced a half-smile. "I understand how you feel, Bob. But I'm not going to start a war here."

"Looks to me like the Germans have already started it, sir," Adm. Casey said. "God knows why, but they *want* to duke it out with us."

Secretary of State Whelkin shook her head. "I don't think so."

The CNO's eyebrows shot up. "They took the first shots," he said. "At the Brits and then at us. And you don't think they're spoiling for a fight?"

SecState raised her index finger. "I'm not disagreeing with you, Admiral. I'm certain that you're right; the Germans *are* looking for a fight. I just don't think they want a *war*."

The room was silent as everyone tried to digest that puzzling remark.

After a few seconds, the president said, "Talk to me, Liz. What's going on in that head of yours?"

Elizabeth Whelkin folded her hands on the table in front of her. "We're trying like hell to avoid a war here, right?"

Nearly every head in the room nodded.

She tilted her head. "Don't you think the Germans know that?" Her gaze traveled around the room, touching on every set of eyes around the table. "Not only do they know it, but they're depending on it."

"Wait a minute," the CNO said. "You're saying they *want* to mix it up with us, but they're counting on *us* to keep it from blowing up into a full-scale war?"

The secretary of state nodded. "That's how I read it."

National Security Advisor Gregory Brenthoven put both hands on the tabletop. "I can think of at least two possibilities that make more sense than that. How about this? Maybe those submarine commanders have gone rogue. They might be operating without authority from their government. Or maybe those Siraji crews that they've been training have seized control and hijacked the damned things!"

The president shook his head. "I don't think so, Greg. If those subs are operating without orders from the German government, where are the apologies? Why isn't Friedrik Shoernberg falling all over himself to kiss up to me? Where are the frantic phone calls denying involvement?"

Brenthoven looked surprised. "He hasn't called you, sir?"

The president shook his head again. "Hell no. I had to call *him*."

"What did he say?"

"He expressed sympathy for the families of our dead and wounded Sailors," the president said.

"No apologies?"

"No apologies. In fact, the bastard half-implied that it was *our* fault."

The CNO sat up. "Our fault? How in the hell does he figure that?"

"It's a free ocean," the president said. "From their angle, their subs were exercising their legal right to transit. Friedrik gave me a whole song and dance about it. By interfering with their passage and shoving a carrier up their noses, we provoked them into defending themselves."

"That's absolute bullshit," the CNO snapped. "Our ships have United Nations authorization to board and search any vessel suspected of violating the arms embargo against Siraj. Those subs are prohibited military hardware. We were totally within our rights to try to stop their delivery."

"That's not how Chancellor Shoernberg sees it," the president said. "It's the position of the German government that our mandate to conduct maritime interception operations is only valid within the boundaries of the Arabian

Gulf. Shoernberg claims we overstepped our authority when we went after his subs in the Arabian Sea."

The national security advisor stared at the secretary of state. "Is that right?"

Whelkin whistled through her teeth and scribbled a rapid note on her legal pad. "That's a tuffy. I'll have to go back and look at the wording of the resolution. It's possible that Chancellor Shoernberg is right. Technically, anyway."

"Technically, my ass," the CNO snapped. "You don't shoot at your allies—your *supposed* allies—over a technicality. The whole self-defense argument is a crock anyway. The *Kitty Hawk* strike group was hit by a coordinated multi-axis attack. From what I've seen of the initial post-mission analysis, the whole thing was a carefully orchestrated attempt to disrupt the defensive formation around a United States aircraft carrier long enough to attack the carrier itself. A damned successful attempt at that."

"Maybe the self-defense claim is Chancellor Shoernberg's way of covering his ass," Brenthoven said. "A whole pack of rogue submarines is pretty damned embarrassing. Could it be that the German government is stalling until they can think of the least damaging angle on this thing?"

The secretary of state shook her head. "Those submarines are not rogue. They are operating under orders."

Brenthoven stared at her. "How can you possibly know that?"

"It's not all that difficult to figure out," Whelkin said. "An entire squadron of German Air Force jets showed up to escort them through the Straits of Gibraltar. Unless you're suggesting that the Luftwaffe has gone rogue as well, I'd say that's a pretty good indication that the German government is calling the plays."

"Don't forget those radar-decoy yachts in the southern Med," the CNO said. "That was a calculated deception, carried out using boats that were leased by the German Navy."

The president's eyebrows went up. "Right. So, we scratch the rogue commander theory. What does that leave us? Can the Germans really be that determined to push us into a war?"

"Not a *war*, Mr. President," Whelkin said. "A *fight*."

Brenthoven rolled his eyes. "Are we back to playing semantics again? Planes, ships, torpedoes, missiles. Burnt bodies floating in the ocean. What difference does it make what you call it? Do you think the families of those dead Sailors care what word we use for it? Are they any less dead if we call it a *fight* instead of a *war*?"

"You misunderstand me," the secretary of state said. "I'm not talking about the choice of words. I'm talking about the *scope* of the conflict."

Brenthoven snorted. "What in the hell does *that* mean?"

The president raised a hand. "Keep your shirt on, Greg. I want to see where Liz is going."

Whelkin turned her eyes to the president. "I think the German government is challenging us to single combat."

The president frowned. "You mean like they did in the Middle Ages? Like jousting?"

"Pretty much, sir," Whelkin said. "But in the Middle Ages, it was primarily used as a display of battle skills, or to decide points of honor." She took a swallow of coffee and carefully wiped the lipstick off the rim of the cup before continuing. "In biblical times, the concept had much greater significance. When the leaders of opposing nations had disagreements, sometimes they would settle them by single combat. The toughest warrior from one country would do battle with the other country's toughest warrior, often while the opposing armies looked on. The warrior who came out on top won the day for his side. It was a pretty good system. Disputes over land and resources could be resolved without the danger and expense of all-out war. Remember the Bible story about David and Goliath? That's a classic example of single combat in its original form."

The president's eyebrows furrowed. "You think that's what the Germans are trying to do here?"

"It fits, sir. They shot up a carrier strike group. That's not the kind of thing we can let slide, right? We've *got* to take some sort of retaliatory action. We can't risk letting the pocket Napoleons of the world think that they can attack our ships with impunity."

"You've got that right," the CNO said. "That's why we've got to chase those bastards down and sink every goddamned one of them. If we don't, it's even money that somebody else will take a poke at one of our carriers next month, or next week."

Secretary Whelkin looked around the room. "The Germans are not stupid. They know that we're going to nail those subs. They knew it before they launched them."

"It's a hell of a risk on their part," Brenthoven said. "How can they be certain that we wouldn't go to war over this?"

"It's not as much of a risk at it seems to be," the secretary of state said. "The Germans know that we'll avoid going to war if we possibly can. They also know that we can't afford to let an attack on one of our carrier strike groups go unpunished. If you put the two ideas together, it's predictable that we will try to destroy those submarines without much further military escalation."

"Single combat," the president said slowly. "The modern version—a handful of their subs against a handful of our ships and aircraft."

"It still doesn't make sense," Brenthoven said. "Selling weapons to Siraj I can understand, even if I don't agree with it. Germany needs a lot of oil fast, and—in exchange for breaking the weapons embargo—Siraj is giving it to them at a fraction of fair market value. That part I can see. But I cannot for the life of me see what the Germans stand to gain from attacking the *Kitty Hawk*."

"That is the question," the president said. "What do the Germans get out of this?"

"Turn the question around, Mr. President," the secretary of state said. "What do we stand to *lose* from this?"

"We live and die by our image over there," the CNO said. "What success we've had in keeping a lid on the Middle East is largely due to our military strength. As long as we appear to be invincible, no Middle Eastern leader will seriously attempt to challenge us. Oh, they'll rant and rave on the six o'clock news and call us dirty names on the floor of the UN General Assembly, but they'll avoid direct conflict. It's not a perfect peace, God knows—some of those guys just can't pass up the chance to shoot at their neighbors—but it allows commerce rather than chaos to be the dominant mode of operation in the Gulf States."

"There's your answer," Secretary Whelkin said. "The Germans have already demonstrated that they can penetrate our carrier strike groups. Right now, their reputation is gaining ground and ours is losing. If we can't prevent them from delivering those subs, they're going to look even stronger, and we're going to look weaker still."

"A new Germany for the new century," the president said. "Re-forged as a world power. Focused, independent, and not afraid to play rough with the big boys."

"This whole thing has been a great showcase for their military hardware," Whelkin said. "Four little submarines have managed to elude one carrier strike group and blow the hell out of a second one."

"I can't argue on that point," Brenthoven said. "So far, they've succeeded in making us look like idiots. And we can't afford to lose credibility in the region."

"I agree," the CNO said. "We can't let even one of those subs get through to Siraj. A big chunk of our deterrence comes from our carriers. Not just the carriers themselves, but the perceptions associated with them. The American aircraft carrier is the *embodiment* of force projection. We've all seen it work when some pissant third-world dictator gets too big for his britches. A carrier shows up a few miles off his coastline, and suddenly he's jumping through hoops to show how enlightened and cooperative he can be. Most of the time, we don't have to fire a single shot. The aura of power reaches out from the carrier like an umbrella and practically blocks out the sun.

"We've got two carriers off the Chinese coast right now. Do you think the Chinese would be minding their P's and Q's if they thought they could hit our carriers with impunity?"

"An excellent point," the president said. "And a *vital* point. I think Admiral Casey is correct. The credibility of our conventional deterrence is on the line here. If we screw this up, it could affect the balance of power in countries all over the planet."

"Okay," said Brenthoven, "we throw everything we've got at those subs." He snapped his fingers three or four times. "I remember reading a proposal for eradicating the Iranian Kilo Class submarines. Something about catching them in the Straits of Hormuz and carpet-bombing the hell out of them with thousand-pound bombs. We could do that. The German subs will have to transit the straits to get into the Arabian Gulf. We can wait and nail them then."

"I'm not sure how Iran would take that," said the secretary of state. "The Straits of Hormuz are right off the Iranian coastline. If we were already at war with Iran, a scenario that your carpet-bombing proposal was apparently designed for—since it calls for attacking Iranian submarines—it wouldn't be an issue. But we're *not* at war with Iran, and we aren't looking to start one. It might be a good idea to think twice before bombing the hell out of their coastal waters."

"It's the wrong kind of response, anyway," the president said. "We've thrown two carrier strike groups at those subs already, and we've gotten our asses kicked. If we're going to salvage our credibility, we need to beat them in a fair fight. They've got four submarines—we send four surface combatants to take them on. No carriers, no bombers, no land-based aircraft. Just our destroyers and frigates against their submarines."

"Mr. President, you can't be serious," the CNO said. "The credibility of our national deterrence is at stake, and you're asking me to fight with one hand tied behind my back?"

The president said, "I want you to look me in the eye and tell me that our Navy is good enough to go one-on-one with the Germans and come out on top. If you can't say that with a straight face, we've got bigger problems than credibility."

"We snatched the *Kitty Hawk* out of there pretty quickly, sir," the CNO said. "I'm not sure if I can get four ships into a position to intercept. I know I've got three Middle East Force deployers on station—two destroyers and a frigate—but I may have to scrounge around to come up with a fourth unit on short notice. Unless you'll let me substitute a submarine. I should be able to get the *Topeka* in position without too much trouble."

The president shook his head. "No submarines. Those bastards have been lucky so far. If they managed to get a shot in on one of our subs, we could end up with nuclear contamination from one end of the Gulf to the other. Besides, the credibility of our sub force isn't in question right now. We need to do this with surface combatants." He looked at Whelkin. "Single combat."

The national security advisor cleared his throat. "Isn't that giving the Germans what they want?"

"We'll give them what they want," the president said. "We'll stick it up their ass and break it off."

"We might end up with only three ships," the CNO said. "Against four submarines."

"Then we do it with three ships," the president said, "but we *do* it. And keep this in mind: if *any* of those submarines make it to Siraj, the Germans win this thing."

Adm. Casey nodded slowly. "Understood, sir."

The president stood up. "I have to go figure out what to tell the American people about this mess."

The door opened and a young Navy lieutenant (junior grade) walked in, carrying a red and white striped folder. He scanned the room quickly and made his way toward the Chief of Naval Operations.

Every eye in the room followed the young officer as he walked. Under the color-coding system of the White House Signals Office, red and white stripes indicated highly classified material of utmost urgency.

The lieutenant (jg) stopped near the CNO, whispered briefly into his ear, and handed him the folder.

No one spoke. Adm. Casey opened the folder and read the single-page document inside. The CNO looked up. "Mr. President, our little mess just got a hell of a lot messier."

The president lifted his papers from the table and straightened them. "Bad news never improves with age, Bob. What have you got?"

The CNO looked down at the folder again. "Sir, about twenty minutes ago, two squadrons of British Sea Harriers exchanged missile fire with a German frigate in the North Sea. The ship was the FGS *Sachsen*, the lead unit of the new *Sachsen* Class guided missile frigates, and pretty much the pride of the German fleet. As of this report, the *Sachsen* was burning but still afloat."

The president rubbed the back of his neck. "Any word on who fired first?"

"The preliminary satellite data suggests it was the Brits, sir. And they don't seem to be going out of their way to deny it."

"They're getting even for what happened to the *York* and the *Chatham.*"

"It certainly looks that way, Mr. President," the CNO said. "Apparently we're not the only ones worried about the credibility of their deterrence."

CHAPTER 25

//SSSSSSSSSS//
//SECRET//
//FLASH//FLASH//FLASH//
//180504Z MAY//
FM COMUSNAVCENT//
TO USS TOWERS//
USS BENFOLD//
USS INGRAHAM//
INFO CTF FIVE ZERO//
SUBJ/USW TASKING/IMMEDIATE EXECUTE//
REF/A/RMG/CNO/150744Z MAY//
REF/B/RMG/CNO/180449Z MAY//
NARR/REF A IS CHIEF OF NAVAL OPERATIONS TACTICAL SUMMARY OF LIVE-FIRE HOSTILITIES BETWEEN UNITED KINGDOM ROYAL NAVY WARSHIPS AND FEDERAL REPUBLIC OF GERMANY (LUFTWAFFE) AIRCRAFT APPROX 13MAY//
NARR/REF B IS CHIEF OF NAVAL OPERATIONS TACTICAL SUMMARY OF LIVE-FIRE HOSTILITIES BETWEEN USS KITTY HAWK BATTLEGROUP AND FOUR DEUTSCHE MARINE TYPE 212B DIESEL SUBMARINES EARLIER THIS MORNING.//
1. (CONF) AS OUTLINED IN REFS A AND B, GERMAN NAVAL UNITS HAVE ATTACKED BRITISH ROYAL NAVY AND U.S. NAVY ASSETS TWICE IN THE PAST FIVE DAYS. IN MOST RECENT ENGAGEMENT, TWO U.S. NAVY HELICOPTERS DESTROYED, USS KITTY HAWK SERIOUSLY DAMAGED. PERSONNEL CASUALTIES HIGH.
2. (CONF) CURRENT THREAT EVALUATION HOLDS ALL FOUR DEUTSCHE MARINE SUBS AS UNDAMAGED AND UNRESTRICTED IN ABILITY TO FIGHT OR EVADE.

3. (CONF) INTELLIGENCE SOURCES BELIEVE DM IS ATTEMPTING TO DELIVER SUBS TO SIRAJ IN VIOLATION OF STANDING UN RESOLUTIONS.
4. (SECR) USS TOWERS, USS BENFOLD, AND USS INGRAHAM ARE DIRECTED TO FORM A THREE-SHIP SEARCH ATTACK UNIT (SAU) AND PROCEED SOUTH AT MAXIMUM AVAILABLE SPEED. SUBJECT SUBMARINES ARE DECLARED HOSTILE. TOWERS, BENFOLD, AND INGRAHAM ARE DIRECTED TO ENGAGE AND DESTROY ALL DM SUBMARINES WITHIN COMMANDER U.S. NAVAL CENTRAL COMMAND S AREA OF RESPONSIBILITY.
5. (SECR) COMUSNAVCENT WILL MAKE ALL EFFORTS TO LOCATE AN ADDITIONAL SURFACE ASSET TO REINFORCE SAU. IN THE INTERIM, USS TOWERS IS DESIGNATED AS SAU COMMANDER.
6. (SECR) AT LEAST ONE DM SUBMARINE HAS SUCCESSFULLY ENGAGED AND DESTROYED CARRIER-BASED USW AIRCRAFT USING SUB-LAUNCHED SURFACE TO AIR MISSILES. TAKE ALL POSSIBLE PRECAUTIONS WHEN DEPLOYING AIRCRAFT IN THE VICINITY OF TARGET SUBS.
7. (SECR) ALL UNITS ARE ADVISED THAT DM SUBMARINES HAVE SHOWN EXCEPTIONAL TACTICAL SKILL AND CREATIVITY, HIGHLY PROFICIENT EXPLOITATION OF ENVIRONMENTAL CONDITIONS, AND A PREDILECTION FOR DEPLOYING ELECTRONIC DECOYS. EXPECT COORDINATED, ZERO-NOTICE, MULTI-AXIS ATTACKS AND BE PREPARED TO DELIVER SAME TO DM SUBMARINES.
8. (UNCL) GOOD LUCK AND GOOD HUNTING! ADMIRAL ROGERS SENDS.
//180504Z JUN//
//FLASH//FLASH//FLASH//
//SECRET//
//SSSSSSSSSS//

USS *TOWERS* (DDG-103)
CENTRAL ARABIAN GULF
FRIDAY; 18 MAY
0911 hours (9:11 AM)
TIME ZONE +3 'CHARLIE'

There was a full-length mirror bolted to the bulkhead outside the wardroom. Across the top of the glass was a blue decal depicting the eagle-and-anchor emblem of the U.S. Navy, followed by a short paragraph in white block lettering:

CHECK YOUR MILITARY APPEARANCE. ARE YOU SETTING A PROPER EXAMPLE FOR YOUR SUBORDINATE PERSONNEL?

LOOK LIKE A LEADER. THINK LIKE A LEADER.
BE A LEADER.

Sonar Technician Chief Theresa McPherson paused to examine her reflection in the mirror. She was a bantam hen of a woman: short, redheaded, and inclined toward plumpness. Thirty-five minutes a day on the treadmill kept her within Navy body-fat standards, but her round face and full cheeks made her seem chubby no matter how trim she kept her body.

She suppressed a sigh. Her face was a preview of the years ahead. The women of her family all put on weight in their late thirties, and some day—when she no longer had the energy to struggle against her genes and the general entropy of middle age—she would become just as round as the others. That day might not be too far in coming. She didn't need the streaks of gray in her hair to know that her fortieth birthday was careening toward her like a juggernaut.

She turned her attention to her uniform. Her short-sleeved khakis were crisply starched, the creases sharp and precisely aligned. Despite her chipmunk cheeks, there were no bulges at the hips of her khaki trousers, and the buttons of her shirt lay flat against her belly. She was winning the battle, for now at least. And maybe that was all she could expect: to win one battle at a time. She straightened her belt buckle a fraction and stepped away from the mirror.

Two quick steps brought her to the wardroom. She rapped on the doorframe and then opened the door far enough to stick her head in.

Capt. Bowie was sitting in his customary spot, the middle seat on the far side of the table that ran down the center of the room. He looked up and motioned to a chair. "Come on in, Chief. Grab yourself a cup of coffee and have a seat."

Chief McPherson skipped the coffee and took a chair near the middle of the table.

The captain turned back to a stack of papers laid out on the table in front of him. "I hope you'll excuse me," he said with the ghost of a smile. "I want to make sure that my homework is finished before the thundering hoard arrives."

The chief nodded automatically, despite the obvious fact that the captain wasn't looking at her. "Of course, sir." She checked her watch. "I'm early anyway."

She resisted the temptation to give the room the once-over. She'd been to meetings here at least two dozen times, but the wardroom was so unlike the rest of the ship that just walking through the door was always a bit of a shock. *Towers* was a warship, and that meant she was built for utility rather than aesthetics. Outside of the wardroom, the bulkheads and overheads were crowded with pipes, valves, ventilation ducts, cable runs, electrical junction boxes, and damage control equipment—so much so that it would have been difficult to locate two square feet of exposed wall space. If such an empty spot had existed, some naval engineer would undoubtedly have found a way to shoehorn in a fiberoptic relay terminal or a casualty power transformer.

Inside the door of the wardroom was a different matter. The walls were paneled in richly grained walnut. (Yes, *wall* was the right word; *bulkhead* was a shipboard term, and the dark wooden paneling bore no resemblance to the utilitarian white-painted steel bulkheads found elsewhere on the ship.) In place of the cable runs and pipes that lined the overheads on the rest of the ship, the wardroom boasted an acoustic tile ceiling that would have looked at home in a restaurant or business office.

Equal parts conference room, classroom, dining room, and social parlor, the wardroom on *Towers* (as on every warship) was the nexus of all officer activity. Here, the commissioned officers held training sessions, conducted high-level briefings, and entertained the occasional civilian dignitary or head of state.

A score of other details made the wardroom—and to a lesser degree the officers' staterooms—markedly different from the rest of the ship. Up here, the officers dined on real china—inlaid with the ship's crest. Down on the Mess Decks and in the Chief Petty Officer's Mess, the enlisted crew members ate their meals off fiberglass trays. The officers' eating utensils were of finely patterned silver—also engraved with the ship's crest. The enlisted crew used unpatterned stainless steel flatware. The wardroom napkins were starched linen, in place of the paper napkins used by the rest of the crew.

Chief McPherson didn't begrudge the officers the few perks they received, and she didn't think that most of the crew did either. General consensus treated the wardroom as an upscale version of the Chief Petty Officer's Mess, but Chief McPherson knew that it was more than that. It was, among other things, a symbol: a line drawn in the dirt that clearly delineated the distinction between the enlisted crew and the officers who commanded them.

In ages past, the line between commissioned officers and their enlisted subordinates had been so obvious that it had needed no elaboration. Officers had been the military's version of the aristocracy: educated, frequently wealthy, and well mannered to the point of gentility. By contrast, enlisted men had often been illiterate, ill mannered, and so nearly destitute that the majority had lived from payday to meager payday.

Over the years, such distinctions had faded far enough to blur the line between officers and their subordinates. The typical twenty-first–century petty officer was college-educated, technically skilled, well mannered, and financially solvent. In point of fact, the wealthiest man currently stationed aboard *Towers* was a second class Electronics Warfare Technician with a bachelor's degree in economics and an uncanny flair for predicting the ups and downs of the securities market.

The extravagant (by comparison) trappings of the wardroom served as a subtle reminder to the crew, and to the officers themselves, that the line between officer and enlisted was still in place—and that it was there for a reason.

* * *

Chief McPherson focused her attention on the trio of oil paintings that hung in a neat row on the wall behind the captain's chair. The center, and largest of the three, was a portrait of the ship's namesake, Vice Admiral John Henry Towers. Obviously based on a photograph taken early in the man's career, the face staring out of the portrait had the sort of square-jawed, wavy-haired good looks that were more readily associated with motion picture heroes than with actual warriors. But the man had *been* an actual warrior; only the third airplane pilot in the history of the U.S. Navy, Towers had been designated *Naval Aviator Number 3* in 1911. Present at the very birth of military aviation, he had guided the development and growth of the Navy's fledgling air wing through two world wars.

To the left of the admiral's portrait was a painting of the first ship to carry the name of Towers. Shown plowing through heavy seas under a storm-darkened sky, the old *Adams* Class guided missile destroyer looked resolute and powerful, and yet—at the same time—tiny and frail against the thrashing might of the waves. Fluttering from the old ship's starboard yardarm were the signal flags *November* and *Yankee*: the tactical signal for "*I Stand Relieved.*"

On the opposite side of the admiral's portrait hung a painting of the current USS *Towers*. Also shown slicing through a stormy sea, the new ship flew the signal flags *Charlie* and *Lima* from the short yardarm on the port side of her shark-fin mast, and the flags *Bravo* and *Zulu* from the starboard yardarm. The four flags formed two tactical signals: "*I Assume the Watch*," and "*Job Well Done!*"—the new ship's answer to the message sent by her older sister.

The low, angular profile of the stealth destroyer looked more like something out of a science fiction movie than the sister of the older ship. But, appearances aside, sisters they were. Despite the fifty-odd years of technological development that separated them, both ships shared the same DNA. As guided missile destroyers in the United States Navy, both ships had been designed with the tin can Sailor's credo in mind: *Go anywhere, do anything, battle any foe.*

With thirty years of service spanning the Vietnam War and the Cold War, the old *Adams* Class DDG had more than met the challenge raised by those words. With fewer than eighteen months of duty under her belt, the new *Towers* had a long way to go before she could begin to live up to her name.

* * *

The wardroom door opened, and the executive officer, Lieutenant Commander Pete Tyler, filed in, followed in short order by the ship's Operations Officer, Lieutenant Brian Nylander; the Combat Systems Officer, Lieutenant Terri Sikes; and the Navigator/Administrative Officer, Lieutenant (junior grade) Karen Augustine. Each of the officers greeted the captain and found a seat at the wardroom table.

The XO leaned over in Chief McPherson's direction and whispered, "Where is your boss?"

The chief glanced at the door. "On the way, sir. He won't be late. He never is."

"He'd better not be," the XO said out of the side of his mouth. "He's your ensign; it's your job to train him."

There was a hint of amusement in the XO's eyes, but Chief McPherson knew that the man was only half-joking. As the captain's second-in-command, the XO was charged with making sure that the ship operated in accordance with the captain's orders and policies. One of those policies involved ensuring that junior officers were never—*never* late for meetings. *Especially* not meetings that had been called by the captain.

Due to the oddities of the Navy command structure, that put Chief McPherson in a bit of a predicament. Her Division Officer, Mr. Cooper, was a brand-spanking-new ensign (as were most other Divo's). He was a commissioned officer, albeit a very junior one, and that made him Chief McPherson's boss. She was required to follow his orders, despite the fact that she had nearly twenty years of experience, and he had virtually zero. Ens. Cooper was a hard-charger and a quick learner, but he was also young and *very* wet behind the ears. By naval tradition, the chief was expected to train her own boss and mold him into a good officer, which made her responsible for his actions, even though she was his subordinate. A good chief petty officer, it was reasoned, could use knowledge and experience to guide a young officer into correct action—which ultimately meant that the XO would kick Chief McPherson's ass up around her shoulder blades if her boss didn't show up for the captain's meeting on time.

She stifled the urge to look at her watch or the door again. "My Fearless Leader will be here, sir. Count on it."

The door opened again, but it wasn't Ens. Cooper. Lieutenant Alan West, the Supply Officer, walked in and took the chair closest to the coffeepot.

Now Chief McPherson did look at her watch. Her boss had about three minutes. She was just about to get up and use the phone to try to track him down when the door opened and Ens. Cooper walked in.

As soon as the ensign found a chair and pulled it up to the table, the XO cleared his throat. "Ah, Captain. We're ready to begin."

Capt. Bowie looked up from his paperwork and scanned the group of men and women seated around the table. "Where's the Chief Engineer?"

"The CHENG is down in Main Engine Room number one," the XO said. "The engineers are finishing up the installation on the new fuel oil purifier, and he's overseeing the work. I told him he could take a pass on the meeting, and I'd catch him up later."

The captain digested this bit of information for a few seconds. Then he shook his head. "Sorry to second-guess you, Pete, but I need him up here for this."

The XO nodded. "Yes, sir." He stood up and walked to the phone.

* * *

A couple of minutes later, the Chief Engineer showed up, his coveralls streaked with grease. He nodded toward the captain. "Sorry I'm late, sir. I thought I had a get-out-of-jail-free card, but I guess I misplaced it."

The captain waved him to a chair. "I'll let you slide this time, but next time you'll have to bring a note from your mom."

Everyone chuckled politely.

The captain held up a hand for silence. "How many of you have been staying on top of the secret message traffic?"

Every hand in the room went up.

"Good," the captain said. "Then you all know what's been going on with that wolfpack of German submarines."

Everyone nodded, and there were gentle murmurs of assent.

"Excellent," the captain said. He picked up a stack of papers and began passing copies around the table. "Because we've just received orders to form a Search Attack Unit with USS *Benfold* and USS *Ingraham*. We've been designated as commander for the SAU. You can read these at your leisure, but I'll give you the short version for now. Our orders are to proceed south at all speed, intercept the German submarines, and destroy every one of them."

The Supply Officer accepted his copy of the orders and stared blankly at it. "Sir? Are we at war with Germany?"

"Not yet, SUPPO," the captain said. "And maybe not at all. This may be an isolated reprisal for the attack on the *Kitty Hawk* strike group.

"What I want right now is an up-to-the-minute status report. Are we ready for this? What equipment is broken? Which systems are degraded?" He turned to the Chief Engineer. "You first, CHENG. If we can't drive, we can't fight. What's the latest on the engineering plant?"

"The engines are in top shape," the CHENG said. "So are the generators. Prairie Masker is looking good. The installation on One Alpha Fuel Oil Purifier is about ninety percent complete. With a little luck we'll have it back on line in a couple of hours." His eyebrows narrowed slightly. "I'm not crazy about the compressor on air conditioning plant number three. I haven't ordered a sound survey yet, but the A-Gang Chief says he thinks it's running a little loud. I've listened to it, and I think he's right. If we can't get it back within specs, we may have to shut it down entirely before we can set Silent Ship."

The captain scribbled a note. "Number three AC feeds enlisted berthing aft, doesn't it?"

The Chief Engineer nodded. "Yes, sir."

"The ambient air temperature is over a hundred degrees," the captain said. "If we have to shut three AC down for long, aft enlisted berthing will become an oven. I don't want the crew sleeping down there when it gets like that."

"It will be uncomfortable, sir. But the crew can learn to live with it."

"I'm sure that's true," the executive officer said. "But it's hard to sleep when it gets that hot. And when the crew loses sleep, they make mistakes. We're about to take on a pack of hostile submarines that have stomped the shit out of every surface ship that has crossed their path. Mistakes are something we cannot afford."

"I agree," the captain said. He looked at the Supply Officer. "SUPPO, make sure the engineers get whatever parts they need to fix that compressor. And if they need something we don't carry on board, send out a logistics request, and we'll have it sent out by helo. We just jumped to the top of the Navy's logistics priority list." He looked around the table. "All of you, get your wish lists to the SUPPO before evening chow. It just became Christmas on Happy Warship *Towers*, and the Navy supply system has been designated as your official Santa Claus."

The captain looked at the XO. "Pete, assign one of our bright junior officers to come up with a plan for moving the enlisted personnel out of aft berthing, just in case we can't get three AC to play right."

The XO nodded. "Sounds like a good job for the Admin Officer."

Lt.(jg) Augustine made a thumbs-up gesture. "Piece of cake, sir. We can spread the personnel out to other berthing spaces with empty racks. Move a few into officer and chief petty officer overflow berthing. If worse comes to worst, we can drag mattresses and sheets down to some of the electronics spaces. Those spaces are nice and chilly."

"Good," the captain said. "Now, OPS, what have you got for me?"

The Operations Officer looked up from his copy of the new orders. "Operations department is clean and green, Captain. The biggest problem I have to report is a sticky cipher lock on the starboard door to CIC. Other than that, we're just ducky."

"Just ducky," the Combat Systems Officer said under her breath in a mocking tone. "We're just *ducky* here. *Ducky*, I tell you."

"You're next, CSO," the captain said. "You're the one with all the cool bullets and bombs. What's broke and what ain't?"

The Combat Systems Officer sighed and consulted her palm-top computer. "We've got that bad Tomahawk in VLS cell twenty-two. Should be zero tactical impact, at least while we're hunting submarines. The Aegis backup computer has a bad high-volt power supply. Tactical impact is just loss of a redundant system. Supply department has a replacement on board, but we've been holding off, because we don't have sixty thousand dollars left in this quarter's repair budget. But if we really do have a blank check for parts, we can draw the new power supply from stores and have the backup computer on line in less than an hour." She used a plastic stylus to scroll down the screen on the tiny computer. "As far as Undersea Warfare goes … all the sonars are up; we've got a full bag of sonobuoys; all the ASROCs and torpedoes look good. I'd say we're ready to go hunt some submarines."

Chief McPherson nodded imperceptibly. Her equipment was in good shape, and her people were trained.

"That's just what I wanted to hear," the captain said. "And now we can move on to our next order of business: tactical planning. How are we going to go about this business of hunting down these submarines? And, perhaps more importantly, what tactics are we going to use when we encounter them?"

Ens. Cooper spoke up. "Ah, Captain … as the Undersea Warfare Officer, that would be my ball of wax …"

The captain nodded for him to continue. "Absolutely, Pat. What do you have in mind?"

Ens. Cooper swallowed visibly. "First, I suggest a thorough review of our tactical USW doctrine. Our teams are pretty sharp right now, but it never hurts to polish up. Then I recommend we select the proper tactics for engaging diesel submarines in shallow water, and we construct two or three training scenarios utilizing the On-Board Trainer. If we run each scenario twice a day, we should be razor-sharp by the time we get far enough south to commence our search."

Heads nodded around the table, but Chief McPherson felt her muscles tighten. Her boss's plan sounded great, but she knew that it had a hole in it—a big one. She chewed the inside of her lower lip for a few seconds. Would it be better to point it out now? Or should she wait and do it in private, so as not to embarrass Ens. Cooper in front of the other officers? Of course, if she waited to bring the problem to his attention, he would have to come back to this same table some time in the future with his hat in his hand and admit his mistake. That might be even more embarrassing for him.

The chief glanced up to discover that the captain was staring at her with a strange look on his face. Then it hit her. The captain already *knew* there was a problem. *That* was why he'd summoned her to a meeting that was otherwise all commissioned officers. He not only knew that there was a problem; he knew that she would spot it. And, obviously, he expected her to have a hand in fixing it.

She cleared her throat. "Uh … Captain? If I may?"

The captain nodded. "Of course, Chief."

She continued. "Captain, the USW Officer's plan is a good one, but I'm afraid that I have to disagree with one major part of it."

Ens. Cooper stared at her, obviously shocked at the idea that his own chief petty officer would contradict him in front of the captain. "Um … which part do you … um … disagree with, Chief?"

Every eye in the room was on the chief now, and she was suddenly conscious of just how far out of her territory she was. "I don't think we can afford …" She stopped, swallowed, and started again. "I don't think we can afford to trust our tactical USW doctrine in this situation. In fact, I think we have to *avoid* using our tactical doctrine at all costs."

The USWO rubbed behind his ear, a puzzled look on his face. "Help me out here, Chief. I'm trying to understand what you're saying."

"I know it sounds crazy," the chief said. "But think about it, sir. Nearly every tactic in those books has been shared with NATO. Search patterns. Attack patterns. The timing of our zigzag plans. Even the spacing of our sonobuoys. The lion's share of our doctrine was designed for use in cooperation with NATO. The Germans have been members of NATO since the get-go—which means they've already read our playbook. If we follow our doctrine, they already know what we're going to do before we even do it."

Capt. Bowie nodded. "I think you hit the bull's-eye, Chief. Excellent job. That explains how the Germans managed to clean *Kitty Hawk*'s clock so easily."

The XO's eyebrows went up for a few seconds. Then, he clapped his hands and rubbed them together briskly. "Sooooo ... I guess we start by throwing the old book out the window and coming up with some new tactics."

"I agree, sir," the Combat Systems Officer said. And when we do get something hammered out, we can punch it into the Link and shoot it over to *Benfold* and *Ingraham* and see if they can suggest any improvements."

The captain nodded. "Good call." He turned back to the chief. "You've been doing this half your life—got any pet theories you want to try out against some no-shit hostile subs?"

Chief McPherson nodded. She'd been right. *This* was why the captain had invited her to this meeting. "I might just have one or two ideas gathering dust at the back of my brain, Captain."

The captain smiled. "I kind of suspected that you might."

The chief glanced at Ens. Cooper. His face had whitened visibly. She could nearly hear the thoughts tumbling around in his head. All of his knowledge of Undersea Warfare had come from studying tactical doctrine. Now, those neatly bound tactical manuals were useless to him. Even his training in the Undersea Warfare Evaluator's course had been based entirely on the tactics written into the manuals. Outside of scheduled exercises, which were—again—based upon the doctrine contained in the manuals, he had no experience chasing submarines. He had no personal knowledge to fall back on, no pet tactical theories based on hard-won expertise. And now, the captain was asking him to forget everything he had studied and start from scratch.

Apparently catching the USW Officer's expression of near terror, the captain said, "You look like you just stepped off a cliff, Pat, and you're waiting to hit bottom."

The USWO didn't say anything.

"Don't worry," the captain said. "We're going to be making this up on the fly, so anything we do is right. It may not work, and it might get us killed, but—since we have to shit-can the play book—nobody will be able to say that we were wrong."

CHAPTER 26

U.S. NAVY CENTRAL COMMAND (USNAVCENT)
BAHRAIN
FRIDAY; 18 MAY
1025 hours (10:25 AM)
TIME ZONE +3 'CHARLIE'

Admiral Vincent Rogers, Commander Fifth Fleet, leaned back in his chair and squeezed the bridge of his nose between thumb and index finger. The ever-present stack of paperwork on his desk seemed to grow every time he took his eyes off it for a few seconds. Maybe it was reproducing itself through some mechanism of parthenogenesis that had heretofore lain dormant in paper products—perhaps a recessive gene hidden deep in the paper's DNA that had somehow been activated by the stifling Middle Eastern heat.

Rogers ran his fingers through the iron-gray stubble of his flattop haircut. Eight days shy of his fifty-seventh birthday, he was an old man to the Sailors he commanded, but—to his own way of thinking—he was far too young to be chained to a desk full of reports, operational summaries, force projection studies, feasibility matrices, and whatever the hell else had found its way into his *Urgent* stack.

There were two quiet knocks on his door.

Adm. Rogers sat up. "Enter."

The door opened, and his chief of staff, Commander Troy Moody, stepped into the office. Moody carried a yellow folder in his left hand. Under the color-coding system used by the USNAVCENT staff, yellow was reserved for SITREPs, or situational reports, from ships assigned to Fifth Fleet's command.

The admiral's eyes stayed locked on the yellow folder. "Say, Troy, I was just wondering … whatever happened to that paperless Navy we were supposed to be headed for? Remember that?" He pointed to his desktop computer and then to his laptop computer and finally to his palm-top. "As I recall," he said, "*these* were supposed to get rid of *those*." He pointed to the fat stack of papers on his desk. "That was a great idea. Whatever happened to it?"

Moody smiled. "Um ... I believe that *paper* covers *computer*, sir."

"What the hell does that mean?"

Moody held out the folder to the admiral. "You remember the rules, sir. Rock smashes scissors. Scissors cut paper. Paper covers rock. Well, somebody did a study, and it turns out that paper covers computer as well."

Adm. Rogers accepted the folder. "By extrapolation, I assume that means that rock smashes computer."

Moody pointed to the desk. "It certainly does, sir. Unfortunately, that still leaves paper."

The admiral sighed. "No way around it, I guess." He opened the folder. "What have you got here, Troy?"

"A SITREP from USS *Antietam*, sir."

"I can see that," the admiral said. "But I don't feel like wading through four pages of minutiae in search of whatever little nugget of wisdom you found buried in there. Just give me the *Reader's Digest* version." He closed the folder. "What's going on with *Antietam*?"

"They've completed repairs to their starboard rudder nearly a week ahead of schedule, sir. Barring problems during shakedown, they're ready to put to sea now. I know you've been trying to scare up a fourth ship for your Search Attack Unit, sir. Looks like *Antietam* is going to be available after all."

The admiral nodded. "Excellent work, Troy. The CNO has been up my ass for two days to come up with another ship."

"So I understood, sir."

"Good man. Now, get on the horn and tell the admin weenies to cut steaming orders for *Antietam*."

"Already done, sir. They won't be final until you sign them, of course, but I've taken the liberty of starting the ball rolling, just in case you decided to assign *Antietam* to the SAU."

The admiral nodded. "Excellent."

"I didn't think you'd want to waste any time," Cmdr. Moody said. "*Antietam* still has to do a quick shakedown after her rudder repairs. They'll really have to drop the hammer to catch up. The SAU has a head start, and those guys are hauling ass."

Rogers looked at his chief of staff. "Whiley will catch 'em," he said. "He's up for admiral after this tour, and he's not going to pass up a chance to play war hero. They can use the sprint south as their shakedown. Then, if the rudder gives them any trouble, they can turn back to port and let the SAU continue on without them. But that's not going to happen. Whiley won't let it happen. He'll be there, all right. You can bet your ass on it."

"One more thing, sir," Cmdr. Moody said. "Captain Whiley is a senior full-bird captain, sir. He's going to want to assume command of the SAU. I don't imagine Captain Bowie is going to like the idea of giving it up."

"Bowie'll shit a brick," the admiral said, "but there's nothing I can do about that. Whiley outranks him seven ways from Sunday. If Whiley wants SAU Commander, it's his."

"*Antietam* is an air-shooter, sir," Moody said. "I've been looking back through the daily OPSUM messages; that crew hasn't done anything but Anti-Air Warfare for a long time. Undersea Warfare is a highly perishable skill. If you don't use it, you lose it. If Captain Whiley is smart, he'll let the *Towers* run the show."

The admiral smiled. "*If* he were smart. Have you met Whiley?"

"No, sir."

"He's a dip-shit," Adm. Rogers said. "Don't quote me on that. Oh, he did all right with those Iranian MiGs last month, but the man is a weasel at heart."

Cmdr. Moody kept a carefully neutral face. "No comment, sir."

The admiral's smile grew even wider. "Good man! Now, get *Antietam* on the horn, and let's kick their ass out of port."

CHAPTER 27

M-1 WASHINGTON HERALD TRIBUNE THURSDAY

Two Bodies Found in Van May be Linked to Attack on British Embassy

WASHINGTON (AP) — A security guard discovered the bodies of two men believed to be connected to the British Embassy attack in the cargo section of a green Chevrolet utility van about 8 a.m. today.

Neither of the bodies has been identified, but Lt. Sharon Crane of the Arlington County Police Department has verified that they appear to match the descriptions of two WizardClean employees who have been missing since May 6, when the British Embassy in Washington was attacked, killing 68 people and critically injuring 49 others. A third WizardClean employee, identified only as a 19-year-old Navy man, also has been missing since May 6.

A Pentagon source verified that the three WizardClean employees are believed to be linked to the recent biological warfare attack on the British Embassy.

Sgt. Raymond Wilchoaski, a bonded employee of the Meta-Shield Security Group, discovered the bodies during a security check of the Park Safe multilevel parking structure in Arlington.

"The van checked in to long-term parking 11 days ago," said a spokesman for Meta-Shield. "The driver paid for three weeks in advance, so the vehicle didn't attract our attention until customers began complaining of a bad smell up on Level Four. One of our officers investigated and discovered the bodies."

Wilchoaski was unavailable for comment.

The Meta-Shield spokesman refused to comment on rumors that Wilchoaski has been placed in medical quarantine for possible exposure to a life-threatening infectious disease. The spokesman confirmed that the van in question was registered to WizardClean Inc., a Washington-based company specializing in professional floor and carpet cleaning.

The county's chief medical examiner has refused to speculate on the cause of death for the two men and has declined to confirm that the third floor of the Park Safe garage is undergoing chemical decontamination. Autopsies will be performed on the bodies, the medical examiner said.

See **EMBASSY** Page M-3

LONDON
FRIDAY; 18 MAY
0928 hours (9:28 AM)
TIME ZONE +1 'ALPHA'

Andrew Smythe Harrington (OBE) was a top-echelon analyst with the British Secret Intelligence Service, better known to the world as the SIS, or "the Firm." Nearing fifty, he looked closer to thirty, and—he admitted to himself as he twisted in his chair to ease the kink in his lower back—felt closer to sixty. Handsome in an Errol Flynn sort of way, Harrington had garnered a reputation as something of a ladies' man (which he most certainly was *not*) and an exceptional chess player (which—all modesty aside—he most certainly *was*). But Harrington liked to refer to his real talent in life as *"a gift for seeing the obvious."*

His office was on the third floor of SIS headquarters at Vauxhall Cross. Unlike the toweringly elegant Century House, which had served as the headquarters for the Secret Intelligence Service until 1995, the Vauxhall Cross complex was an architectural polyglot of cylinders, cubes, and truncated pyramids that had led its detractors to nickname it *Legoland*.

Harrington was entitled to a corner office on the top floor, both by seniority and by the influence conferred by his *Order of the British Empire*. But he had rejected a large, prestigious office in favor of a smallish cubicle with no windows. His job was to think, and he took that job very seriously. To ensure that his thinking was as efficient as possible, he avoided distractions wherever he could, including windows, unnecessary decorations, and the attractive female secretary that so many of his peers seemed to find indispensable.

He scanned the American newspaper article for the third time and then placed it carefully on top of the neat stack of papers in the center of his desk. There were over four hundred pages in the stack. Police reports, USAMRIID and CDC contagion projections, toxin concentration counts from the embassy after decontamination, medical reports from Walter Reed Hospital, regional threat assessments, a forensic analysis of the T2 trichothecene mycotoxin, and traffic analyses of known and suspected terrorist movements before, during, and after the attack. Also in the stack were the only three documents that really mattered: a copy of the visitors log from the British Embassy in Washington, a transcript of the interview of one Mr. Larry S. Burke, shift supervisor for the carpet cleaning company, and the Washington newspaper article.

Harrington laid his hand on top of the little stack. Everything was right here, in those three little bits of paper, as difficult to miss as the fox in the proverbial henhouse. How was it possible that no one else had seen it?

The carpet cleaning company, WizardClean, had dispatched a three-man crew to the British Embassy. But only two men had shown up to do the job. The Washington police were still searching for the third man, the missing Sailor, who hadn't been seen since the night of the attack.

But Seaman Apprentice Jerome Gilbert was not the key to the puzzle. He had been added to the work crew just an hour or so before the attack. It was extremely unlikely that he could have been in on the plot. In all probability, Gilbert had been dead well before the two attackers had reached the embassy.

That meant the real third man was still missing, the regular third man for the WizardClean work crew assigned to the embassy. A twenty-eight-year-old Arab American named Isma'il Hamid. According to the shift supervisor from the carpet cleaning company, Hamid had reported for work with the rest of his crew, but he'd been too sick to go out with the truck.

Harrington picked up the transcript of the supervisor's interview with the Arlington police, flipped to the fourth page, and scanned down to the relevant section.

Detective Scot J. Barnes: ARLINGTON PD [3127]	You said Mr. Hamid showed up for his shift, but he was too sick to work?
Witness Larry S. Burke: WTN-16/CA-23077	That's right. Sick as a dog, the poor bastard. Throwing up all over the place, and you could tell he was in major pain. He was trying not to show it, that whole macho Arab thing, but his stomach was hurting him so bad he could hardly breathe. He couldn't even walk right. He was in rough shape.
Detective Scot J. Barnes: ARLINGTON PD [3127]	But he tried to work his shift anyway?
Witness Larry S. Burke: WTN-16/CA-23077	Yeah. Hamid tried to play it off like he had the stomach flu. Said he'd taken some Pepto Bismol, and it was getting better. He wanted to go out with the truck.
Detective Scot J. Barnes: ARLINGTON PD [3127]	And you wouldn't let him?

Witness Larry S. Burke: WTN-16/CA-23077	Hell no I wouldn't let him. His crew was assigned to the embassy. That's a big contract. Important people. I couldn't have him puking all over the fucking place. I sent the new guy, the Gilbert kid, out with the truck in Hamid's spot.
Detective Scot J. Barnes: ARLINGTON PD [3127]	Did Hamid seem to get upset about that?
Witness Larry S. Burke: WTN-16/CA-23077	Upset? There's your understatement of the year. He was fucking furious! Started yelling at me in Arabian, or Egyptian, or one of them rag-head languages. Excuse me. I mean some kind of Iranian talk, or something. Shocked the hell out of me when he started going ballistic on me. Hamid was always one of the quiet ones. Hard worker. Good attitude. I could use a half-dozen more workers just like him.
Detective Scot J. Barnes: ARLINGTON PD [3127]	Did he calm down after you sent the truck out?
Witness Larry S. Burke: WTN-16/CA-23077	Not really. He collapsed. His knees just sort of folded, and he went down like a sack of bricks. He didn't look like he was breathing right. That's when I called 911. The paramedics said it was his appendix. He had it bad, like it was rupturing, or something. The paramedics said he'd have been dead in another half-hour or so.
Detective Scot J. Barnes: ARLINGTON PD [3127]	Thank you. Now, tell me more about this Jerome Gilbert.

Harrington closed the transcript and returned it to the stack. Hamid had been slated as the third man in the attack; Harrington had no doubt of that.

The FBI and Washington police were searching for Hamid, and the American immigration authorities were watching the airports for him. But Harrington was nearly certain that Hamid was neither hiding nor trying to flee.

He pulled a telephone directory from his desk drawer and thumbed through to the government section. He found the listing he was looking for under Army Medical Directorate. It took him nearly ten minutes of conversations with underlings to actually lure a doctor to the telephone, and then another two minutes to explain who he was. At last, Dr. Kenneth Hale seemed to be prepared to answer his questions.

"I'll try not to keep you long, Dr. Hale," Harrington said.

"I appreciate that," Dr. Hale said. "I am busy on the best of days, and this doesn't happen to be a very good day at all."

Harrington kept his voice carefully neutral. With another telephone call or two, he could have easily compelled Dr. Hale to appear in person. He hoped that wouldn't be necessary. "Doctor, I'd like to discuss the human appendix for a moment."

"What would you like to know?"

"First of all," Harrington said, "how difficult is an appendectomy? And what is the normal postoperative recovery time?"

"The procedure is fairly straightforward," the doctor said. "In most cases, the patient recovers very quickly and can be discharged in two or three days."

"I see," Harrington said. "I'd like to discuss a hypothetical patient. Let's assume that an otherwise healthy young man, between the ages of twenty and thirty, underwent an appendectomy on Saturday a week ago. Is it safe to assume that he would be back on his feet by now?"

Dr. Hale laughed. "Back on his feet? By now, he'd probably be kicking footballs."

"Ah," Harrington said. "But what if there were complications?"

"These days, there are almost never complications with an appendectomy. It is, as I said, a fairly straightforward procedure, with an excellent postoperative prognosis."

"But suppose," Harrington said, "that the young man in question did not seek medical attention."

"He would," the doctor said. "An inflamed appendix can cause pain of the highest magnitude. The average person would be unable to ignore that sort of pain and unable to function in the face of it."

"But suppose our hypothetical young man has extraordinary willpower," Harrington said. "Or assume that he was unable to seek medical attention in a timely manner, for whatever reason."

"Then," Dr. Hale said, "we would be looking at an entirely different scenario. The patient's appendix might perforate, or rupture. There could be all sorts of complications. Intraperitoneal abscess, pylephlebitis, wound infection, diffuse peritonitis, and possibly, but not likely—appendiceal fistula. Some of these conditions are potentially lethal."

"And how long would treatment typically take, in such a case?"

"Perhaps three weeks," the doctor said. "Even longer if there are surgical complications as well."

Harrington smiled, although no one was around to see it. "Thank you very much, Dr. Hale. You have been *extremely* helpful."

He broke the connecton, waited for about three seconds, and then dialed the number for the Operations Directorate.

It was answered on the first ring. "This is Keating."

Harrington cleared his throat. "Yes, George, Andrew Harrington here. I know where to find Isma'il Hamid."

"Where?"

"In the hospital, recovering from his appendicitis."

"Andrew, my friend, you are looking down a blind alley," Keating said. "The recovery time for an appendectomy is only two or three days. Hamid would have been treated on Sunday the sixth. He would have been released by Tuesday at the latest. No one even knew to look for him until Wednesday. He was well and truly gone by then."

"I thought so too," Harrington said. "And apparently, so did everyone else, since the American police reports don't mention a follow-up with the hospital that treated Hamid's appendicitis."

"You can't blame anyone for that," Keating said. "With a few thousand leads to track down, that would have been at the bottom of my priority list too."

"Have another look at the transcript of the interview with the shift supervisor at WizardClean," Harrington said. "Mr. Hamid tried to ignore the pain and complete his shift. The supervisor attributed Hamid's tenacity to cultural machismo, but he was wrong. Hamid expected to be dead in a few hours from exposure to the T2 mycotoxin. And, after all, what are a few hours of agony when one is about to sit at the right hand of Allah?"

"All right," Keating said. "Hamid tried to tough his way through. But his body was obviously weaker than his spirit, because he collapsed. What does that tell us that we didn't know before?"

"Perhaps nothing," Harrington said. "But how long did Hamid suffer before he collapsed? How long did he manage to hide his pain before it got the better of him?"

"I have no idea," Keating said. "Does it matter?"

"It may. I believe that Mr. Hamid may have held out long enough for his appendix to burst. And the recovery period for *that* is not two or three *days*, but *three weeks* or more. If I'm right, Hamid is flat on his back in a hospital bed somewhere. It shouldn't be terribly difficult to find out which bed and which hospital."

"I understand," Keating said. "I'm on it."

CHAPTER 28

TORPEDO: THE HISTORY AND EVOLUTION OF A KILLING MACHINE

(Excerpted from an unpublished manuscript [pages 121–122] and reprinted by permission of the author, Retired Master Chief Sonar Technician David M. Hardy, USN)

On December 7, 1941, six aircraft carriers of the Japanese Imperial Navy launched nearly 400 aircraft in a sneak-attack bombing raid against the U.S. Pacific Fleet based in Pearl Harbor, Hawaii. Twelve American warships were sunk or beached, including every battleship in the Pacific Fleet. Another nine ships were heavily damaged. Over twenty-four hundred Americans were killed. A significant portion of the damage can be attributed to conventional aerial bombs, but the real killer of the day was the air-launched torpedo. Carried beneath the fuselages of *Kate* bombers, the Japanese torpedoes cut through the shallow waters of the harbor like knives, leaving swaths of fire and death in their wakes. America was at war again, and again it had begun with torpedoes.

* * *

Twenty-three years later, in the Tonkin Gulf, off the coast of Vietnam, the American naval destroyer USS *Maddox* was attacked by three North Vietnamese patrol boats. The high-speed attack boats fired at least four torpedoes at the American ship, as well as several rounds from their 14.5mm deck guns. The torpedoes all missed, and USS *Maddox* returned fire with her own guns. Two days later, North Vietnamese patrol boats conducted torpedo attacks on another American naval destroyer, USS *Turner Joy*. As in the attack on USS *Maddox*, the *Turner Joy* came away from the engagement without serious damage. President Lyndon B. Johnson saw the attacks as justification for increasing U.S. military presence in Vietnam. The ensuing escalation ultimately led to what we now know as the Vietnam War.

Critics of Johnson (and the war) accused the president of stretching the incident out of proportion and (essentially) fabricating an excuse to go to war with the North Vietnamese. The arguments over the war and President Johnson's role in escalating it continue to this day, but two facts remain undisputed: America was at war again, and it had begun (again) with torpedoes.

CHAPTER 29

SOUTHERN ARABIAN GULF
(STEAMING TOWARD THE STRAITS OF HORMUZ)
FRIDAY; 18 MAY
1330 hours (1:30 PM)
TIME ZONE +4 'DELTA'

Chief McPherson adjusted the four-point harness that held her in the flight seat and leaned forward far enough to see over the shoulders of the pilot and copilot. The green flight suit she wore over her khakis tugged uncomfortably at her collarbone as she craned her neck to look through the helicopter's windshield. The helo was new, less than a year into its service life, but the Plexiglas windshield was already beginning to take on a vaguely frosted look—the inevitable product of a thousand tiny scratches born of countless collisions with the desert sand that always seemed to ride the back of the hot Middle Eastern wind.

The chief scanned the wave tops as they slid by a thousand feet below. Their destination, USS *Antietam*, was down there somewhere—supposedly close now, but she couldn't see the ship yet.

She stole a glance to her right, where Capt. Bowie sat belted into his own flight seat. He seemed lost in thought, but—from the way the muscles in his neck were bunching up—they weren't pleasant thoughts.

Up in the cockpit, the pilot keyed his mike. "*Antietam*, this is *Firewalker Two-Six*. I am on final approach. Request your numbers, over."

The reply came back a second later. "*Firewalker Two-Six*, this is *Antietam*. My numbers are as follows … Winds are thirty degrees off my port bow at twenty-seven knots. Pitch is one degree. Roll is one degree. My SPY radar is silent aft. All HF antennas within thirty degrees of your approach vector are silent, over."

The pilot nodded and looked over his shoulder. "Captain, everything is looking good. We're going to head for the barn."

Capt. Bowie nodded. "Understood."

The pilot keyed the mike again. "*Antietam*, this is *Firewalker Two-Six*. Copy all. Your numbers look good. Request green deck, over."

"We're going the wrong way," Capt. Bowie said. He spoke softly, and it was difficult to hear him over the wail of the twin turbine engines and the syncopated thump of the helo's rotors.

Chief McPherson leaned closer to him. "Sir?"

The captain looked up. "Just thinking aloud," he said. He jerked a thumb over his left shoulder toward the tail of the helo—toward the southern end of the Arabian Gulf. "My ship is back *that* way, steaming toward the bad guys at top speed." He pointed in the direction of the helo's nose. "Meanwhile, I'm flying *this* way—away from my ship and away from the threat—so that we can go drink coffee and make polite conversation with the man who's about to snatch the rug out from under us."

The chief thought for a few seconds and said, "We don't know that, sir. Captain Whiley may be planning to leave you in command of the SAU. That's certainly the smart thing to do."

"He's going to take command," Capt. Bowie said. "That's why we're being summoned to *his* ship. He wants to do this on *his* turf, where *he* is the captain, and I'm just a visiting commander."

That, Chief McPherson knew, was likely to be true. According to naval custom, there could only be one captain aboard any warship, and that was the commanding officer. The instant Capt. Bowie's foot touched the deck of *Antietam*, he would revert to his actual rank of commander and remain as such until he departed the ship.

Capt. Bowie cocked one eyebrow. "Of course, if I were in a position to do the same thing to *him*, this is probably how I would do it. It's actually a half-decent piece of political maneuvering, even if it does piss me off."

Chief McPherson nodded once and turned back to look through the windshield again. After a few seconds, she spotted the *Antietam*, still steaming south toward her rendezvous with the other ships in the Search Attack Unit. From a thousand feet up, the aging Aegis guided missile cruiser looked like a bathtub toy—a trick of perspective that would soon change, the chief knew. In fact, at 566 feet, the cruiser was 37 feet longer than the *Towers*.

Approaching from the cruiser's bow, the pilot flew down the ship's starboard side and made a tight buttonhook turn to the right, lining up with the flight deck and shedding unneeded altitude with the same neat maneuver. The toy-sized ship began to grow rapidly in the helicopter's windshield.

The voice of *Antietam*'s radio talker came over the speaker. "*Firewalker Two-Six*, this is *Antietam*. My deck is green, over."

The pilot keyed his mike. "*Antietam*, this is *Firewalker Two-Six*. Copy your green deck. I am making my approach, over."

* * *

Less than a minute later, the helo touched down on the ship's gently rolling deck with a thump that was barely audible over the din of the rotors. It was as smooth a landing as the chief had ever seen. Of course, it should have been; the seas were calm, and the relative winds across the deck were nearly ideal. But not all shipboard landings were so easy. Navy pilots and flight deck crews were trained to make landings under unbelievable conditions, on heavy seas, in low visibility, with the ship bucking and rolling, the winds shifting freakishly, and maybe an engine failure thrown in for good measure.

A few seconds after they were down, a young enlisted man wearing a purple flight deck jersey and a cranial-style flight deck helmet opened the door from the outside. The roar of the helo's rotors grew instantly louder. The Sailor threw Commander Bowie a quick salute and shouted, "Welcome aboard, Commander. Can you please follow me, sir?"

Cmdr. Bowie gave the man a thumbs-up and reached to unbuckle his safety harness. Being senior, the commander was first out, followed a few seconds later by the chief. They followed the purple-jerseyed Sailor across the flight deck at a quick trot, heads ducked to avoid the helicopter's thundering rotor blades.

The Sailor led them to a watertight door, which he opened for them. They stepped through, and the Sailor stepped in after them and dogged it closed. The noise level dropped dramatically.

"Welcome aboard, sir," the Sailor said again—at a more reasonable volume this time. "The captain is waiting for you in the wardroom. If you'll follow me, please."

Cmdr. Bowie nodded. "Thank you, son."

The Sailor led them through a series of passageways and up several ladders to officers' country. When he came to the door of the wardroom, he knocked, opened the door, and held it for them, but he didn't enter.

They stepped past him into the wardroom. It was even fancier than the wardroom aboard *Towers*, one of the perks—no doubt—of having a senior full-bird captain as commanding officer.

Captain Stuart Whiley stood when they entered the room and beckoned them further into his inner sanctum. He was a short, wiry man in his late forties. His crisply starched khakis were impeccably tailored, and his brush-cut hair was a shade of black so improbably deep that it was almost certainly colored. His movements were quick and adroit. He smiled, showing a mouth full of very white teeth, and extended a hand. "Welcome aboard, Commander."

Cmdr. Bowie gripped the offered hand and shook it. "Thank you, Captain. You've got yourself a fine-looking ship here."

Capt. Whiley nodded and released the commander's hand. "Kind words coming from the man who drives the most advanced ship the Navy has to offer."

He made introductions around the table. "This is my XO, Commander Don Palmer." A tall, blond man stood up and offered his hand. "And this is Commander Rachel Vargas, CO of the *Benfold*." A trim woman with copper skin and deeply chiseled cheekbones stood up and shook Cmdr. Bowie's hand. She smiled. "Commander Bowie and I are old steaming buddies. I've been keeping him out of trouble for years." She looked him in the eye. "Good to see you, Jim."

The last person at the table was a stocky redheaded man. He stood up and stretched out his hand. "This is the CO of *Ingraham*, Commander Mike Culkins."

Cmdr. Bowie shook his hand. "Mike and I know each other too. We did our first Divo tours together on the *Bunker Hill*. I coached Mike on ship handling, and he taught me how to drink too much without falling down."

Cmdr. Culkins grinned. "A skill that remains useful through the years."

"Well," Capt. Whiley said, "looks like this is old-home week for you three." His smile was theatrical, and it didn't fool anyone.

His eyes lit on the chief, as though noticing her for the first time. He paused for a second. "Perhaps your chief will be more comfortable down in the CPO Mess."

Cmdr. Bowie looked at his chief. "Will we be starting immediately?"

The captain nodded. "We're ready to begin now, unless you'd rather change out of your flight suit first."

Cmdr. Bowie shook his head. "I'm fine, sir. Ready to start when you are."

"Good," Capt. Whiley said. He motioned to the table, which was laid out with trays of deli-style sandwiches. "I thought we'd have sandwiches and coffee while we work." He smiled again. "Sort of a power lunch."

"Looks great, sir," Cmdr. Bowie said. "But if we're going to get started right away, I'd prefer that Chief McPherson stay up here. With your permission, of course. I brought her along because she's been chasing submarines for the better part of twenty years. I know that I wouldn't want to plan a sub hunt without her input."

Capt. Whiley's smile narrowed perhaps a millimeter. "Fine," he said with a quick nod. His tone of voice said that it was anything *but* fine. "We'd be foolish to ignore that sort of expertise." He looked at the chief. "Make yourself at home, Chief. Welcome to *Antietam*'s wardroom." His eyes carried not the barest glimmer of the welcome that he'd just offered her.

Chief McPherson took the nearest seat. "Thank you, sir. I hope I contribute something worthwhile."

"I'm certain that you will," the captain said. "Chief petty officers are the backbone of the Navy. I've always said that, and I've always believed it. They're the subject matter experts."

"Thank you, sir," the chief said. She noticed that Capt. Whiley was making no move to summon his own Chief Sonar Technician.

Cmdr. Bowie found a chair, and as soon as he was seated, Capt. Whiley walked to the far end of the room. A projection screen hung from the ceiling. He pulled a pen-shaped laser pointer from his shirt pocket and picked up a small remote control unit from the corner of the table. He pressed a button on the remote, and the lights dimmed. He pressed another button, and a ceiling-mounted projector flared to life. A map of the Middle East appeared, extending from the northern tip of the Arabian Gulf—at the top left-hand corner of the screen, to the Gulf of Oman and Northern Arabian Sea—near the lower right corner of the screen. "Ladies and gentlemen," he said, "this is our playground."

The map, and the images that followed, were crisp, brightly colored, and had a professional edge to them. It rapidly became obvious that the briefing material had been prepared by someone who knew what they were doing, undoubtedly using slick commercial software. And Capt. Whiley had studied his material well. He used the laser pointer to great advantage as he worked his way through screen after screen of images and charts.

Chief McPherson put down the sandwich she had been nibbling on and watched the captain's presentation with a growing sense of alarm. First off, this was not a tactical planning meeting; it was a dog and pony show. It was becoming increasingly apparent that Whiley had not invited them here to brainstorm tactics and search plans. He'd brought them here to wow them with his plan—one that he'd already formulated—meaning that it probably wasn't up for debate. Taken by itself, that was bad enough, but it wasn't the worst of it. Whiley's planning was straight out of the textbook.

The chief shifted uncomfortably in her seat. There were three commanding officers in the room, besides Whiley himself. Surely they wouldn't leave it up to her to say something. She was the only non-commissioned officer present, and Whiley had already made it perfectly clear that she was less than the dust beneath his chariot wheels. If she opened her mouth, he would stick his foot down her throat. And pissing off a full-bird captain would not be a good way to start her afternoon.

She was about to take her chances and say something anyway, when Cmdr. Bowie spoke up. He cleared his throat. "Ah, Captain? If I may?"

Whiley continued for a few seconds before the interruption filtered through to his brain. He stopped in mid-sentence and stared at Cmdr. Bowie. "Can I do something for you, Commander?"

Cmdr. Bowie cleared his throat again. "Yes, sir. I can't help noticing that your search and attack plans follow Navy doctrine pretty closely."

Whiley smiled. "Thank you for noticing that, Commander. I pride myself on keeping abreast of the latest tactics. Train like you fight, and fight like you train. Anything else will get your ass shot off."

"Yes, sir," Cmdr. Bowie said. "Ordinarily, I would agree with you one hundred percent. But we're dealing with an unusual case here, Captain. We're taking on submarine crews that are trained in NATO tactical procedures. If we try to use NATO strategies against them, we're going to get our heads handed to us."

Capt. Whiley's cheeks reddened visibly, even in the semidarkness. He opened his mouth to speak, but Cmdr. Vargas, commanding officer of the *Benfold*, jumped in. "With all due respect, Captain, I have to agree with Commander Bowie. So far, every ship that has tangled with these guys has followed standard doctrine, and all they've got to show for it is a string of downed aircraft, dead Sailors, and broken ships. We're the last line of defense here, sir. We can't afford to make the same mistakes they did."

Capt. Whiley pressed a button on the remote, and the lights snapped on without warning, half-blinding everyone in the room. "Are you two seriously suggesting that we flush years of battle-tested doctrine down the toilet and start over from ground zero?"

Cmdr. Culkins piped up. "We wouldn't exactly be starting from ground zero, sir. Commander Bowie and his USW team have already cranked out some preliminary tactics. Commander Vargas and I have been helping them plug the leaks, and I must say they look pretty sound to me."

Capt. Whiley's eyes narrowed. "Do they now? And I assume you've worked out some method of *testing* these new tactics *before* you encounter the enemy? An enemy, I might add, that has already sent one ship to the bottom and put two others in dry dock."

Cmdr. Bowie shook his head. "No, Captain. There isn't time to test them, but I still think it would be safer to avoid …"

Capt. Whiley's voice rose. "Did I hear you right, Commander? Did you actually say '*safer*'? How can it possibly be *safe* to chuck everything we've learned about USW in the trash can and substitute a bunch of untried theories? Good god, man, these new tactics you're trying to shove on me haven't even been tested in *simulations*, have they?"

"No, sir."

Cmdr. Palmer, Capt. Whiley's executive officer opened his mouth to say something and then snapped it shut. He obviously had an opinion on one side or the other, but it looked as though he had decided that it was safer to keep it to himself.

"So, in a nutshell," Capt. Whiley said, "you have no idea whether or not your ideas are tactically sound." He looked around the room, the scorn on his face as evident as it was in his voice. "Am I really the only person who's bothered by this little technicality? Safety comes from doing what works. Well, we know what works, and we are damned well going to do it. I am NOT going to jeopardize four United States Navy warships, *and* their crews, so that you can try to armchair quarterback your way through an engagement with proven hostile forces! You can forget that business, right now, mister. You can *all* forget it!"

Chief McPherson got to her feet. Every eye in the room snapped to her. "Captain? Request permission to speak, sir."

Breathing heavily, Capt. Whiley stared at her for a few seconds. "What is it?"

Chief McPherson swallowed and tried with limited success to still the trembling in her knees. "May I show you something, sir? It will illustrate an important point that needs to be taken into consideration, no matter whose search plans get used."

"Very well," Whiley snapped. "But make it fast. We don't have time for much more of this nonsense; those submarines are getting closer every second."

The chief nodded. "I understand that, sir. In fact, what I have to say hinges on that very thought." She reached across the table toward the captain. "May I borrow your laser pointer, sir?"

Capt. Whiley glared at her, and for a half-second he seemed to consider refusing to give her the pointer. But apparently he couldn't think of an even remotely viable reason for refusing such a simple request, so he dropped the pointer into her outstretched palm.

"Thank you, sir." The chief flicked the power button on the pointer and directed the beam toward the all-but-forgotten video screen. The computerized projection was nearly washed out by the fluorescent overhead lights, but enough of a ghost image was visible to make out the Straits of Hormuz and the neat black arcs and lines that represented Capt. Whiley's assessment of the tactical situation.

In the lighted room, the dot of the laser pointer appeared more pink than red. Chief McPherson maneuvered the pink dot back and forth in a semicircle, tracing and retracing a curved black line on the captain's programmed projection.

"As I understand it, sir, this is the farthest-on circle for time fourteen hundred local. Is that correct, sir?"

"Yes," Capt. Whiley said. "Yes, it is."

"And you computed it using the formula for diesel submarines found in standing Navy USW doctrine?"

"Of course I did."

The chief swallowed again. "Sir, with all due respect, it's not only wrong, it's not even in the ballpark."

The captain grabbed a stack of hardcopy printouts of radio messages lying on the table and began to rifle through it. "You sound pretty sure of yourself, Chief. Am I to assume that you have better access to satellite intelligence data than I do? I assure you that my data is up to the minute!"

"I'm certain that it is, sir. But you've calculated the rate of travel for the subs at fifteen knots for the first hour and five knots for every hour after that."

The captain nodded. "In accordance with tactical doctrine, Chief. Now, will you please make your point?"

"Captain, those speed figures are based on the fact that a normal diesel submarine operating on batteries can only sprint for about an hour before its batteries begin to go flat. After that, it has to slow down drastically, or it won't have enough battery power to run even basic systems."

The captain crossed his arms. "I know this, Chief. In fact, I'd venture to say that every person in this room knows it. That's just about the first thing the Navy teaches you in Surface Warfare Officer school. But I'm sure we all appreciate the refresher training." He reached for his pointer. "Can we continue, now?"

The chief took a breath. "Captain, that theory doesn't apply to the Type 212 diesel submarine. The 212s are equipped with an air-independent propulsion system. Basically, they're a modified version of the hydrogen fuel cells used on the space shuttle. They can produce about 300 kilowatts of power for … well, never mind that. The point is, sir, the 212Bs can do nineteen or twenty knots submerged for days at a time." She directed the laser pointer back toward the screen and drew a huge curve, far outside the captain's neat black arc. "If we recalculate the farthest-on circle for a continuous speed of twenty knots, it will fall way out here somewhere." She flicked the laser pointer off and handed it to the captain. "Sir, those submarines are already outside of your containment area. If we go looking where doctrine tells us to, we're going to be searching where those subs have already been. We *can't* follow doctrine, Captain. If we try, we've already lost the battle."

Capt. Whiley stood without speaking, and for nearly a minute the room was silent. Then Whiley's eyes focused on Chief McPherson, and he nodded. "Thank you for pointing out the error in my calculations, Chief. We will, naturally, recompute the farthest-on circles using speeds appropriate for the 212 diesel submarine."

Cmdr. Bowie said, "Captain, with regard to the rest of the standing doctrine …"

"With regard to the rest of standing doctrine, there will be no change."

"But sir …"

"But nothing, Commander. A single miscalculation is hardly sufficient cause to dump the entire body of our Navy's accumulated knowledge of Undersea Warfare."

"Sir," Cmdr. Culkins said, "the Germans will be able to predict our every move."

"So what?" Whiley snapped. "Every baseball team in America plays by the same set of rules, from the same book. No secret strategies. No tricky little surprises. But somebody loses and somebody wins, every single time. Same rules. Same bases. Same ball. Because one team is faster, and better trained, and better coached, and—most important—they want it more." He glared at everyone in the room. "*That* is how we will win this fight. We will follow *proven* doctrine, and we will be smarter, faster, and deadlier than those goddamned submarines. Those are my orders, and they are not subject to negotiation." He slammed the laser pointer down on the tabletop. "Any questions?"

He obviously didn't expect any questions, but Cmdr. Culkins raised his hand. "What kind of backup can we expect on this mission, sir?"

"Backup?"

"Yes, sir. Can we get P-3 assets? How about a friendly sub to run interference?"

Capt. Whiley shook his head. "There will be no backup. We have been ordered to complete this mission utilizing only assets organic to our four ships. No P-3s, no friendly submarines, no cavalry. We're on our own, here."

Cmdr. Bowie frowned. "Can we go back to Fifth Fleet and ask them to rethink this one? USS *Topeka* is not that far away, and I'm sure USNAVCENT can whistle up a couple of P-3s, sir."

Capt. Whiley leaned over the table. "Admiral Rogers assures me that my orders come from the president himself, through the Chief of Naval Operations. I intend to follow those orders to the letter. And *that* means that every one of *you* will follow *my* orders without question, and absolutely without fail. Am I making myself clear here?"

He waited several seconds. "Good. You are dismissed. Return to your ships and make ready for combat!"

As they filed out of the wardroom, Chief McPherson leaned near her skipper and whispered, "We're all going to die, sir."

CHAPTER 30

WHITE HOUSE PRESS ROOM
WASHINGTON, DC
FRIDAY; 18 MAY
3:30 PM EDT

White House Press Secretary Lauren Hart stood at the podium and leaned close to the bank of microphones. "Ladies and gentlemen," she said, "the President of the United States."

The men and women of the news media came to their feet as President Chandler strode into the room. The usual smattering of polite applause died away when he reached the podium.

White House Chief of Staff Veronica Doyle watched from just inside the door.

Camera flashes began popping at irregular intervals. The president looked out over the assembled press corps and marshaled his thoughts. "Good afternoon," he said finally. "As most of you are no doubt aware, five days ago, a squadron of German war planes engaged in an extended sea battle with two warships of the British Royal Navy. One of the British ships, HMS *York,* was sunk as a result, and the other ship, HMS *Chatham,* was severely damaged. Four German aircraft were destroyed. Over two hundred British Sailors were killed, as well as the pilots of the downed German planes.

"Last night, shortly before midnight eastern daylight time, two squadrons of British Sea Harriers conducted coordinated missile strikes on a German warship in the North Sea, apparently in retaliation for the earlier attacks on *York* and *Chatham.* The German guided missile frigate FGS *Sachsen* sustained major damage. Eighty-six German Sailors were killed along with one British pilot, who failed to eject when his aircraft was destroyed.

"There has been a great deal of speculation in the media as to who fired the first shot, and—more to the point—what led the German and British navies into conflict to begin with.

"I'm afraid that I can't shed much light on the first question. Analysts from the Pentagon and the Naval War College have been over the available data in detail, and they are no closer to knowing who pulled the trigger first. And, since both countries have denied initiating the hostilities, it seems likely that we will never know who fired first.

"But I *can* answer the second question. HMS *York* and HMS *Chatham* were conducting a naval blockade against four submarines of the German Navy. And they were carrying out that blockade at my request."

The room broke into an uproar of voices as the journalists leapt to their feet and began shouting questions. A male voice cut through it all. "Mr. President, can you tell us about the attack on USS *Kitty Hawk*?"

The president held up a hand and waited for silence. It was several minutes in coming. Only when it became clear that he was not going to say another word until order was restored did the journalists take their seats.

Eventually, the president nodded. "I asked Prime Minister Irons to blockade the Strait of Gibraltar to prevent the passage of the German submarines. I made the decision to do so on the basis of compelling evidence that the government of Germany intends to deliver those submarines, and other high-tech weaponry, to the Middle Eastern nation of Siraj, in clear violation of international law and standing United Nations sanctions."

Once again the press corps erupted into a clamor of confused questions. And, once again, the president held up his hand and waited for silence.

"As I mentioned, we have compelling evidence of Germany's intentions," he said finally, "and we have made arrangements to deliver that evidence to the United Nations Security Council. I am confident that, upon reviewing the evidence, the UN will take appropriate action to prevent the German government from arming a nation known to support terrorists.

"Unfortunately, the wheels of international diplomacy turn slowly. By the time the United Nations can react to this situation, Germany's first shipments of military hardware will have reached their destinations in Siraj." The president paused for a second to let his words sink in.

"Abdul al-Rahiim styles himself as the president of Siraj, but the world knows better. *You* and *I* know better. Abdul al-Rahiim is a dictator and a tyrant. He is a lawless brute who rules by violence and by the *threat* of violence. He has repeatedly demonstrated his willingness to use military force against his neighboring countries and against the very people he claims to govern.

"Until this point, the United Nations has chosen to contain his abuses through restrictive political and economic sanctions, enforced largely by a multinational naval blockade. Though many people—and I include myself on the list—have advocated for more direct action against the government of Abdul al-Rahiim, the UN's sanctions have had significant success in keeping a lid on his oppressive regime.

"But those efforts will all come to nothing if we allow this tyrant to rearm his military. Think of the damage he was able to do with aging ex-Soviet military hardware. And then imagine what he could do with state-of-the-art weaponry. Imagine what the Middle East will look like if Abdul al-Rahiim finds himself in possession of cutting-edge submarines, fighter jets, and missile systems.

"The United States cannot—*will* not—stand by and watch as advanced weapons systems are handed over to Siraj. And so I asked Prime Minister Irons for assistance in blocking the delivery of four technologically advanced submarines. The resulting blockade ended in the attack on HMS *Chatham* and HMS *York*.

"Early this morning, United States Navy warships operating on my orders attempted to intercept the German submarines in the Gulf of Aden, south of the Middle Eastern country of Yemen. A naval battle ensued. An aircraft carrier, USS *Kitty Hawk*, suffered serious battle damage, and two U.S. Navy helicopters were shot down. Twenty-one American Sailors were killed: fifteen aboard the *Kitty Hawk*, plus the air crews of both helicopters.

"I spoke at length with Chancellor Shoernberg on the phone, shortly after we received word of the attack on USS *Kitty Hawk*. He formally declined to apologize for the attacks on our ships or the ships of the Royal Navy. Chancellor Shoernberg also refused to comment on Germany's intentions with regard to Siraj. In the hours since our phone conversation, the chancellor has rejected all attempts to open a diplomatic dialogue."

The president gripped the edges of the podium and stared directly into the television cameras. "I do not wish to believe that a long-trusted ally has turned against the United States, but it is becoming increasingly difficult to view the actions of the German government in a friendly light." His eyes narrowed. "To Chancellor Shoernberg, President Bremen, and the Federal Assembly of the German government, I say this: I have already dispatched ships to intercept and sink the four submarines in question. It is neither my desire nor my intention to threaten a sovereign nation with a long history of peaceful ties to the United States, but we *will not* permit aggression against our citizens or our military forces to go unpunished. We remain open to a diplomatic solution, but we will take whatever steps we deem necessary to prevent the delivery of those submarines to Siraj. Chancellor Shoernberg, turn back those submarines!"

The president turned and walked toward the door. Flashbulbs began popping furiously and an entire choir of reporters began shouting, "Mr. President! Mr. President!"

Press Secretary Hart stepped up to the podium. "The president thanks you all for coming. He regrets that he cannot answer questions at this time."

* * *

"That's not going to hold them for long, sir," Veronica Doyle said as the president passed her on his way out the door.

"I don't expect it to," the president said. "But it should put that son of a bitch Shoernberg in the hot seat for a while."

CHAPTER 31

WASHINGTON, DC
FRIDAY; 18 MAY
4:42 PM EDT

The laminated hospital ID badge hanging from the breast pocket of his lab coat identified him as Dr. Richard Warren. He looked like any one of the fifty young interns and residents who frequented the wards on the third floor of Columbia Memorial. He wore the usual stethoscope draped around his neck, and his face had the slightly harried appearance that seemed to mark most doctors young enough to still be scrambling for a foothold in the world of HMO-driven medicine. But his name was not Richard Warren, and he was not a doctor. And the two men who walked behind him were not hospital orderlies, despite their green scrubs and hospital IDs.

To the casual eye, all three men blended in perfectly with their surroundings. A careful observer might have noticed that the trio moved with the animal grace of athletes, or that their eyes swept the hallway with the mechanical precision of radar scanners. But—thanks to the closure of DC General, the patient load at Columbia Memorial was nearly forty percent over rated capacity, and the third-floor staff had its hands full just staying on top of emergencies.

The man who was not Dr. Warren stopped at the nurse's station and flipped through the rack of stainless steel clipboards until he found the chart for Room 31, Bed 4. The floor nurse glanced up from her own paperwork just long enough to register his lab coat and ID. He nodded without speaking, and she returned to her work.

The patient's name was Isma'il Hamid. His diagnosis was listed as diffuse peritonitis and inflammatory bowel obstruction, secondary to perforated appendicitis. He was on a regimen of high-dose antibiotics and, according to his chart, was responding well to treatment.

The counterfeit doctor closed the chart and returned it to the rack. His pair of bogus orderlies followed him down the hall toward Room 31.

* * *

About twenty minutes later, the orderly delivering dinner to Room 31 discovered that Bed 4 was empty. Isma'il Hamid was gone.

CHAPTER 32

U.S. Department of State

Executive Summary on Siraj

Section VII Impact of Sanctions [Synopsis and Recommendation(s)]

1. Synopsis:

A. In last week's statement to the United Nations Security Council, Siraji President Abdul al-Rahiim accused the UN of playing politics with hunger. "My people are starving," he said. "The sanctions against my country are squeezing the life out of my citizens. You sit in judgment over what you refer to as my *excesses*, and yet you ignore the fact that it is *your resolution* and *your sanctions* that condemn the Siraji people to slow death."

When reminded that food, medicine, and humanitarian supplies are exempted from standing UN sanctions, Abdul al-Rahiim had no comment.

(See Appendix-B, Tab-C for a full transcript of President Abdul al-Rahiim's remarks.)

B. Even as Abdul al-Rahiim claims that his people are suffering, he persists in obstructing humanitarian supplies intended for the citizens of Siraj. Despite Abdul al-Rahiim's protests, his regime continues to export food in exchange for hard currency. In many cases, the exported foodstuffs are diverted directly from humanitarian shipments. Less than a week ago, ships charged with enforcing the UN blockade against Siraj seized the container ship MV *City of Light* outbound from the Siraji port city of Zubayr. Among the cargo were 1,500 metric tons of rice and over 1,200 tons of powdered baby formula, baby bottles, and other nursing supplies. The seized materials were all earmarked for resale overseas, and all items could be traced back (by lot and batch numbers) to supplies delivered to Siraj in humanitarian shipments. Kuwaiti authorities continue to report seizures of supply trucks traveling overland out of Siraj. In most cases, the supplies in question can be traced directly back to shipments of humanitarian goods.

C. Not since Saddam Hussein have we seen a Middle Eastern leader whose motives are so unambiguously mercenary. Abdul al-Rahiim has built twenty-one palaces for himself since the UN blockade against his country was imposed. He continues to use all resources at his disposal to rearm the Siraji military and to finance his opulent lifestyle. His priorities are clear, and they do not include the welfare of the Siraji people.

2. Recommendation(s):

A. It is overtly obvious that relaxing or lifting the sanctions against Siraj will bring no relief to the inhabitants of the country. Such a move will only offer an already dangerous man increased leverage for destabilizing this politically fragile region. State recommends no change in U.S. position regarding the standing UN sanctions against Siraj.

AIR FORCE ONE
FRIDAY; 18 MAY
7:03 PM EDT

President Chandler dropped the state department summary on the briefing table and settled into his plush, gray-leather swivel chair. Except for the seat belts and the obvious fact that ordinary office furniture was rarely bolted to the floor, the chair would have looked at home in any high-powered corporate boardroom.

At its cruising altitude of thirty-six thousand feet, the huge Boeing 747-200B was slicing easily through the bright morning sky. So far, the flight had been free of turbulence. Even so, the president fastened his seat belt almost immediately after sitting down. He would have preferred to leave the seat belt off, but safety protocols dictated otherwise. There were people in the world who would attack the presidential jet if given the chance, and the pilots might be forced to take evasive maneuvers with little or no warning.

As long as the captain of the aircraft kept the "Fasten Seat Belts" light turned off, anyone else on the plane was free to sit without buckling in. This was a minor source of irritation to Frank, but as one of the pilots had once pointed out, the president's safety was a matter of immediate national security. The lives of the president's staff and the press corps, as valuable as they were, could not be considered a national security issue.

Of course, the president could have ignored the safety guidelines. Many presidents had. But there were too many people who spent their lives trying to protect him—too many whose jobs and training would require them to sacrifice their own lives in order to save his. He owed it to them to do what he could to protect himself. And that meant, among other things, fastening his seat belt even when he didn't feel like it.

He gave the belt an extra tug. It was a nice seat belt, as seat belts went. Like every one on the plane, the buckle was embossed with the presidential seal.

Satisfied that he had done his tiny part to comply with the safety protocols, the president looked up at the small group of people on the opposite side of the briefing table.

National Security Advisor Gregory Brenthoven sat directly across from him, flanked on the left by White House Chief of Staff Veronica Doyle, and on the right by Undersecretary of State Lawrence Mitchell.

The president leaned forward and rested his arms on the briefing table. "Let's start with China."

Brenthoven glanced at his notebook. "Both sides have stepped up their military air presence over the Taiwan Strait, sir. About three o'clock this morning local time, a pair of Taiwanese Mirage 2000s made simulated attack passes on three Chinese J-10s. Nobody actually launched, and none of the aircraft crossed the invisible line down the middle of the strait, but they traded lock-ons with their fire control radars and generally crowded the hell out of each other."

"Playing chicken?"

"That's all it is so far, Mr. President," Brenthoven said. "But both sides are flying about three times as many sorties as usual, and they all appear to be carrying full wartime weapon load-outs. Having that much military hardware flying around creates a lot of opportunities for mistakes. This could turn into a shoot-out in about a split-second."

The president looked at Undersecretary Mitchell. "Larry, your boss has been back and forth between Taipei and Beijing about a dozen times recently. What does the water feel like over there? Is this whole thing just posturing? Or do you think they could be gearing up for a fight?"

"The diplomatic rhetoric is hard-line as hell on both sides of the strait, Mr. President. China is about a half-inch from threatening outright war if Taipei continues to move toward a formal referendum on independence. And the new Taiwanese government is openly referring to this latest Chinese ballistic missile test as *nuclear blackmail.* The Taiwanese army is repositioning land-based missile launchers and recalling reserve personnel for combat training. And China is mobilizing army units for their largest military exercise in ten years. The Chinese government says that the timing is a coincidence, but nobody's buying that."

The president nodded. "What about the naval side of things?"

"We're keeping a close eye on the infrared picture for both navies," Brenthoven said. "Our satellites can detect the heat plumes when their ships light off their engines. So far, the deployed force levels for both navies look pretty much status quo. No sign that anyone is rushing to put more ships to sea, but that could change pretty quickly."

"How quickly?" the president asked.

"It would take either side about two hours to put a significant patrol force to sea," Brenthoven said. "And about twelve hours to scramble most of their frigates, destroyers, and submarines. The newer gas turbine ships can get under way in about an hour, but the older steam-powered ships will require the better part of a day to light off their engineering plants, heat up their boilers, and get up a head of steam."

"How many ships are we talking about?"

Brenthoven scanned his notes again. "China has what the CNO likes to call a 'frigate navy,' sir. Their order of battle includes about four hundred patrol boats, missile boats, and torpedo boats, but they have fewer than fifty major combatant ships. Taiwan is severely outnumbered with regards to patrol, missile, and torpedo boats but has roughly the same number of major combatants as China. However, from a qualitative standpoint, Taiwan's ships are a lot more modern and generally a lot more mission capable. If it comes down to a gunfight, they're pretty evenly matched. Taiwan has the edge in shore-launched anti-ship missiles, though. And that could well tip the balance in a major naval engagement. The Chinese military has concentrated more on ballistic and surface-to-surface missiles than on anti-ship missiles. That's going to cost them if they try an amphibious invasion of Taiwan."

"An amphibious invasion?" UnderSecretary Mitchell asked. "I didn't think China had enough amphibious transport ships to do the job."

"They don't, Mr. Secretary," Brenthoven said. "According to our latest assessments, China can only move about one division at a time, and that's not enough to seize and maintain a decent foothold if the Taiwanese resistance is even half as good as we think it would be."

Doyle nodded. "At least we don't have to worry about the Chinese mounting an invasion."

"That's not necessarily true," the national security advisor said.

The president stared at him. "Make up your mind, Greg. The Chinese either *have* the amphibious capacity to mount an invasion, or they *don't*. Which is it?"

"They ... *might*, sir," Brenthoven said. "If you count strictly military assets, they certainly don't. But a few years ago, the RAND Institute's National Security Research Division published a report on the military aspects of a China-Taiwan confrontation. The report referred to something called a *reverse Dunkirk* tactic. The short of it is, China has a large number of commercial vessels that could be pressed into service as troop ferries, along with a few thousand smaller civilian craft, all of which could be used to transport small numbers of troops."

"Will it work?" the president asked.

"About half of the military experts say no, and the other half say yes, sir. A lot of it depends on Taiwan's anti-ship missiles, and on whether or not Taiwan can gain air superiority over the strait."

"So it still comes down to a coin toss," Doyle said.

Brenthoven nodded. "Pretty much. But if that coin gets tossed, a lot of people will die, no matter which way it falls."

The president exhaled through his teeth. "What can we do to prevent that coin from being tossed?"

"We're already doing it, sir. Our carrier-based F-18Es are flying regular sorties over the straits too. They're sticking to the neutral zone between Taiwanese and Chinese airspace, but their presence is sending a pretty strong signal. The Chinese know that Taiwan will gain air superiority over the strait if we help them. China can't launch an effective invasion if Taiwan owns the sky over the strait."

"Once again we've got our finger stuck in the dike," the president said. "If we pull the carriers out, do you think the Chinese will actually try anything?"

Brenthoven shrugged. "The Pentagon thinks an invasion scenario is possible but extremely unlikely."

"So we can't rule it out," the president said.

"No, sir."

The president sighed. "Okay. We keep working the diplomatic angle, but we leave the carriers in place, for now at least."

He leaned back. "Germany."

Undersecretary Mitchell spoke up. "The diplomatic situation between Germany and Britain is deteriorating rapidly, Mr. President. Chancellor Shoernberg has publicly refused to apologize for the attack on HMS *York* and HMS *Chatham.* He claims that Britain defaulted on all existing treaties and agreements the second the Royal Navy tried to impede the passage of German submarines through international waters. He's calling for a formal apology from Prime Minster Irons, and he's demanding reparations for the aircraft that were destroyed and the pilots who were killed. He's really pitching a fit over the German warship, the *Sachsen.*"

"Reparations? I don't see *that* happening," Doyle said.

"I don't either," Mitchell said. "The average British man on the street has blood in his eye right now. They were already mad as hell over the attack on their embassy. They're ready to hurt somebody, and the shooting match with the Germans has just given them a target for all of that anger. Prime Minister Irons is addressing Parliament this afternoon. The grapevine says she's going to ask for suspension of diplomatic ties with Germany."

The president grimaced. "Not good. When countries stop talking ..."

"They have a tendency to start shooting," the national security advisor finished. "Sad, but true, Mr. President. And from the looks of things, both sides are gearing up for it. Military bases on both sides of the English Channel have been ordered to increased states of readiness, and air activity for both countries has picked up by about fifty percent."

"Is the naval operating tempo increasing as well?"

"Not yet, sir," Brenthoven said. "But that's probably coming."

"What's the latest on the submarines?"

"No word on their current location, sir. Fifth Fleet has assigned four ships to intercept them south of the Strait of Hormuz. I have to tell you, Mr. President, it's going to take a lot of luck to pull this off."

"Unfortunately," Doyle said, "luck has been in rather short supply around here lately."

The president nodded. "Right now, we're looking at about eighteen different ways the world could go to shit."

Undersecretary Mitchell smiled weakly. "Well, at least it can't get any worse."

CHAPTER 33

USS *TOWERS* (DDG-103)
SOUTHERN STRAITS OF HORMUZ
FRIDAY; 18 MAY
2200 hours (10:00 PM)
TIME ZONE +4 'DELTA'

Chief McPherson ran her fingers down the back of one of the Mark-54 torpedoes. She'd been chasing submarines for nineteen and a half years, first as an Ocean Systems Technician Analyst, then as a Sonar Technician, but she had never fired a torpedo.

The weapon's anodized metal skin was smooth and cold, perhaps as cold as the bottom of the sea. As cold as the torn, lifeless bodies of the German Sailors would be.

First would come the fire, the shaped charge blasting through the steel hull, burning everything its white molten plasma jet passed close to. Then the sea would burst in through the broken hull, flooding compartments with the roar of a tidal wave, drowning the few men not already killed by the explosion, or crushing them to a pulp. And then the cold would come, the intense cold of the sea. Quenching the fierce heat of the man-made volcano, leaching the warmth from the still-twitching bodies of the crew, until everything—the twisted steel, the mangled flesh, the terrified screams of dying men—were all the same temperature as the frigid water of the ocean bottom.

*　　*　　*

Behind her, the air drive motor started up with its characteristic hiss. The huge armored door to the torpedo magazine began to swing slowly open.

Chief McPherson looked over her shoulder. Who would be coming into the magazine at this time of night?

She popped to attention as soon as she recognized the figure standing in the widening gap of the doorway. "Good evening, sir."

Capt. Bowie smiled and stepped into the magazine. "Carry on, Chief."

The chief relaxed and turned back toward the rack of stowed torpedoes. She laid her hand on the top weapon again. "I can see their faces, sir."

The captain waited a second before asking, "Whose faces?"

"The faces of the German submarine crews." She took a heavy breath and released it. "I've been chasing subs as long as I can remember, and I've always pictured them as these sort of dark, foreboding shapes, sneaking through the depths, hiding in the shadows." She patted the torpedo twice with the palm of her hand. "I've been training to kill submarines, and talking about killing submarines, and planning the best ways to kill submarines since I was nineteen years old. And now that I'm going to actually do it, I can't picture the submarines at all any more. All I can see are the faces of those German Sailors. Faces of people I've never even met before ... never *will* meet."

The captain nodded slowly. "What do these faces look like?"

Chief McPherson's eyes locked on the captain's for a half-second and then flitted away. "Young, sir. Trained and confident. More than a little scared, but trying like hell to be brave. But young. Too goddamned young to die." She looked up at her captain again. "They look like the faces of *our* crew, sir. And in a few hours, I'm going to have to kill them."

The captain was silent for several seconds, and Chief McPherson began to wonder if she had said too much. "I'm sorry, Captain," she said, finally. "Maybe this is a woman thing. I shouldn't have said anything. I'll do my job when the time comes. I'll be ready, sir."

"I know you will," the captain said. He laid his own hand on the back of a torpedo. "And don't worry. It's not a woman thing. It's a human thing. And believe me, Chief. You are not the only one feeling it."

CHAPTER 34

USS *TOWERS* (DDG-103)
NORTHERN GULF OF OMAN
(SOUTH OF THE STRAITS OF HORMUZ)
SATURDAY; 19 MAY
1830 hours (6:30 PM)
TIME ZONE +4 'DELTA'

In Combat Information Center, Ens. Patrick Cooper stood near the Computerized Dead-Reckoning Tracer and looked down at the digital flat-screen display that covered the unit's entire upper surface. Five feet wide and nearly six feet long, the CDRT display screen was much too large to fit on a regular operator's console. It *had* to be large, because Anti-Submarine Warfare was complex and intricate. Displayed on a normal-sized operator's console, a typical ASW engagement would clutter the screen with so many tracking symbols and trial target geometries that it would quickly become impossible to sort anything out. The large CDRT display allowed the symbols to spread out enough to remain legible.

Cooper shifted his weight from his left leg to his right. The large size of the display had a downside. It was impossible to see the entire screen clearly from a sitting position. To take in the complete display, it was necessary to stand close to the unit and look down, directly into the screen. Consequently, the CDRT was the only watch station in Combat Information Center without a chair for the operator. Cooper had been on watch for less than an hour, and he could already feel his leg muscles beginning to tighten up. The hours of standing made for some long watches.

Ens. Cooper shifted his weight again and scanned the display. Friendly ships appeared on the display as small green circles, each with a single line sticking out from its center, like the stick of a lollipop. The lines were called *speed vectors*. The direction of each vector indicated the course of the ship it represented, and its length indicated the ship's speed through the water. Fast-moving ships had long speed vectors; slower ships had shorter vectors. The circles and lines were called NTDS symbols, short for Naval Tactical Data System. (Although the NTDS system itself had long been superseded by more advanced technology, its easy-to-read catalog of symbols had carried its legacy into the twenty-first century.) The particular NTDS symbol that represented USS *Towers* was marked by a bright green cross that divided the circular part of the symbol into four equal quadrants.

Each symbol on the display was trailed by a small three-character code in capital letters: the tactical call sign for that particular ship. Today, *Towers'* call sign was Y7M, pronounced "Yankee Seven Mike."

To Ens. Cooper, the deployment of ships looked excellent. Spaced at eighty percent of their predicted sonar ranges, *Towers*, *Benfold*, and *Ingraham* formed a moving wall of acoustic sensors. They would sweep west in a locked-step zigzag pattern, searching every inch of water between themselves and the probable position of the enemy subs. In the *"pouncer"* position, *Antietam* would run behind the advancing barrier. When a submarine was detected, *Antietam* would come to flank speed and drive around the end of the formation to engage the unsuspecting sub with Vertical Launch Anti-Submarine Rockets. Then, while the sub was on the run, *Antietam*'s helicopter, *Samurai Seven-Nine*, would swoop down out of the sky like a hawk and drop a torpedo right off the target's bow. Running at high speed to escape the ASROC, the sub should run right into the helo's torpedo before it even had time to react.

It was a good plan, maybe even a *great* plan. Unfortunately, it was right out of the book. Ens. Cooper felt uneasy about his captain's idea of abandoning established doctrine. But the thought of facing an enemy who knows your moves ahead of time had him really scared. No matter how good the Pouncer Plan looked on the color-coded screen of the CDRT, it bordered on suicide.

* * *

A voice broke over the encrypted Navy Red radio circuit. "All units, this is SAU Commander. Execute Passive Search Plan Delta, over."

Ens. Cooper grabbed the red telephone-style handset of the Navy Red terminal and keyed the mike. "SAU Commander, this is *Towers*. Roger. Executing Search Plan Delta, out."

Over the next few seconds, *Ingraham* and *Benfold* both acknowledged the signal.

Now it begins, Ens. Cooper thought. He leaned over the CDRT and waited for the Sonar Supervisor's contact report.

For the next few hours, Cooper was the ship's USWE, or Undersea Warfare Evaluator. It would be his job to coordinate the actions of the *Towers* USW team: cross-referencing contact reports from the ship's sonars, targeting information from the fire control computers, oceanographic data—particularly the thermal structure of the water and the topographic shape of the ocean bottom—predicted acoustic ranges, non-acoustic sensor information, the locations of friendly or neutral ships and aircraft, and an almost overwhelming array of other variables that could affect the tactical situation. And to make matters more interesting, much of the data was based on computer projections, not all of which would be correct. The USWE was expected to take this mishmash of information, swirl it around in his head for a bit, discard some pieces of it, latch on to others, and come up with a mental picture of the tactical situation. Then, if the contact was designated as hostile, the USWE would supervise the programming and launching of USW weapons. If the USWE's tactical picture was accurate enough, those weapons should get close enough to the target submarine for their acoustic seekers to lock on, and (hopefully) destroy the bad guys. Conversely, if the USWE's tactical picture was too far off the mark, the ship's weapons wouldn't be properly placed or programmed, and the submarine would eat their lunch.

Hunting submarines was still more art than science, and the best computers in the world—while they could help him—could not do the job alone. Ens. Cooper smiled nervously to himself. He might not have Chief McPherson's years of experience, but he was good at this part. At least he had been in school. He'd been the best USWE in his class, and his tactical awareness had been excellent. He'd killed the sub in sixty or seventy percent of the tactical simulations the course instructors had thrown at him—a far better record than anyone else in his class.

Of course, this was not a simulation. The enemy subs out there were real, and their weapons were real. If Cooper guessed wrong at a critical juncture, people would die. The wrong people. *His* people.

Which meant that he couldn't let that happen.

* * *

The search continued. Seconds dragged into minutes. Then the minutes began to stack up.

He keyed his mike. "Sonar—USWE, testing Net One One."

The Sonar Supervisor answered instantly. "Read you Lima Charlie, USWE. How me?" (Lima Charlie was net-speak for Loud and Clear.)

Ens. Cooper keyed his mike again. "Read you same, Sonar."

There was nothing wrong with the communication circuit.

He tapped a fingertip on the glass display screen of the CDRT. Why hadn't sonar reported anything yet?

* * *

Ten more minutes passed, and Ens. Cooper keyed his mike again. "Sonar—USWE, report all contacts."

The Sonar Supervisor's reply came a few seconds later. "USWE—Sonar, my tracks are as follows: *Ingraham,* designated Friendly Surface Zero One, bears three-one-five. *Benfold,* designated Friendly Surface Zero Two, bears two-one-seven. *Antietam,* designated Friendly Surface Zero Three, bears zero-niner-four. Sonar holds negative passive or active POSS-SUB contacts at this time."

The ensign chewed on this for a few minutes. Could the subs have slipped by them already? Were the Sonar Technicians searching in the right place? He keyed the mike again. "Ah … Sonar—USWE, your Threat Axis is two-eight-zero. Your Search Sector is two-five-zero to three-one-zero."

The Sonar Supervisor's voice carried a note of annoyance. "Sonar copies, sir. I promise you, if we get anything, you'll be the first to know."

"USWE, aye." Ens. Cooper let his finger off the mike button. He was getting his first glimpse of real Undersea Warfare, and it was a waiting game. Hours, maybe days of searching between contacts, most of which would ultimately turn out to be biologics or distant shipping traffic.

The Tactical Action Officer keyed his mike. "USWE—TAO. Now do you understand why we call it U-S-W?"

"Sir?"

The TAO chuckled. "It stands for Unbelievably … Slooooooow … Warfare …"

Ens. Cooper smiled wanly. "USWE, aye."

"Roger *that,*" the Sonar Supervisor said over the net. "Do you know the definition of USW, sir?"

Cooper said, "I know the definition that's in the book, Sonar. What's your version?"

"Six months of boredom, followed by thirty seconds of sheer terror."

Although no one could see him, Ens. Cooper nodded. "Point taken, gentlemen. I'll try to be patient. But if you get *anything* … "

"You have my word, sir," the Sonar Supervisor said. "We won't keep it a secret."

* * *

Three hours and about six cups of coffee later, Chief McPherson showed up to relieve the watch. The hours of uneventful searching had dulled Ens. Cooper's enthusiasm a bit, and the idea of hitting his rack was starting to sound pretty attractive.

The chief yawned and took a sip from her own coffee. "What have you got, sir?"

The ensign echoed her yawn. "Not a hell of a lot, Chief. We're about two and a half hours into Passive Search Plan Delta. No luck so far." He looked up at the clock. "We don't roll over to a new Zulu-day until after your watch, so you don't need to worry about updating call signs or loading new-day crypto."

He yawned again and was about to start a rundown of all surface contacts being tracked by radar and sonar, when the Sonar Supervisor's voice came over the net. "USWE—Sonar, request clear-or-foul, bearing three-zero-seven."

Cooper slapped his palm on the CDRT's trackball and slewed the cursor over to three-zero-seven. His heart skipped a beat. There were no surface symbols on the plot anywhere near that bearing; the SPY-1 radar had no contacts. But it might still be a small craft. Sometimes wooden boats, especially those with low profiles, didn't show up very well. He keyed his mike. "Bridge—USWE, request a visual clear-or-foul, bearing three-zero-seven."

The reply came back in less than ten seconds. "USWE—Bridge, your bearing is clear. Lookouts report no surface contacts to thirty degrees either side. Mast-mounted sight shows negative visual and negative infrared."

Ens. Cooper swallowed. Instantly awake, his fatigue and boredom were forgotten. He keyed his mike. "Sonar—USWE, bearing three-zero-seven is clear. Tag it, bag it, send it to fire control, and then call it away."

A few seconds later, speakers for the 29-MC announcing circuit crackled to life all over CIC. "All stations—Sonar has passive broadband contact off the port beam, bearing three-zero-seven. Initial classification: POSS-SUB, confidence level low."

Even before the contact had popped up on the CDRT screen, Ens. Cooper was punching the button that patched his comm headset into Navy Red. The sync pulse warbled crazily in his ear for a second until the ship's encryption system synchronized with the encryption system aboard *Antietam*. He cleared his throat before keying the mike. "SAU Commander, this is *Towers*. Contact report to follow. Time, seventeen fifty-one Zulu. My unit holds passive broadband contact, bearing three-zero-seven. Initial classification: POSS-SUB, confidence level low, over."

Less than a second later, Capt. Whiley's voice came over the scrambled radio net. "SAU Commander, aye. Your contact designated *Gremlin Zero One*. My unit will launch *Samurai Seven-Nine* in approximately five mikes. Alert status of your aircraft, *Firewalker Two-Six* upgraded to Ready-Five, over."

"SAU Commander, this is *Towers*, roger, out." As soon as he punched out of the radio circuit, Ens. Cooper keyed back into the USW control net aboard *Towers*. "TAO—USWE, the SAU Commander has upgraded our helo alert status to Ready-Five."

The TAO's voice came back immediately. "TAO, aye. Break. ASTAC—TAO, set Helo Ready-Five."

The current Ready-Five helicopter, *Samurai Seven-Nine* was sitting on *Antietam*'s flight deck, spinning its rotors up for launch at that very second. It would be in the air in five minutes or less—time the screening ships would use to build a firing solution and refine their classification of the contact.

Cooper shifted his attention to the CDRT. Now came the tough part. The next four or five minutes would be crucial. He needed to know what the submarine, designated *Gremlin Zero One*, was up to—before *Antietam*'s helo was in the air.

The first piece of the USW puzzle was in place; they knew the contact's bearing. Instead of a tidy NTDS symbol, the contact appeared on the CDRT display as a red line extending from the center of the symbol for USS *Towers* to the edge of the screen. The angle of the line was 307 degrees: the bearing of the contact from *Towers*. The contact could be anywhere along that line of bearing, at a range of anything from a couple of hundred yards, to hundreds of thousands of yards. To localize him further, they would need to know his range. For an effective firing solution, they would also need to know the target's course and speed, but that could be estimated with a good degree of accuracy once they knew the contact's range.

Cooper keyed his mike. "UB—USWE, got anything yet?"

The Underwater Battery Fire Control Operator keyed up. "USWE—UB. That's a negative, sir. The sonar track is looking pretty good, but it's going to take me a while to nail this guy down off passive broadband alone. If you want something quick, I'm going to need a turn."

"USWE, aye."

If they'd had passive narrowband frequency data on the contact, the fire control computer could have calculated the target's range based on minute changes in Doppler as the submarine moved through the water. Without frequency information, they were restricted to Target Motion Analysis. While it would eventually give them the information they needed, TMA could take twenty minutes or more and would require them to turn at least once (and maybe twice) to feed the computer enough changes in bearing rate to do its magic. But turning wasn't an option right now. He couldn't afford to open up a hole in the formation. If he did, the submarine could slip through it and get inside the screen's defenses—which was exactly what had happened to *Kitty Hawk*.

The ensign stared at the colored symbols on the CDRT. Every thirty seconds, another red line appeared, each one tagged by a tiny set of digits that represented the Zulu time of that particular bearing update. The red lines accumulated slowly. Using only bearings, this was going to take a long time. Too long.

He exhaled fiercely. "Shit." He keyed his mike. "Sonar—USWE, have you got any kind of narrowband on this contact at all?"

"No discrete tonals, sir. The target is showing a tightly packed cluster of frequencies up around 550 hertz, but it's so garbled I can't do anything with it. Everything else I've got is too broad and diffused to track or classify. We are definitely not getting anything we can use for Doppler. Request permission to go active, sir."

Cooper's answer was immediate. "Negative, Sonar. Remain passive. If we spook this guy, he'll pop off a shot at us and run like hell."

Chief McPherson nodded. "Good call, sir. No sense in tipping our hand this early in the fight."

Cooper tapped his fingers on the face of the CDRT. "Thanks, Chief. What do you think about having Sonar adjust the depth of the towed array, to see if we can get some useful narrowband?"

Chief McPherson shook her head. "Never violate the second rule of USW, sir: 'If you've got contact, don't screw with *anything*.'"

"We're running out of time, Chief. *Antietam*'s helo is going to be airborne in ..."—he checked his watch—"about two minutes."

"It's your call, sir," the chief said. "Until we finish our watch turnover, you're still the USWE. But if it were me, I'd say screw the helo. That's a LAMPS III bird, strictly re-detect and attack. They're not set up for search. They've got no business launching until we have the contact localized."

A hand squeezed Ens. Cooper's shoulder. He looked around to find the captain standing behind him. "Listen to your chief, Pat. I can't count the number of times I've seen somebody lose contact because they were futzing with equipment line-up, trying to get a better picture."

"What do I tell the SAU Commander when he starts screaming for amplifying contact data?"

"You let me worry about Captain Whiley," Capt. Bowie said. "You follow your search plan and keep your eyes open. And don't get tunnel vision."

"Sir?"

"There are four subs out there. Don't let yourself get wrapped around the axle over one contact, especially if it's POSS-SUB low. We still don't have any real classification data on this guy. We don't even know his range. He might still turn out to be an Omani fishing boat way the hell and gone outside of radar range, and his signal's caught in the surface duct."

"I've seen it happen, sir," Chief McPherson said. "More than once. Just be ready to shift gears on a second's notice if we get any new information on the contact."

The ensign nodded. "I'll remember that." He looked up. "Are you ready to assume the watch?"

The captain said, "Hang on to it for a while, if you want to, Pat. This is your first no-shit bad guy, and he showed up on your watch. In my book, that means you get to chase him down. This will be your kill … if you want it."

Ens. Cooper swallowed heavily. He was frankly surprised that the captain wasn't pulling him off in favor of a more experienced USWE. He suspected that he'd been given the watch for the first leg of the search because the captain hadn't anticipated any action so early in the hunt. But now the captain was trusting him with the safety of the ship—saying as much right in front of the CIC crew. True, the captain and Sonar Chief would be close at hand, in case he screwed up, but it was still a pretty clear vote of confidence from the old man. He felt a surge of nervous pride.

"I want it, Captain." He turned to the chief. "This one is mine, Chief. You can have the next one."

Chief McPherson took a step backward and crossed her arms. "Your show, boss."

Ens. Cooper looked at the chief out of the corner of his eye. "Okay, I know the *second* rule of USW. What's the *first* rule?"

The Sonar Chief smiled. "USW is hard. If you're stupid, it's impossible."

The ensign raised an eyebrow. "You're making this up as you go along."

"No, sir, I am not."

Cooper opened his mouth to speak, but he was interrupted by a burst of warbling tones from the Navy Red secure radio circuit, followed by a voice transmission. "SAU Commander, this is *Benfold*. Contact report to follow. Time, seventeen fifty-four Zulu. My unit holds passive broadband contact, bearing three-two-five. Initial classification: POSS-SUB, confidence level low. Believe this contact correlates to *Towers*' *Gremlin Zero One*, over."

Capt. Whiley's reply was as rapid as before. "Roger, *Benfold*. SAU Commander concurs. Designate your contact *Gremlin Zero One*, over."

Ens. Cooper forgot whatever it was he'd been about to say. He was too busy punching keys on the CDRT. A bright blue line popped up, extending from the center of *Benfold*'s NTDS symbol to the edge of the screen. The blue line crossed the most recent bearing line from *Towers*. His keyed-in commands instructed the computer to plot a hostile-submarine NTDS symbol (a red V-shape with a dot in the center) directly on top of the intersection of the blue line from *Benfold* and the red line from *Towers*. It was called a cross-fix. That's where the submarine was. "Gotcha, you little bastard." He keyed his mike. "All Stations—USWE, we're in business. Break, UB, stand by for range updates from the CDRT."

"UB, aye."

Every thirty seconds, the CDRT updated the range and bearing to the contact. After only two updates, the underwater battery fire control computer had a rough estimate of the submarine's course and speed. Each set of bearing updates refined the solution. The *search* was about to become the *chase*.

* * *

Capt. Whiley's voice broke over the Navy Red radio circuit. "All units, this is SAU Commander. I am executing Pouncer Maneuver—now, now, NOW!"

Cooper watched on the CDRT. Sure enough, the symbol for *Antietam* was increasing speed and heading toward the southern flank of the formation. The symbol representing *Antietam*'s helo, *Samurai Seven-Nine*, cut around the northern end of the formation—to approach the sub from an unexpected angle. According to the tactical plan, the helo's altitude would be above 2,000 feet; high enough so the submarine's sonar wouldn't be able to detect the sound of his rotors.

The plan was going perfectly.

Whiley's voice came over Navy Red right on schedule. "All units, this is SAU Commander. My Anvil is away—now, now, NOW!"

* * *

Anvil (USS *Antietam*):

A small armored hatch snapped open on the cruiser's forward missile deck, exposing the weatherproof membrane that covered the upper end of a vertical launch missile cell. A millisecond later, the membrane was shattered as *Antietam*'s Vertical Launch Anti-Submarine Rocket (ASROC), code-name Anvil, blasted out of its missile cell and roared into the night sky on a silvery-orange pillar of fire.

Although it came out of the launcher like any other missile, the ASROC's flight profile was like no missile in the world. Instead of diving toward the surface of the ocean to begin a sea-skimming run, or turning toward its target and accelerating to an intercept point, the ASROC heeled itself over at a forty-five–degree angle and began boosting toward the top of a pre-programmed ballistic arc.

Ten thousand feet above the ocean, it hit the top of that arc, and any passing resemblance it had to an ordinary missile vanished. An electronic module inside the weapon sent trigger pulses to a pair of explosive blocks in the airframe. The explosives detonated instantly, shattering the steel restraining bands that held the missile together, and splitting the fiberglass airframe into two pieces. The missile literally came apart in midair, and from the expanding cloud of discarded debris fell the ASROC's payload: a specially configured Mark-54 torpedo.

The torpedo dropped toward the sea like a stone, completing the downward half of the ballistic arc as it hurtled toward its rendezvous with the waves. As the weapon fell past two thousand feet, a parachute deployed, slowing its rate of descent just enough to prevent damage when it hit the water.

Falling somewhat slower now, the weapon slammed into the ocean with enough force to shatter its nose cone along a series of pre-stressed structural points—absorbing a little more of the shock and protecting the delicate sonar transducer in the nose of the weapon.

As it sank through the ocean, seawater rushed in through small vents, completing the electrical circuit for the weapon's salt-water batteries. The batteries transmitted power to the weapon's computer, and the computer (in turn) sent signals to other systems, lighting off the sonar sensors, pre-arming the warhead, and taking control of the fins and stabilizers.

All of this happened very quickly. Less than six seconds after its launch from USS *Antietam*, the torpedo's turbine engine spun to life. The weapon calculated its depth and position, and then accelerated toward the start point for its search pattern.

* * *

USS *Towers*:

"USWE—Sonar, we have weapon startup. It's *Antietam*'s ASROC, sir, and it looks like they got it right in the pocket."

A friendly-weapon symbol appeared in blue on the CDRT. Ens. Cooper kissed the tip of his finger and touched it to the glass screen directly over the symbol. "Come on, baby, acquire ... acquire ..."

A half-minute later, the Sonar Supervisor's voice came over the net. "USWE—Sonar, *Antietam*'s weapon has acquired the target. Looks like it's starting its attack run now."

Ens. Cooper clapped his hands. "All right!"

Chief McPherson stared at the CDRT without saying anything.

Capt. Bowie watched her for a few seconds. "What is it, Chief?"

The chief shook her head. "Something's not right here, Captain."

Ens. Cooper looked at her. "What?"

"The sub isn't doing anything," Chief McPherson said. "He's got a torpedo screaming up his ass, and he's not doing anything about it. No evasion, no flank speed, no nothing …"

"It's a decoy!" Ens. Cooper shouted. He nearly broke a finger jabbing the button for Navy Red. "SAU Commander—*Towers*, it's a decoy! I say again, your target is a mobile decoy! Recommend you take immediate evasive action!"

From across CIC, a Radar Operator yelled, "TAO, I've got two, no … make that three missile pop-ups! Bearing two-two-zero!"

The TAO yelled, "Use the goddamned net!" Into his own comm-set mike he half-shouted, "All Stations—TAO, we have in-bound Vipers! I say again, we have missiles in-bound! This is not a drill! Weapons Control, shift to Aegis ready-auto. Set CIWS to auto-engage. Break. EW, I need your best course for minimized radar cross-section, and stand by to launch chaff!"

The Electronics Warfare Technician's response came a half-second later. "TAO—EW, standing by on chaff. I have active H-band seekers on all three missiles. Looks like Exocet SM-39s, 'November Variants.' EW recommends we avoid jamming, sir. I say again, recommend we do not jam. The November birds have home-on-jam capability."

The captain sprinted for his chair at the center of CIC, between the giant Aegis display screens. Three missile symbols were rapidly closing on the ships. It was still too early to determine which ships had been targeted. He pulled a comm-set over his head and keyed up. "Give me a plot on the pop-up point for those missiles."

A hostile-submarine symbol appeared on the screen in flashing red.

"What's the range? Can we hit that bastard with ASROC?"

Ens. Cooper keyed up. "Captain—USWE. Range to missiles' point of origin is fifty-five thousand yards, sir. No way we can hit it with ASROC."

"Damn it!" the captain shouted. "TAO, what's the estimated time-on-top? When are those bastards going to hit us?"

Before the TAO could answer, the captain punched the button to jumper his comm-set into the 1-MC General Announcing Circuit. When he keyed the mike, his voice came out of speakers all over the ship. "This is the Captain speaking. We have three in-bound Vipers off the port bow. All hands rig for impact. This is not a drill."

The ship heeled over as the bridge began to maneuver to minimize the ship's radar cross-section.

The TAO said, "Vipers are not targeted for *Towers*, Captain. All three are locked on *Antietam*. Estimated time-on-top is ninety seconds."

As the words left his lips, a second set of hostile-missile symbols popped up on the screen. Three more Exocet missiles—all bound for *Antietam*.

The captain keyed his comm-set. "Weapons Control, this is the Captain. Can we get some birds up there to help *Antietam* out?"

The response was a few seconds in coming. "Captain—Weapons Control. Negative, sir. *Antietam* is fouling our range. As low as those Vipers are to the water, we'd have to shoot through *Antietam* to get to them."

The Air Supervisor spoke up. "*Antietam* is firing, sir. Two salvos of surface-to-air missiles, looks like six and six."

The captain nodded.

Antietam was following *shoot-shoot-look-shoot-shoot* doctrine for incoming Vipers: fire two missiles at each Viper, take a peek with radar to see if they've been destroyed, and then fire two more missiles at each Viper that survived the initial salvo.

Capt. Bowie nodded at the Aegis display screen and said quietly, "Whiley, you stubborn bastard, still playing it by the book. And look what it's got you."

The battle seemed to unfold in slow motion on the big display screens. Six friendly-missile symbols and three hostile-missile symbols vanished as *Antietam*'s first salvo took out three of the incoming Vipers. Ten seconds later, the scenario repeated itself as *Antietam*'s second salvo of six destroyed the remaining three in-bound Vipers.

The *Towers* CIC team began to cheer.

"I'll say this for Whiley," the captain said, "that son of a bitch can shoot!"

The cheers were suddenly chopped off by a voice over the 29-MC speakers. "All Stations—Sonar has multiple hydrophone effects off the port bow! Bearings three-one-five, and three-one-seven. Initial classification: hostile torpedoes!"

"Crack the whip!" Ens. Cooper said into his comm-set. "Bridge—USWE. We have in-bound hostile torpedoes. I say again—crack the whip!"

"Bridge, aye!"

In the background came the muffled wail of the gas turbine engines as they spun up to flank speed.

The Officer of the Deck's voice broke over the 1-MC. "All hands stand by for heavy rolls while performing high-speed evasive maneuvers."

The deck began to heel to starboard as the big destroyer whipped into the first in a series of tight, high-speed turns. The *crack-the-whip* anti-torpedo maneuver would take the ship through a rapid succession of near-hairpin turns, designed to create multiple propeller wakes at very close intervals. A torpedo attempting to follow a ship through the aftermath of a crack-the-whip maneuver would find itself faced with a confusion of wakes to choose from, not to mention a wall of acoustic interference as the millions of bubbles churned up by the ship's screws collided, collapsed, and popped. Coupled with the towed acoustic decoy system called Nixie, the maneuver was highly effective. Some tactical analysts rated its probability of success at nearly seventy percent. And in the world of torpedoes, it didn't get any better than that.

Ens. Cooper gripped the edge of the CDRT to maintain his footing as the deck surged first one way, and then the other. The symbols on the screen had devolved into a mad little dance as every ship in the formation executed its own torpedo evasion maneuvers.

"*Antietam* is outside the screen," he said quietly. He braced one hip against the side of the CDRT and let go with his right hand so that he could key his mike. "Captain—USWE. Both of the enemy torpedoes are locked on *Antietam*, and *Antietam* is outside of our defensive screen."

He stared at the CDRT's tactical display, and then looked over his shoulder at the big Aegis display screens. They all told the same story. From the wild movement of her tactical symbol, it was obvious that *Antietam* was running her own crack-the-whip maneuver. It was just as obvious that the maneuver was going to fail. The hostile torpedoes had been fired from too short a range. They had far too good a sniff of the cruiser's real acoustic signature to be distracted by decoys and tricky maneuvers.

Ens. Cooper watched helplessly as the flashing red hostile-torpedo symbols began to merge with the symbol that represented *Antietam*.

* * *

DMA37 Torpedo:

Powered by a four-stage axial-flow turbine and a sophisticated planetary gear drive train, the German torpedo was capable of slightly over fifty knots. And at the moment, it was using every scrap of that power to close the range to its target.

The target was fast, but not fast enough. And it was tricky, but not tricky enough.

Inside the torpedo's acoustic seeker head, an array of 152 miniature sonar transducers were bombarded by a powerful source of white noise. Under other circumstances, the interference might have been enough to mask the target entirely, but the target was close, and the acoustic seeker could still detect it clearly through the cacophonous barrier of sound energy.

The transducers detected another sonar contact, with acoustic characteristics that closely resembled the target. For a few milliseconds, this confused the targeting algorithm running through the torpedo's digital processors. Two targets to choose from, both displaying acoustic characteristics within acceptable parameters, both easily within the weapon's attack envelope. It could strike either target in a matter of seconds.

With no compelling criteria to use for target selection, the torpedo's computer did exactly what its programmers had intended: it locked on to the closer of the two potential targets and started the final arming sequence on its warhead.

Slightly less than ten seconds later, the weapon's acoustic sensors determined that it was nearing optimum range for detonation. The torpedo dove to twelve meters, a depth calculated to place it beneath the hull of the target. The algorithm's calculations were precise; the torpedo reached the twelve-meter mark at the exact instant that the target's acoustic signal strength reached its peak. The torpedo was under the target.

The warhead contained 250 kilograms of hexagon/RDT/aluminum high-explosive. It detonated with a destructive force equivalent to nearly 500 kilos of TNT.

The target was vaporized.

* * *

USS *Towers*:

"Holy shit!" the Sonar Supervisor shouted over the net. "They just blew up the *Antietam*'s Nixie! The torpedo fell for the decoy! Yeah! Fuckin'-A!" The sonar team was cheering in the background.

Ens. Cooper jabbed his comm button. "Sonar—USWE. Can it! Maintain net discipline! This is no time to get excited anyway. There's still another torpedo out there, and there's no way *Antietam* can get her backup Nixie fish deployed in time."

* * *

USS *Antietam*:

About five seconds later, the second of the DMA37 torpedoes proved Ens. Cooper right. With the other distracting target out of the way, it dove to an optimum depth of twelve meters, slid neatly under *Antietam*'s hull, and detonated.

The explosion flash-vaporized a huge volume of water directly beneath the cruiser's keel, simultaneously ripping and burning an enormous hole through the steel hull plates of the ship's bottom. The keel, the structural backbone of the ship, fractured like bone under a sledgehammer. With its spine shattered and nearly all support snatched out from under its hull by the still-expanding bubble of vaporized water, the cruiser bent near the middle, and then broke. The sound was unbelievable, an ear-rending cacophony of tearing metal and roaring water, punctuated by the screams of the injured and dying. The over-burdened steel hull plates separated completely, ripping the old ship in half.

The aft section of the ship rolled over on to its starboard side and began to sink immediately.

The forward half of the ship remained afloat somehow, without power, as the generators had been destroyed along with the engineering spaces. Fires raged through the powerless steel hulk that—ten seconds ago—had been a United States warship.

* * *

Samurai Seven-Nine:

"Jesus Christ," the copilot whispered. "Oh Jesus ..."

The pilot stared down at the flaming remains of their ship. "SENSO, did you get a fix on the spot where those Vipers left the water?"

In the rear of the helo, the Sensor Operator stared blankly into space, too stunned to even answer.

The pilot keyed the mike of his inter-phone and shouted, "Goddamn it, Perkins! Snap out of it! We don't have time for this shit!"

The Sensor Operator jerked as though he'd been slapped. "What? What? I'm sorry, what did you say, sir?"

"Did you get a fix on the spot where those Vipers left the water?"

The Sensor Operator scanned his console. "Um, I think so. Ah ... yes, sir. I've got a fix."

"Good," the pilot said. "Shoot me a fly-to point."

The SENSO nodded. "Yes, sir." He used his trackball to roll a cursor to the screen coordinates that corresponded to the point where the missiles had popped up on radar. He punched a button. "Fly-to point coming up now, sir."

"Got it," the pilot snapped. He tweaked the cyclic and the collective, swinging the helo around until his instruments showed that they were pointing toward the appropriate spot in the ocean. "Start your weapons check-off list," he said. "Cut corners if you have to, but get that weapon ready now! The longer we wait, the farther that sub's going to be from the spot where he launched those missiles. We're only going to make one pass. We're going to make it low, and we're going to shove a torpedo up that bastard's ass."

"Yes, sir!"

The copilot keyed the radio. "SAU Commander, this is *Samurai Seven-Nine.* I am prepping for an attack run, over."

The pilot looked at him out of the corner of his eye. "Who're you talking to?"

"SAU Commander."

The pilot jerked his head in the direction of what was left of USS *Antietam.* "SAU Commander just got his ass shot off. We're on our own, Larry."

"Who's the next most senior captain?" the copilot asked. "He's the next in the chain of command, so he's the SAU Commander now."

"Fuck the chain of command," the pilot snarled. "Our people are dead or dying down there. We've got maybe sixty seconds to kill the bastards that did it. After that, they'll be outside the search envelope of our torpedo."

"Weapon is ready, sir," said the Sensor Operator. "Standing by to launch on your order."

A voice came over the radio. "All units, this is the commanding officer of USS *Towers.* I am assuming SAU Commander at this time. I say again, I am assuming SAU Commander at this time, over."

The pilot pitched his aircraft into a shallow dive. "Weapon away on my mark"

"Aye-aye, sir."

The ocean rushed up toward them. "Here we go," the pilot said. "Launch—now, now, NOW!"

The Sensor Operator jabbed a button. The airframe of the helo jerked as it was suddenly relieved of its five-hundred–pound burden. "Weapon away, sir!"

The pilot pulled back on the stick. "Eat that!"

"Oh shit!" the Sensor Operator shouted. He began pointing frantically out the window at a bright flare of light down on the water. "Missile emergence! We've got a missile coming out of the water, bearing three-three-zero!"

"Chaff!" the pilot screamed as he threw the helo into a wild side-slip. "I need chaff right fucking ..."

He never finished the sentence. The sub-SAM came through the port side of the aircraft, just forward of the sonobuoy launchers. The detonating warhead flash-fried the air crew, even as it blasted the fuselage of the helicopter into burning bits of wreckage.

* * *

<u>USS *Towers*</u>:

"TAO—Air Supervisor. *Samurai Seven-Nine* just dropped off the scope. We lost his IFF signal and all communications. Looks like he went down, sir."

"TAO—Bridge. Lookouts are reporting a fireball on *Samurai Seven-Nine*'s last bearing. I concur with the Air Supervisor; *Samurai Seven-Nine* is down."

Capt. Bowie slammed his fist down on the arm of his chair. "Damn it! What the hell were they doing below two thousand feet? They had specific orders to stay high enough so the subs couldn't hear their rotors. If they had followed their orders, they'd still be alive."

The TAO looked up at the Aegis display. "All right, guys. We need a break here …"

As if in answer, the Sonar Supervisor's voice came over the net. "USWE—Sonar, we have weapon start-up. It's a Mark-54. Looks like *Antietam*'s helo managed to get off a shot, sir."

Chief McPherson nudged Ens. Cooper's elbow. "Ask them if it's acquired, sir."

The ensign nodded. "Sonar—USWE. Has the helo's weapon acquired?"

"USWE—Sonar. Affirmative, sir. Sounds like it locked on right after it started up. They must have dropped it right on top of the target."

Ens. Cooper gritted his teeth and held up his fingers to show that they were crossed.

The Sonar Supervisor's next report came over less than a minute later. "USWE—Sonar. We have a loud underwater explosion, bearing two-eight-two. Sounds like secondary explosions on the same bearing. I think *Antietam*'s helo got themselves a submarine!"

"USWE, aye," Ens. Cooper said. "I hope you're right, but we don't have any confirmation yet. But even if you are right, there are still three hostile submarines out there somewhere. This engagement may not be over, so stay sharp!"

"Sonar, aye!"

But the engagement was over. The ships continued searching, even while they were rendering assistance to the stricken *Antietam*, but the submarines had disappeared again.

CHAPTER 35

U.S. NAVY CENTRAL COMMAND (USNAVCENT)
BAHRAIN
SATURDAY; 19 MAY
2240 hours (10:40 PM)
TIME ZONE +4 'DELTA'

Cmdr. Moody stood at the foot of the admiral's desk with a yellow folder in one hand and a green folder in the other.

Adm. Rogers looked up at the clock. "What do you suppose would happen if we actually knocked off before midnight some night?"

Cmdr. Moody's eyebrows went up. "One of us would turn into a pumpkin, sir."

"Which one?"

"I don't know, sir. I'd have to check the duty roster. But I think it's your turn."

"Figures," the admiral said. He sighed. "What have you got for me, Troy?"

Moody opened the yellow folder and flipped through several pages, scanning rapidly. "The latest SITREP from USS *Towers*, sir. Per Captain Bowie's orders, *Benfold* and *Ingraham* are continuing to render assistance to *Antietam*. The fires are out. They're still pulling people out of the water. Dead, mostly, but every once in a while they come across another survivor. So far, they have forty-one confirmed dead, but it'll probably be quite a while before we get an accurate casualty count. There are still over a hundred missing. Captain Bowie also thinks there may be air pockets trapped in the sunken part of *Antietam*'s hull. There could be survivors down there. He's requesting a team of emergency divers to survey the wreck and conduct rescue dives if they locate any survivors."

The admiral nodded. "Bowie's a good man. Drop what you're doing and get on the horn to OPS. I want a dive team in the air ten minutes ago."

Moody smiled. "I've already taken the liberty, sir." He glanced at his watch. "They should be airborne just about now. In the meantime, the *Towers* and a couple of the helos have set up a defensive screen around the rescue operations, but Captain Bowie is asking for a relief force. He's eager to get back to the hunt."

The admiral nodded. "I'm working on that. One way or the other, we'll have somebody down there to cover for them before tomorrow morning. Then we have to figure out how to get *Antietam* towed back in to port. Or what's left of her, anyway. Any further sign of the subs?"

Cmdr. Moody shook his head. "Not yet, sir. But *Ingraham*'s helo did a fly-by of the area where they thought one of the German submarines went down. They found a field of floating debris, an oil slick, and a half-dozen bodies. No survivors. Looks like *Antietam*'s helo got a kill after all. And that makes us even, again. Three ships—three subs."

"Even isn't good enough," the admiral said. "It's not *nearly* good enough."

Moody nodded. "Understood, sir."

Adm. Rogers leaned back in his chair and closed his eyes. "You've got two folders there, Troy. What's in the other one?"

Moody opened the green folder. "It's an incoming *Personal-For* message from Captain Whiley, sir."

The admiral opened his eyes. "I told Captain Bowie to keep Whiley on bed rest until we can arrange to helo him and his crew back to shore. He's in no shape to be up and around."

Cmdr. Moody shrugged. "Apparently Captain Whiley doesn't agree with your diagnosis, sir. He's asking you to put him back in command of the SAU."

The admiral sat up. "Is he fucking crazy?"

"I have no opinion on that, sir."

The admiral leaned back and closed his eyes again. "Drop that message in the burn bag, son. I'm not even going to dignify it with an answer."

CHAPTER 36

USS *TOWERS* (DDG-103)
STRAITS OF HORMUZ
SUNDAY; 20 MAY
0700 hours (7:00 AM)
TIME ZONE +4 'DELTA'

The executive officer, Lt. Cmdr. Tyler, was the last to arrive. He nodded in the captain's direction and took a seat at the wardroom table. His eyes were bloodshot. He looked like he hadn't slept in a week.

"Just got in a message from USNS *Arapaho*," he said. *Arapaho* was the ocean-going tug that was rigging the battered remains of the *Antietam* for towing. "The last of *Antietam*'s casualties have been evacuated to Bahrain. They're continuing search and rescue operations in the surrounding waters, but they don't expect to find any more survivors. That's the bad news. Here's the good news: the team of rescue divers you requested finally arrived. They've completed their initial survey of the wreck, and you were right; there are survivors down there. The dive team has located two groups of survivors. Somebody in one of the groups is communicating with the divers by tapping out Morse code signals on the hull. There are eleven people in that group. The other group, unfortunately, doesn't have anyone who knows Morse. They're banging on the hull too, but the divers can't make heads or tails out of what they're trying to say. So they can't tell how many people are in the second group." The XO smiled tiredly. "The situation looks good for getting both groups out." He shrugged. "And the divers may get lucky and find more survivors down there who haven't been able to communicate."

Chief McPherson shuddered involuntarily at the thought of being trapped in the hull of a sunken ship. The emergency battle lanterns would only last a few hours, and then would come a darkness blacker than anything she could imagine. After a while, the small volume of air trapped in the pocket would become stale, and then foul, and finally impossible to breathe. And the air pocket might not even hold. The unstable wreck could shift, bleeding precious air out through some newly formed crack. The water might gradually find its way into the space, slowly flooding the compartment until all the air was gone. The chief swallowed heavily and tried to push these thoughts from her mind.

Capt. Bowie nodded toward the XO. "Thanks for the update, Pete." He looked at the team of men and women assembled around the table. "I've already said a few prayers for the crew of *Antietam*—the unharmed ones, as well as the injured, and the missing, and the dead. I intend to say a few more. I know that you all have different religious beliefs, and that some of you don't believe in God in any form. But I would take it as a personal favor if you would find the time over the next few days to say a few words of prayer for the crew of *Antietam*."

Every head around the table nodded slowly.

"Thank you," the captain said. "Now, I'd like to turn this meeting over to Chief McPherson."

Chief McPherson stood up. "Thank you, Captain." She walked to a pair of charts that had been taped to the wall. The first was a navigational chart of the Arabian Gulf region. The second was a geographic map of the world. She nearly smiled; her visual aids were a far cry from Capt. Whiley's whiz-bang computer graphics. She pointed to the chart of the Arabian Gulf. "We are currently steaming through the Straits of Hormuz at thirty knots. Our sonars are degraded by our speed, and we are generating quite a bit of noise, which makes us vulnerable to submarine attack. But it's a calculated risk, and the captain has decided to take it. The German Type 212B diesel submarine has a maximum submerged speed of only twenty knots." She pointed to the northern end of the Straits of Hormuz on her chart. "The idea is to outdistance the submarines and establish a choke point at the northern end of the straits, before the subs can get there."

"Works for me," the XO said. "Then what?"

"Well, that's what we're here to figure out, sir. The next time we encounter those subs, we have got to give them something unexpected. And therein lies the problem. Whatever it is can't *look* like something they're not expecting."

Ens. Cooper frowned. "I'm not following you, Chief."

"Look at it like this," the chief said. "In the three battles that have occurred so far, the German submarines have met only with variations of NATO tactics. By now, they are probably convinced that the U.S. Navy is too hidebound by doctrine to try anything creative. Hopefully, that means they'll be expecting more of the same. Therefore, whatever the SAU tries should break the rules of NATO tactical doctrine without *looking like* it's going to break them."

The XO's eyebrows went up. "So we have to hit them with something that's *not* in the NATO tactical doctrine, but it has to look like something that *is* in the NATO doctrine?"

Chief McPherson nodded. "Yes, sir."

"I think everyone's got the idea, Chief," the captain said. "Move on."

"Yes, sir. If the subs run flat-out at their top speed of twenty knots, the earliest they can possibly reach the choke point is 1100. At thirty knots, we can be on station nearly forty minutes ahead of them—more than enough time to get in position to intercept."

The chief pointed to a series of penciled X-marks on the world map. "I've done a little math here. And based on the timing of the various sightings and skirmishes with the submarines, I calculate that they are covering an average distance of 13.5 nautical miles per hour. Although they are undoubtedly traveling at a higher rate of speed, the deceptive maneuvering they're using has reduced their actual speed through the water. All that zigging and zagging slows down their progress. If they continue their deceptive maneuvering, I estimate that the subs won't reach the choke point until some time after 1700 this evening. As I say, the SAU will be in position by 1020 hours, just in case the Germans decide to forgo their tricky maneuvering routine, in favor of achieving maximum possible speed through the water."

She looked around the table. There were no questions, so she continued. "We want our setup to duplicate our previous deployment of forces as closely as possible." She pointed to the Arabian Gulf chart again. "I recommend we put *Benfold* and *Ingraham* here and here, spaced at eighty percent of their predicted sonar ranges, just like before. They'll use the same locked-step zigzag pattern that we used before, forming a two-ship version of the moving barrier. Last time we used three ships in the barrier, but the Germans know that we are down a ship, so they'll expect our formation to be one ship short."

The Combat Systems Officer, Lt. Sikes, tapped a pencil against her palm. "When do we pull the rabbit out of the hat?" she asked. "So far, this looks like what we did when we got our butts shot off."

Chief McPherson grinned. "That's exactly how we want it to look, ma'am. The good old U.S. Navy, too dumb to learn from its mistakes, trying the same old plan—even after it's fallen on its face." She pointed to a spot on the chart, behind the formation. "The Germans will assume that *Towers* is back here in the Pouncer position, running behind the advancing barrier—ready to charge around the end of the formation at the first sign of trouble." She moved her finger to a different point on the chart. "This is where the rabbit comes out of the hat. Because *Towers* will actually be way down here, in *front* of the formation, where they won't be expecting her."

Ens. Cooper furrowed his brow. "It won't matter what the Germans are expecting. They're going to *see* us. One peep through a periscope, and they're going to know that we're not on the back side of the formation. The jig will be up long before those subs are within weapons range."

The chief waved a hand toward the Operations Officer. "Sir?"

Lt. Nylander stood up. "Thank you, Chief." His eyes traveled from face to face. "Chief McPherson and I have worked this out. The Germans will not see us, because we're going to make the ship invisible."

The Combat Systems Officer waved her pencil around in circles like a wand. "See? I knew there was some hocus-pocus in here *somewhere*. Rabbits out of hats, invisible ships. Maybe we should levitate the Chief Engineer as a finale."

"Watch it," the CHENG snapped.

"Patience," the captain said. "There is a method to this madness."

The Combat Systems Officer caught herself before another quip left her mouth.

"Thank you, sir," the Operations Officer said. He looked around the table again. "What's the best way to hide a cat?" he asked.

"Stick it in the microwave," the CHENG said softly. The Combat Systems Officer elbowed him in the ribs.

"Close," said the Operations Officer. "You put it in a room full of *other* cats."

"The Straits of Hormuz is a major shipping lane, and dozens of oil tankers go through every day, in both directions. If we want to disappear, all we have to do is become a tanker."

"Child's play," the Operations Officer said. "We rig deceptive lighting, so we look like an oil tanker in the dark. We secure the SPY radar and every other piece of electronics that transmits anything on military frequency bands. That still leaves us the Furuno radar, for safety of navigation, but Furunos are carried by two-thirds of the merchant ships in the world. The Germans will *expect* a tanker to carry a Furuno, or something like it."

The Chief Engineer was nodding now. "We can configure the engineering plant for turn-count masking. If we run one engine a little faster that the other one and offset the difference in thrust by angling the blades of the propellers differently, we'll get a loud, mushy blade signature. With a bit of experimentation, I'll bet we can make ourselves sound like an old tanker with a poorly maintained screw."

Ens. Cooper tugged at his lower lip. "This is all well and good, as long as the subs show up in the evening, at or after sunset. What if they turn up at lunchtime? By the chief's calculations, that could happen if they run at high speed. We might fool them with tricky lighting after dark, but no amount of fan dancing can make a destroyer look like a merchant ship in broad daylight."

"It's a risk, sir," Chief McPherson said, "but a *calculated* risk. Once they make it out of the straits and into the gulf, it's going to be a hell of a lot harder to find them. They'll have a lot more room to maneuver, and a lot more places to hide. Our best chance is to bottle them up *before* they get out of the straits, and they know that as well as we do. They've got to be expecting us to try for a choke point at the northern end of the straits."

"I'm sure you're right," Ens. Cooper said. "But what's to stop them from running the choke point at high noon?"

"Sub skippers don't like to attack when visibility is good," the chief said. "It's too easy for a lookout to spot a periscope, or for an aircraft to see the silhouette of the sub's hull through the water. Given the choice, a submarine commander will either attack after dark, or as close to sunrise or sunset as he can get. The human eye has trouble picking out detail under changing light conditions."

Ens. Cooper nodded. "They hit the Brits after dark, and they hit *us* after dark. When did they hit the *Kitty Hawk*?"

"Just as the sun was coming up," the executive officer said.

"So they'll probably try to run the choke point after the sun goes down?" the ensign asked.

"That's what we're hoping, sir," the chief said. "As I said, it's a calculated risk. If they decide to crash the party early, we shoot about a dozen ASROCs in their general direction to keep their heads down, and we run like hell."

"Fair enough," the ensign said.

The Combat Systems Officer looked thoughtful. "We should lay a sonobuoy barrier to the south," she said. "Passive buoys only, so the subs won't be able to detect them. The subs will have to pass through the barrier to transit the straits, and we'll see them coming."

"We'd need to launch a helo to monitor the buoys," the XO said.

The captain shook his head. "Negative. No helos. The Germans have displayed an excellent ability to localize low-flying aircraft from the sound of their rotors. I don't want to take a chance at tipping our hand. One sniff of a helo and those subs will be alerted."

"What if we don't launch it?" the Operations Officer asked. "If we're in the mood to be tricky, why don't we leave the helo on deck, lights out, and rotors not turning? The flight crew can sit in the helo and monitor the buoys in the dark, right from the flight deck. If they keep their engines spun up for a rapid launch, they could still be at Ready-Five."

"Yeah," said the CHENG, "but they'll be burning fuel the whole time they sit there. What if we have to launch, and the helo's nearly out of gas?"

"We could hot-pump the helo," Ens. Cooper said. Hot-pumping was a method of refueling helicopters on deck, with their engines running and their rotors still turning. It was a technique most often used when a helo needed to land, take on fuel, and get back into the air as quickly as possible. "The rotors are usually spinning when we hot-pump a helo," he said, "but there's no reason that they *have* to be."

"Good point," the captain said. "We'll keep their tanks topped off constantly. If we do have to launch, they'll have a full bag of fuel."

* * *

The discussion continued for another fifteen minutes before it became clear that they were rehashing the same ideas. The captain looked around the table. "Anybody see any good reasons why this plan won't work?"

No one said a word.

"Does anyone have a better idea, or a refinement that we haven't discussed?"

Again, no one had anything to say.

The captain stood up. "All right, then. I'll run through this with the COs of *Benfold* and *Ingraham*, and give them a chance to poke holes in it. But unless one of them thinks of something that we missed entirely, this is the plan we run with."

CHAPTER 37

USS *INGRAHAM* (FFG-61)
NORTHERN STRAITS OF HORMUZ
SUNDAY; 20 MAY
1844 hours (6:44 PM)
TIME ZONE +4 'DELTA'

Auxiliary Machinery Room #3 was a labyrinth of piping, pumps, relay panels, and electrical junction boxes. The compartment was home to several critical engineering systems, including high- and low-pressure air compressors, the fresh-water distillers of the potable water system, and #4 and #5 fire pumps. But through the center of the maze ran the most important piece of equipment in the compartment: the propeller shaft, known to the engineering crew who maintained it as simply *the shaft.*

Over two feet in diameter, the huge steel shaft performed much the same function as the drive shaft on a car, only instead of carrying power from the transmission to the rear axle, this shaft carried power from the ship's main reduction gears to the screw that drove the ship through the water.

Gas Turbine System Technician–Mechanical Third Class Michael Carpenter laid his hand against the housing for the line shaft bearing that supported the shaft. He could feel the throbbing vibration of the huge propeller, right through the thick steel housing of the bearing's oil sump. Of all the spaces on the ship, *this* was where you could feel the power of the turbines the best. You could hear it better in the Main Engine Room, where even the acoustic enclosures could not eliminate the jet engine scream of the twin General Electric LM-2500 gas turbines. But you could feel it better here, in AMR #3.

Standing in the bilge next to the line shaft bearing, with only about a half-inch of steel hull plating between his feet and the ocean, Carpenter could feel the hiss and rumble of the water as it passed under the hull. Just a few yards aft of where he was standing, the tremendous bronze screw churned the water into froth as it drove the ship forward.

The sample valve was located on the bottom of the oil sump. Carpenter unclipped the locking arm from the hand wheel of the sample valve and pulled a glass sample bottle from the left hip pocket of his coveralls. As Engineering Messenger of the Watch, part of his job was to take regular oil samples from key pieces of engineering equipment. The oil lab, which operated twenty-four hours a day, would test the samples for seawater, metal filings, dirt, or other contamination that could degrade the lubricating property of the oil. Carpenter opened the valve a crack and waited as the dark amber liquid began to ooze into his sample bottle. Hot oil-scented air surged up from the open valve, the signature aroma of heavy machinery at work.

Something flew past his head and ricocheted off the bearing housing. It startled him, and he jerked away involuntarily. The object fell into the bilge. It was a balled up piece of paper.

Carpenter turned in time to dodge a second paper projectile that was also aimed at his head. Standing a few feet away was Seaman Wayne Harris, a general wise-ass and Carpenter's best friend.

Harris grinned, showing his mulish front teeth. "Hey shit-for-brains, let's go up to the starboard break and smoke a ciggy-butt." His voice was loud. It had to be to carry over the sounds of the machinery.

"I've got to get this oil sample up to the lab," Carpenter said.

"So get a move on," Harris said. "We can swing by the lab on the way up."

Carpenter checked the oil level in the sample bottle out of the corner of his eye, not willing to turn his back entirely on Harris, who was a bit of a prankster. The bottle was about two-thirds full. "What's the rush?"

"Your Hot-a-malan girlfriend is up there taking a smoke break. She usually likes to smoke two, so she doesn't feel like she wasted the trip. If we hurry, we can catch her."

Gitana Delgado was Guatemalan, not *Hot*-a-malan, as Harris insisted on calling her. And she wasn't Carpenter's girlfriend. Not that he would have minded …

It struck Carpenter for about the thousandth time how lucky Harris was that Gitana Delgado didn't take his nickname for her personally. With a word or two in the right direction, she could have nailed him for sexual harassment, or maybe even racial discrimination. The Navy didn't play games with either one of those subjects. If you had opinions on someone's gender or ethnic background, you had damned well better keep them to yourself. Gitana could get Harris into serious trouble if she wanted to. Carpenter smiled. For that matter, she could probably kick Harris's ass. Gitana spent a lot of time in the gym, and everybody knew that Harris's most developed muscle was his mouth.

Carpenter looked around suddenly, as he felt the hot oil flow over his fingers. Damn. He had overfilled the bottle. He shut the valve quickly and tried to get the lid on the sample bottle without spilling any more than he had to. As soon as the lid was on tight, he pulled a rag from his back pocket and wiped the bottle down. He slid the bottle into his hip pocket and surveyed the mess. He hadn't spilled much. Just a few ounces. Nothing major.

He flipped down the locking arm and pinned the sample valve in the locked position. That done, he knelt down and used his rag to mop up the tiny puddle of oil in the bilge. There. No harm done.

He looked up at Harris. "All right, I'm done. We have to make a quick stop by the lab, and I have to tell the Engineer of the Watch that I'm taking a quick smoke break."

"Stop dragging ass," Harris said. "My lungs are overdosing on oxygen."

Carpenter bumped into Harris on purpose as he walked toward the ladder. "Sorry. Excuse me. Pardon me. Coming through."

Harris followed him. "Shithead!" A few seconds later, the watertight door closed behind him with a bang.

* * *

Down in the bilge beneath the line shaft bearing, a fresh spot of oil appeared on the steel deck. After a second or two, it was joined by another one. And then another. The sample valve on the bottom of the oil sump was locked in its current position. It was nearly closed, but the disk was not completely sealed against the seat. The drip became a trickle.

CHAPTER 38

USS *TOWERS* (DDG-103)
NORTHERN STRAITS OF HORMUZ
SUNDAY; 20 MAY
2115 hours (9:15 PM)
TIME ZONE +4 'DELTA'

Chief McPherson swirled the last bit of coffee around the bottom of her cup and glared at the dark liquid with accusatory eyes. She knew the coffee was cold, and she could see the grounds in it. She thought for a second about getting a fresh cup, but she would be going off watch in about a half hour, and she didn't want the caffeine kicking in just when she was trying to catch a few winks. Not that she'd sleep for long anyway. She'd be back in CIC in an hour or two. She was having a hard time staying away, even when she wasn't on watch. In fact, she probably wouldn't hit her rack at all. Maybe she'd just catch a catnap in a chair at one of the unused consoles.

She was very careful not to actually do the math in her head. Because, when she did, she'd have to admit to herself that she had been awake for two days and counting. The logical part of her mind knew that dedication and willpower only went so far. Her energy reserves were running low, and she'd have to put in some major sack time in the not-too-distant future. But she was all right for now. Or, rather, she would be after a little nap.

She looked up at the big red digits on the CIC battle clock. She and the sonar watch teams were due for turnover at 2145—in a little less than thirty minutes—and that nap was starting to look better all the time. With any luck, the subs wouldn't show up during the watch turnover, the way they had the last time.

She slurped the last swallow of coffee and made a face when the cold, sludgelike liquid hit her taste buds. She was in the process of picking stray grounds off the tip of her tongue when it hit her. She stared dumbly at the

CDRT for several seconds with her tongue still sticking out. *Last time, the subs had struck during the watch turnover. But what about the time before that?*

Her tongue retreated into her mouth. She punched keys on the CDRT, calling up a history of encounters with the German submarines. The data she was looking for came up quickly. The subs had tangled with the *Antietam* SAU at 2152, right in the middle of watch relief for the 2200–0200 watch. The day before, in the Gulf of Aden, they'd nailed the *Kitty Hawk* strike group at 0647, during the turnover for the 0700–1200 watch.

The pattern fell apart when she looked at the attack on the British ships in the Straits of Gibraltar. That one had taken place at 0348, and the Brits wouldn't have been turning over the watch then.

Or maybe they *had* been …

In the late 1990s, in response to reduced manning, the U.S. Navy had shifted from six watches a day to five. Instead of the traditional rotation, with six four-hour watches per day, the Navy now ran a five-section rotation, with four five-hour watches and one four-hour watch—the 2200–0200.

What if the Brits were still running an old-style six-watch rotation? That would put the Gibraltar Straits attack, which had occurred at 0348 hours, right in the middle of the 0400–0800 watch turnover!

The chief stared at the list of attacks on the CDRT and shook her head slowly. "Every time," she said softly. "You crafty bastards hit us during watch turnover every single time. Right when we were at our most disorganized. And you were even smart enough to account for the differences between our watch rotation and the British rotation."

She glanced up at the battle clock above the Aegis display screens again. The large red digits read 21:22. The early birds would start trickling in about ten minutes from now, but the majority of the reliefs would show up at about 2140. She keyed her mike. "TAO—USWE, I think I know when the subs are planning to attack, sir."

The Tactical Action Officer on watch was Lt. Nylander, the Operations Officer. His voice sounded as tired as Chief McPherson felt. "USWE—TAO. Practicing a little black magic over there, Chief?"

"No, sir. Just your run-of-the-mill crystal ball. And if you'll step over here to the CDRT, I'll show it to you."

"On my way," the TAO said.

* * *

Two minutes later, he keyed his mike. "Bridge—TAO. Call away GQ."

"TAO—Bridge. Say again?"

"Bridge—TAO. Call away General Quarters. Do it now! We're about to be attacked. I'll give you the details in a minute."

"Bridge, aye!"

The raucous growl of the General Quarters alarm began to blare from every 1-MC speaker on the ship. After a few seconds, the alarm was replaced by the amplified voice of the Officer of the Deck, "General Quarters, General Quarters. All hands man your battle stations. Set Material Condition Zebra throughout the ship."

The alarm and announcement were repeated, and as soon as the speakers fell silent, the TAO keyed into Navy Red. "All units, this is SAU Commander. Post-mission analysis of every encounter with the hostile submarines shows that the Germans have attacked during scheduled watch turnovers on every single occasion. I say again—the Germans have shown a preference for attacking during scheduled watch turnover. Recommend all units set General Quarters and prepare for USW action, over."

The ship's standard for manning battle stations and setting material condition Zebra (all watertight doors and hatches closed) was seven minutes. It was just a few minutes before taps, and a goodly portion of the crew would be asleep already. They'd be lucky to do it in twelve or fifteen minutes. The TAO decided to try to speed things up by getting the crew's attention. He keyed into the 1-MC and spoke to the entire ship. "This is the Tactical Action Officer. We have reason to believe that the ship will be attacked by hostile submarines within the next ten to fifteen minutes. This is the real thing, people. Get to your stations *now*! The safety of this ship depends on it."

* * *

The XO made it to CIC in about two minutes, followed by the captain about three seconds later. They were both still zipping coveralls and tying shoes as they gathered at the CDRT. The XO rubbed his left eye. "What have you got, Brian?"

The TAO nodded toward Chief McPherson. "Chief? It was your idea, you tell them."

Chief McPherson pointed to the flat screen display. "The Germans always attack during watch turnover, sir."

The CO ran a hand vigorously over his hair several times. "Are you sure?"

"Yes, sir," the chief said. "They've done it every single time. With us and with the British Navy."

Seats were filling all around CIC, as watchstanders in various stages of battle-dress took their stations. Over the 1-MC, the Damage Control

Assistant's voice said, "This is the DCA from CCS. General Quarters time—plus four minutes. All stations expedite setting Zebra."

The captain looked up at the battle clock. It read 21:31. "Well, Chief, we'll know if you're right in the next fifteen minutes or so."

* * *

CCS reported that all stations were manned with material condition Zebra set at 2135. The TAO nodded. Eight minutes was not bad, considering the circumstances.

* * *

A couple of minutes later, *Benfold* reported ready for battle, followed by *Ingraham* a minute or so after that.

* * *

The critical moment, 2145, came and went with no sign of the submarines. By 2155, everyone was stealing glances at the clock. At 2158, Chief McPherson said, "Come on … I know you're out there …"

Another minute passed. The chief was about to say something when a message came in over Navy Red. "SAU Commander, this is *Ingraham.* Contact report to follow. Time, twenty-one fifty-nine Zulu. My unit holds passive broadband contact, bearing three-one-five. Initial classification: POSS-SUB, confidence level low, over."

Chief McPherson looked at the CDRT. "Three-one-five? That's on the other side of the formation. How in the hell did they slip past us?"

The TAO keyed up Navy Red. "SAU Commander, aye. Your contact designated *Gremlin Zero One.* My unit standing by to launch *Firewalker Two-Six* when contact is localized. Request you confirm your *Gremlin* is northwest of formation, over."

"SAU Commander, this is *Ingraham.* Affirmative. *Gremlin Zero One* is behind the formation and outside the straits. Believe contact has penetrated our barrier. Request permission to break formation to pursue, over."

"*Ingraham*, this is SAU Commander. Stand by, over."

The TAO looked at Capt. Bowie. "What do you think, sir? Do we let *Ingraham* break formation?"

The captain turned to Chief McPherson. "How about it, Chief? Did those subs sneak by us?"

Blue lines of bearing were beginning to appear on the CDRT, angling away from *Ingraham*'s NTDS symbol. "I don't know, sir," the chief said. "It looks like they did, but … maybe *Ingraham*'s *Gremlin* isn't one of the subs. Maybe it's a fishing boat, or something too small to give a decent radar return. We need to find out if they've got any narrowband frequencies we can use to classify this guy."

The XO looked at the TAO. "Brian, ask *Ingraham* if they're getting any narrowband."

The TAO nodded. "*Ingraham*, this is SAU Commander. Interrogative narrowband tonals, over."

The reply came back a few seconds later. "SAU Commander, this is *Ingraham*. Negative narrowband tonals at this time, over."

"How about small craft?" the chief asked.

The TAO went out over Navy Red again. "*Ingraham*, this is SAU Commander. Interrogative surface small craft in the area of *Gremlin Zero One*, over."

"SAU Commander, this is *Ingraham*. Negative small craft in area of my *Gremlin*. My radar did show one motorboat near the initial bearing of my contact, but I am now seeing over thirty degrees of bearing separation. Do not believe my *Gremlin* is a small craft, over."

The XO said, "That's it, then. I say we let them break formation, Captain. If those subs have gotten past us, they're either going to slip away or jam a torpedo up our ass. We need to jump on this sucker before it gets away."

The captain nodded. "Looks like we just proved Patton's old adage: *No plan ever survives contact with the enemy*. I hate to throw this one out the window, but we can't take a chance on even one of those subs getting by us. Let *Ingraham* go, Brian. And tell them we're standing by to assist."

The TAO said, "Yes, sir." He keyed up Navy Red. "*Ingraham*, this is SAU Commander. You are cleared to break formation to pursue your *Gremlin*. *Towers* is standing by to assist, over."

"Wait a second," Chief McPherson said. "Ask them what their contact looks like, sir."

The TAO's eyebrows went up. "What?"

"What it looks like," the chief said. "Is it strong or weak? Fuzzy or discrete? What are its acoustic characteristics?"

The TAO cocked his head to one side. "Uh … *Ingraham*, this is SAU Commander. Interrogative acoustic characteristics of your *Gremlin*, over."

The reply took nearly a minute. "SAU Commander, this is *Ingraham*. My Sonar Operators describe the contact as strong and discrete broadband, with diffused swaths of narrowband that are too broad and indiscrete to track or classify. Target is showing a tightly packed cluster of frequencies up around 550 hertz, but it's too muddled to process, over."

Chief McPherson slapped the CDRT. "I knew it!" She looked up. "Captain, that's a decoy!"

"Where the hell did it come from?"

"I don't know, sir. Maybe that motorboat launched it; they don't weigh more than fifteen or twenty pounds. But what they're tracking sounds like a perfect description of the one we had earlier—the one that suckered *Antietam* out of the formation."

Capt. Bowie snapped his fingers and pointed to the TAO. "Tell them! Do it quick!"

The TAO keyed up Navy Red. "*Ingraham*, this is SAU Commander. *Gremlin Zero One* evaluated as a mobile decoy. Return to formation immediately, over!"

"*Ingraham*, aye!"

On the CDRT, the *Ingraham*'s NTDS symbol began to swing back toward the hole it had left in the formation. She was almost back in position when the net crackled with an incoming message from the Sensor Operator aboard *Firewalker Two-Six*. "USWE—SENSO, buoys five and six are hot. We hold narrowband tonals consistent with Type 212 diesel submarines. Initial classification: POSS-SUB, confidence level high!"

Immediately afterward, a call from the pilot came over the HAWK-Link. "SAU Commander, this is *Firewalker Two-Six*. Request permission to break hot-pump."

The TAO keyed his mike. "*Firewalker Two-Six*, this is SAU Commander. Break hot-pump. Stand by for green deck."

He turned to the captain. "Request permission to launch the helo, sir."

The captain nodded. "Do it."

The TAO keyed up again. "*Firewalker Two-Six*, this is SAU Commander. Your contact designated *Gremlin Zero Two*. You have green deck. Launch when ready."

Less than a minute later, the helo keyed the HAWK-Link again. "SAU Commander, this is *Firewalker Two-Six*. I am up for *Towers* control. My fuel state is three hours plus four zero minutes. Three souls aboard. My load-out is one Mark-54 torpedo and a mixed rack of sonobuoys, over."

"Roger, *Firewalker*," the TAO said. "Break. *Ingraham*, this is SAU Commander. Alert status of your aircraft, *Gunslinger Four-One* upgraded to Ready Five, over."

Ingraham acknowledged.

Capt. Bowie said, "Tell *Firewalker* to clear to the east until we get our VLAs off. Then prep us a couple of ASROCs, and let's take this show to town."

"TAO, aye."

"USWE, aye."

"Keep an eye out," the captain said. "There are two more subs out there."

As if in answer to his words, the speaker rumbled again. "SAU Commander, this is *Firewalker Two-Six*. New contact! Buoys nine and ten are hot. I hold narrowband tonals consistent with Type 212 diesel submarine. Initial classification: POSS-SUB, confidence level high! Looks like another one is trying to run the barrier, sir."

The TAO answered immediately. "*Firewalker Two-Six*, this is SAU Commander. Your new contact designated *Gremlin Zero Three*, over."

The chief keyed the net. "TAO—USWE. Recommend we target both *Gremlins* with ASROC, and assign *Benfold* to target both subs as a backup."

The TAO looked at the captain. "Sounds like a good call to me, sir."

The captain nodded.

"USWE—TAO. Good call. Target both *Gremlins* with VLAs and inform me as soon as you have a firing solution."

"USWE, aye."

Chief McPherson scanned the unfolding tactical picture on the CDRT. *Towers*, *Benfold*, *Ingraham*, and *Firewalker Two-Six* were shown in blue. The contacts designated *Gremlins Zero Two* and *Zero Three* appeared as red V-shaped hostile-submarine symbols. To the northwest, behind the formation, was the symbol for the motorboat that might or might *not* have launched the acoustic decoy. It was shown in white, for neutral. The boat appeared to be loitering harmlessly, but they couldn't count on that. The chief clicked on the motorboat symbol and upgraded its status from neutral to potentially hostile. Its color changed to a lighter shade of red than the submarines. That done, she spoke into her mike. "UB—USWE. I need the status of your firing solutions on contacts *Gremlin Zero Two* and *Gremlin Zero Three.*"

"USWE—UB. Just a second, Chief. My processors are updating now." There was a brief pause, and then, "USWE—UB. I hold an excellent firing solution on *Gremlin Zero Two.* I am just starting to get tracking data on the second submarine."

Per the chief's recommendations and the captain's orders, the TAO got on Navy Red and directed *Benfold* to target both submarines with ASROCs.

"USWE—UB. I hold excellent firing solutions on both contacts."

"UB—USWE. Stand by. Break. TAO—USWE. Request batteries released."

The TAO looked at the captain, who nodded. "USWE—TAO. You have batteries released."

"USWE, aye. Break. UB—USWE. Kill *Gremlin Zero Two* and *Gremlin Zero Three* with Vertical Launch Anvils."

"UB, aye. Going to launch standby on weapon one. Launch ordered. Weapon away—now, now, NOW!" On the third *now*, the entire ship shuddered as the first ASROC missile blasted its way out of the forward vertical launch system. "Anvil one is away, no apparent casualties. Going to launch standby on weapon two. Launch ordered. Weapon away—now, now, NOW!" The ship shuddered again as another ASROC missile rocketed out of its cell. "Anvil two is away, no apparent casualties."

* * *

The second ASROC hadn't even pitched over into its ballistic arc when the Officer of the Deck's voice came over the net. "TAO—Bridge. Lookouts are reporting two bright flashes, bearing three-four-four. We're getting confirmed infrared signatures from the mast-mounted sight cameras. Flight profiles consistent with small missiles."

"TAO, aye."

"TAO—Surface. Three-four-four is the bearing to that motorboat. Recommend we re-designate that contact as hostile."

"TAO, aye. Break. All Stations—TAO, we have in-bound Vipers! I say again, we have missiles in-bound! Weapons Control, shift to Aegis ready-auto. Set CIWS to auto-engage. Break. EW, give me your best course for minimized radar cross-section. Stand by to launch chaff!"

The Electronics Warfare Technician responded a half-second later. "TAO—EW, standing by to launch chaff, but I don't think it'll do any good, sir. I'm showing negative active missile seekers at this time. These Vipers are possible heat seekers, or maybe they're laser-guided."

"EW—TAO. Understood. Stand by to launch torch rounds, just in case they're heat seekers."

"EW, aye."

The TAO keyed the net again. "Air—TAO. Where are these missiles heading?"

* * *

Scorpion II (mid-flight):

The two missiles streaking through the night were beam-riders, German-built Scorpion II laser-guided anti-tank missiles. Both were targeted on *Benfold*, and they closed their target at just under three-quarters the speed of sound. They had been fired from well inside the minimum range of *Benfold*'s SM-2s, so the luckless destroyer would not have the option of launching her own missiles to intercept.

The target began launching chaff. A half-dozen blunt projectiles rocketed away from the ship. Four of them exploded at predetermined distances, spraying clouds of aluminum dust and metallic confetti into the air to create clusters of false radar targets. The remaining two projectiles were torch rounds: self-igniting magnesium flares designed to seduce heat-seeking infrared guided missiles.

The Scorpions blew past the expanding chaff clouds with zero hesitation. Aluminum dust could fool radar, but the Scorpion missiles had no radar. The missiles ignored the torch rounds for the same reason. With no infrared sensors, the Scorpions couldn't even see the heat signatures from the flares, much less be distracted by them. In fact, the Scorpions couldn't see anything but the narrow beams of their laser directors. Their seeker heads were amazingly simple, and—in this situation—that made them amazingly effective.

The target ship's Close-In Weapon System opened fire. The six-barreled Gatling gun spewed a fusillade of 20mm tungsten bullets into the darkness, cutting the first of the incoming Scorpions into bite-sized chunks. The defensive Gatling gun spun to cover the other incoming missile, but it was too late. The second Scorpion had reached its target.

* * *

USS *Benfold*:

The missile slammed into the destroyer's starboard bridge wing, passing through an inch-thick window before detonating. The expanding cloud of shrapnel and fire ripped through the pilot house like a tornado, killing everyone in the bridge crew except the Helmsman. Badly burned, deafened by the concussion, and blinded in one eye, the twenty-two-year-old deck seaman struggled to his feet and stood amongst the wreckage and the smoldering bodies of his shipmates.

Driven so far into shock that rational thought was an alien concept, the young Sailor became only dimly aware of the searing pain coming from the area of his left hand. *Perhaps it's still on fire,* he thought, but even that idea felt detached and unimportant. He slowly raised the wounded arm so he could inspect it with the eye that still seemed to be working. But the hand wasn't there. Someone had taken away his hand, and left in its place a bleeding stump. Splinters of bone protruded from the mangled wrist, and blood shot from the mass of torn flesh and cartilage in a pulsating jet that was fascinating to watch. The Helmsman sank to his knees, and then lay down on the scorched deck, surrounded by the bodies of the bridge crew. *Just for a minute,* he thought. *I'll just rest here for a minute, until my head clears.* He closed his one good eye.

* * *

Out on the forecastle, *Benfold*'s 5-inch deck gun opened fire, hurling six shells at the enemy motorboat in rapid succession.

The little boat zigged and zagged with insane abandon as the sky began to rain exploding naval artillery shells. The boat was small, fast, and incredibly agile. Through some combination of skill and luck, it slipped unharmed through the barrage of steel and fire.

Benfold's big gun began barking continuously, pumping out shell after shell, pausing only long enough between firing for the gun's auto-loading system to raise the next shell and ram it into the barrel.

The ninth round caught the motorboat, blasting it into thousands of burning fragments no larger than a pack of cigarettes. The tenth and eleventh rounds were already in the air. Both landed and detonated in the same stretch of water that the motorboat had recently occupied. But the target was gone, and the exploding shells succeeded in killing only saltwater.

* * *

Anvil (USS *Towers*):

The nose cone of *Towers*' first ASROC shattered on impact, and the Mark-54 torpedo came to life and detached itself from its parachute.

Placement of the weapon was nearly textbook perfect. It acquired its target on the first pass and accelerated to attack speed before the submarine could even maneuver.

The water was shallow in the straits, and the shock wave of the explosion was magnified, sending a base surge of displaced water fountaining thirty feet into the air. *Gremlin Zero Two* was obliterated.

* * *

Anvil two didn't meet with the same level of success. At the top of the weapon's ballistic arc, the second VLA's airframe jammed and didn't separate properly. The torpedo couldn't detach itself, and the entire missile assembly fell out of the sky well down range of its target. Falling ten thousand feet without a parachute, the faulty weapon disintegrated on impact with the water.

* * *

USS *Towers*:

The Sonar Supervisor's voice came over the 29-MC: "All Stations—Sonar has multiple hydrophone effects off the starboard beam! Bearings two-six-zero and two-six-five. Initial classification: hostile torpedoes!"

Ens. Cooper stabbed at the mike button. "USWE, aye! Break! Bridge—USWE. Crack the whip! We have in-bound hostile torpedoes. I say again—crack the whip!"

"Bridge, aye!"

The whine of the gas turbines increased in pitch and volume as the engines wound up to maximum rpm.

The Officer of the Deck's voice came over the 1-MC. "All hands stand by for heavy rolls while performing high-speed evasive maneuvers."

The deck tilted sharply to port as the ship veered into the first evasive turn.

* * *

USS *Benfold*:

Capt. Vargas punched the button that patched her comm-set into the 1-MC. "This is the Captain speaking from CIC," she said. "The bridge has been knocked out by a missile hit. I need a damage control team and medical personnel on the bridge *now*. CCS take rudder and engine controls. Engineering Officer of the Watch, establish communications with CIC on Net One Zero, and stand by for maneuvering orders. Get to it people! That is all." She released the mike button.

The TAO's console lost power. He was about to report the failure when the call came in.

"TAO—Weapons Control. Aegis is down hard!"

"What the hell happened?" the TAO snapped.

"We lost primary and alternate power to the computers, sir. Probably one of the automatic bus-tie transfers, since they're about the only pieces of gear common to both primary and alternate legs of power. The Combat Systems Officer of the Watch says his people are checking prints and chasing cables now. As soon as they find the bad ABT, they can rig casualty power."

"TAO, aye. What's your estimated time of repair?"

"The CSOOW is calling for ten minutes, sir. They might be able to cut that in half, if they get lucky and find the bad ABT quickly."

"We don't have ten minutes," Capt. Vargas said. She looked up at the darkened Aegis display screens. "We don't even have *five* minutes."

The TAO nodded. "I know that, ma'am." He keyed his mike. "Weapons Control—TAO. With Aegis down, two-thirds of your consoles are dead. Send your unused operators down to assist the CSOOW's crew on chasing cables. Let's try to speed this up."

"Weapons Control, aye."

Capt. Vargas looked at the TAO. "Go out to SAU Commander on Navy Red. Tell him we've taken a hit to the bridge, and we've lost Aegis. We will not be able to make the backup VLA shots he ordered."

The TAO nodded. "Yes, ma'am." He punched in to the secure radio channel and started his report.

* * *

USS *Ingraham*:

Captain Culkins gritted his teeth as *Benfold*'s status report came over the speaker. "Well, ain't this a pretty picture," he said quietly.

Ingraham's CIC was about half as well equipped as the ones on her more powerful sister ships. But her crew was well trained, and the gear they did have was good, even if it wasn't quite state-of-the-art. She might not have the most impressive weapons and sensors in the Search Attack Unit, but at least her combat systems hadn't crapped out in the middle of the battle.

Capt. Culkins allowed himself a tiny, humorless smile. Okay, maybe that last bit had been a bit below the belt. *Benfold* had just taken a missile hit right in the face; some equipment was bound to be knocked off-line. It was just a hell of a time to lose Aegis, the heart of the destroyer's combat system.

Culkins shook his head and keyed into Navy Red. "SAU Commander, this is *Ingraham*. Request permission to break formation and close *Benfold*'s position. We can provide missile defense coverage until *Benfold* gets her Aegis system back on line, over."

"*Ingraham*, this is SAU Commander. Roger. You are cleared to break formation. Keep an ear in the water, though. Those subs are still out there."

"You don't hear that every day," *Ingraham*'s Tactical Action Officer said. "A frigate providing missile coverage for a destroyer. My, my, how the mighty have fallen."

"Don't enjoy it too much," Capt. Culkins said. "Those are our people dying over there."

"Of course, sir," the TAO said. All traces of mockery were gone from his voice. "I'm sorry. I didn't mean ..."

"Don't sweat it," the captain said. "It's an honest mistake. I went down that road myself, for a couple of seconds."

"Yes, sir."

* * *

USS *Towers*:

"USWE—Sonar. Hostile torpedo number one has broken acquisition. Looks like we fooled it."

On the CDRT, Chief McPherson watched the symbol for one of the enemy torpedoes go astray. She keyed her mike. "Sonar—USWE. What's the status of the second torpedo?"

"Still closing, Chief. It's sticking to us like peanut butter sticks to the roof of your mouth."

"USWE, aye. Break. TAO—USWE. We have evaded the first torpedo, but the second torpedo is still locked on. We're not going to shake this one, sir."

"TAO, aye." Lt. Nylander looked at the captain. "Any ideas, sir?"

"One," the captain said. "A crazy idea that one of my academy buddies came up with about a hundred years ago. I have no idea if it'll work, but it's not like we've got a lot to lose." He looked up at the Aegis display screens. "The torpedo is coming dead up our stern, right?"

"Yes, sir."

"All right," the captain said. He keyed his mike. "Bridge—Captain. Come right thirty degrees and steady up."

"Bridge, aye. Coming right thirty degrees."

The ship began to turn.

"The idea," the captain said, "is to get the torpedo to come in from your quarter, about thirty degrees off your stern."

The TAO watched the tactical displays. "What does that do for us, sir?"

"Nothing, by itself," the captain said. "But we know the torpedo is programmed to dive under our hull and detonate. So we have to give him as little hull as possible at the critical moment. It won't eliminate the damage, but—with a little luck—it might keep this fucking torpedo from blowing us in half."

"Captain—Bridge. We are steadied up on new course zero-six-five."

"Captain, aye. Stand by for my orders. When I give the command *hard to starboard,* I want you to throw the rudder over hard to starboard, then go all-ahead flank on the port engine, and all-back on the starboard engine. Got that?"

"Bridge, aye. Copy all, sir. Standing by for your order."

"Good," the captain said. He keyed his mike again. "USWE—Captain. I need to know when that torpedo is going to hit us. I know you can't give me an exact answer, but I want Sonar's best guess, based on signal strength and elapsed run-time. Understand?"

"Uh … I think so, sir. That is, yes, sir. Do you want us to give you a count-down?"

"That's an excellent idea," the captain said.

* * *

USS *Ingraham*:

"TAO—Air. I've got three missile pop-ups! Bearing two-seven-five!"

The Electronics Warfare Technician confirmed the report a few seconds later. "TAO—EW, standing by on chaff. I have active H-band seekers on all three missiles. Classification: Exocet SM-39s, 'November Variants.'"

"TAO, aye. Break. Weapons Control—TAO. Let me know the second you get fire control lock on those Vipers."

"TAO—Weapons Control. We are locked on and tracking all three Vipers. Request batteries released."

Capt. Culkins keyed the net. "This is the Captain. You have batteries released."

* * *

Out on the forecastle, the Mark-13 missile launcher rotated up to the *zero* position and an SM-1 surface-to-air missile rode up the vertically aligned rail to lock into place on the launcher's single arm. Nicknamed the one-armed bandit, the Mark-13 system was an unwieldy-looking contraption, but it was fast. Although it could handle only one missile at a time, it could load and launch fast enough to keep up with most twin-armed launchers.

The one-armed bandit slewed around and pointed the nose of its missile in the direction of the enemy Vipers. With a brilliant flash of light and an unholy roar, the SM-1 leapt off the rail on a trail of fiery smoke. The launcher swung back around to the zero position, and another missile slid up the rail.

* * *

USS *Towers*:

"Torpedo impact in approximately ten seconds," Chief McPherson said over the net. "Nine ... Eight ..."

"Bridge—Captain. Hard to starboard!"

"Bridge, aye!"

The ship heeled over sharply, and the bow swung to the right as the rudder shot around to the hard-over position. A fraction of a second later, the ship began to shudder as the blades on the starboard propeller rotated from full ahead to full astern, reversing the direction of thrust on the starboard side of the ship. The bow came around even faster, and the ship heeled over even farther as it reefed into the turn.

Chief McPherson shouted into her mike, "Three ... Two ... One ... Impact!"

* * *

DMA37 Torpedo:

The acoustic signal strength from the transducers was close to optimal. The torpedo dove toward twelve meters and slid under the target's hull, exactly according to the targeting algorithm in its computer. But the calculations were off somehow. The target signal strength peaked before it should have and was falling off rapidly by the time the torpedo reached twelve meters.

The target had made a violent turn toward the torpedo at the last second, and the torpedo overshot its mark, rocketing under the hull and beginning to come out the other side before it could correct its course.

Had the DMA37 been a hair smarter, it might have aborted the arming sequence and swung back around for another pass at the target—one with better placement. But the arming conditions had been met, however briefly, and the computer followed its program. The detonating signal reached the warhead, and 250 kilograms of high-explosive erupted into an expanding sphere of fire and death.

* * *

USS *Towers*:

For an instant, the underwater explosion illuminated the darkened ocean like a flash of lightning. A microsecond later, the shock wave smashed into the port side of the destroyer, lifting the stern completely out of the water, and rolling the ship far onto its starboard side.

With a shriek of rending metal, hull plates buckled and collapsed. The ship's stern seemed to hang in the air for a second, apparently suspended on a mushrooming bubble of steam and fire. The keel began to bend.

Then the spell was broken, and the stern crashed back into the waves, throwing plumes of seawater fifty feet into the air. The whipsaw effect torqued the keel in the other direction, and the steel backbone of the ship groaned like a wounded animal, a resonating sound that rose through the deck plates at an incredible volume. But the keel held.

Towers rolled a little farther onto her starboard side and then sluggishly, she rolled back to port. She settled onto her wounded side and began to take on water.

* * *

Emergency battle lanterns came on automatically as power failed through two-thirds of the ship. The lanterns cast circles of light in the darkened passageways, raising the illumination level from Stygian blackness to something approaching evening twilight. The engines had fallen silent, but the semidarkness was far from quiet. The screams of injured Sailors echoed through the passageways, their cries competing with the shouts of damage control crews and the torrential rumble of the rising floodwaters.

* * *

CIC was a shambles. Capt. Bowie climbed to his feet. His ears were still ringing, and a gash across the left side of his forehead leaked blood across his face and into his eyes. He clamped his left hand over the laceration and used his right hand to wipe the blood from his eyes as best he could. He blinked and strained to see in the near darkness. "TAO!"

Lt. Nylander's voice came from behind him. "Here, sir!"

The captain turned to see the Tactical Action Officer struggling to get to his feet. The lieutenant winced and clutched at his right knee. Then he stood with a visible effort, holding on to the edge of a console for support.

"Establish comms with CCS. I need damage reports, casualty reports, and a report on the status of damage-control efforts. I want to know how long before we can make way and how long before we can fight."

"Aye-aye, sir!"

The captain reached for his comm-set and then realized that he had lost it. He looked around and selected a face at random. "Surface!"

"Yes, sir!"

"See if we can go out over Navy Red. If we can't fight, maybe we can still run this show from the sidelines."

"Aye-aye, sir."

A minute later, the Surface Radar Officer made his report. "The HF transmitters are out, Captain. We can hear, but we can't transmit. The techs are working on it now, but we don't have an ETR yet."

The captain nodded. "Very well."

A very young and timid voice asked. "Captain? Are we going to sink, sir?"

The captain made no move to locate the owner of the voice. The young man was scared, and he had every right to be. There was no sense in singling him out. "No, son," the captain said. "We are not going to sink. We're going to kill those bastards. Every goddamned one of them."

* * *

USS *Ingraham*:

Ingraham's first SM-2 reached its intercept point with one of the Vipers bound for *Benfold*, and a distant flash in the sky told the story. Radar confirmed the kill a second later. "Splash one!" the Weapons Control Officer shouted. Then, a few seconds later, "Splash two! Splash three!" He clenched his fists and waved them in the air. "We got 'em all!" He let go with a loud wolf whistle. "And *that* ... ladies and gentlemen ... is how it is done!" The CIC crew began to cheer.

Capt. Culkins smiled. "Nice shooting." This fight was far from over, but he could let them have a few seconds of self-congratulatory fun. They'd earned it.

He keyed up Navy Red. "SAU Commander, this is *Ingraham*. We have splashed all three of *Benfold*'s inbound Vipers, over."

There was no reply.

Capt. Culkins keyed up again and repeated his message.

Again, there was no answer.

This time, he went out to *Benfold*. "*Benfold*, this is *Ingraham*. Radio check, over."

"*Ingraham*, this is *Benfold*. Read you Lima Charlie, over."

Capt. Culkins frowned. *Towers* must have been hit pretty hard; they were off the air. He went out over Navy Red again. "*Benfold*, this is *Ingraham*. SAU

Commander has taken damage and cannot respond via Navy Red. You are next in seniority. Are you prepared to assume SAU Commander at this time, over?"

The reply took nearly a minute. Rachel Vargas must have been tearing her hair out over there. No commanding officer ever wanted to turn down a position of command, especially in the heat of combat, but her bridge was knocked out and most of her weapons and sensors were off line. When she finally answered, the frustration in her voice was palpable. "*Ingraham*, this is *Benfold*. I'd love to take the ball, but I'm in no shape to run with it. This one is all yours, Mike. Good luck, over."

"*Ingraham*, aye. Break. All units, this is the commanding officer of USS *Ingraham*. I am assuming SAU Commander at this time. I say again, I am assuming SAU Commander at this time, over."

He released the mike button and scanned the tactical plot. He didn't have much of a SAU left to work with. *Benfold* was out of it for the moment and so was *Towers*. That left *Ingraham* and *Towers'* helo, *Firewalker Two-Six*. His own helo, *Gunslinger Four-One*, was at Ready Five. He could launch it in a matter of minutes if he had to. He decided to hold off on that for the moment. So far, helicopters hadn't faired very well against the submarines. It wouldn't pay to risk both of the SAU's remaining air assets at the same time.

He keyed up Navy Red. "*Firewalker Two-Six*, this is SAU Commander. Say your current status, over."

"SAU Commander, this is *Firewalker Two-Six*. My fuel state is three hours plus zero two minutes. Three souls aboard. My load-out is one Mark-54 torpedo and a mixed rack of sonobuoys. I am currently monitoring passive buoys, tracking one POSS-SUB contact, designated *Gremlin Zero Three*, over."

"SAU Commander, aye. Do you have a firing solution on contact *Gremlin Zero Three*, over."

"SAU Commander, this is *Firewalker Two-Six*. That's affirmative. I've got this guy tagged and bagged. Give me batteries released, and I'll bring you his head on a plate, over."

Capt. Culkins thought about this for a few seconds. "*Firewalker Two-Six*, this is SAU Commander. You have batteries released. You are authorized to drop below two thousand feet only long enough to make your attack. Your approach and return are to be made above Angels Two, over."

"This is *Firewalker Two-Six*. Copy all. Out."

Capt. Culkins swallowed. The Navy had sent helicopters after these submarines three times, and three times the helos had been blasted out of the sky. He hoped like hell he hadn't just ordered *Firewalker*'s air crew to their deaths.

* * *

***Firewalker Two-Six*:**

The pilot's name was Lieutenant Clinton Brody, or just *Clint* to his buddies. He scanned his instrument panel and keyed his inter-phone. "Start your weapons check-off list," he said to the Sensor Operator. He looked over at his copilot, Lieutenant (junior grade) Julie Schramm. "Here's the plan, Jules. We stay above Angels Two for the approach. As soon as we start our attack dive, you launch a pair of flares. My guess is the sub will pickle off a heat seeker with our name on it the instant he detects our rotor wash. The flares will give the missile something to play with. As soon as our weapon is away, we bank hard to port, climb like hell, and you pop off two more flares. Got it?"

His copilot nodded. "Piece-o-cake, boss."

"Good. Now, go ahead and make your reports."

The copilot keyed her radio. "SAU Commander, this is *Firewalker Two-Six.* I am prepping for my attack run, over."

"SAU Commander, aye. Good hunting."

About a minute later, the Sensor Operator reported that the weapon was ready to drop. "Standing by to launch on your order, sir."

"All right, let's do this," the pilot said. He nudged the stick forward, pitching his aircraft into a dive. "Weapon away on my mark"

"Aye-aye, sir."

The copilot punched a button. "Flares away." Two brilliant flashes of light appeared at the edges of their peripheral vision and rapidly fell away behind the aircraft.

In the darkness the ocean was invisible. But it was down there all right, rushing up to meet them at breakneck speed.

"Stand by ..." the pilot said, watching the numbers on his altimeter unwind. "Launch—now, now, NOW!"

The Sensor Operator smashed his thumb down onto the firing button, and the aircraft lurched as the torpedo dropped clear. "Weapon away, sir!"

The pilot pulled back on the stick, and the helo began to climb. "Pack a bag, kids, 'cause we are out of here!"

The copilot punched another button. Two more flares ignited and fell away into the darkness. "Flares away!"

"Here it comes!" the Sensor Operator shouted. "Missile-emergence, bearing one-three-six!"

"Holy shit!" Lt. Brody said as he jogged his aircraft into a sharp bank to the left, still fighting for every inch of altitude he could get. "The welcoming committee doesn't fuck around!"

Something caught his attention at the lower threshold of his hearing. His copilot was mumbling something. Her words were very soft, and he had to strain to make them out over the hammering of the rotors. "Hail Mary, full of grace … Hail Mary, full of grace … Hail Mary, full of grace …"

He looked over his left shoulder. "Where's the missile?"

"I don't know, sir!" the SENSO said. "I lost it!"

"Well find it!"

Below them, a circle of the night sky flashed yellow-white as the heat-seeking missile homed in on one of the flares and detonated.

"See that?" Lt. Brody said. "No big deal when you fly with the pros." His cocky tone of voice gave no hint of the fact that he'd just been hit by a nearly overpowering urge to urinate.

The SENSO held his headphone closer to his ear. "We've got weapon start-up, sir." A few seconds later, he added, "Looks like good placement, sir. The weapon has already acquired."

For the briefest of instants, a patch of ocean two thousand feet below lit up like daylight.

"Bull's-eye!" the Sensor Operator shouted. "Loud underwater explosion with multiple secondaries! I think we just bagged us a submarine!"

"Outstanding!" Lt. Brody said. "Now comes *Miller Time* …"

His copilot looked at him. "Now comes *what*?"

"Miller Time," the pilot said. "You know … the old beer commercials …"

Lt.(jg) Schramm shrugged. "Must have been before my time, boss."

The pilot raised an eyebrow. "It all becomes clear, now. You're the brilliant young Jedi apprentice, and I'm the toothless old codger who must educate you in the ways of the Force."

"I don't know about the *toothless* part …" the copilot said, "but the rest of it sounds dead on the money."

"Uh … sir?" the SENSO said. "I hate to interrupt all that official pilot talk, but I think I'm getting a sniff on the third submarine."

The pilot stared over his right shoulder. "Get out of town, kid."

"I'm not joking, sir. Buoys three and four are coming up hot. I've got narrowband tonals consistent with a Type 212 diesel submarine. I think the other member of this wolfpack is about to crash the barrier."

"You're not shitting me?"

The SENSO's eyes were locked on his display. "No, sir. This guy is getting stronger all the time."

The pilot looked over at his copilot. "You wouldn't happen to have a spare torpedo in your pocket, would you?"

"Afraid not."

"Damn it!" the pilot said. "Make the call to the SAU Commander. Tell him we've got another sub in our sights, and we are fresh out of torpedoes!"

* * *

USS *Towers*:

Chief McPherson listened to *Firewalker*'s contact report and shook her head. *Ingraham* was the only unit left that was capable of engaging the sub. But the frigate was not equipped with ASROC. *Ingraham* would have to close the submarine to within a few thousand yards and conduct a torpedo attack using her over-the-side torpedo tubes. An iffy proposition at best. The last place a surface ship wanted to be was within weapons range of a hostile submarine.

The chief stared at the dark screen of the powerless CDRT as if it still had the capacity to show her something. If she'd been in Cmdr. Culkins' shoes, she would have launched *Gunslinger Four-One*. Of course, the launch itself would take about five minutes. Add to that another ten minutes for the helo to get into attack position. Fifteen minutes minimum before the helo would be able to engage the submarine. Fifteen minutes was a long time. The sub could launch more Vipers, or it might disappear again. Cmdr. Culkins wouldn't want to take that risk. He would go after the submarine himself, despite the risks.

Perhaps thirty seconds later, the SAU Commander responded to *Firewalker*'s contact report, and all of the chief's predictions came true.

"*Firewalker Two-Six*. All units, this is SAU Commander. Your contact designated *Gremlin Zero Four*. Maintain track and pass targeting data to all units. Break. All units, this is SAU Commander. *Ingraham* is detaching from the formation to pursue and engage *Gremlin Zero Four*. Wish us luck, over."

Chief McPherson's eyes stayed glued to the useless screen of the CDRT. "Come on, baby," she whispered quietly. "You've got the ball. Now bring it on home to mama."

CHAPTER 39

USS *INGRAHAM* (FFG-61)
NORTHERN STRAITS OF HORMUZ
SUNDAY; 20 MAY
2247 hours (10:47 PM)
TIME ZONE +4 'DELTA'

Engineman First Class Donald Sebring, the Engineering Officer of the Watch, stared at a cluster of instruments on the Propulsion and Auxiliary Control Console. "Oh, come on, not now ..."

He keyed his mike. "Bridge—CCS. We've got high vibrations on the output side of the main reduction gears. In accordance with standard EOSS procedures, recommend slowing one major speed while we investigate."

The reply came almost immediately, but it wasn't the bridge; it was the commanding officer. "CCS, this is the Captain. Conduct your investigation but do not reduce speed. You are directed to maintain speed at all costs."

The captain's words took Sebring by surprise. Maintain speed? The casualty response was clearly outlined in the Engineering Operational Sequencing System. EOSS called for a reduction in speed while investigating out-of-tolerance vibrations. Didn't the CO realize that he was risking the entire engineering plant?

Petty Officer Sebring switched channels and keyed his mike again. "Messenger—CCS. We have high vibrations on the output side of the MRGs."

"CCS—Messenger, high vibrations on the output side of MRGs, aye." The voice belonged to Fireman Sandra Cox. "Do you want me to walk the shaft?"

Sebring keyed his mike again. "Messenger—CCS. That's affirmative. Walk the shaft starting at the MRGs and report ASAP."

"Messenger, aye."

Walking the shaft was an engineering term for visually inspecting every inch of the ninety-four-and-a-half–foot propeller shaft—from the Main Engine

Room, where it coupled with the output side of the main reduction gears—to Shaft Alley, where it passed through the watertight seals of the stuffing box and out through the bottom of the hull into the ocean. With luck, the Messenger's inspection would turn up something simple, like a broken pipe or a shifted bracket rubbing against the shaft.

On Sebring's first ship, a mop bucket had gotten loose during a high-speed turn and had somehow managed to wedge itself under the shaft. The metal sides of the bucket had formed a natural resonating chamber, amplifying the vibrations of the spinning shaft until it sounded like the mating cry of a brontosaurus.

The memory brought a flicker of a smile to Sebring's lips, but any trace of humor was driven instantly from his mind by the angry buzzing of an alarm on the Damage Control Console.

A half-second later, the DC Console Watch shouted, "Smoke alarm in AMR #3!"

Sebring switched back to the bridge circuit and keyed his mike. "Bridge—CCS. We've got a smoke alarm in Auxiliary Machinery Room #3. Report to follow."

"CCS—Bridge. Copy your smoke alarm in AMR #3. Call it away."

Sebring grabbed the flexible microphone stalk for the general announcing circuit and swung it down near his face. There was a brass bell bolted to the bulkhead to the right of his console. He grabbed the lanyard, pressed the microphone button, and rang the bell rapidly eight times, paused for a couple of seconds and then gave three distinct rings of the bell to indicate that the casualty was in the aft portion of the ship. The sound of the bells and his voice blared from 1-MC speakers all over the ship. "Smoke, smoke, smoke. We have a smoke alarm in Auxiliary Machinery Room #3. Away the Flying Squad. Provide from Repair Three." He rang the bell again and repeated the message. And then he shoved the 1-MC microphone away.

"DC Console Watch, start your plot."

"Already started, boss."

Sebring glanced at the clock. Because of the possible presence of smoke, the Flying Squad would have to wear Self-Contained Breathing Apparatuses to enter AMR #3. Of course, at General Quarters, they would already be wearing their SCBAs. But they would still have to light off their breathing gear and conduct seal checks. Figure one minute for that, plus another minute to haul ass to AMR #3, check the door for heat and pressure, and enter the space. It would be at least two minutes before any damage reports started coming in. By that time, the Damage Control Assistant would have shown up and taken control of the investigation and repair efforts.

Sebring keyed his headset mike again. "Messenger—CCS. Continue your walk down of the shaft, but skip over AMR #3. The Flying Squad will handle that space."

"CCS—Messenger. Continue my walk-down of the shaft, but skip over AMR #3, aye."

Sebring looked at the readouts from the vibration sensors. The vibrations were getting worse. This didn't look much like a runaway mop bucket.

He heard it in the distance at first—a low, slow groaning sound that reminded him vaguely of whale songs. But this sound didn't taper off to silence the way that whale songs did. It grew continually louder until Sebring could feel it resonating through the very deck plates. And then it grew louder still, loud enough to rattle the glass faceplates of the dials on his console. And he began to realize what the sound must mean.

Sebring looked at his watch. Where in the hell was the Damage Control Assistant? The DCA should have been running this show. Where was he?

"CCS—Flying Squad. Four SCBAs lit off, time two-two-one-eight. Door checks are complete. We are entering the space."

Sebring nodded unconsciously. "CCS, aye."

The second report came almost immediately, at a near shout as the Flying Squad leader struggled to be heard over the noise of the strange groaning vibration. "CCS—Flying Squad. We have heavy smoke in AMR #3. We are preparing to scan with Nifty."

Nifty, or NFTI, was the Naval Firefighting Thermal Imager: a handheld infrared viewer that could spot sources of heat even in total darkness.

"CCS, aye." Sebring was only half-listening to the reports of the Flying Squad. The groaning was still growing louder, and its accompanying vibration was beginning to rattle the entire ship. He was picturing AMR #3 in his mind now, and he knew what the Flying Squad was going to find.

The door behind him rattled as the dogging lever came up. Lieutenant (junior grade) Mark Wu, the ship's Damage Control Assistant, came through, dogging the door behind himself. "Sorry I'm late," he said. "I shouldn't have had that damned chili. It's killing my stomach. I can't seem to get more than fifty feet from the head."

He walked up behind EN1 Sebring. "Give me a pass-down."

He was interrupted by a half-shouted voice over the speaker. "CCS—Flying Squad. The line shaft bearing is smoking! I say again, the main line shaft bearing in AMR #3 is smoking. It's so hot that it whited out my Nifty. Recommend we rig a fire hose to attempt seawater cooling."

Sebring keyed his mike. "Flying Squad—CCS. Negative. Do not attempt to cool the bearing. Evacuate the space and wait for orders."

"Good call," the DCA said. "If that bearing is hot enough to zap the Nifty, it'll explode when cold water hits it."

Sebring switched circuits and keyed up again. "Repair Three—CCS. Set primary fire boundaries around Auxiliary Machinery Room #3."

The repair locker phone talker acknowledged and repeated back his order.

The groaning sound was a roar now, and the entire ship was rattling like an old car on a dirt road.

Sebring pulled off his headset and handed it to the DCA. "You've got to talk to the captain, sir. He won't listen to me."

Lt.(jg) Wu pulled the headset on and keyed the mike. "Captain—DCA. The main line shaft bearing in AMR #3 is burning. Recommend we stop engines and lock the shaft immediately to prevent serious damage to the engineering plant."

The CO's voice came back immediately. "DCA—Captain. Negative. We are in pursuit of a hostile submarine. You are ordered to maintain speed."

The DCA keyed his mike again. "Captain—DCA. If that bearing locks up while the shaft is still turning ..."

The captain cut him off. "I know we can wreck the plant, Mark. I also know what can happen if we don't sink this damned sub. Two minutes, Mark. That's all I need to get within firing range. You give me two more minutes of speed, and then you can trash the whole plant."

Wu keyed his mike. "DCA, aye."

He looked down at Sebring. "What do you think? Will that bearing hold together for another two minutes?"

Sebring shrugged. "I have no idea, sir. I've never even heard of anyone running flank speed with a burned line shaft bearing. I'm amazed that it's held this long."

* * *

For a little while, it seemed as if the captain might actually get his two minutes. But suddenly, there was a brief but harsh metallic scraping sound, followed immediately by the shriek of tearing metal.

In AMR #3, the burning bearing seized up, grinding the spinning propeller shaft to an abrupt halt.

In the Main Engine Room, *Ingraham*'s gas turbine engines continued to crank forty-one thousand horsepower of torque into the input shaft of the main reduction gears. But the reduction gears couldn't turn, because the output shaft was locked in place. The transverse frames that supported the reduction gear housing began to buckle under the strain, as the howling turbines attempted to turn the entire main reduction gear, housing and all.

The monstrous stress ripped open welds between plates of the ship's hull, and the sea came flooding in. The MRG housing cracked, spraying lubricating oil all over the engine room, and throwing off hot steel shrapnel like a bomb.

A fist-sized chunk of broken gear caught the Upper-Level Watch in the left cheek. Moving at the speed of a meteor, it tore the side of his head off without even slowing down. His limp body fell off the catwalk and into the rapidly flooding bilge.

* * *

Ingraham drifted to a stop and wallowed at the mercy of the waves. The chase was over. The submarine was gone.

CHAPTER 40

OVAL OFFICE
WASHINGTON, DC
SUNDAY; 20 MAY
4:03 PM EDT

"Just a second, Bob," President Chandler said. "Let me go secure." He inserted the magnetically coded encryption key into the slot on his STU-6 secure telephone unit and gave it a half-turn clockwise. The key clicked as it locked into place, and a brief series of warbling tones came out of the earpiece while the phone synced up with the encryption algorithm in a twin phone on the desk of the Chief of Naval Operations. The red "clear" lamp went out, and the green "secure" lamp came on.

"Okay, Bob," the president said. "We're in the green. I assume you're calling to give me an update on the sub hunt. How are we looking?"

"It's the old joke, Mr. President," Adm. Casey said. "Good news and bad news."

"What's the good news?"

"We have clear battle damage assessment. *Towers* took out one of the submarines. Her helicopter took out another one."

"So there's only one hostile sub left?"

"Yes, sir."

"Excellent," the president said. "What's the bad news?"

"*Towers* and *Benfold* are both shot up pretty badly, and *Ingraham* is totally out of the picture. Somebody is going to have to write a bunch of those 'The U.S. Navy regrets' telegrams, sir. Quite a few of our young men and women out there are coming home in body bags."

"We're paying a hell of a price," the president said. "But we can still win this thing, can't we?"

The CNO sighed. "I don't know, sir. *Towers* has already restored her electrical power, and *Benfold* should be back under way within an hour or so. How much speed they can make still remains to be seen. Maybe they can catch that sub. Then again, maybe not."

"If they catch it, can they kill it?"

"I think so, Mr. President. I damned sure hope so."

"You aren't exactly filling me with confidence here, Bob."

"With all due respect, sir, if you want more confidence you've got to give me more assets. It's not too late to get a couple of P-3s out there. Then I could pretty much guarantee you a kill."

"I can't do that, Bob," the president said. "We've got to show that we can go toe-to-toe with the best the Germans can offer up and still come out on top."

"I understand that, sir. But what if that sub gets by us? Why risk losing when there's still a chance to guarantee a win?"

"Goddamn it, Bob! Can't you see what this is about? In the minds of the people, perception is reality. Shoernberg is making a power play here, and he's only thrown a few cards on the table to do it. If we have to call up the militia, the Boy Scouts, and the Air National Guard to catch one lousy German submarine, he *wins*. Shoernberg will have successfully demonstrated that the United States cannot win in a fair fight against German military hardware and tactics. He'll come out of this flexing his muscles, and we'll end up looking weak. And about twenty minutes after the dust settles, every pocket Napoleon in the developing world is going to start wondering if the U.S. is really so tough after all.

"We've only got one choice here, Bob. We've got to take Friedrik Shoernberg's little power play and shove it so far up his ass that he can't remember what he had for breakfast. He sends out four submarines; *none* of them get through. Not *one* of them! Then he only has two choices: escalate the conflict or back down. And I don't think he's stupid enough to escalate."

"Mr. President, if what you say is true, then we need to *guarantee* a kill on that last submarine," the CNO said. "And, if you need a guaranteed kill, you've got to let me throw some more assets into the hunt."

"No, Bob. *How* we kill that submarine is every bit as important as whether or not we kill it at all."

"That's what you keep telling me, sir," the CNO said. "But I've got two ships out there that have already had the shit shot out of them, and I'm asking them to take on a killer submarine without backup."

The president sighed. "Okay, Bob. Let's try it this way ... In a one-on-one fight between a surface combatant and a submarine, who wins?"

"Whoever shoots first, sir."

"Exactly. And who *shoots* first?"

"Whoever gets contact first."

The president chuckled. "You're going to make me drag this out of you, aren't you? All right, you stubborn bastard, who gets contact first?"

"Three times out of five, it's going to be the submarine, sir."

"So, if a surface ship mixes it up with a submarine, three times out of five, the ship gets its doors blown off. Would that be a safe assumption?"

"Pretty much, sir."

"And anybody who has a clue about Undersea Warfare knows this?"

"Yes, sir."

"Okay, how many of our ships have the Germans sunk so far?"

"One, sir, if you count the *Antietam*."

"I do *not* count the *Antietam*," the president said. "She isn't sunk, and she isn't going to be. In fact, we're going to repair her and keep her in service."

"With all due respect, sir, that doesn't make any sense. We can build a Flight-Three *Arleigh Burke* with every bit as much firepower and a thirty-year service life for what it would cost to put *Antietam* back together. Why waste that kind of money on a cruiser that's over twenty years old?"

"Perception," the president said. "Perception. The political value will be tremendous. Think about how it will look to the man on the street ... Submarines kill surface combatants three times out of five, but *not* when they take on the United States. We go one-on-one, ship-to-sub, and we kill *everything*. The Germans lose *every* single unit they send out, but *all* of our ships make it home. Every single one of them lives to fight another day. In a fight where the Germans have the inherent advantage, Shoernberg loses it all. He comes away with no military victory, no propaganda coup, no bragging rights. Nothing."

"And you think he'll tuck tail and go home?"

"If he does, maybe we can stitch NATO back together for a few years," the president said.

"What if he doesn't, sir? What if Chancellor Shoernberg comes out with guns blazing?"

"Then we teach him a lesson that his country has already learned twice."

The line was silent for nearly a full minute before the president spoke again. "Bob, we can't afford to lose this one."

The CNO's voice was very quiet. "I know, Mr. President. I know."

CHAPTER 41

U.S. NAVY CENTRAL COMMAND (USNAVCENT)
BAHRAIN
SUNDAY; 20 MAY
1740 hours (5:40 PM)
TIME ZONE-4 'DELTA'

The shore version of the admiral's Flag Plot bore very little resemblance to the sort found on aircraft carriers. Gone were the radar consoles and radio handsets, replaced by computer terminals and desks with secure telephones. The walls—uncluttered by piping and cable runs—were decorated with bronze and wooden plaques bearing the names and coats of arms of nearly every ship, submarine, and aircraft squadron that had ever served within the U.S. Naval Central Command's area of responsibility. The large tactical display screens that dominated the east wall were of civilian design: the type used by corporations for training or briefing large groups of people. But despite the obvious physical differences, the shore and ship versions of Flag Plot were more alike than they were different. The tools were different, but the conversations that took place over the secure telephones tended to cover the same subjects that were discussed over shipboard secure radio circuits. The tactical symbols that peppered the big civilian-built display screens were from the same catalog of symbology used on ships.

The Duty Intelligence Officer, Lieutenant Commander Calvin Fisk, didn't give the differences or similarities of ship and shore facilities even a passing thought. In addition to his other duties, he had an inch-thick stack of reports and message traffic to plow through. Luckily, most of the information was routine, meaning that he could skim some of the pages—checking only for significant changes in matters of tactical interest.

One message grabbed his attention. It was a contact locator report from SUCAP (Surface Combat Air Patrol), the squadron of fighter jets dedicated to monitoring—and if necessary, engaging—hostile and unknown surface craft operating in the Gulf region.

According to the report, three unmarked fishing trawlers had spent several hours cruising around off the coast of Siraj. Ordinarily, this wouldn't have even been worth mentioning, but the SUCAP aircraft had spotted the trawlers several times, and none of the boats had ever made any visible efforts to deploy fishing nets.

Lt. Cmdr. Fisk looked up from the stack of paperwork. He wasn't particularly concerned, but it was a little strange. He picked up the phone and punched the extension number for the Plot Supervisor.

"Plot Supe."

"This is the Duty Intelligence Officer," Fisk said. "I'm holding a SUCAP locator report on some Siraji fishing boats that are acting a bit on the squirrelly side. I'm sending a copy your way. I want each reported position for the boats recorded on the master tactical plot. I also want you to update the positions of the boats if any new reports come in."

"Will do, sir," the Plot Supervisor said.

As soon as he hung up the phone, Fisk realized that he hadn't mentioned the lack of nets. It probably wasn't important anyway.

He summoned an orderly. "Here," he said, handing the young Sailor the SUCAP message. "Make a copy of this. Put the original back on the *Read Board* and take the copy over to master tactical plot and give it to the Plot Supervisor.

"Aye-aye, sir." The orderly turned and walked away with the message.

The Duty Intelligence Officer went back to his stack of reports and didn't give the fishing boats another thought.

* * *

Four hours later, the on-coming Plot Supervisor examined the master tactical plot as part of his preparations for assuming the watch. He pointed to the track history for Lt. Cmdr. Fisk's fishing trawlers. "What the hell were these guys doing?"

The off-going Plot Supervisor shrugged. "Fishing, probably. The intel officer got a bug up his ass and made me put them on the plot." He laughed. "Why? Do you think they're fishing in a manner that poses a threat to the security of the United States of America?" The last part was in an exaggeratedly masculine voice that was obviously meant to mimic the overly histrionic narrators used in Navy training videos.

The on-coming Plot Supervisor didn't smile. "I don't think they're fishing at all," he said. He pointed to the track history. "Look at all these course changes, like they were weaving a blanket, or something. If they were fishing, they ran over their own nets at least a dozen times. Where are they now?"

The off-going Plot Supervisor yawned and stretched. "They pulled back into Zubayr about forty minutes ago. Why? What do *you* think they were doing?"

"You've got me by the short and curlies," the on-coming supervisor said. "But you can bet your ass it wasn't fishing."

CHAPTER 42

USS *TOWERS* (DDG-103)
SOUTHERN ARABIAN GULF
SUNDAY; 20 MAY
2140 hours (9:40 PM)
TIME ZONE +4 'DELTA'

Capt. Bowie addressed the small group of men and women gathered around the wardroom table. "I apologize for calling this meeting at such a late hour, but we may very well be in combat again by tomorrow morning, and that means we have to make our preparations tonight." His eyes lit on the commanding officer of USS *Benfold*, and he nodded in her direction. "I'd like to thank Commander Vargas, and her USW Officer, Lieutenant (junior grade) Sherman, for accepting my invitation to join us tonight. I know that they have personnel casualties and damage-control issues to deal with back on their own ship, and I can appreciate how difficult it must have been to tear themselves away."

Cmdr. Vargas nodded. "I'm glad to be here, Captain. This really isn't an easy time to leave my ship, and I have to confess that I was tempted to send Lieutenant (jg) Sherman by himself. But I have a top-notch exec, and I'm certain that my ship is in the best of hands. Still, I had to do some soul searching before deciding to come. Here's what made up my mind ... Our SAU is down to two ships now, both of which are damaged. We have a tremendous amount of firepower at our command, but very little of it can be brought to bear against a submerged submarine, which tells me that we probably can't outrun this guy, and we certainly don't outgun him. If we're going to sink that submarine, we're going to have to out-think him." She looked around the table. "And since this is where most of that thinking is going to take place, this is where I need to be tonight."

Capt. Bowie nodded. "Well said, Commander. Well said." He looked at the XO. "I've asked my executive officer, Lieutenant Commander Tyler, to kick us off with an outline of our current status. Pete?"

The XO nodded. "Thank you, sir." He paused for a second and briefly consulted some notes that he'd made on a yellow legal pad. "The torpedo hit that we took on the port side did a number on us. We have a hole in the hull, to the port side of the keel. We've estimated its size at about twenty feet by fifteen feet, but we don't know the actual dimensions of the hole, because the compartments that it opens onto are all flooded to the overheads. If we had time, we could ask for a team of divers to conduct an underwater survey of the damage, but time is the one thing we haven't got. However large the hole is, we know that it's added four inches to our draft in the aft end of the ship, and it's given us a five-degree permanent list to port. We considered counter-flooding some compartments on the starboard side, to balance out the list and improve our stability, but we're already hauling around enough flooding water to slow us down.

"To make matters worse, the hydraulic oil power module for the port shaft has at least a dozen leaks from shrapnel damage. We can't control the pitch of the port screw, and right now it's set pretty close to zero. We can spin the port shaft, but, without pitch control, it'll just thrash the water and make a lot of noise; it won't actually give us any headway.

"Between the weight of the flooding water and the loss of the port screw, our top speed is reduced to about eighteen and a half knots. Our engineers are working their asses off to restore pitch control to the port screw, but we can't count on it being ready in time to be of use."

He glanced at his legal pad again. "Personnel casualties, thank God, have been surprisingly light. Three dead, three reasonably serious injury cases—none of them life-threatening—and a couple of dozen minor injuries ... sprained ankles, broken noses, and superficial lacerations, that sort of thing."

The captain touched the bandage over his left eye and gave a grim smile. "Easy for you to say, XO. They're only superficial when it's not *your* head."

The XO reddened. "Of course, sir. The point is, we have a few personnel shortages, but we're not cut so short that we can't steam or fight." He checked his legal pad one last time. "That's about it for now, sir. We've taken some lumps, but we're not out of the fight."

The captain nodded. "Thanks, XO. Commander Vargas, could you give us a quick rundown on your own status?"

"Of course, Captain," Cmdr. Vargas said. "I didn't bring my notes, but I think I can wing it." She thought for a few seconds. "I'm afraid that our personnel casualties were a bit heavier than yours. The rocket attack killed all six members of my bridge crew. The Helmsman was still alive when our stretcher team got to him, but he died on the way down to Sick Bay." She paused again before continuing. "Our Ship Control Console is totally wrecked, but we've worked out a system of steering from the bridge. The Conning Officer has to relay his course orders to the Secondary Control Console in After Steering, and his speed orders to Propulsion Control Console in CCS. It's awkward, but it works. The explosion blew out most of the windows, so the watch team is constantly getting about twenty knots of hot desert wind right in the face. Not pleasant, but they're dealing with it.

"Let's see ..." she said. "What else?"

"The helo," Lt.(jg) Sherman said softly.

"Right," said Cmdr. Vargas. "Thanks. Since *Ingraham* is down for the count, we've borrowed their helo, *Gunslinger Four-One*. We don't have a helo hangar, but I figure that any aircraft that costs thirty million dollars should be able to survive for a day or two strapped to our flight deck." She gave a tired smile. "Our flight deck crew wanted the air crew to feel at home, so they went out and painted a welcoming sign on the door to the helo control tower. It's one of those big blue road signs, like the ones you see near highway off-ramps. It's got those three symbols on it that mean gas, food, and lodging." Her voice trailed off. "I think that's it."

"Thank you, Commander," the captain said. "I guess we're ready for the tactical part of the brief. Ready, Chief?"

Chief McPherson unrolled a navigational chart of the Arabian Gulf and laid it on the table. "Yes, sir." On the chart, in colored marker, she had drawn a series of lines and symbols describing the current tactical situation. The last known position of *Gremlin Zero Four* was marked by a red datum symbol. The datum was now two and a half hours old, and a black dashed circle enclosed it at a scaled range of fifty nautical miles. Based on the submarine's maximum submerged speed of twenty knots, this dashed line—or farthest-on circle—represented the farthest that it could have possibly traveled in two and a half hours. "This chart is already time-late," Chief McPherson said. "A contact moving at twenty knots will travel two thousand yards in three minutes. Therefore, every three minutes, the radius of the farthest-on circle increases by two thousand yards, or one nautical mile. The piece of ocean that we have to search grows by a corresponding amount. Our top speed is limited to eighteen and a half knots. So, if the sub is running away at top speed, we'll never catch him. If he's headed northwest toward Siraj at a dead run, every three minutes he gets a hundred and fifty yards farther ahead of us. The longer we chase him, the farther ahead he's going to get."

Lt.(jg) Sherman shook his head. "In theory that's true, Chief. But your own calculations show that these 212s have only been covering an average distance of 13.5 nautical miles per hour. No doubt this guy *can* outrun us, but—based on the performance they've shown so far—I don't think he will."

"We were his last roadblock," the chief said. "If I were him, I'd forget about sneaking around. I'd be hauling ass toward the Siraji coastline. There's nothing between him and Zubayr but open water."

"Maybe he doesn't know that," Ens. Cooper said.

Chief McPherson gave her boss an uncertain look. "German intel on our positioning has been pretty damned good. Which probably means that sub is getting downloads from reconnaissance satellites. If he is, he already knows there aren't any more ships in his way."

"That could be," Capt. Bowie said. "But he can't possibly know whether or not we're planning to send P-3s after him."

"That raises an excellent question," Cmdr. Vargas said. "Why *aren't* we trying to get some P-3s? Captain Whiley is out of the game; why are we still trying to fight this thing with one foot in a bucket?"

Around the group, heads nodded in silent agreement.

"I don't know," Capt. Bowie said. "I asked Admiral Rogers that same question. He told me that the answer was classified at a need-to-know level *way* above his head. He hinted that the CNO had told him that it was a matter of the highest national security."

Cmdr. Vargas ran her fingers through her hair. "They won't give us backup, and the reason *why* they won't give it to us is a matter of national security. What kind of sense does that make?"

Capt. Bowie's eyebrows went up. "I don't know, Rachel. But think about this: Three nations, all of whom are members of NATO *and* the United Nations, have been in direct military conflict for the past few days. A lot of political and military alliances are on the chopping block. There's no telling what kind of bizarre diplomatic maneuvers are going on right now, or what might upset the apple cart."

Lt.(jg) Sherman said, "Maybe the Saudis have clamped down on their airspace until this thing blows over. The French did that when Reagan ordered the bombing of Libya, back in the 1980s."

"That's possible," Capt. Bowie said. "But for right now, the brass hats don't want us to know the reason. So we move on, and we work with what we've got."

Cmdr. Vargas said, "What we've got is a big piece of water and damn few assets to search it with. Anybody got any ideas on where to start?"

"I think we should sprint up to the north end of the pond," Lt.(jg) Sherman said with a weak smile, "or maybe I should say 'hobble' … and set up a blockade off the coast of Siraj. Then we nail them when they think they're on the home stretch."

"Not a bad idea," Capt. Bowie said. "We may use that as our fall-back plan, but I hate to let the sub get that close to Siraj. If he slips by us then, we've lost him. We need to catch him down at this end of the pond, if we can."

Cmdr. Vargas nodded. "I agree with you, in theory. But there aren't any choke points between here and Siraj. If we sweep the western side of the gulf, the sub can run up the eastern side. If we sweep the middle, he can slip past us on either side. We just don't have enough assets to string a barrier all the way across the gulf."

"Maybe we don't have to," Ens. Cooper said thoughtfully. "Maybe it's not as big a pond as we think it is."

Capt. Bowie looked at him. "What have you got, Pat?"

Ens. Cooper stared at the chart. "I have to wonder where those subs have been refueling."

"The intel weenies say they topped off in Port Suez," Chief McPherson said. "Just after they transited the canal."

"That would get them down the Red Sea and through the Gulf of Aden," Ens. Cooper said. "But they wouldn't have made it across the Arabian Sea, and *certainly* not all the way up to the Straits of Hormuz."

Capt. Bowie nodded. "Good call, Pat. They must have fueled up again some time after they mixed it up with the *Kitty Hawk* strike group. If we can figure out where, we can make a decent guess at where that last sub is going to run out of gas."

Ens. Cooper ran a fingertip across the chart and brought it to a stop on an island at the southwest end of the Arabian Sea. "I'm betting it was here, Captain. The island of Socotra."

The captain scratched his chin. "How did you come up with *that*?"

"Look at this entire operation, sir. The Germans put a lot of work into planning this. They didn't leave a lot to chance."

"I can't argue with that. But how does it tell us where they stopped for fuel?"

"They had to plan for the possibility that word would be out by now," the ensign said. "In which case ports that are friendly to the United States would be closed to them."

"Makes sense to me," the XO said.

Ens. Cooper nodded. "They would have mapped out their fueling stops ahead of time, and I'll bet you they stuck to ports that don't have close ties to the U.S." He used his finger to trace a rough arc on the chart. "They would have been running low on fuel somewhere in here." Only two countries fell within the arc he was tracing on the chart: Oman and Yemen. "That gives us two likely candidates, and Oman—if you've been following the news—has been kissing up to our government for months now. They're trying to wheedle their way into 'favored nation' status, so we'll lift the technical embargo that's keeping their communications and computer infrastructure in the dark ages. I figure they don't want to risk screwing that up, so they'll probably steer clear of anything that even *smells* like conflict with the U.S. That leaves our buddies down in Yemen, and they *have* been known to play footsie with enemies of the United States. Remember when the USS *Cole* was bombed back in 2000? That happened in a port called Aden, and guess what country Aden is in?"

"Yemen," Chief McPherson said.

Ens. Cooper nodded. "Bingo."

"Okay," Cmdr. Vargas said, "admittedly, Yemen is not at the top of our national Christmas card list. But how did you happen to pick this island? Scotroa, was it?"

"*Socotra*, ma'am. And it's mostly a hunch. It's owned by Yemen, but it's far enough away from their coastline that the Yemeni government can deny involvement if anything goes wrong. Plus, it's on an almost direct line from the point where the *Kitty Hawk* encountered the subs, to where the subs entered the Straits of Hormuz."

Capt. Bowie's eyebrows went up.

Chief McPherson smiled. "That's pretty heady stuff, sir. Have you been eating your Wheaties?"

Ens. Cooper frowned. "Why, Chief? Did I say something wrong?"

The chief shook her head. "Not as far as I can see, sir. I think you nailed it."

Cmdr. Vargas tilted her head to one side. "It's still just a guess, but I have to admit, it looks like a pretty damned good one."

"Looks good to me," Lt.(jg) Sherman said.

"Okay," Capt. Bowie said. "We go with Pat's hunch until something better comes along."

Ens. Cooper's eyes widened.

Capt. Bowie laughed. "Don't look so shocked, Pat. We're not so hidebound that we can't recognize good thinking when we see it, even if it does come from the new kid on the block. Now, reach into your hunch generator and see if you can pull out the next place that sub is going to take on fuel. He's got to be thirsty by now. Where's he going to stop for a drink?"

Ens. Cooper studied the chart. After a few seconds, he said, "Qatar."

Cmdr. Vargas looked at Capt. Bowie. "Where did you find this kid? The Psychic Hotline?"

"It's within the sub's range, if it fueled up in Socotra," Ens. Cooper said. "The current regime is not particularly friendly to the United States. It's even roughly in line with the sub's last known position and the Siraji port of Zubayr."

"What about Iran?" Lt.(jg) Sherman asked. "They're not big fans of the U.S., and they've got tons of coastline that a sub could slip up to."

"Iran doesn't like us much," Ens. Cooper said, "but they hate Siraj a lot more. Those guys have been sniping across the border at each other for thirty years. I doubt the Iranian government would jump through hoops to break an arms embargo against one of their long-running enemies."

"I'll admit," Cmdr. Vargas said, "that Qatar is copping an attitude toward us. But would they risk international censure to help out Siraj?"

"They might, if the money was right," Ens. Cooper said. "But, if they're smart, they won't let the submarine pull into any of their ports. They'll keep it at sea, so they can claim ignorance if things go bad."

Capt. Bowie frowned. "Does Qatar have any oilers configured for at-sea replenishment?"

Ens. Cooper shook his head. "Not that I know of, sir. But they don't need one. All they have to do is pull up to an oil platform."

"An interesting theory," Lt.(jg) Sherman said, "but subs don't run on crude oil. They're going to need diesel, and oil platforms aren't set up to refine crude oil into fuel."

"Actually, oil platforms *do* have diesel tanks," Ens. Cooper said. "For their generators and the small boats that work the rigs—that sort of thing."

Chief McPherson whistled slowly through her teeth. "You *have* been eating your Wheaties!"

Cmdr. Vargas nodded. "You could be right."

Capt. Bowie nodded also. "Maybe the pond isn't as big as we thought."

CHAPTER 43

OVAL OFFICE
WASHINGTON, DC
MONDAY; 21 MAY
1:07 AM EDT

The president held the receiver to his ear and verified that the green "secure" lamp was lit before speaking. "Okay, Emily. We're green."

The voice of British Prime Minister Emily Irons warbled slightly as it came through the encrypted phone. "I appreciate you taking my call at this hour, Frank. I should have checked the time difference before phoning."

"Don't give it a second's thought," the president said. He did his best to suppress a yawn. Emily Irons wasn't known for wasting time on pleasantries, and she *never* called without a compelling reason. It was worth getting up before the roosters to hear anything she had to say.

"What's on your mind, Emily?"

"The attack on my embassy," she said.

The president automatically sat up straighter and tightened the belt of his robe. "I'm listening."

"The attack was planned by Abdul Kaliq, the Siraji minister of defense, and financed by the government of Siraj through a series of blind bank transactions in the Cayman Islands."

The president felt a twinge, deep in his bowels. "You're certain?"

"There's no room for doubt, Frank. I've seen the proof."

"Are you going to take it to the UN?"

"No," she said. "I'm going to handle the matter myself."

"I see," the president said. "Do you mind if I ask how you found out who was behind the attack?"

The British prime minister paused before answering. "That's a bit of a sticky question, I'm afraid. I must ask you to trust me when I tell you that you will be *much* happier if you don't *ever* know the answer to that question."

It was the president's turn to pause. "I had a homeland security briefing yesterday evening. It seems that there was a third man involved in the attack on your embassy—a Mr. Isma'il Hamid. He was struck down by a ruptured appendix before he could carry out his part of the plan. My intelligence people tell me that Hamid disappeared from his hospital bed at Columbia Memorial just about a half-hour before the FBI showed up to take him into custody. The hospital staff is certain that Mr. Hamid was far too sick to escape under his own power. You wouldn't have any idea where Mr. Hamid disappeared to, would you?"

Emily Irons sighed into the phone. "Frank, I'm a little deaf in my left ear, and I didn't hear that question. But, whatever it was, *both* of our lives will be much less complicated if you *never* ask it again."

"I see," the president said again. He rubbed his eyes. "No, Emily, I *don't* see. I'm not trying to be rude, but surely you didn't call me just to tell me that you can't *tell* me anything."

"Friedrik Shoernberg *knew* about the attack on my embassy, Frank."

"What?"

"The BND, the German Federal Intelligence Service, had advanced intelligence on Abdul Kaliq's plan to attack my embassy. I know for a fact that Shoernberg received a detailed brief on the attack at least a week before it happened."

Frank swallowed. "You'll have to excuse me, Emily, but I find that a little hard to believe. I'll grant you that Friedrik has made some pretty dicey decisions lately, but the idea that he would …"

"He *knew*, Frank. The bastard *knew* the Sirajis were planning to murder my people, and he didn't raise a finger to stop it."

She paused for a few seconds. When she resumed speaking, her voice had a strangely formal quality to it. "Under its current regime, the Federal Republic of Germany constitutes a clear and present danger to the security and the sovereignty of the United Kingdom. In a few hours, I intend to ask Parliament for a formal resolution authorizing war with Germany."

The president sat in silence for nearly a minute. "Are you certain you want to do this?"

"The Germans attacked my ships, in clear violation of Article 5 of the NATO Charter," the British prime minister said. "And under Article 5, member nations of NATO are required to take whatever action is necessary to restore the security of the North Atlantic Treaty area." Her voice took on a hard edge. "The charter doesn't say we're *authorized* to take action, Frank. It says we are *required* to take action. Article 5 also requires other signatory nations to assist any NATO country that has come under attack. I'm going to take the fight to Shoernberg's door, Mr. President. And I expect the backing of the United States."

The president closed his eyes. "I assume you're going to petition the other NATO countries as well …"

"Of course," Irons said.

"You'll have trouble getting support," the president said. "Shoernberg is claiming that your ships fired first at Gibraltar. Without concrete evidence, it'll be difficult to prove that Germany struck the first blow."

"The German government *knew* about the biological warfare attack on my embassy, Frank. They didn't warn us, and they didn't do anything to prevent it. And now they're selling weapons to the very people who attacked us."

"I know," the president said. "But both of our countries lost a lot of popularity in NATO when we took on Iraq. Some of our NATO partners will *want* to believe Germany's claim that your ships fired first at Gibraltar. And you'll have to reveal your intelligence sources if you're going to prove that Friedrik Shoernberg knew about the embassy attack ahead of time. From what you've told me, I suspect you're not going to be able to reveal your sources. That'll give France all the excuse it needs to side with Germany. Belgium will probably follow Germany on this as well. Italy could go either way. They gave us nominal support during the liberation of Iraq, but they've bucked us on nearly everything since. Turkey's another coin toss. They're still mad at us because we wouldn't let them beat up the Kurds in northern Iraq."

"Greece will back us," Irons said. "So will Portugal, and Poland. And I think we can convince the majority of the others."

"Maybe you're right, Emily," the president said. "Maybe you *will* be able to persuade most of the others. But at what cost? NATO is going to come apart at the seams. Do you really want that?"

"Of course not," she said. "But the NATO alliance is worthless if we can't call upon it to live up to its charter. Either NATO protects its members, or it doesn't. And if it doesn't, it isn't an alliance at all. It's just a lot of high-sounding words on paper."

"What if I can take Shoernberg down?" the president asked. He gripped the phone more tightly as the words came out of his mouth, and he wished instantly that he hadn't said them.

"What do you mean?" Irons asked.

The president gritted his teeth. In for a penny, in for a pound …

"Suppose I can take Shoernberg's regime out of power … That would remove the threat to your country, wouldn't it? The German people aren't really your problem. It's Shoernberg and his cronies."

"How would you go about it?"

"For starters," the president said, "I squash his last submarine like a bug. And if necessary, I order a surgical strike on the air base where the Germans are staging fighter jets for delivery to Siraj. I don't let so much as a slingshot get through to Siraj."

"Go on."

"Then I rake Friedrik over the coals. I stand before the United Nations General Assembly and formally accuse him of violating everything from standing UN resolutions, to international law, to Article 5 of the NATO Treaty. I pull down his pants in front of the media. I paint him as not only a criminal, but an *incompetent* criminal. It's not bad enough that he violates international law, but he's not even smart enough to do it *successfully*."

"That won't be enough to push him out of power."

"No. But it's a start. Siraj won't be supplying Germany with oil, because Germany won't be delivering any weapons. My analysts tell me that the German economy is going to take a nosedive without that oil. They're going to have one hell of an energy shortage, complete with power rationing—maybe even blackouts. I'll crank up import tariffs on German-made products and squeeze their economy even harder. Once the crunch is really on, the German people will be screaming for Shoernberg's head on a stick. I'll have the CIA dig up every scrap of dirt that Shoernberg or his people ever touched. If one of them ever stole a candy bar, cheated on his taxes, or pinched a secretary on the rump, we'll plaster it all over the six o'clock news. We'll humiliate him every morning and discredit him every evening. Hell, I don't *know* what all we'll do. I'm just freewheeling here. I've never played dirty politics before. But I've got some smart people working for me, Emily. So do you. We'll turn them loose on this."

The prime minister paused before speaking. "I don't think it will work, Frank."

"Maybe it won't," the president said. "But it's certainly worth trying. Anything is better than war. You know what happened the *last* two times your country butted heads with Germany …"

"This situation isn't remotely similar," Irons said. "We're not going to drag the entire world into this. It won't happen that way again. The world has changed too much."

"We'd like to believe that," the president said. "But we can't be sure."

He took a deep breath and exhaled slowly. "If war with Germany cannot be avoided, the United States will honor its obligations of treaty and its long-standing friendship with Great Britain. But I beg you, Emily ... give me a chance to prevent this war."

"You sink that submarine, Mr. President," the British prime minister said, "and *then* we'll talk."

CHAPTER 44

GUNSLINGER FOUR-ONE
CENTRAL ARABIAN GULF (OFF THE COAST OF QATAR)
MONDAY; 21 MAY
0758 hours (7:58 AM)
TIME ZONE +3 'CHARLIE'

Lieutenant Vincent Brolan yawned hard enough to make his ears ring. "I fucking hate dawn patrol," he said, for about the eighth time that morning. "I mean I really fucking *hate* it."

"I know you do, Vince," the copilot said. "And you really hate spending all that flight pay that you get for flying it."

Brolan eased his aircraft, *Gunslinger Four-One,* a little closer to the oil platform. They were close enough to see the workers going about their morning routines, doing whatever the hell it was that oil rig workers did. A few of the workers turned at the sound of the helo's rotor blades, and some of them even waved. Most of them paid no attention whatsoever. Helicopters were a dime a dozen in the gulf.

Lt. Brolan leaned his helmet against the port-side window and felt the vibration of the engines resonating through his skull. "Lucky Number Seven is a bust," he said. "Let's move on to our next contestant."

The copilot, Lieutenant (junior grade) Enrico "Henry" Chavez, pointed down at the platform. "Don't you think we ought to swing around and check out the back side?"

"It's a waste of time, Henry. There's nobody home." Under his breath, he said, "This *whole thing* is a waste of time."

"We ought to do this by the numbers, Vince. That sub has got to be hiding somewhere."

"Yeah? Well if it ever *was* here, it's long gone by now."

"Come on, Vince. You know our orders."

In the rear seat, the Sensor Operator, Aviation Warfare Systems Operator Second Class Linda "Mojo" Haynes, listened to the exchange and didn't say a word. As the only enlisted member of the flight crew, she made it her business to stay out of disagreements between the officers.

The pilot let out a heavy sigh. "All right, okay, I'm turning already." He banked the helicopter into a broad turn that would take them around behind the oil platform.

As they rounded the corner of the platform, it slid into view: a fat black cigar shape riding low in the water, tethered to the platform by a web of lines and hoses.

"Jackpot," the SENSO said over the intercom. "There's our submarine."

Lt.(jg) Chavez reached up to key his mike, when a pair of nickel-sized holes surrounded by spider webs blossomed on the Plexiglas windshield to the left of his head. Simultaneously the helicopter was jarred sharply several times, as though someone with a hammer was banging on the fuselage.

"Holy shit!" Chavez shouted. "They're shooting at us!"

Lt. Brolan swung the helo into a tight turn away from the station and put on the speed. A stream of tracers leapt up from the oil platform and blasted through the air where the helo had been a split second before. Brolan keyed his radio. "This is *Gunslinger*. I'm under fire!"

Lt.(jg) Chavez half turned in his seat and keyed his intercom. "Hey, Mojo. You okay back there?"

"I think I just peed my pants, sir!"

"Don't feel like the Lone Ranger, kid!"

Lt. Brolan jogged the helo to the right just in time to avoid another burst of machine-gun fire. He shouted into the radio, "My aircraft is hit and still receiving hostile fire!"

"*Gunslinger Four-One*, this is SAU Commander. Evade and return to home plate. Help is on the way, over."

Lt. Brolan jerked the stick to the left, but a series of rapid-fire hammer blows to the airframe told him that he hadn't been quite fast enough. A chattering vibration started to come from the tail boom, and the indicator needles on several instruments began to swing crazily.

"I'm hit again!" Lt. Brolan shouted into the radio. "*Gunslinger* is hit again! We are still taking fire!"

"*Gunslinger Four-One*, this is SAU Commander. Can you tell me what kind of fire are you taking, over?"

"How the fuck should I know? Some kind of machine gun!"

Chavez keyed the radio. "SAU Commander, this is *Gunslinger Four-One*. We have located *Gremlin Zero Four*, moored to oil platform *Golf*. Our aircraft has taken several hits from one or more automatic weapons. Damage report to follow, over."

He switched over to his intercom. "Mojo, I need a damage report. Give me a rapid survey; we'll check for little stuff in a minute."

A few seconds went by, but he didn't receive an answer. He keyed the intercom again. "How's it looking back there?"

No answer.

Chavez turned far enough in his seat to see into the rear of the cabin. Petty Officer Haynes was slumped over in her seat, her head hanging limply, bobbing and rolling with each movement of the aircraft. A dark stain was spreading across her chest, but against the olive drab of her flight suit, it was impossible to tell if it was blood. The helo took a particularly violent bump, and the young woman's head lolled far enough to the side so that her face was partially visible. A dark red bubble formed over one nostril, broke, and then another one began to form. It was blood all right.

Chavez keyed his intercom. "Mojo is hit!"

Lt. Brolan was silently chanting, "Come on baby … come on baby … come on baby …" With a rapid interplay of hand and foot work, he managed to throw his crippled helo far enough to the side to avoid another hail of bullets. At least he thought he had avoided it; the airframe was rattling so badly that they might have taken a hit and not been able to feel it. He keyed his intercom. "How bad is she?"

"I don't know," Chavez said. "But it doesn't look good." He keyed the intercom again. "Mojo, can you hear me? Come on, Mojo, talk to me. You're gonna be okay; you've just got to hang on for a few minutes."

He switched back to the radio. "SAU Commander, this is *Gunslinger Four-One.* My SENSO is hit. I can't tell how bad, but it looks like a chest wound. I'm going to need a medical crew standing by as soon as I hit the deck, over."

"Roger, *Gunslinger.*"

Another burst of gunfire came from the oil platform, but this one fell short, the tracers dropping harmlessly into the ocean at the ends of their trajectories.

"I think we're out of it," Lt. Brolan said. "I think we're …" The tension in his voice was easing. He looked up. "What's our damage like?"

"I can't tell," Lt.(jg) Chavez said. "My dials are all over the place. But I think I'm smelling oil."

Lt. Brolan nodded. "Yeah, I smell it too. Think we can make it back to the barn?"

The radio kicked in. "*Gunslinger Four-One*, this is SAU Commander. We are approaching at all speed. Return to home plate, over."

Brolan stared at the radio as if it were from another planet. "No shit."

Chavez thumped his instrument panel, where a red tattletale was flashing. "Oh shit! I'm showing a '*chip-light*' on engine one."

"Is it for real? Or are your instruments taking a dump?"

"You want to chance it?"

Lt. Brolan shook his head. "No way."

According to the flashing tattletale, a sensor in the oil sump had detected metal filings in the starboard engine. If the sensor was reporting an actual condition (instead of an erroneous reading caused by instrument damage), the engine could seize up, tearing the aircraft apart, or even exploding like a bomb.

"Shut down engine one," Lt. Brolan said. "I'll mow the lawn," he said under his breath. "I'll help the kids with their homework. I will *never* look at another woman again ..."

The aircraft took on a shudder so violent that it jarred Brolan's teeth. Only four hundred feet up, they were starting to lose altitude. The cyclic and collective were becoming less responsive with every second, and now he'd been forced to shut down one of his two engines. He hoped the increasingly powerful stink of burnt oil was coming from the now-dead starboard engine. If it was coming from the transmission casing or the port engine, they were going to have to ditch in the ocean. And no matter what the Navy's air-sea survival courses taught, he knew that the odds for surviving a helo ditch were not good at all.

The copilot keyed up the radio. "SAU Commander, this is *Gunslinger Four-One.* My starboard engine is out, and I am losing altitude." He glanced at his Tactical Air Navigation screen before continuing. "My ETA to *Benfold* is three mikes. Request emergency green deck, over."

The reply came over the radio a few seconds later. "*Gunslinger Four-One*, this is SAU Commander. *Towers* is designated as your home plate. You have emergency green deck on *Towers.* Do *not* attempt to rendezvous with *Benfold*, over."

Pilot and copilot both stared at the radio. "What the hell are they thinking?" Chavez asked. He immediately keyed the radio. "SAU Commander, this is *Gunslinger Four-One.* I have an emergency. My SENSO is injured, I am down one engine, and my aircraft is about to fall out of the goddamned sky, over!"

On the TACAN, *Benfold* was approaching at thirty-five knots. *Towers* was limping after her at eighteen and a half knots. *Benfold* would be within range a hell of a lot sooner.

"*Gunslinger Four-One*, this is SAU Commander. I acknowledge your emergency. Your ETA to *Towers* is six mikes. You are *not*, I repeat *not* authorized to rendezvous with *Benfold*. Their deck is red to you, over."

"This is *Gunslinger Four-One*. Roger, out."

Lt.(jg) Chavez looked out his side window at the ocean, only about three hundred feet below and coming up way too fast. "I sure hope those guys brought some body bags."

CHAPTER 45

USS *TOWERS* (DDG-103)
CENTRAL ARABIAN GULF (OFF THE COAST OF QATAR)
MONDAY; 21 MAY
0812 hours (8:12 AM)
TIME ZONE +3 'CHARLIE'

The executive officer looked at Capt. Bowie. "You sure about this, Jim? If those guys have to ditch, all we'll be able to do is steam around in circles and try to fish the body parts out of the water. It will take an act of God to get *one* of them out of that thing alive."

Capt. Bowie nodded slowly. "I know."

"*Benfold* can recover that aircraft in …"

The captain cut him off. "By the time *Benfold* recovers the helo, that submarine will be gone. Right now, if they pull out all the stops, they might get lucky and catch it on the surface. With a busted screw, we can't get there in time."

"What if we can't get to the *helo* in time?"

"We will," the captain said quietly.

"But, what if we don't? That air crew is going to die …"

Capt. Bowie wheeled around. "Do you think I don't know that? Do you *really* think for a second that I don't know that?"

The XO didn't say anything.

"How many people are dead already?" the captain snapped.

"I don't know, sir."

"We lost three to that goddamned torpedo, not counting the wounded. *Benfold*'s whole bridge crew was wiped out; that's six more. Plus our three, that makes nine. One on the *Ingraham* makes it ten. Call it an even hundred and fifty on the *Antietam*. And let's not forget the *Kitty Hawk*; they lost fifteen, plus two entire air crews—that would be six more. And how many have the Brits lost? Nearly all hands on the *York*. Their crew would be, what? Two hundred?

Two seventy-five?" He covered his eyes with his left hand and rubbed his temples with thumb and fingertips.

When he dropped his hand, his voice was much softer. "We will do everything we can to save the crew of that aircraft. But those subs have racked up an unbelievable body count. We sink that bastard, *priority one*. Everything else is a secondary consideration. If it costs us three more lives, then we pay the price." He turned away and half-whispered, "We pay the price."

* * *

They stood in silence for several moments, until the TAO interrupted. "Captain, *Gunslinger* is on final approach."

"Is the crash-and-smash crew standing by?"

"Yes, sir, and Sick Bay is prepped to receive casualties."

The captain punched keys on his console, and views from each of the three flight deck cameras popped up on the Aegis display screen. The video was black-and-white but very high resolution. Even so, the helo appeared as a blur at first, a gray and white smudge against black waves.

The pilot had bought himself some time by jettisoning his torpedo and ejecting his load of sonobuoys. Somehow the helicopter was still managing to claw its way through the air, darting and fluttering like a sparrow with an injured wing.

* * *

The crippled aircraft came in from the aft starboard corner of the flight deck, and it was immediately apparent that its angle of approach was all wrong. The LSE (short for Landing Signal Enlisted) tried to wave the helo off, but it was obvious that it didn't have the power to gain altitude for another approach.

The helo's tail wheel caught the edge of a flight deck net, and the belly of the aircraft slammed into the deck, crushing the landing gear.

The pilot cut power instantly, but the helo rolled far enough onto its port side for the rotors to scrape the deck. The blades shattered, and shrapnel flew in all directions.

A hand-sized chunk of the rotor hit the chock-and-chain man just below the right knee, shattering the bone and nearly amputating his leg. A larger piece of rotor hit the front window of the helo control tower, turning the safety glass to an instant network of spider webs. A smaller piece dealt the LSE a glancing blow to the side of the head, dropping him to his knees, but his cranial helmet reduced the impact to merely bruising force.

Miraculously, though pieces of the shattered rotors ricocheted off the deck and bulkheads, no others found human targets.

The crash-and-smash team started moving the instant the helo was on deck—one team spraying the wrecked aircraft with firefighting foam, and another rushing up to access the cabin and rescue the crew.

The pilot and copilot, both of whom could walk with assistance, were out in less than a minute. The SENSO, Petty Officer Haynes, had to be carried out on a stretcher.

* * *

The Helo Control Officer watched as his crash-and-smash team continued to blanket the downed aircraft with foam. "We're going to have to push it over the side," he said.

"We need the captain's permission to do that," the LSE said.

"Of course we do," the HCO said. "But it's not like he's going to have a choice. No way that bird is leaving the flight deck under its own power. Maybe if we were back in the States, they could crane it off and haul it back to the squadron for a rebuild. But right now, it's blocking the flight deck, and we can't launch or recover *Firewalker* until it's gone."

* * *

His words proved prophetic. Ten minutes later, the captain ordered a fifty-man working party to muster on the flight deck. Working together under the orders of the HCO, they rocked the damaged aircraft back and forth until they could roll it off the deck.

Gunslinger Four-One slipped over the side. The crippled helo floated only for a few seconds before disappearing beneath the waves.

CHAPTER 46

USS *BENFOLD*
CENTRAL ARABIAN GULF (OFF THE COAST OF QATAR)
MONDAY; 21 MAY
0818 hours (8:18 AM)
TIME ZONE +3 'CHARLIE'

The image on the left Aegis display screen was a live video feed from the *Benfold*'s mast-mounted sight. The high-resolution black-and-white camera was focused on oil platform *Golf*.

Capt. Vargas pointed to the screen. "Look at those bastards. Going about their business-as-usual routine, just as innocent as you please. And not a hint of the fact that they just cut one of our aircraft to ribbons a few minutes ago."

"Can't say I blame them for playing nice," Lt.(jg) Sherman said. "A couple of shots from our 5-inch gun, and they'll be visiting Allah in person. A helo is one thing, but they're not stupid enough to risk mixing it up with a destroyer."

"Looks like the sub is gone," Capt. Vargas said, still watching the screen as *Benfold* swung around to check out the back side of the oil platform.

"It hasn't had time to go very far, ma'am," said the USWE. He started punching buttons on the CDRT. "I'm setting datum at the northern edge of the oil platform, since that's the last known location of the sub." He punched another few keys and watched the display screen. "Okay, here's our farthest-on circle. I'm building in the assumption that the sub got under way about fifteen minutes ago, or within five minutes of the last sighting by *Gunslinger Four-One*. Based on a maximum submerged speed of twenty knots, that sub has to be within ten thousand yards of the oil platform."

The captain nodded. "What's our predicted sonar range?"

"About forty-five hundred yards," the USWE said. "But I'd rather err on the side of caution and base our search plan on thirty-five hundred yards."

"We can cover the search area in three parallel passes," the captain said.

"My thoughts exactly, ma'am."

"Do it. Execute your search plan."

"Aye, aye," the USWE said. He keyed his mike. "Sonar—USWE. Go active on sonar. Commence your search. Remember how shallow the water is and adjust your depression angles accordingly."

"Sonar, aye."

"UB—USWE. I expect to gain contact within the next few minutes, and the water is too shallow for ASROC. We don't know what side of the ship this guy is going to show up on, so go ahead and prep an over-the-side shot for the port and starboard torpedo tubes."

"UB, aye. Recommend we configure both weapons for shallow runs, minimum initial search depths, and minimum ceiling depths."

"Good call, UB," Lt.(jg) Sherman said. "Make it so."

He watched the CDRT, waiting for the first sign of the submarine. "We've got you now, you son of a bitch," he said softly. "The fat lady is about to sing, because this opera is over."

* * *

But twenty minutes later, when *Benfold* came to the end of her search run, there was still no sign of the submarine.

Capt. Vargas laid her hand on Lt.(jg) Sherman's shoulder. "How did he get past us, Alex?"

Her USWE stared at the CDRT, still devoid of submarine contacts. "He didn't, ma'am. He *couldn't* have."

"Then he's still here."

"I don't think so, Captain. We would have picked him up."

"You can't have it both ways, Alex," the captain said. "The sub is either still here, or it got past us. Which is it?"

"He's here, Skipper."

"Then maybe he's under the oil platform, blending in with its sonar return," the captain said.

Sherman furrowed his eyebrows. "I don't think he can do that, Captain. Between the scaffolding, and the piping, and the pumps, there's an awful lot of equipment down …" He stopped. "What did you just say, ma'am?"

"I said, 'He might be under the oil platform … '"

Lt.(jg) Sherman shook his head rapidly. "Not that part, ma'am. The other part."

Captain Vargas shrugged. "I don't know. I think I said something about the sub blending in with the oil platform's sonar return."

Sherman snapped his fingers. "Not the oil platform, the *bottom*."

"You think the sub is sitting on the bottom?"

"Could be, Skipper."

"Wouldn't sonar have picked him up when we ran over the top of him?"

"No, ma'am," the USWE said. "The SQS-53D's automatic gain control clips the bottom return out of the signal when it processes it. If it didn't, the system would show a sonar return in all directions; our scopes would be saturated. If the sub is sitting on the bottom, his signal could be getting clipped out along with the bottom signal."

"Can we just shut the automatic gain control off, or bypass it?"

"No, ma'am. The bottom return would saturate our scopes, and we'd be completely blind."

The captain stared at him. "You're telling me that the American people spent millions of dollars on a sonar that *refuses* to see the submarine?"

"I'm afraid so, Skipper."

"And that submarine could be directly underneath us at this very second?"

"That would be a hell of a coincidence, but yes, ma'am. It's certainly possible."

"*There's* a case of our tax dollars hardly at work. Can we call him up on the underwater telephone and invite him to come out and play?"

Lt.(jg) Sherman's eyebrows went up. "That's not a bad idea ..."

"Great," the captain said, her voice dripping with sarcasm. "Now all we have to do is find someone who speaks German."

Sherman smiled. "Actually, Skipper, what we need is someone who speaks *Submarine*." He keyed his mike. "Sonar—USWE. Does your On-Board Trainer's sample library contain a recording of a Mark-54 torpedo?"

"USWE—Sonar. Yes, sir. It does."

"Sonar—USWE. Can you patch an audio signal from the OBT into the underwater telephone?"

The reply took several seconds. "Uh ... yes, sir. I guess so. Is that what you want me to do?"

"Affirmative, Sonar. Go ahead and rig the patch and load the Mark-54 recording, but do not transmit until I give the word."

"Sonar, aye."

The captain nodded slowly. "You're going to broadcast a fake torpedo signal and scare the sub off the bottom?"

"That's the idea, ma'am. When the sub hears that torpedo start up, he's going to assume that we've detected him somehow, and that he's about to get a high-explosive enema. He'll be off the bottom, running his torpedo evasion maneuvers in nothing flat."

"He's going to launch a counter-battery attack as soon as he detects our weapon."

"Yes, ma'am. That's how we're going to locate him. As soon as he shoots, we'll put a torpedo down his firing bearing."

"So we have to draw fire from his torpedo to get a firing solution for our own torpedo?"

"I know it's a risky plan, Captain. I just can't think of a better one."

Capt. Vargas didn't speak for over a minute. Finally, she said, "Neither can I. Looks like we do it your way, Alex."

"Yes, ma'am." Lt.(jg) Sherman keyed his mike. "Sonar—USWE. Commence transmitting your recorded torpedo signal and keep it up until I tell you to stop."

"Sonar, aye. Transmitting now."

The next two reports came back-to-back, less than thirty seconds later. "USWE—Sonar has active 53 Delta contact off the starboard quarter, bearing one-five-five. Initial classification: POSS-SUB, confidence level high!" Before the USWE could acknowledge, the Sonar Supervisor started in on his second report. "All Stations—Sonar has multiple hydrophone effects off the starboard quarter! Bearings one-five-five and one-five-seven. Initial classification: hostile torpedoes!"

"Holy Christ!" the USWE shouted. "This guy is right up our ass." He keyed the net. "Bridge—USWE. Crack the whip! I say again, crack the whip!"

"Bridge, aye!"

The Sonar Supervisor's voice came over the 29-MC. "The first torpedo has acquired! Torpedo is close aboard!"

The turbines began to spin up, and the ship started to turn.

It was too late.

* * *

The DMA37 torpedo slipped under the hull and detonated directly beneath the destroyer's after fuel tanks. The shallow, hard-packed sand bottom reflected a great deal of the shock wave back toward the surface—toward *Benfold*—effectively doubling the destructive power of the warhead. The magnified explosion ripped through the steel hull plates, rupturing the fuel tanks. Sixty thousand gallons of diesel fuel marine erupted into flame, instantly transforming USS *Benfold* into an inferno.

The blazing steel hulk had barely settled back into the waves before a second torpedo darted in and hammered the ship again.

When the smoke and spray from the base surges of the explosions cleared, all that remained to mark the last position of USS *Benfold* was a debris field and a burning oil slick.

* * *

USS *Towers*:

Capt. Bowie stood on the forecastle and watched the scattered pieces of *Benfold*'s debris field slide past the bow wake and drift aft. The desert wind was hot, and it carried enough sand to sting his cheeks. He felt, rather than saw, the executive officer walk up behind him. He spoke without looking over his shoulder. "Any more survivors yet?"

"No, sir," the XO said. "Just the one man. A kid, really. I just came from Sick Bay. He can't be more than eighteen or nineteen. Doc says he's got burns over about 40 percent of his body."

"He's not going to make it, then," the captain said.

"Probably not, sir."

The captain nodded once, but didn't say anything. It didn't make sense. It shouldn't have happened. Despite the damage to her bridge, *Benfold* had been operating at near full capacity, with her speed, maneuverability, and firepower undiminished. Her captain, Rachel Vargas, had been a skilled tactician and a master of sea-maneuver warfare. Her USW team had been well trained and well prepared. And now they were all gone.

The thoughts turned slowly over and over in Capt. Bowie's brain, but they refused to become real for him. The U.S. Navy hadn't lost a warship in combat since World War II. And now a ship under his command was gone, and—except for one burned and dying teenager—every human being on board was dead. All three hundred thirty-seven of them.

Capt. Bowie shifted his eyes to the horizon. *Gremlin Zero Four—God, what an innocuous sounding designation for such a ruthlessly efficient killer*—was still out there.

The captain turned toward the XO. "I'm going to head down to Sick Bay for a few minutes. Get a hold of the Navigator and have him plot a course to the coast of Siraj, using our best speed."

"Aye-aye, sir."

Capt. Bowie walked down the port side, toward the door that would lead him down to Sick Bay. He knew that he should go to CIC instead. They needed him there. His crew was looking to him for the plan, the stroke of tactical genius, the rabbit out of the hat that would let his crippled ship take on a cunning and deadly enemy and somehow emerge triumphant.

But that could wait, for a few minutes at least. He could spare two minutes for the last surviving member of a United States warship.

* * *

The Chief Hospital Corpsman met him at the door to Sick Bay. "He's already gone, sir. We did everything we could, but he just slipped away from us. I'm sorry."

"Not your fault, Doc," the captain said. "What was his name?"

"His uniform was mostly burned off when they pulled him out of the water. We couldn't find any ID. We … don't know his name, sir."

The captain nodded and walked away. "Thanks, Doc," he said over his shoulder. Bowie headed for CIC. He shook his head as he walked. They didn't even know the kid's name.

CHAPTER 47

WHITE HOUSE SITUATION ROOM
WASHINGTON, DC
MONDAY; 21 MAY
03:14 AM EDT

Adm. Casey looked at the president. "It's confirmed, sir. USS *Benfold* is gone. It looks like all hands were lost."

"I thought *Towers* picked up a survivor," Gregory Brenthoven said.

"They did," the CNO said. "He died shortly after he was pulled out of the water."

The president shook his head slowly. "Jesus … When was the last time we lost a ship with all hands?"

Adm. Casey thought for a second. "I believe that would have been 1968, sir. A nuclear fast-attack submarine, USS *Scorpion,* suffered some kind of accident in the mid-Atlantic and went down with all hands. Ninety-nine dead, if my memory serves me."

"That was an accident," the president said. "What about in combat?"

"I'm not sure, sir. Certainly not since the Second World War."

The president closed his eyes and ran both hands slowly through his hair, fingers combing from front to back. "So much for my total victory, huh? Germany loses everything, and we get away clean as a hound's tooth. It sounded so goddamned brilliant. What the hell was I thinking, Bob? Did I really think those guys could just sail out there, sink a bunch of cutting-edge killer subs, and sail home in time for lunch?"

No one attempted to answer.

After a few seconds, the president opened his eyes. "All right, I guess that puts us in damage-control mode. What have we got left that can stop that submarine?"

"*Towers*, sir," the CNO said.

"I can't leave it to them anymore," the president said. "They're beat to shit. I need to put enough assets out there to guarantee a kill. What have we got in-theater?"

The CNO took a breath and exhaled heavily. "Nothing, sir. What's left of *Kitty Hawk*'s strike group is at least twenty hours too far south and west. Even if we turn them around now, that sub will be in Zubayr before they can get through the Straits of Hormuz. My P-3s in Saudi are pinned down by a sand storm. If it clears in the next couple of hours or so, I can get them up into the northern Gulf, but even *that* will probably be too late."

The national security advisor asked, "What about that nuclear submarine you wanted to send after them?"

"We had to clear the *Topeka* out of the Gulf. With four ships up there hurling torpedoes right and left, we couldn't risk a blue-on-blue engagement with a friendly sub."

"Those nuke subs are *fast*," Brenthoven said. "Get it back up there!"

The CNO shook his head. "They're not *that* fast. *Topeka* is too far out of position."

"What you're telling me," the president said, "is that I made my bed, and now I have to lie in it."

"I didn't say that, Mr. President," the CNO said.

"But it's true, nevertheless ..."

"I'm afraid so."

CHAPTER 48

USS *TOWERS* (DDG-103)
NORTHERN ARABIAN GULF
MONDAY; 21 MAY
2318 hours (11:18 PM)
TIME ZONE +3 'CHARLIE'

The Chief Engineer dropped heavily into one of the chairs at the wardroom table. His coveralls were streaked with grease and his face and hands were filthy. "My boys have managed to restore pitch control to the port screw, but it's got a lot of vibration in it. Obviously, we can't tell for sure without divers, but I think the screw itself is pretty chewed up. It must have taken some direct damage from the torpedo hit. We're not going to be able to run it at full speed, and frankly, Captain, that screw is going to howl like a dog whenever we run it."

"How much difference will it make in our speed if we run the damaged screw?" Capt. Bowie asked.

The Chief Engineer shrugged. "We won't have exact figures until we put some power to it, but I'm guessing about five or six knots. We can do eighteen and a half on the starboard screw. With both screws going, I'd expect to see between twenty-three and twenty-five knots."

"But we'll be noisy as hell …"

"I'm afraid so, sir."

"Stealth or speed," the XO said. "That's a hell of a choice to have to make when you're chasing a submarine."

"It's not really much of a choice, sir," Chief McPherson said. "If we don't beat that sub to the Siraji coast, we're out of the ball game. Stealth or no stealth, I think we're going to have to sprint like hell to get ahead of the sub."

"What's that kind of noise going to do to our sonar ranges?" the captain asked.

"We'll be blind as a bat, sir," Chief McPherson said. "At least while we're sprinting. Sonar will be back to normal as soon as we slow down and drop the port screw off line again."

"Noisy and blind," Ens. Cooper said. "What a great way to chase a submarine."

"I agree, sir," Chief McPherson said. "It's certainly not my first choice, but if we try it quiet and slow, that sub is going to be tied to a pier in Zubayr before we even get up to the north end of the gulf."

The XO whistled through his teeth. "It looks to me like we are damned if we do, and double-dog-damned if we don't."

"Anybody got any brilliant suggestions?" the captain asked.

No one had any.

The captain stood up. "Okay," he said. "Bring the port screw on line and head for Al-Kufah with the best speed we can manage. No matter how noisy the coach is, Cinderella cannot be late for the ball."

* * *

An hour later, Chief McPherson knocked on the door to the captain's stateroom.

"Enter."

The chief opened the door. "Captain? May I have a word with you?"

"Come on in," the captain said. "What's on your mind?"

"Sir, I just came from Sonar Control. We are making a *lot* of noise. The sub is going to see us a hundred miles away."

The captain said, "No choice, Chief. We've got to have the speed."

The chief nodded. "I realize that, sir. The problem is we sound like a destroyer with a bad screw."

"I've talked to the Chief Engineer, and he tells me there's nothing we can do to quiet that screw."

The chief nodded. "I understand, sir. So I think we should take it in the opposite direction. If we can't make *Towers* quiet, we should try to make her as noisy as possible."

The captain frowned. "And then the sub will be able to detect us even *farther* away."

"Yes, sir," Chief McPherson said. "But will it be able to *classify* us?"

"What do you mean?"

"When I went through Acoustic Analysis, they taught us a simple rule for spotting U.S. subs on a sonar gram: 'If you look at the gram, and there's nothing on it, you're probably looking at a U.S. nuke.'"

"I'm not following you, Chief."

"When a Sonar Operator looks at a contact that's generating big fat broadband and lots of narrowband tonals, he's not thinking U.S. nuke. He's thinking merchant ship. He's thinking beat-up old tanker with worn-out engines. He's thinking *anything* but U.S. nuke. Ordinarily, he would be correct. If we play it right, I think we can take advantage of that kind of thinking."

"We make ourselves so noisy that no Sonar Operator in his right mind would even *think* about classifying us as a stealth destroyer?"

"Yes, sir."

"Chief, have you ever read Poe?"

"Sir?"

"Edgar Allen Poe. He was one of the early horror writers. Some say that he's still never been equaled."

"I read *The Telltale Heart* in high school. And what was that poem? *The Raven*, I think …"

"I had in mind a different story," the captain said. "Your idea smacks of Poe's *Purloined Letter*. You should read it, when this is over. It's a story about how to hide things in plain sight."

"I'll do that, sir."

The captain nodded. "Good. Now, let's see how obnoxiously noisy we can make ourselves."

CHAPTER 49

U.S. NAVY CENTRAL COMMAND (USNAVCENT)
BAHRAIN
TUESDAY; 22 MAY
0147 hours (1:47 AM)
TIME ZONE +3 'CHARLIE'

"Zubayr is a ghost town," the off-going Duty Intelligence Officer said. "No surface traffic in or out of the harbor in the past twenty-four hours."

Caught in mid-yawn, Lt. Cmdr. Fisk drew back. "What? That can't be right. Half of Siraj's surface traffic goes through Zubayr. It's always crawling with activity."

The off-going DIO was a heavyset lieutenant with a bad comb-over. "I know. Weird, isn't it? Maybe it's some obscure Islamic holy day."

"I don't think so," Fisk said. "State would have given us a heads-up. Has Siraji air activity slacked off?"

The lieutenant shook his head. "Business as usual, air-wise."

"Has surface traffic been affected in any other Siraji ports?"

The off-going Duty Intelligence Officer shook his head again. "No. Normal shipping density everywhere except Zubayr."

"That doesn't make any sense," Fisk said.

"I'm just giving you the skinny. There hasn't been so much as a kayak in or out of Zubayr harbor all day." The lieutenant looked at the master tactical plot. "The last movement we show was yesterday morning. Three fishing trawlers pulled in, and then everything got quiet."

"Three fishing trawlers?" Lt. Cmdr. Fisk stared at the master tactical plot. "Oh shit." He looked up. "Plot Supervisor, get me SPECWAR on the line. Do it now!"

The off-going DIO held his hands up. "Whoa, cowboy! Why are we calling in the Special Warfare Unit?"

"They need to see this plot," Fisk said.

"Why? What in the hell is going on?"

"I hope like hell I'm wrong," Fisk said. "But I think the Sirajis have just laid a minefield across the approach to Zubayr."

CHAPTER 50

USS *TOWERS* (DDG-103)
NORTHERN ARABIAN GULF
TUESDAY; 22 MAY
0328 hours (3:28 AM)
TIME ZONE +3 'CHARLIE'

The noise was incredible. Steaming at her maximum (damaged) speed of twenty-three knots, the *Towers* was generating an unholy racket. True to the Chief Engineer's prediction, the port screw was howling like a banshee, but the damaged propeller wasn't the only voice singing in the choir. Every pump, every fan unit, and every piece of engineering equipment was running at maximum speed. And (where possible) the acoustic suppression systems had been disabled. On the bottom of the hull, the *masker belts*, which were designed to inject low-pressure air into the sea to acoustically decouple the ship's engine noise from the water, had been turned off. The *prairie air* system, which performed a similar function for the ship's propeller signature by injecting air through tiny capillaries in the propeller blades, had also been turned off. In the galley, the garbage disposal was running continuously, as were the paper shredders in Radio Central. The decibel level was so high that the Chief Hospital Corpsman had asked the captain to issue an order requiring all crew members to wear earplugs.

The noise levels in CIC were slightly lower, but only slightly.

"So much for that stealth bit," the TAO said.

The captain cupped a hand to an ear and shouted, "What?"

The TAO opened his mouth to repeat himself, but the captain held up a hand. "Just kidding. I heard you."

"Do you think this is working?" the TAO asked.

The captain shrugged. "Hard to say. We haven't gotten our asses blown off, so I guess that's a good sign."

"That's what I keep telling myself, sir," the TAO said. "And then I catch myself straining to hear the sound of high-speed screws. Sometimes I think I can hear a torpedo approaching, but it always turns out to be my ears playing tricks on me. Maybe it's caused by the same portion of the brain that makes you think you hear the phone ringing every time you climb into the shower."

"It won't be much longer now," the captain said. "We're almost close enough to the Siraji coast to start our search."

"It can't come a second too soon," the TAO said. "I never appreciated how wonderful silence could sound."

Navy Red began to warble with an incoming message. The captain reached up and cranked the volume to maximum so that he could hear the radio over the noise.

"*Towers*, this is COM Fifth Fleet. Have your Charlie Oscar stand by for the president, over."

Navy Red was patched into the overhead speakers, so everyone in Combat Information Center heard COM Fifth Fleet's voice. Eyebrows went up all over CIC. President? *The* president? And he wanted to talk to their CO?

The captain turned to the TAO. "Slow the ship down and try to cut down on some of the racket. I'd hate for my first and probably *only* conversation with the commander in chief to be a shouting contest."

The TAO nodded. "Aye-aye, sir." He keyed his own mike and began issuing orders.

But the noise level was still largely unabated when the captain keyed up Navy Red. He spoke a little louder than usual, in the hopes that his raised voice would carry over the clamor. "COM Fifth Fleet, this is the Charlie Oscar of *Towers*. I am standing by for the president, over."

The noise began to ease off as crew members rushed to silence the offending pieces of equipment.

After a few seconds, the president's trademark baritone came over Navy Red. "Am I speaking to Captain Samuel H. Bowie?" Even through the modulations of the encryption software, the voice was instantly recognizable.

"Yes, sir, this is Captain Bowie, over."

"Let's dispense with the radio jargon, shall we, Captain? I don't know much about it, and this is hardly the time to learn."

"Yes, sir," Capt. Bowie said. "By all means."

"Good," the president said. "Now, may I call you Sam?"

"Um … I don't really answer to that, sir. Most people call me Jim."

The president's chuckle came over the line. "Was Colonel Bowie a relation of yours?"

"Not as far as I know, sir. But I grew up in San Antonio, so the nickname was pretty much inevitable."

"It's a good name anyway," the president said. "Your namesake was a warrior and a patriot. It's a compliment to have your name associated with his."

"I've always thought so, Mr. President," the captain said.

The president paused for a few seconds. "Now Jim, as you've probably guessed, I don't make it a habit of calling my Navy captains at sea. You don't call me in the Oval Office, and I generally try to return the courtesy." He laughed briefly at his own attempted joke. Then he chopped it off, and the humor was gone from his voice. "So the fact that I'm calling you in the hour before battle must tell you something of how important this is."

"Yes, sir," the captain said.

"I know that this mission has personal importance to you. The lives of your crew are at stake, and—obviously—your own life as well. The recent loss of the USS *Benfold* is also, no doubt, on your mind—as it should be. Your comrades-in-arms have fallen at the hands of the enemy that you are set to face, and if there is an element of vengeance in your thinking, I don't believe that anyone could criticize you."

"I must admit that it's a factor, sir."

"If you said otherwise, I'd be inclined to doubt your word," the president said. "But there is a larger picture here, and the stakes are greater than you perhaps imagine. If Germany manages to deliver that submarine despite the concerted efforts of our Navy, it will seriously damage the credibility of our naval deterrence. It will also prove to many of the nations who are watching that German military hardware, and German military tactics, and German military training are the equal to—if not superior to—our own. To say that this will alter the balance of power in Europe would be a gross understatement. But even that is not the worst of it. I've spoken at length to Prime Minister Irons, and she makes no secret of the fact that she is preparing for war with Germany. I don't believe I need to remind you of what happened the *last* couple of times England and Germany went to war with each other."

"No, sir."

"We may have a chance to prevent that war," the president said. "If you can send that last submarine to the bottom, we can paint this whole thing as a military disaster for Germany. Really rub the German government's nose in it: in the United Nations, in the media, and in the eyes of the man on the street. If we can do that, I think I can talk Prime Minister Irons into accepting a symbolic defeat of Germany, in lieu of the real thing."

The noise level was dropping rapidly now, and that was a good thing, because the president's voice became softer. "I hate to put the pressure on you,

Jim, but this may well be the most important naval engagement of our time. It's the bottom of the ninth, and you're our last batter."

"We'll do our best to put it over the back fence, Mr. President," the captain said.

"I know you will, Jim. May God bless USS *Towers* and all who sail in her. Good luck and good hunting."

The speaker warbled again, and Navy Red dropped sync. The president was off the line.

CIC was silent for nearly a minute, and then Capt. Bowie clapped his hands together. "TAO, let's get *Firewalker* airborne. Then tell the engineers to drop the port screw off line and set Quiet Ship." He looked around CIC. "It's show time, folks. Time to kill us a submarine."

CHAPTER 51

USS *TOWERS* (DDG-103)
NORTHERN ARABIAN GULF (OFF THE COAST OF SIRAJ)
TUESDAY; 22 MAY
0358 hours (3:58 AM)
TIME ZONE +3 'CHARLIE'

The helo pilot's voice came over the Navy Red speaker in Combat Information Center, "SAU Commander, this is *Firewalker Two-Six*. I am up for *Towers* control. My fuel state is three hours plus four zero minutes. Three souls aboard. My load-out is one Mark-54 torpedo and a mixed rack of sonobuoys, over."

"Roger, *Firewalker*," Chief McPherson said. "Proceed to your fly-to points and begin seeding your buoys. You are at the edge of Siraji airspace, so keep your eyes peeled and don't wander outside our missile envelope. You might get some company up there, over."

"This is *Firewalker Two-Six*. Copy all. Roger, out."

The chief switched her comm-set from Navy Red to the USW tactical net. "Sonar—USWE. Go active. Stay sharp and change your equipment lineup every couple of minutes until we find the combination that gives us contact."

"Sonar, aye."

The chief looked at the CDRT and ran through the tactical situation in her mind. She wanted to be sure that she hadn't missed anything.

Navy Red warbled. "*Towers*, this is COM Fifth Fleet. I hate to follow the president's pep talk with bad news, but intelligence estimates indicate that you are steaming into a Siraji minefield, over."

The XO looked up. "A minefield? How much more good news can we stand?"

"Tell me about it," the captain said. He keyed up Navy Red. "COM Fifth Fleet, this is *Towers*. Understand my unit is steaming into a minefield. Request estimated boundaries of the field and any known safe transit lanes, over."

"*Towers*, this is COM Fifth Fleet. I am transmitting boundaries of the minefield to you now. There are currently no known safe transit lanes, and I do not have time to get a mine sweeper up there before you encounter the field, over."

The XO snorted. "This just keeps getting better."

The TAO said, "Captain, the parameters of the minefield just showed up in the link."

An irregular geometric shape appeared on the Aegis display screens, a series of thin red lines connected at each end to form a lopsided trapezoid off the coast of the port city of Zubayr. The NTDS symbol for *Towers* showed the destroyer a little less than a mile and a half south of the edge of the minefield.

"Nothing like cutting it close," the XO said. "They could have waited another six minutes or so, and we'd have found out by ourselves."

The captain keyed up Navy Red. "COM Fifth Fleet, this is *Towers*. I am in receipt of your minefield coordinates. I would have liked to have known about this sooner. I almost steamed into this thing blind, over."

"*Towers*, this is COM Fifth Fleet. Sorry about that. We just confirmed this info about two minutes ago. You were the first to know, over."

"COM Fifth Fleet, this is *Towers*. Roger, out." The captain punched out of Navy Red and walked over to Chief McPherson at the CDRT. "How are we looking, Chief?"

The chief tapped the screen with her fingertip. "Farthest-on circles put *Gremlin Zero Four* somewhere south of this line, Captain." She indicated a dotted arc on the display, just south of the minefield. "Assuming he's been traveling at maximum submerged speed since he torpedoed the *Benfold*, he could be inside our own Torpedo Danger Zone in the next ten minutes or so."

"Are you expecting to gain contact immediately?"

"Not really, sir," the chief said. "So far, he's depended a lot on deceptive maneuvering; I'd be surprised if he makes a straight run for home. But he might just *want* to surprise us, so we're prepared for it."

She pointed to a series of small green circles, each with a lightning bolt–shaped line coming out of its top at a forty-five–degree angle. "*Firewalker Two-Six* is laying a passive sonobuoy field to the south. When *Gremlin Zero Four* breaks the barrier, he'll be inside torpedo range."

"I hate to wait until he's that close," Capt. Bowie said. "Are you sure we can't get ASROC to work here? I thought the new shallow-water configuration was supposed to be pretty effective."

The chief shook her head. "It is, sir. But this water is too shallow even for the modified ASROCs. They'll end up buried in the sea bottom."

"Is there any way to reprogram the ASROCs?" the XO asked.

"I wish we could, sir," Chief McPherson said. "But it's not a software issue. It's a physics problem. We call it *dynamic overshoot*. An ASROC missile drops its torpedo from an altitude of about ten thousand feet. Even with the parachute pack to slow it down, when it hits the water, an ASROC-launched torpedo is moving *fast*. The saltwater batteries start the motor up almost immediately after the weapon splashes down, but the torpedo is still sinking fast. The computer takes control of the rudder fins and elevator fins and starts leveling off the torpedo as quickly as it can—sort of like a pilot trying to pull an airplane out of a steep dive. If the water is deep enough, the torpedo levels itself off and goes into its search pattern. If the water is too shallow, the weapon slams into the sea bottom before it can level off. Maybe the bottom is soft mud, and it buries itself. Maybe the bottom is hard-packed sand, and the torpedo is demolished by the impact. Either way, the torpedo is history."

The XO scratched his chin. "And this water is definitely too shallow?"

"Yes, sir," the chief said. "An ASROC torpedo will hit the water, run its motor for maybe ten seconds, and then crash into the bottom. It'll make a bunch of noise, but it won't do anything useful."

The XO's eyebrows went up. "If the water is so shallow, what's going to keep our tube-launched torpedoes from hitting the bottom? Or any torpedo dropped by the helo?"

Chief McPherson held up two fingers. "Two things, sir. First: over-the-side torpedoes and helo-dropped torpedoes hit the water with only a slight nose-down angle, so they're much closer to being level when the motor starts up. And second: they don't fall as far, so they don't build up much inertia. Our torpedo tubes are only about twenty feet above the water. The helo drops its torpedoes from an altitude of only a few hundred feet, not ten thousand feet like an ASROC. They're not moving all that fast when they hit the water, so they don't sink very far before they can level off."

"I see," the captain said. "And there's no way to program the ASROCs to drop their torpedoes from a lower altitude? Or maybe program the ASROC torpedoes to strike the water at a shallower angle?"

"Sir, it would take a complete redesign of the ASROC missile," Chief McPherson said. "A team of engineers with a billion-dollar budget could probably figure out how to do it if they had a couple of years to play around with the idea. But there's nothing we can do here and now."

"So we're stuck with over-the-side torpedoes," the XO said.

"Afraid so, sir. We'll have *Firewalker* running interference for us. If we get lucky, he'll be able to put a torpedo on *Gremlin Zero Four* before the sub knows what's up."

"Or he'll get blown out of the sky by a sub-SAM, like *Antietam*'s helo did."

"That's one of the risks, sir. But by the time the sub is close enough to shoot at *Firewalker*, he'll also be close enough to shoot at us. We're all going to be in the line of fire."

"We can't afford to forget about Vipers," the XO said. "The 212B can carry three Exocet missiles. They're supposed to fire them one at a time, but these bastards have shown a preference for launching them all at once."

"There were four subs left when we got into this fight," Capt. Bowie said. "That makes twelve Exocets. We saw them shoot nine, so there are three left."

"There *might* be three left, sir," the TAO said. "We've sunk three out of the four submarines. There's an excellent chance that this guy has launched one or more of his birds."

"Forget percentages," the XO said. "Until he's dead, as far as I'm concerned, this guy is armed with Exocets. Hell, with the kind of luck we've been having, he's got a couple of extras lying around for a rainy day."

Chief McPherson half-smiled. "Good thing it doesn't rain much in the Middle East, sir. Or we'd be screwed."

The XO glared at her for a couple of seconds, and then turned to the Tactical Action Officer. "TAO, I want Aegis ready-auto, CIWS set to auto-engage, and the Electronics Warfare guys standing by to jam or launch chaff. Set Tac-Sit One; I want all four .50-caliber mounts manned, and both 25mm chain-guns. Make sure that the 5-inch gun is loaded with HE-rounds. We have no friendly units within weapons range. If anything out there so much as farts, I want a missile, a torpedo, or a 5-inch shell shoved up its ass before its sphincter can slam shut."

"Aye-aye, sir." The TAO keyed into the tactical command net and began issuing orders.

* * *

Towers steamed back and forth, a wounded but determined sentry guarding the harbor against the approaching enemy. The crew settled in for a long wait, but less than twenty minutes had passed when the call came from the Electronics Warfare module. "TAO—EW, I have six active J-band radar seekers! We have in-bound missiles from the coast. First cut looks like Siraji HY-1 Silkworms."

The TAO was about to acknowledge the report when the Electronics Warfare Technician cut him off with a follow-up report. "TAO—EW. Make that twelve! We have a second flight of six. I say again, we have *twelve* in-bound Vipers! Request permission to initiate jamming protocols."

"EW—TAO. Initiate jamming and stand by on chaff. Break. Air—TAO, can you confirm inbound Vipers?"

"TAO—Air. That's affirmative, sir. We just picked them up about two seconds ago. Twelve inbounds!"

"TAO—aye! Break! All Stations—TAO, we have in-bound Vipers! I say again, we have missiles in-bound! This is not a drill! Weapons Control, verify that we are in Aegis ready-auto and CIWS is set to auto-engage."

"TAO—Weapons Control. Affirmative, boss. We are locked and cocked. Bring 'em on!"

"TAO—EW. Standing by on chaff. Recommend new course three-one-zero to minimize our radar cross-section."

The TAO looked up at the Aegis display screens. Twelve hostile-missile symbols had appeared, and all of them were rapidly closing on the *Towers*. "TAO, aye. Break. Bridge—TAO. Come right to new course three-one-zero."

"Bridge, aye! Coming right to three-one-zero."

All around CIC, operators began glancing up from their own consoles to steal looks at the big screens. Twelve missiles? They'd *never* trained for that many at one time.

"This is going to get ugly," an unidentified voice said.

"All right, people," the captain said. "Stay focused. Do your jobs, and everything will be okay."

Suddenly, three of the missile symbols veered away and disappeared off the display.

"TAO—Air. Splash three."

"Maybe that jamming gear is finally going to pay for itself," the XO said.

The TAO frowned. "Why only three? We're transmitting a broadband jamming strobe. It should be hitting all of those Vipers at the same time. If Silkworm missiles are impervious to jamming, we shouldn't have gotten any of them. If they're vulnerable to jamming, we should have gotten them all."

"Not necessarily," the XO said. "Remember, Siraj has been under an arms embargo for nearly two decades. Their arsenal is composed of what they had prior to the embargo, supplemented by whatever hardware they've been able to smuggle in. Those Silkworms they're launching may span three or four generations of technology."

"Launching chaff," the EW announced. His voice was followed by a rapid series of muffled thumps. "Six away."

"So far, so good," the TAO said.

The captain keyed his mike. "Weapons Control—Captain. How much longer until the Vipers come within our missile-engagement range?"

"Vipers are entering the Auto-Engage Circle right … about … *now*, sir."

The Aegis computers transmitted pre-launch programming data to eighteen SM-3 missiles, two for each of the enemy missiles remaining. This *shoot-shoot-look-shoot-shoot* doctrine would remain in effect until *Towers* expended fifty percent of her available SM-3 missiles. Then the Aegis computer would automatically fall back to a *shoot-look-shoot-shoot* doctrine, firing only one initial missile at each incoming Viper before checking to see if it had been destroyed.

On the forecastle, nine armored hatches flipped open in rapid succession, and nine SM-3 missiles blasted free of their launch cells and climbed into the darkness on actinic pillars of fire. The combined roar of the solid-fuel missile boosters reverberated through the ship like the rumble of an earthquake.

At the exact same instant, nine other armored hatches popped open on the after-missile deck, and nine more surface-to-air missiles leapt into the sky. Dividing the missiles between the launchers was a standard consideration built into the Aegis computer program. By assigning the missiles in equal or nearly equal proportions from both launchers, the Aegis computers could maintain a measure of redundancy.

The Air Supervisor's voice came over the net. "Splash one! Splash two! Splash three!" As he watched, the tally of destroyed missiles continued to mount. A few seconds later, he said, "Looks like we got 'em all!"

"Round One goes to *Towers*," the TAO said quietly.

Round Two was only seconds in coming. "TAO—EW, here comes the second salvo! I have six active J-band radar seekers! Wait! Six more! I have twelve in-bound Vipers."

The Air Supervisor confirmed the report immediately. "We've got them on SPY! I confirm, twelve Vipers in-bound!"

Capt. Bowie keyed his mike. "Air—Captain. Backtrack the trajectories of those Vipers! I want to know where they're coming from. Break. Weapons Control, stand by on guns. As soon as we get some coordinates, I want you to pound the hell out of those missile launchers!"

"With pleasure, sir!"

The twelve new hostile-missile symbols appeared on the Aegis display screens and began to close on the ship's symbol at alarming speed.

"TAO—Air. We've got party crashers, sir. Two Bogies inbound from the north. No modes, no codes, and no IFF."

The TAO watched as two unknown-aircraft symbols popped up on the tactical display. "TAO, aye. What's their flight profile?"

"They're coming in low and fast, sir. They're still over land, but I expect them to go feet-wet in about thirty seconds. In the meantime, they're hugging the ground."

"They're trying to sneak in under our radar," the XO said. "I guess their mamas didn't tell them that SPY sees all the way down to the ground."

"Air—TAO, copy all. Break. EW—TAO, can you classify those Bogies by their radar emitters?"

"TAO—EW, I could if they were showing me anything. So far, both of them have been as quiet as church mice."

"Right out of the old Soviet tactical book," the captain said. "Low, fast, and quiet. They won't point their radar at us until they're ready to illuminate us for missile-lock."

"They meet all the requirements for an auto-engage," the TAO said. "Aegis will take them out as soon as they come into missile range."

The captain shook his head. "Negative. Prohibit auto-engage on all Bogies."

"But, sir," the TAO said, "you said yourself they're going to shoot us as soon as they get missile-lock."

"We can't shoot them," the captain said. "Not now, anyway. The Rules of Engagement won't let us. We can't even technically classify them as hostile."

"Captain, I don't understand," the TAO said. "The Sirajis have already launched two dozen missiles at us. What more do we need?"

"For one thing," the captain said, "we don't even know for certain that those planes are Siraji."

"They're coming out of Siraji airspace, and they're flying strike profiles," the TAO said.

"Not good enough," the captain said. "We fly planes through Saudi air space all the time, but it doesn't make our planes Saudi. As much as I hate to say it, under U.S. Rules of Engagement, flying low and fast without radar is not considered a hostile act. As soon as one of them launches or lights off his fire control radar, they all become fair game. Until then, keep an eye on them but concentrate on your Vipers."

The TAO sighed. "Aye-aye, sir."

Three hostile-missile symbols disappeared from the Aegis display screens.

"TAO—Air. Splash three more. Two of them got jammed, and the third one got suckered by chaff."

"TAO, aye. Break. EW—TAO. Nice job. Stay on it."

The ship gave a rapid sequence of shudders, accompanied by a series of thunderous roars.

"TAO—Weapons Control. Eighteen more birds away, no apparent casualties. Targeted two each on the inbound Vipers."

"TAO, aye."

A trio of red octagonal symbols appeared on the tactical display, each of them superimposed over a different part of the Siraji coast. "Captain—Radar Supervisor, I've got cross-fixes on three of the enemy missile launchers, sir!"

"Punch them into the link!" the captain said. "Weapons Control, you have batteries released. Engage those missile launchers, now!"

A few seconds later, the ship jerked as the 5-inch deck gun fired for the first time. The report of the big gun was astonishingly loud, even in the insulated confines of CIC. The gun quickly fell into a rhythm, punching out a high-explosive shell every three seconds, with a series of teeth-rattling booms.

The TAO keyed his mike. "Air—TAO. What's going on with those inbound Bogies?"

"They've sheared off, sir, but they're not bugging out. They're staying outside of our engagement circle but just barely. I think they're waiting for their shore-based Silkworm launchers to saturate our defenses. Or they could be hoping we'll run out of missiles."

The captain said, "At the rate we're using up SM-3s, either one could be a good bet. Keep an eye on them, son. They might decide they want a piece of this fight at any second."

"Aye-aye, sir."

* * *

On the Aegis displays, eighteen friendly-missile symbols merged with the nine flashing red symbols that represented inbound Vipers. For a few seconds, the converging array of symbols made a confusing knot on the screen, and then they began to disappear as the Aegis computers sorted out which missiles had been destroyed and which were still providing valid radar returns. When the display finished updating itself, only two missile symbols remained—both shown in flashing red.

"TAO—Air. Two of the Vipers have gotten past our first salvo of interceptors." There was another quick series of shudders, followed by the thunder of launching missiles. "Four more birds away, no apparent casualties. Targeted two each on the inbound Vipers."

"TAO, aye."

Twenty seconds later, the interceptors merged with the inbound Vipers on the tactical display, and—when the display updated itself—one of the Viper symbols remained, still closing rapidly.

"Shit!" the Weapons Control Officer shouted. "TAO—Weapons Control, one of the Vipers got through. It's kicked into terminal homing phase, and it's too close to re-engage with missiles."

"It's up to CIWS, now," the XO said.

* * *

As if in answer, the forward Close-In Weapon System locked onto the incoming missile and opened fire. The six-barreled Gatling gun rapped out a burst of 20mm tungsten rounds. Somewhere out in the darkness, a brief flash of exploding fuel announced the destruction of the Viper.

"TAO—Weapons Control. Got the bastard!"

"Good job," the TAO said. "Break. Air—TAO, what's the status of our Bogies?"

"They're just inside our missile range, sir. And still circling."

"Don't lose track of them," the TAO said. "And watch for more Vipers."

* * *

The next missile attack wasn't long in coming. "TAO—EW, I've got five more inbounds! Make that ten; they're all getting off a second bird!"

"God damn it!" the Radar Supervisor shouted. "I've got 'em too! Confirm, ten inbound Vipers! How many are they going to throw at us?"

* * *

"TAO—Weapons Control. I think we've got a kill on one of the missile launchers, sir. I'm shifting my fire to the other two cross-fixes. I'm going to need position data on the remaining three sites pretty quick here, sir."

"I'm working on it, sir!" the Radar Supervisor shouted.

Capt. Bowie keyed his mike. "Radar Supervisor, this is the captain. Calm down, son. I need you to keep a clear head right now."

"Yes, sir! I mean, I'll try, sir!"

* * *

The 5-inch gun continued to hammer out high-explosive rounds every three seconds or so.

Navy Red warbled. "*Towers*, this is *Firewalker Two-Six*. My buoys five and six are hot! We hold narrowband tonals consistent with a Type 212 diesel submarine. Initial classification: POSS-SUB, confidence level high!"

The XO's voice was incredulous. "How in the hell do they do that? How do they always manage to show up just when the shit is hitting the fan?"

The captain keyed Navy Red. "*Firewalker Two-Six*, this is *Towers*. Take your shot. Try to make it a good one."

On the Aegis display screen, three of the ten incoming-missile symbols winked out.

"Splash three Vipers," the Air Supervisor said over the net. "Chalk up two to jamming and one to chaff."

A quick series of rumbles announced the launch of another salvo of missiles. "TAO—Weapons Control. Ten more birds away, no apparent casualties. Targeted two each on the first three inbound Vipers and one each for the remaining four Vipers."

The odd report stopped the TAO cold. He keyed his mike. "Weapons Control—TAO, why did we only launch one interceptor on the last four Vipers?"

"We've expended more than fifty percent of our SM-3 inventory," the Weapons Control Officer said. "The computer has throttled us back to a *shoot-look-shoot-shoot* doctrine."

"Fifty percent?" the TAO said. "We carry ninety-two SM-3 missiles. How in the hell can we be at fifty percent of our inventory?"

"Fifty percent of ninety-two is forty-six, sir," the Weapons Control Officer said. "We've launched fifty missiles."

The TAO looked at the captain.

The captain nodded. "Stick with it. The shooting's not over yet."

"Well," said the XO, "at least we know what those Bogies have been waiting for."

* * *

"*Towers*, this is *Firewalker Two-Six*. My weapons check-off list is complete. I am prepping for my attack run, over."

The TAO keyed Navy Red. "*Towers*, aye. Good hunting, *Firewalker*."

The captain's eyes traveled over the faces of the men and women of the CIC crew. "Cross your fingers and say a prayer," he said. "If *Firewalker* pulls this off, the show's over, and we're out of here."

"Amen to that," the XO said.

Firewalker Two-Six's buoy cross-fixes began popping up on the CDRT. Chief McPherson rolled the trackball until her cursor was centered over the first cross-fix symbol and began playing connect-the-dots. The CDRT's computer gave her a rough course of three-five-seven at an estimated speed of sixteen knots. *Gremlin Zero Four* was headed north, toward the minefield. Toward Zubayr harbor and safety.

* * *

The TAO watched on the Aegis display screens as *Firewalker Two-Six*'s green friendly-aircraft symbol vectored across the screen toward the red V-shape of

Gremlin Zero Four's hostile-submarine symbol. He cocked an ear toward the speaker, expecting to hear *Firewalker*'s attack report at any second.

But the next report came from the Weapons Control Officer. "TAO—Weapons Control. Scratch another Silkworm launcher. Shifting to the next target at this time."

"Two down," the TAO said.

"We're not getting them fast enough," the captain said. "At this rate, we're going to run out of SM-3s before they run out of Silkworms."

The Air Supervisor's voice came over the net. "TAO—Air. The Bogies are moving!"

"TAO, aye. Are they closing us?"

"Negative, sir," the Air Supervisor said. "They've going after the helo!"

"TAO—EW, the Bogies just lit off their radars! French-built. Thomson-CSF Cyrano IVM series. That makes our Bogies either Mirage F-1s or Mirage F-50s."

"There aren't any F-50s in-theater," Capt. Bowie said. "So our bad guys are F-1s, which means we still can't shoot them. They might be Siraji, but they might also be from Iran, Jordan, or Kuwait. Mirages aren't exactly rare in this part of the world."

The TAO keyed Navy Red. "*Firewalker Two-Six*, this is *Towers*. Watch your back, you've got two Bogies inbound from the north, over."

"*Towers*, this is *Firewalker*. Copy inbound Bogies. Keep them off my back for another thirty seconds, until I get off my shot, over."

"We'll try, *Firewalker*," the TAO said. "But the Bogies have not satisfied Rules of Engagement criteria to be designated as hostile."

* * *

On the Aegis displays, ten friendly-missile symbols merged with seven flashing red Viper symbols. When the display finished updating itself, the flashing red missile symbols were gone.

The Air Supervisor's voice came over the net. "TAO—Air. Splash seven! We got them all!"

* * *

The Tactical Action Officer was about to key his mike to acknowledge when another report came in.

"TAO—EW, Bogies just lit up their fire control radars!"

"That's it!" the captain said. "Batteries released! Take them out!"

The TAO keyed the net. "Weapons Control—TAO, Bogies have been designated as hostile. You have batteries released. Engage and destroy!"

Without waiting for acknowledgment of his order, the TAO shifted to Navy Red. "*Firewalker Two-Six*, this is *Towers*. The Bogies are setting you up for an attack! Abort your torpedo launch and get the hell out of there!"

"Just another three seconds," *Firewalker Two-Six*'s copilot said over Navy Red. "Here it comes ... Weapon away—now, now, NOW!"

* * *

Under the starboard side of the helicopter's fuselage, solenoid-controlled latches snapped open, releasing *Firewalker Two-Six*'s torpedo. The weapon dropped like a rock until its parachute pack deployed a fraction of a second later, slowing the torpedo's rate of descent and drawing it into a slightly nose-down angle for optimum water insertion.

The copilot keyed his mike. "*Towers*, this is *Firewalker Two-Six*. My torpedo is away. I am going evasive to avoid Bogies."

* * *

"TAO—Air. Bogies are launching. I count two missiles, both targeted on the helo."

The ship shuddered as two SM-3s blasted out of their missile cells and turned toward the enemy jets.

"Can we intercept their missiles?" the captain asked.

"Not a chance, sir," the TAO said. "By the time our birds get there, *Firewalker* will already be toast."

The little drama played itself out on the Aegis display screen, two hostile-missile symbols merging with the helicopter symbol. Somewhere out in the night sky, twisted metal and burning flesh were falling toward the darkened wave tops. On the screen, *Firewalker Two-Six*'s symbol changed to a last-known-position marker, and the helicopter and its crew of three were gone.

"TAO—Weapons Control. Our birds have acquired the Bogies."

Seen from the Aegis display screen, the destruction of the enemy jets was no more dramatic than the loss of the helo had been. Two friendly-missile symbols converged on two hostile-aircraft symbols. Each of the missile symbols touched the symbol for one of the hostile aircraft, and the Bogies were gone. The destruction of two aircraft depicted in the sterile exchange of computer icons. No hint of the fire and violent death that those symbols represented.

"I hope they suffered," the XO said. "I hope those bastards shit their pants when they saw our missiles coming, and I hope they burned and bled and screamed for Allah—all the way down to the water. And I hope their souls fry in hell!"

Capt. Bowie laid his hand on his second-in-command's shoulder and quietly said. "That's enough, Pete." He gave the shoulder a quick squeeze. "I understand what you're feeling, but we don't have time for that."

As if on cue, the Weapons Control Officer's voice came over the net. "TAO—Weapons Control. Silkworm launcher number three is down for the count. Shifting to launcher number four."

* * *

Out on the forecastle, the 5-inch gun fell silent for a second, swung to cover its new target, and began hammering out another barrage of shells.

* * *

The Sonar Supervisor's voice came over the tactical net. "USWE—Sonar, we have weapon start-up. It's *Firewalker*'s torpedo, sir. Placement looks pretty good."

A friendly-weapon symbol appeared in blue on the CDRT.

Chief McPherson keyed her mike. "Sonar—USWE. Has the weapon acquired?"

"USWE—Sonar. That's affirmative. *Firewalker*'s weapon has just now acquired the target. It's a tail-chase, Chief. Even odds as to whether it can catch the sub."

"USWE, aye."

* * *

U-307:

"Kapitan!" the Sonar Operator shouted. "The American torpedo has acquired us!"

"Calm down!" Gröeler snapped. "Estimated range?"

"Close aboard, sir! The signal strength is high. Estimated range—less than fifteen hundred meters."

"Very well," Gröeler said. He nodded, as though he had been expecting this. The Americans were good—far better than he had thought. He had three missing U-boats to prove it. But this wasn't over yet.

He turned to the OOD. "Officer of the Deck, I have the Conn!"

"Officer of the Deck, aye!"

Gröeler barked, "All engines ahead one-third, slow to five knots! Left standard rudder, steady new course three-one-zero!"

The boat began to heel over as the Helmsman executed his orders. "Sir, my rudder is left fifteen degrees! Coming to new course three-one-zero. All engines ahead one-third! Slowing to five knots!"

The Officer of the Deck stared at Gröeler. "*Five knots*, Kapitan? Sir, how can we outdistance a torpedo at five knots?"

Gröeler held up a hand. "Launch two static noisemakers," he said. "Then wait thirty seconds and launch two mobile decoys. Set one of the mobile decoys for low speed and the other for high speed."

The Officer of the Deck stared at his kapitan for another second. Then he blinked and turned to the Countermeasures Control Panel. "Aye-aye, sir. Launching static noisemakers now!"

A pair of pneumatic hisses followed by a pair of metallic thumps announced the ejection of the two countermeasures.

* * *

The Officer of the Deck began punching buttons rapidly, programming the mobile decoys as his kapitan had ordered. His hands trembled as he worked. *Five knots? They should be racing away at flank speed, not waiting for the torpedo to catch them!*

* * *

"The American torpedo is too close," Gröeler said. "There is no time to run. It will catch us before we go a thousand meters. Our only chance is to fool it."

"Launching mobile decoys, now!" the Officer of the Deck reported. There was another pair of hisses and thumps as the second set of countermeasures was ejected.

"Excellent," Gröeler said. "Diving Officer, ten degrees up-angle on the bow planes. Make your depth twenty-five meters."

"Diving Officer, aye! Sir, my bow planes are up ten degrees. Coming to new depth two-five meters."

"Steady on new course three-one-zero," the Helmsman called out.

"Very well," Gröeler said. He looked at his Officer of the Deck. "We give the torpedo two static noisemakers to activate its anti-countermeasure algorithm." He spoke in a quiet, unhurried voice, as though unaware that death was rushing toward them. "Then we give it a pair of mobile decoys—not so easily identifiable. The torpedo is faced with two invalid targets and three possibly valid targets. Two of them move slowly and do not seem to be actively evading. The third moves away at high speed."

The American torpedo was close enough now to be heard with the naked ear. The growling whine of its high-speed screws resonated through the hull of the submarine like the buzzing of an insanely powerful electric razor. The sound grew rapidly louder as the torpedo approached.

The Officer of the Deck's eyes darted frantically around the control room, as though searching for somewhere to run. There was, of course, nowhere to go. "The torpedo …" His voice came out in a squeak. He stopped himself and tried again. "The torpedo will acquire the high-speed decoy and attack it instead of us?"

Utterly calm, Gröeler turned back to the tactical display. "I estimate that we will find out the answer to that question in approximately one minute."

* * *

USS *Towers* (DDG-103):

The Sonar Supervisor's voice came over the 29-MC announcing circuit. "All stations—Sonar has multiple active 53 Delta contacts off the starboard quarter, bearing one-five-five. Initial classification: POSS-SUB, confidence level low."

Chief McPherson keyed her mike. "Sonar—USWE, what have you got?"

"USWE—Sonar, I'm tracking five separate contacts. Unless I miss my guess, we're looking at a cluster of decoys, Chief. Two of my contacts are dead in the water, so they're probably static countermeasures. The other three are all showing motion. Looks like two are moving slowly, and one is getting the hell out of Dodge."

The chief keyed her mike again. "Sonar—USWE. Watch your net discipline. The fast-moving contact is probably our submarine, trying to outrun *Firewalker*'s torpedo. But I want you to maintain a track on all three of your mobile contacts until we get a clear classification. Your two low-speed contacts are designated Alpha and Bravo. Your high-speed contact is designated Charlie. Tag all three contacts and send them to fire control."

"Sonar, aye. Slow-movers are designated Alpha and Bravo. Fast-mover is designated Charlie. All three contacts are tagged. Transmitting them to fire control now."

"USWE, aye. Break. UB—USWE. You should be getting contact data on three POSS-SUB contacts in a few seconds, designated Alpha, Bravo, and

Charlie. We believe Alpha and Bravo are decoys, and Charlie is our submarine, but we don't have final classification yet. Prep the starboard tubes for an over-the-side torpedo shot and stand by to launch it on zero-notice."

Before the Underwater Battery Fire Control Operator had a chance to reply, the Sonar Supervisor's voice came over the net again. "USWE—Sonar. *Firewalker*'s torpedo has acquired contact Charlie, the fast-mover. Torpedo is accelerating to attack speed now."

The Sonar Supervisor's next report came over the 29-MC announcing circuit almost immediately. "All stations—Sonar has loud underwater explosion off the starboard quarter, bearing one-six-zero."

Chief McPherson keyed her mike. "Sonar—USWE. Are you detecting secondary explosions?"

The answer was a few seconds in coming. "USWE—Sonar. Negative. We did not detect secondaries. But we have no echoes on contact Charlie."

Chief McPherson keyed her mike. "USWE, aye." She released the mike button. This was the tricky part. When a torpedo killed a submarine, there was usually a string of secondary explosions following the initial detonation of the warhead. Fuel tanks, battery cells, and the submarine's torpedoes, all going off in explosions of their own. The lack of secondaries wasn't conclusive proof that the submarine hadn't been destroyed. It was possible for the submarine's hull to crack and fill with water *without* setting off a string of secondary explosions. But it was rare, and—when it did happen—it turned battle damage assessment into a guessing game.

Had *Firewalker*'s torpedo killed the sub? Or had it destroyed a decoy? Was their mission complete now? Or was the sub still lurking out there, waiting for a chance to kill them?

The answer was not long in coming.

"USWE—Sonar. Contact designated Bravo has increased speed and turned toward the minefield. We're detecting shaft and blade signatures consistent with a Type 212 series submarine."

The chief banged her fist on the CDRT. "Damn! He tricked us again!" She keyed her mike. "Sonar—USWE. Copy all. Your contact Bravo is now re-designated as *Gremlin Zero Four*. Break. UB—USWE. Contact Bravo is now re-designated as *Gremlin Zero Four*."

"USWE—UB, copy all. Be advised that *Gremlin Zero Four* is at the very edge of our torpedo engagement envelope. I hold a firm fire control solution. If we're going to shoot this guy, we need to do it soon."

Chief McPherson looked at *Gremlin Zero Four*'s track history on the CDRT's display screen. The submarine was heading straight for the minefield.

"USWE, aye. Break. TAO—USWE. Sonar holds a solid track on *Gremlin Zero Four*, and UB has a firm fire control solution. Request batteries released."

The TAO's voice came back at once. "USWE—TAO. You have batteries released. Kill contact *Gremlin Zero Four*."

"TAO—USWE, Batteries released, kill contact *Gremlin Zero Four*, aye. Break. UB—USWE. Kill contact *Gremlin Zero Four* with over-the-side torpedo."

"UB, aye. Going to *Standby*. Going to *Launch*. Torpedo away—now, now, NOW!"

The Sonar Supervisor's report followed a second later. "USWE—Sonar, we have weapon start-up."

A blue friendly-weapon symbol appeared on the CDRT. Chief McPherson watched it begin to move toward the hostile-submarine symbol that represented *Gremlin Zero Four*. "Go get the bastard," she whispered.

The 29-MC speakers thundered to life. "All Stations—Sonar has hydrophone effects off the starboard quarter! Bearing one-five-three. Initial classification: hostile torpedo!"

"Damn! He's shooting down our line of bearing!" Chief McPherson said. She keyed her mike. "Crack the whip! Bridge—USWE. We have an inbound hostile torpedo. I say again—crack the whip!"

"Bridge, aye!"

With a rising wail, the ship's gas turbine engines spun up to flank speed.

The Officer of the Deck's voice blared over the 1-MC. "All hands stand by for heavy rolls while performing high-speed evasive maneuvers."

The deck heeled to starboard as the big destroyer came sharply about for the first high-speed turn demanded by the crack-the-whip torpedo evasion maneuver.

Chief McPherson latched on to the edge of the CDRT as the deck tilted one way and then the other. On the screen, she could see new POSS-SUB symbols appearing. *Gremlin Zero Four* was launching another set of decoys.

* * *

After nearly five minutes of evasive maneuvering, the Sonar Supervisor's voice came over Chief McPherson's headset again. "USWE—Sonar. The hostile torpedo has not acquired. Looks like we dodged the bullet."

"USWE, aye," the chief said into her mike. "Looks like we're not the only ones." On the CDRT, it was obvious that *Gremlin Zero Four*'s tricky little maneuver with the decoys had worked again. The submarine had managed to evade their torpedo.

She paused to reassess the tactical situation. With half an ear, she heard the Electronics Warfare Operator report six more inbound Vipers, followed a few seconds later by the rumble of launching SM-3s. She keyed her mike. "UB—USWE, do you hold a good track on *Gremlin Zero Four*?"

"USWE—UB. That's affirmative. I've got a firm solution on the target, but the submarine is outside our torpedo engagement envelope now. We're going to have to close the range before we can shoot again."

"USWE, aye."

Updated tracking data for *Gremlin Zero Four* was coming through on the CDRT display. Chief McPherson slewed her cursor over to the most recent position symbol for the submarine and began punching keys. "Shit!"

She punched into the tactical net. "TAO—USWE. Based on current course and speed, I hold *Gremlin Zero Four* as entering the minefield in less than one minute."

Capt. Bowie was at her side before she had even released the mike button. "Are we within torpedo range?"

The chief shook her head. "Negative, sir. We need to get closer. But, as soon as we close within range, he's going to shoot at us again."

"We can't let that sub get away," the captain said.

"I know, sir."

"We don't have much of a choice," the captain said. "Shift the sonar to Kingfisher mode. We're going into the minefield."

"Sir, with all due respect, that's not going to work," Chief McPherson said. "The Kingfisher software is designed to detect mine-sized objects only. It will clip out anything with a cross-section larger than about six feet. We won't be able to see the submarine, sir."

"Then we'll alternate: two sweeps in Kingfisher mode, and one sweep in Search mode. Your operators will have to look sharp; they're only going to see the mines two-thirds of the time, and the target one-third of the time. Understand?"

Chief McPherson's eyebrows went up. "I understand, sir." She pointed to the CDRT display. "The submarine is entering the minefield now."

The Tactical Action Officer appeared at the captain's elbow. "Sir, Silkworm launcher four is out of business. We're shifting fire to site number five."

Capt. Bowie nodded. "We need to knock those last two launchers out quickly. We're headed into the minefield."

"Sir?"

The captain patted the TAO on the shoulder. "Let chief here worry about the mines. You just keep the heat on those missile launchers."

"Aye-aye, sir."

* * *

Another report came over the Tactical Action Officer's headset, snatching his attention away from the submarine and the minefield.

"TAO—EW. I have two active J-band radar seekers! And there's the second flight, two more. Make that *four* inbound Vipers."

"TAO, aye. Break. Air—TAO. Can you confirm incoming Vipers?"

"Affirmative, sir," the Air Supervisor said. "SPY confirms, four Vipers inbound!"

"TAO, aye. Break. EW—TAO. Jam and chaff at will. We won't be able to maneuver in the minefield, so forget about minimizing our radar cross-section."

"TAO—EW. Copy all. Launching chaff."

The TAO looked up at the four inbound missile symbols on the tactical display. "TAO, aye."

* * *

Out on the forecastle, the 5-inch gun continued to pound out high-explosive shells.

* * *

The Sonar Supervisor's voice came over the 29-MC speakers. "All Stations—Sonar. Mine off the port bow! Bearing three-one-two. Recommend turn to starboard!"

Chief McPherson keyed the net. "Bridge—USWE. Emergency Mine! Come right to new course three-four-zero!"

"Bridge, aye!" The ship heeled over in nearly instant response to the order.

They had been on the new course less than a minute when the next report came. "All Stations—Sonar, mine off the starboard bow! Bearing zero-one-five. Recommend turn to port!"

Chief McPherson keyed the net. "Bridge—USWE. Emergency Mine! Come left to new course three-one-five!"

"Bridge, aye!" The ship heeled over to port and began to come about.

The XO looked at their progress on the Aegis display. "This is turning into a drunkard's walk."

"Yes, sir," the TAO said. "But it looks like it's working."

* * *

Chief McPherson watched the CDRT. The ship's track history was very nearly a blind stagger through the minefield, but they were slowly closing the range to the target. They would be within the torpedo engagement envelope soon, close enough to shoot at the submarine again. But what good would it do them? The sub commander had obviously figured out how to outfox their torpedoes. If they shot another torp at him, he'd just evade it with his tricky little decoy tactic. Not only that, but he was certain to return fire with his own torpedo, and *Towers* couldn't exactly evade in the middle of a minefield.

There had to be a way to trick him, the way he was tricking their torpedoes. Some way to disguise or hide a torpedo until it was too close for the sub to evade. The Germans had been using decoys of nearly every sort imaginable since this whole crazy chase had started. If only she had some decoys of her own …

In the background, she heard the rumble of another set of missiles launching. They must still be trading punches with the shore-based missile launchers.

Too bad she couldn't launch her own missiles. If only the water was deep enough for ASROCs. She could keep the sub distracted with an over-the-side shot, and—while he was busy evading the torpedo—she could drop an ASROC right off his bow. She could …

She stopped. Wait a minute … Maybe she could do it *backward* … Keep the sub distracted with ASROCs long enough to sneak up on him with an over-the-side torpedo.

She felt herself grin as she reached for the mike button. "UB—USWE. How long until the target is within our torpedo engagement envelope?"

* * *

U-307:

"Kapitan!" the Sonar Operator shouted. "I have splash transients and hydrophone effects, bearing two-six-five. Initial classification: hostile torpedo! Estimated range—less than two thousand meters."

"Very well," Gröeler said. "All engines ahead one-third, slow to five knots!" He glanced at the double dotted lines on the tactical display that indicated the zigzagging pattern of the clear lane through the minefield. "Right standard rudder, steady new course one-four-zero!"

The boat began to come about. "Sir, my rudder is right fifteen degrees! Coming to new course one-four-zero. All engines ahead one-third! Slowing to five knots!"

Gröeler was about to order the launching of the first pair of decoys, when the Sonar Operator shouted again.

"Kapitan! All hydrophone effects have ceased. Hostile torpedo has shut down."

Gröeler turned to stare at the man. "What?"

"The torpedo has shut itself down, sir. Its motor started up, ran for maybe fifteen seconds, and shut down."

"That doesn't make any ..."

The Sonar Operator cut him off. "Kapitan! I have new splash transients and hydrophone effects, bearing three-zero-zero. Initial classification: hostile torpedo! Estimated range—less than one thousand meters."

Gröeler took three quick steps to the sonar console. The Sonar Operator was correct; the high-speed blade signature of an American Mark-54 torpedo was clearly visible on the screen. He verified the bearing to the new torpedo and decided that his current course was still viable. He turned toward the Officer of the Deck. "Launch two static noisemakers. Then wait thirty seconds and launch two mobile decoys. Set one of the mobile decoys for low speed and the other for high speed."

The OOD, who was now familiar with the tactic, had already been reaching for the Countermeasures Control Panel. "Aye-aye, sir. Launching static noisemakers now!"

A pair of hisses and thumps marked the ejection of two decoys.

"Kapitan!" the Sonar Operator said. "I have splash transients and hydrophone effects, bearing zero-five-zero. Initial classification: hostile torpedo! Estimated range—two thousand meters."

Gröeler looked at the sonar display. The previous torpedo had shut down, just like the first one. Its signature began to fade from the screen. The first torpedo's signature was also fading but still visible. The third torpedo signal was bright and strong, bearing zero-five-zero, exactly as the Sonar Operator had reported.

What were the Americans trying to do? He opened his mouth to order a course change, when his Sonar Operator reported yet another torpedo. Where were these torpedoes coming from, and why were they all shutting down so quickly?

"Kapitan?" It was the Officer of the Deck. "Do you wish me to launch more decoys, sir?"

"Yes," Gröeler said. "Launch two ..." He stopped himself. "No ..."

"These Americans are crafty," he said. "They drop their useless ASROCs all around us, to force us to expend our decoys. Then, when we have no decoys left, they will fire their torpedoes. Launch no more decoys until I give the order."

* * *

USS *Towers* (DDG-103):

Chief McPherson watched the tactical display on the CDRT. It was working! *Gremlin Zero Four* had stopped reacting to the ASROC attacks. A distant rumble announced the launch of another ASROC. Hot on its heels came two more rumbles, as a pair of SM-3 missiles climbed into the sky in search of incoming Vipers.

The chief keyed her mike. "UB—USWE. Kill contact *Gremlin Zero Four* with over-the-side torpedo."

"UB, aye. Going to *Standby*. Going to *Launch*. Torpedo away—now, now, NOW!"

The Sonar Supervisor's report confirmed the launch almost immediately. "USWE—Sonar. We have weapon start-up."

A blue friendly-weapon symbol popped up on the CDRT and began moving toward *Gremlin Zero Four*'s hostile-submarine symbol. There were several friendly-weapon symbols on the screen. "That's right," she whispered. "Keep your eyes on the right hand, and you'll never even see what the left hand is doing."

Another rumble, and another ASROC climbed into the sky.

* * *

U-307:

"Kapitan …" The Sonar Operator's voice sounded strange. "This one is not shutting down."

Gröeler turned toward him. "What?"

"This torpedo is not shutting down," the Sonar Operator said.

Gröeler stepped over to the sonar console. "Which torpedo?"

The operator pointed at the screen. The display was a nearly unintelligible mishmash of torpedo signatures, all faded to varying degrees. All except one. The torpedo signature at bearing one-seven-eight wasn't fading at all. It was getting stronger rapidly.

Gröeler could hear it now, the electric-razor whine of high-speed propellers. The sound quickly growing to a howl.

Gröeler gripped the Sonar Operator's shoulder. "Give me an estimated range!"

"Extremely close aboard! Less than five hundred meters!"

"Decoys!" Gröeler shouted. No. It was too late for decoys.

"Belay that order! Counter-battery fire! I want a torpedo in the water NOW! Firing bearing one-seven-eight!"

The Fire Control Officer acknowledged his order and began to punch buttons with the speed of a touch-typist. "Torpedo away!" he shouted after a few seconds. "Firing bearing one-seven-eight!"

The water-jet ejection system emitted its characteristic burbling vibration as it propelled the torpedo out of its tube. The sound was almost lost under the shriek of the American torpedo.

The Fire Control Officer turned toward his kapitan. "Sir! What do we do now?"

Gröeler stared back at him. "Now? Now, we die ..."

The bulkhead to his left imploded, the metal first fracturing and then vaporizing under the incredible heat of the Mark-54 torpedo's plasma-jet explosive. Gröeler was blown from his feet and incinerated before his lifeless body hit the deck.

The pressure inside the dying submarine dropped instantly, as the hungry fireball sucked up all of the available air. A millisecond later, the sea crashed through the broken hull and pulverized everything inside.

The broken pieces of *U-307* tumbled to the bottom of the sea.

* * *

USS *Towers* (DDG-103):

The 29-MC speakers thundered to life. "All Stations—Sonar. Loud underwater explosions with secondaries, bearing zero-zero-two! I think we got the bastard!"

A cheer went up in Combat Information Center, followed by what seemed to be a collective sigh of relief.

The 29-MC speakers thundered to life again. "All Stations—Sonar has hydrophone effects off the starboard bow! Bearing zero-zero-five! Initial classification: hostile torpedo!"

Chief McPherson's eyes jerked back to the CDRT. *Oh shit! It wasn't over yet!* She keyed her mike. "TAO—USWE. We can't evade in a minefield! Look at the plot, sir! We've got mines on both sides of us!"

* * *

Capt. Bowie stared at the hostile-torpedo symbol flashing red on the Aegis display screen. There was nowhere to run. They couldn't evade. The torpedo screaming toward them was a German-built DMA37, the same model that had broken the *Antietam* like a child's toy. The same model that killed the *Benfold.*

The seconds dragged on, and the captain gradually became aware that nearly every pair of eyes in CIC was locked on him. He was their commanding officer, and their eyes were begging him to lead them out of this trap. He kept his eyes on the tactical display. There was nowhere to go.

The XO nudged him, "Jim?"

Capt. Bowie stood without speaking. They were surrounded by mines. If they tried to run, they were nearly certain to hit one. If they *didn't* run, the torpedo was going to kill them anyway. With a little more time, they could map the minefield with their Kingfisher sonar—find a clear passage out into safe waters.

He started to open his mouth and then stopped himself. A clear passage ... They didn't have time to find one. Could they make one?

He keyed his mike. "Weapons Control—Captain. Forget that last missile site. Train the 5-inch gun directly off the bow. Use maximum elevation and reduced powder charges. I want those rounds to fall as close to the bow as possible. HE-CVT, fused to go off when they hit the water."

"Sir?"

"No questions, just do it. In fact, I want every gun we've got, including the .50-cals and the chain-guns pointed into the water off the bow. Maybe we can blow ourselves a safe path out of here."

* * *

Two hostile-missile symbols vanished off the Aegis display screens, leaving two more inbound missiles.

"TAO—Air. Splash two more Vipers. Both of them to jamming. No takers on the chaff."

"TAO, aye."

The ship gave two shudders, accompanied by the roar of two missiles launching.

"TAO—Weapons Control. Two birds away, no apparent casualties. Targeted one each on the inbound Vipers."

"Screw the missiles," the captain said. He keyed his mike. "Weapons Control, this is the Captain. Let Aegis handle the missiles. We've got an inbound torpedo that we *can't* shoot down. Concentrate on blowing us a path out of here."

"Weapons Control, aye."

The gunfire increased in intensity as the rest of the ship's guns joined the 5-inch. The barrage was unholy.

"Captain—Weapons Control. We're pumping everything we've got into the water, sir. You may maneuver when ready."

The captain keyed his mike. "Bridge—Captain. Let's go! Left standard rudder! Get us out of here!"

"Bridge, aye!"

As the ship heeled over into its turn, the XO leaned near the captain's ear. "Do you think this'll work?"

The captain shrugged. "Frankly, I have no idea. I just know that it's better than sitting back there waiting to die!"

A thundering boom rattled the ship.

"TAO—Bridge. Close-aboard explosion off the port bow."

Another explosion followed immediately.

"TAO—Bridge. Close aboard explosion dead off the bow."

All around CIC, watchstanders began exchanging glances. Maybe this really *was* going to work …

On the Aegis display screen, the speed vector for *Towers*' NTDS symbol was pointed back out of the minefield. They were turned around now and headed for safety. The ship's symbol inched toward the bright red line that represented the border of the minefield.

"TAO—Air. Splash one more Viper. We still have one inbound, and it's too close for another missile shot."

"TAO, aye. We'll have to let the aft CIWS mount handle it."

Another explosion rocked the ship, this one much closer than the others had been. The shock wave rolled the ship hard to starboard, and circuit breakers began to trip, cutting off electrical power to parts of the ship.

"TAO—Weapons Control. Aegis is down! Primary computer is off line! I'm taking control of the backup computer and reloading in alternate configuration."

"Weapons Control—TAO. What's the status of the aft CIWS mount?"

"Just a second, sir," the Weapons Control Officer said. "It's … uh … It's … I can't tell, sir! I lost my data feed from CIWS! I can't tell if CIWS is up or down!"

* * *

HY-1 Silkworm (mid-flight):

The missile was an ugly thing. It bore little resemblance to the sleek, dartlike airframes of the German and American missiles. Its blunt nose, fat cigar shape, and stubby wings gave it the same general lines and proportions as a 1950s airliner. Seen in the daylight and under other conditions, it might have seemed comical.

But in the darkness, it was invisible, except for the yellow-blue streak of glare that trailed its engine exhaust.

It was a capable machine, despite its comic appearance, and there was nothing even remotely amusing about the 454 kilograms of high explosive packed in its warhead.

The missile made a last-second course correction and darted in for the kill.

* * *

USS *Towers* (DDG-103):

The aft CIWS spun on its mount and pointed its six barrels at the incoming missile. With a sound akin to a lawn mower, the high-tech Gatling gun spun its barrels up to speed and unleashed a burst of 20mm rounds. A fraction of a second later, the cluster of hardened tungsten bullets slammed into the incoming missile, and the HY-1 Silkworm missile disintegrated in an expanding cloud of fire and shrapnel.

The CIWS mount swung back around to its zero position and waited for another target.

* * *

"TAO—Bridge. We are clear of the minefield."

Chief McPherson nearly broke her finger jamming the mike button. "Bridge—USWE. Crack the whip! I say again, crack the whip!"

"Bridge, aye!"

The ship heeled abruptly to starboard as the bridge began the series of tight switchback turns that were supposed to throw off the pursuing torpedo.

* * *

"Weapons Control—TAO. Cease fire on all guns!"

"Weapons Control, aye!"

The deck heeled to port as the ship began a switchback turn in the opposite direction. The guns stopped firing, leaving a strange, ear-ringing silence in their wake.

* * *

Over the 29-MC, the Sonar Supervisor shouted, "Hostile torpedo is *still* locked on!"

"Crack the whip!" Chief McPherson said into her mike. "Crack the whip!"

The ship heeled again as the bridge threw the destroyer into a second set of switchback turns.

"It's not going to work," a voice said from over her shoulder.

The chief turned to see Capt. Bowie standing behind her, his eyes glued to the CDRT's tactical display. "It's not going to work," he said again. His voice was quiet, almost as if he was talking to himself rather than her.

The captain swung the microphone of his comm-set up to his mouth and keyed into the tactical net. "Bridge—Captain. Bring the port screw on line! I want all engines ahead flank right *now*!"

The OOD's voice came back over the net immediately. "Bring the port screw on line, all engines ahead flank—Bridge, aye!"

A metallic groan resonated through the ship, and the damaged port screw began to turn. The sound gained rapidly in pitch and volume as the mangled propeller came up to speed, rising from a groan to an ear-splitting shriek that rivaled even the explosive hammering of the now-silent guns.

The sound turned Chief McPherson's blood to ice water. In torpedo evasion, sound was the enemy. An acoustic torpedo could home in on a sound source like a bloodhound sniffing out a fox.

"Captain!" Chief McPherson said. "The torpedo can *hear* that!"

"I know," the captain said. His eyes never wandered from the flashing torpedo symbol on the tactical display.

"Sir! Speed won't help us now! We can't outrun this thing! And it's going to follow that howling screw right up our ass!"

"Let's hope so," the captain said. He keyed his mike. "Bridge—Captain. Starboard engines all stop! Port engines maintain flank speed!"

Chief McPherson stared at her commanding officer in abject disbelief. "Sir! What are you …"

"We can't stop this torpedo from hitting us," the captain said. "But maybe we can control *where* it hits us."

The chief frowned. "You're saying it's safer to get shot in the gut than in the head?"

"That's the idea," the captain said, his gaze still not wavering from the flashing red torpedo symbol. "Of course, a gut shot can kill you too, but it's the only chance we've got." He punched his comm-set into the 1-MC general announcing circuit. When he spoke, his voice came out of every speaker on the ship. "All hands, this is the Captain. Brace for shock!"

* * *

R-92:

The fifth-generation computer that formed R-92's digital brain noted the changes in signal strength caused by the target's evasive maneuvers. R-92 was not fooled by the target's bobs and weaves. Over two-thirds of the 152 miniature sonar transducers in R-92's acoustic seeker head had strong signal locks on the target. And then—improbably—the target signal grew even louder, giving R-92 a better acoustic lock.

R-92 did a range calculation on the target and determined that it was approaching optimum range for detonation. It sent a coded digital pulse to its warhead, initiating the final arming sequence.

R-92 did not know anything about the people it was programmed to kill. It had no understanding of politics, or national boundaries, or the fates of men. The torpedo had no way of knowing that the successful destruction of its target would point the future of the human race toward all-out war, whereas the failure to destroy its target would create a respite in which careful and thoughtful men might still be able to salvage the peace. The machine that was about to become the axis upon which history turned was not aware of history at all.

The weapon checked its depth and adjusted the angle of its elevator fins to take it under the hull of the target. Satisfied that its calculations were accurate, R-92 closed in for the kill.

The torpedo reached its optimum attack depth of twelve meters at the same instant the target's acoustic signal strength hit its peak. R-92's digital brain transmitted one final signal, and 250 kilograms of hexagon/RDT/aluminum high-explosive erupted into an expanding shock wave of fire and vaporized water.

* * *

USS *Towers* (DDG-103):

The torpedo impacted on the port screw, near the after-edge of the huge hole left by the previous torpedo hit. The explosion crashed into the ship like the fist of God, rolling the destroyer onto her starboard side, ripping through the already damaged hull, and letting in tons of seawater.

All over the ship, people and unsecured equipment slid down the swiftly tilting deck toward the starboard side. The angle of the deck was crazy now, and still the wounded ship continued its roll.

* * *

Chief McPherson careened across the deck of CIC, her speed increasing as the slant became even steeper. Her shoulder slammed into the base of an Aegis radar console, and she screamed as she felt her bones shatter with horribly audible crunches.

The ship hung there for what seemed an eternity, wallowing on her starboard side, as though considering whether or not to complete the death roll and give herself up to the waves.

Someone screamed, "We're going under!"

But then, with agonizing slowness, the wounded ship began to right herself. She finally settled, with a heavy list to port—where the water was still pouring in.

* * *

Capt. Bowie tried to claw his way to his feet. His left knee was badly wrenched, broken maybe, and every movement brought nauseating waves of pain.

"The nets are down," he hissed. "TAO, get a messenger to CCS! I want damage control teams down there now!"

He turned to the XO, who was just beginning to try to stand. "You all right, Pete?"

The XO's face was a mask of pain. His arms were wrapped tightly around his chest. He staggered but managed to stand. "Broken … ribs … I think." He gritted his teeth and stood up a little straighter. "Yes, sir, Captain. I'm okay."

The captain stared at him for several long seconds before speaking. "Good. See what you can do to put this place back together; the Sirajis might not be done shooting at us." He took a painful step and his knee nearly collapsed. His vision narrowed, and he had to grab a console to steady himself. "I'm going up to the bridge and see if I can still get some fight out of this old girl."

The XO nodded. "Yes, sir."

* * *

Chief McPherson lay on the deck, a fetal ball of pain and dizziness. Her comm-set was missing. She tried to turn her head to look for it, and the pain came down on her like an ax. She squeezed her eyes shut, and hot tears ran down her cheeks. She blinked them away.

An Operations Specialist who was just climbing to his feet looked down at her. The young man's right cheek was bleeding, and it was clear that he was going to have two black eyes. "We made it, Chief! We're still here!"

* * *

Hobbling as he was, it took Capt. Bowie ten minutes to make it to the bridge. His left knee was already swelling, and each step he took got a little harder.

He staggered through the airlock and seized the back of the OOD's chair to keep from falling down. "Officer of the Deck?"

The OOD was Lt.(jg) Karen Augustine. Her hair was matted with blood, and she was holding a scrap of bloody T-shirt to her scalp, but her eyes were bright and alert. "Yes, sir?"

The captain glanced down at the helm indicators. "How much speed can you give me?"

The OOD scanned her consoles. "A little less than eight knots, sir. Engineering is working to get us more, but right now, it's a miracle that we can make way at all."

"Eight knots it is," the captain said. "Let's get the hell out of here."

CHAPTER 52

OVAL OFFICE
WASHINGTON, DC
MONDAY; 28 MAY
4:30 PM EDT

The television was a rear-projection model, a big one that slid neatly into a recess in the ceiling when it wasn't needed. The big screen made Friedrik Shoernberg's face look huge.

Veronica Doyle pointed a remote at the screen, and the Chancellor of Germany's face winked out of existence. "I guess that makes it official," she said. "How did you know he'd resign, Mr. President?"

"I gave him a little incentive," the president said. "I assured him that the United States wouldn't seek reparations if he stepped down quietly. And I told him we would back a British attack on Germany if he didn't."

Gregory Brenthoven stared at him. "Tell me you're joking, sir."

The president shook his head. "I'm not joking, Greg. I *did* tell him that, and I was serious. Shoernberg's resignation and a formal apology from the Bundestag were the only things that could keep Emily Irons from declaring war on Germany. If Chancellor Shoernberg had refused to step down, I don't think I could have prevented a war. And if I couldn't stop it, the least I could do was try to end it quickly."

"Lucky for us that you read Chancellor Shoernberg correctly, Mr. President," Doyle said. "You called this play all the way down the line."

"Bullshit," the president said. "Bull … shit." He shook his head slowly. "I predicted that Friedrik would take the easy way out if his ass was on the line. That's the only thing I was right about in this whole god-awful mess."

He looked down at a folder on his desk, bound in dark blue leather and embossed with the presidential seal. He hadn't opened it yet, but he knew what was in it: an operational summary of the entire incident, complete with charts, graphs, and satellite photos. Some of those charts represented dollars spent. Others discussed fuel expended and the amount of ordnance that had been launched. And one of the charts would show him the cost of this fiasco in human lives.

"I was wrong about a lot more things than I was right about," he said softly. "And an awful lot of fine young Americans had to die to show me how wrong I was."

CHAPTER 53

USS *TOWERS* (DDG-103)
CONTINENTAL MARITIME SHIPYARDS
SAN DIEGO, CA
THURSDAY; 21 JUNE
1320 hours (1:20 PM)
TIME ZONE-8 'UNIFORM'

Capt. Bowie stood at the rail of dry dock number four and looked down at his broken ship. Out of the water and up on the blocks, the massive damage to the port side was clearly visible, and it was much worse than even the most pessimistic part of him had suspected. Showers of sparks fell like blue neon rain into the concrete bottom of the dry dock, as shipyard workers cut out mangled sections of steel and welded in new ones.

Many of the crew were gone now—the injured to hospitals for treatment, the dead to their families for burial. Some of the injured would return to *Towers* when their wounds were healed, but not many. The next time the destroyer put out to sea, much of the old crew would be gone, replaced by newcomers to whom the battles that *Towers* had fought would be the stuff of legend.

"She put up a hell of a fight, sir," a voice at his elbow said.

Capt. Bowie turned to find Chief McPherson, her right arm still in a cast from shoulder to wrist.

The chief saluted with her left hand. "It's tough to get used to saluting with the wrong hand."

Capt. Bowie returned her salute with a shadow of a smile. "It won't be for much longer. You'll be out of that thing pretty soon."

"Yes, sir. I'll be all patched up and ready for battle." She nodded toward the ship in the dry dock. "Just like the grand lady down there. Weld on a couple of hull plates, run some wiring, slap on a fresh coat of paint, and we're both as good as new."

She sighed. “We got lucky, sir. If that last sub had gotten past us, the Brits would be gearing up for war right now.”

Capt. Bowie nodded. “We *did* get lucky, Chief. But I think our little tango in that minefield used up the last of my four-leaf clovers.”

“What do you mean, sir?”

“They’re taking her away from me,” the captain said. “I got a heads-up call from SURFPAC this morning. Vice Admiral Hicks is hand-carrying my orders over himself.”

“I’ve never heard of SURFPAC hand-delivering orders before,” the chief said.

“I have,” said Capt. Bowie. “Sometimes that’s how they do it when you’re being relieved of command.”

“What?” the chief said. “Relieved of command? They can’t do that!”

Capt. Bowie smiled. “I’m afraid they can, Chief.”

“They’ve got no grounds to relieve you, sir.”

“Yes they do,” the captain said. “A ship under my command was sunk in combat, and that hasn’t happened since World War II. Not to mention that we lost every helo attached to our SAU. Apparently, the upper command thinks I mismanaged the situation pretty badly.”

“Mismanaged? Sir, with all due respect, that’s bullshit! Nobody could have done it any better than you did.”

Bowie shook his head and stared down into the dry dock at his wounded ship. “I worked for this my whole life,” he said. “I never gave a damn about making full-bird, and I never even *thought* about admiral. I wanted to command a destroyer at sea.” He shrugged. “I was lucky enough to live my dream, for a while anyway. I always knew that my time as CO of *Towers* would go by too quickly. But I never expected to get pulled out of the game early.”

He looked up the pier and pulled his walkie-talkie from its belt holster. “Quarterdeck, this is the Captain. Sound six bells. Admiral Hicks is approaching.”

“Quarterdeck, aye.”

A few seconds later, the ship’s bell rang six times—three groups of two bells each, followed by the Petty Officer of the Watch’s voice over the 1-MC. “Commander, Naval Surface Force Pacific—Arriving.”

Capt. Bowie and Chief McPherson came to attention as the admiral approached. When he was about eight paces away, they both rendered hand salutes, the captain with his right hand and the chief with her left.

The admiral promptly returned their mismatched salutes with a snappy one of his own. “At ease.”

They dropped into slightly more relaxed postures.

Vice Admiral Douglas Hicks had a folder tucked under his left arm. He looked down and tried to brush a smear of dirt off the right leg of his uniform pants. "I shouldn't have worn my whites to a shipyard," he said. He looked up. "But this is an official visit, so it seemed appropriate."

He retrieved the folder from under his arm and held it out to Capt. Bowie. "Do you know what's in here?"

Bowie accepted the folder but didn't open it. "My orders, sir?"

The admiral smiled. "I like you, Jim. But I wouldn't have bothered to trot my fat carcass down here to deliver an ordinary set of orders."

Capt. Bowie started to open the folder and then stopped himself. "I'm not being transferred, sir?"

The admiral shrugged. "That's up to you, son." He nodded toward the folder. "What you have there is what amounts to a blank check. They're orders all right. Signed by the Secretary of the Navy himself."

The captain looked puzzled. "Where am I going, sir?"

"Anywhere you want," the admiral said. "You can take your pick of any O-5 billet in the Navy. And I have it on the highest authority that, if your dream billet is taken, the bureau will move somebody to make room. You think about it for a while and then get back to me when you've made up your mind."

"I don't need to think about it, Admiral. I already know where I want to go." He pointed into the dry dock where cascades of welding sparks were falling. "Right there. I want to do another CO tour aboard the *Towers*."

The admiral grinned. "You just won me fifty bucks. I told my chief of staff to pencil you in for the *Towers*. He said I was nuts." The admiral reached out and shook Bowie's hand. "You're a good man, Jim. And *Towers* is a hell of a ship. I envy you. And on that note, I'll have to take my leave. There's a stack of reports on my desk a foot high, and my name is on every damned one of them."

Capt. Bowie and Chief McPherson came to attention and saluted. The admiral returned their salutes and then turned on his heel and walked briskly back up the pier.

Capt. Bowie radioed the quarterdeck and shortly afterward they were treated to a 1-MC broadcast announcing the admiral's departure.

When the speakers had faded to silence, Capt. Bowie turned to Chief McPherson with a grin. "What do you think, Chief? Are you ready to do it again?"

EPILOGUE

WASHINGTON, DC
FRIDAY; 22 JUNE
3:07 AM EDT

The phone woke President Chandler on the third ring, but it took him five rings to grope for it and get the receiver to his ear.

"Mr. President, this is Lieutenant Feinstein in the Signals Office. The chairman of the Joint Chiefs is requesting your presence in the Situation Room, sir. Something has come up."

The president turned on the bedside lamp and did a quick check to make sure it wasn't shining in Jenny's face. "What kind of something?"

"Sir, it's China."

NAVY TERMS, ACRONYMS, AND ABBREVIATIONS

AAW—Anti-Aircraft Warfare or Anti-Air Warfare.

abeam—Abreast of a ship; to the direct left or right of a ship. "*The buoy was abeam of USS* Decatur."

AC—Air conditioner.

Academy, the—Common Navy slang for the United States Naval Academy. Because of its location in Annapolis, Md., the U.S. Naval Academy is also often referred to as *Annapolis*.

Action Stations—The British Navy's equivalent of General Quarters. See: *General Quarters*.

Aegis—The integrated suite of computers, sensors, and weapons systems aboard modern U.S. Navy guided missile cruisers and guided missile destroyers.

AEW—Airborne Early Warning.

aft—Toward the rear end of the ship, or *stern*.

amidships—The area near the middle of the ship, roughly between the bow and stern. Also referred to as *midships*.

Annapolis—See: *Academy, the*.

ASROC—Anti-submarine rocket: an Anti-Submarine Warfare torpedo mounted to a solid-fuel rocket. Fired from a shipboard missile launcher, an ASROC weapon follows a ballistic trajectory to the vicinity of an enemy submarine. At a pre-calculated point in the flight, the center airframe section of the ASROC splits apart, freeing the torpedo. A small parachute deploys from the tail section of the torpedo, cushioning the weapon's impact with the water. Upon entering the water, the torpedo starts its engine, detaches from the parachute pack, and commences its attack on the enemy submarine. The ASROC system allows a ship to deliver torpedo attacks far outside the normal operating range of ordinary torpedoes. Also see: *Vertical Launch ASROC.*

astern—Behind a ship. "*The tugboat is astern of USS* Hopper."

ASW—Anti-Submarine Warfare.

aye—I understand. (Usually spoken in response to information received.)

aye-aye—I understand and will obey. (Usually spoken in response to an order or instruction.)

battle stations—See: *General Quarters.*

BMOW—Boatswain's Mate of the Watch, or Bo'sun of the Watch.

bow—The very front portion of a ship. (Sometimes jokingly referred to as the "*pointy end*" of the ship.)

bulkhead—A wall, usually steel, aboard a ship. (*Never* referred to as a *wall.*)

BZ—Bravo Zulu. The traditional navy acknowledgment of a job well performed. The term originates from the Allied Signals Book (ATP-1), which contains alphanumeric code groups for transmission by radio, flashing light, or signal flags. The two-letter code "BZ" decodes to read, "well done."

CDRT—Computerized Dead-Reckoning Tracer.

CERT-SUB—Certain submarine: the formal reporting designation for a sonar contact that has been definitively identified as a submarine. Also see: *POSS-SUB* and *PROB-SUB.*

CG—Guided missile cruiser. (U.S. Navy hull designation.)

chaff—A radar decoy system that spreads metallic dust and small pieces of metal foil through the air, creating false targets and/or confusing images for enemy radar systems. Chaff is often deployed by small, self-opening canisters attached to specially designed short-range rockets. Also referred to as *RBOC* and *Super-RBOC.*

CHENG—Chief Engineer, or Chief Engineering Officer. *CHENG* is pronounced to rhyme with *gang.*

Chief Petty Officer's Mess—See: *Chief's Mess.*

Chief's Mess—The cafeteria-like room where chief petty officers, senior chief petty officers, and master chief petty officers eat their meals. The Chief's Mess is equal parts dining room, office, conference room, and lounge. Also referred to as *Chief Petty Officer's Mess* or *CPO Mess.*

CIC—Combat Information Center.

CIWS—Close-In Weapons System, or Close-In Weapon System. *CIWS* is pronounced *see-whiz.*

CNO—Chief of Naval Operations.

CO—Commanding officer.

CPA—Closest point of approach.

CPO—Chief petty officer.

CPO Mess—See: *Chief's Mess.*

crypto—Cryptography, or cryptographic code.

CSO—Combat Systems Officer.

CSOOW—Combat Systems Officer of the Watch. *CSOOW* is pronounced *see-sow.*

CV—Aircraft carrier. (U.S. Navy hull designation.)

CVN—Nuclear-powered aircraft carrier. (U.S. Navy hull designation.)

datum—The last reported position of a submerged submarine whose present location is unknown (i.e., no sensors are currently tracking the sub). Datum for a lost submarine contact acts as the reference point from which search plans will be calculated. In cases where reliable positional information on the submarine is not available, the officer in command of the search may designate a location for datum based on the best available information.

DDG—Guided missile destroyer. (U.S. Navy hull designation.)

deck—The floor, usually steel, aboard a ship. (*Never* referred to as the *floor.*)

Divo—Common navy slang for Division Officer.

dog—1. (noun) A bolt or handle used to close and seal a hatch or watertight door. 2. (verb) The act of sealing a watertight hatch or door. "*He ordered Seaman Hopkins to dog the door.*"

EOOW—Engineer of the Watch, or Engineering Officer of the Watch. *EOOW* is pronounced to rhyme with *meow*.

ETA—Estimated time of arrival.

EW—Electronic Warfare, or Electronics Warfare. May also refer to the Navy technical rating assigned to Electronics Warfare Technicians. For example, a second class petty officer in the EW rating is referred to as an EW2.

farthest-on circle—A circle drawn on a tactical plot to indicate the greatest distance that a submarine could possibly move in a given period of time. Farthest-on circles are usually centered on *datum* (i.e., the last reported position of the submarine) and scaled to account for the maximum possible speed of the submarine. Also see: *datum*.

FFG—Guided missile frigate. (U.S. Navy hull designation.)

forward—Toward the front end of the ship, or *bow*.

galley—The kitchen area of a ship, where meals are prepared. (*Never* referred to as the *kitchen*.)

General Quarters—An advanced state of readiness in which a ship is on alert, all battle stations are manned, and the crew is prepared for combat or emergencies. Also referred to as *battle stations*, or *GQ*.

GQ—See: *General Quarters*.

head—A bathroom or restroom aboard a ship. (*Never* referred to as the *bathroom* or *restroom*.)

helo—Common Navy slang for helicopter.

HUD—Head Up Display, or Heads Up Display.

knot—A nautical mile (6,076.1 feet).

Mess Deck—See: *Mess Decks*.

Mess Decks—The cafeteria-like room where the enlisted Sailors eat their meals. Also referred to as the *Mess Deck*.

midships—See: *amidships*.

mike—Common military radio lingo for *minute*. "*My ETA is three mikes*."

MOOW—Messenger of the Watch.

OIC—Officer in charge.

OOD—Officer of the Deck.

overhead—A ceiling, usually steel, aboard a ship. (*Never* referred to as a *ceiling.*)

PCMS—Passive Countermeasure System: radar-absorbent tiles that can be glued to large areas of a warship to make it harder to detect on radar.

pit—See: *rack.*

POOW—Petty Officer of the Watch.

port—The left side a ship as seen by someone facing the bow. Also see: *starboard.*

POSS-SUB—Possible submarine: the formal reporting designation for a sonar contact that displays some of the characteristics of a submarine, but cannot be definitively identified as a sub. Also see: *CERT-SUB* and *PROB-SUB.*

PROB-SUB—Probable submarine: the formal reporting designation for a sonar contact that has many or most of the characteristics of a submarine, but cannot be definitively identified as a submarine. Also see: *CERT-SUB* and *POSS-SUB.*

QMOW—Quartermaster of the Watch.

rack—A Sailor's bunk or bed aboard a ship. Also referred to as a *pit.* (*Rarely* referred to as a *bunk*, and *never* referred to as a *bed.*)

RBOC—Rapid-Blooming Overboard Chaff. Also see: *chaff* and *Super-RBOC.*

RHIB—Rigid-Hulled Inflatable Boat.

SAM—Surface-to-air missile.

SAU—Search Attack Unit: a small group of ships and/or aircraft designated to hunt down and destroy enemy submarines. *SAU* is pronounced to rhyme with *cow.*

sea puppy—Common Navy slang for an inexperienced junior officer.

SECDEF—Secretary of defense.

SECNAV—Secretary of the Navy.

SENSO—Sensor Operator: an enlisted air crew member (Aviation Warfare Specialist) who operates radar, sonar, and magnetic anomaly detector

(MAD) equipment, interprets acoustic data, and performs search and rescue (SAR) duties as a qualified rescue swimmer.

SPY—Informal nickname for the high-powered AN/SPY-1 radar system found aboard modern U.S. guided missile cruisers and destroyers. Also referred to as *SPY-1* or *SPY radar*.

SSN—Nuclear-powered attack submarine. (U.S. Navy hull designation.)

starboard—The right side a ship as seen by someone facing the bow. Also see: *port*.

stern—The very back portion of a ship. (Sometimes jokingly referred to as the "*blunt end*" of the ship.)

sub-SAM—Submarine-launched surface-to-air missile.

Super-RBOC—Super Rapid-Blooming Overboard Chaff. Also see: *chaff* and *RBOC*.

SUPPO—Supply Officer.

TACO—Tactical Coordinator. *TACO* is pronounced to rhyme with *whacko*.

TAO—Tactical Action Officer.

umbilical—A cable that connects a missile, torpedo, rocket, bomb, or depth charge to the power and computer systems aboard a ship, aircraft, or submarine. In most cases, an umbilical provides electrical power and updated programming information to a weapon right up to the instant of firing, at which time the cable is automatically detached.

USW—Undersea Warfare.

USWE—Undersea Warfare Evaluator.

USWO—Undersea Warfare Officer.

VBSS—See: *Visit, Board, Search, and Seizure*.

Vertical Launch ASROC—An anti-submarine rocket designed to be launched from a shipboard Vertical Launch System. Also referred to as VLA. Also see: *ASROC*.

Vertical Launch System—A modular missile system in which missiles and rockets are housed in vertically mounted "cells" below the deck of a warship. In most configurations, only the armored missile hatches are visible above the deck. Because each cell is a self-contained launcher for the missile it houses, multiple missiles can be launched simultaneously. The Vertical Launch System is widely considered to be the most advanced and capable shipborne missile launching system in the world. Also referred to as VLS.

Visit, Board, Search, and Seizure—A team of specially trained Sailors designated to board and search ships that are suspected of smuggling or violation of international law. Also referred to as VBSS.

VLA—See: *Vertical Launch ASROC.*

VLS—See: *Vertical Launch System.*

wardroom—The dining room where officers eat their meals. Considerably more formal than the Chief's Mess or the Mess Decks, the wardroom is the nexus of all officer activity. On a typical ship, the wardroom is equal parts conference room, classroom, dining room, and social parlor.

XO—Executive officer.

978-0-595-67523-4
0-595-67523-9

Printed in the United States
76697LV00007B/14